STROKE OF MIDNIGHT

SHERRILYN KENYON

AMANDA ASHLEY

L. A. BANKS

LORI HANDELAND

St. Martin's Paperbacks

STROKE OF MIDNIGHT

"Winter Born" copyright © 2004 by Sherrilyn Kenyon.
"Born of the Night" copyright © 2004 by Madeline Baker.
"Make It Last Forever" copyright © 2004 by Leslie Esdaile Banks.
"Red Moon Rising" copyright © 2004 by Lori Handeland.

Excerpt from *Seize the Night* copyright © 2004 by Sherrilyn Kenyon.
Excerpt from *Blue Moon* copyright © 2004 by Lori Handeland.
Excerpt from *The Bitten* copyright © 2004 by Leslie Esdaile Banks.

The poem by Joseph Walsh on p. 83, preceding "Born of the Night," is used with the permission of the author.

ISBN: 0-312-99876-7
EAN: 80312-99876-9

Printed in the United States of America

St. Martin's Paperbacks edition / November 2004

St. Martin's Paperbacks are published by St. Martin's Press, 175 Fifth Avenue, New York, NY 10010.

10 9 8 7 6 5 4 3 2 1

CONTENTS

WINTER BORN

SHERRILYN KENYON

PROLOGUE

It was hard to find an all-powerful, mythical being in a crowd of thirty thousand.

Or at least it was in theory.

At the yearly Dragon*Con science fiction convention in Atlanta, Georgia, however, it was another story entirely. There were two Yodas and a Dragon Rider from Pern checking in at the hotel's front desk while a full regiment of Storm Troopers walked by. There were gods and goddesses, all manner of aliens, warriors, and ladies gathered there. Pandora had even seen the Wicked Witch of the West cruise by on her motorized broomstick.

Since she'd sat down ten minutes ago, Pandora had counted nine Gandalfs, and if she didn't miss her guess, there were at least two dozen elves, fairies, orcs, goblins, and assorted others gathered around, talking on cell phones, or smoking just outside the hotel doors.

And one mustn't forget the entire cabal of vampires and demons walking around handing out fliers for people to come to their room for a "blood party" and Buffy film fest.

Not to mention she'd already been invited twice to the Klingon Homeworld in Room 316 at the Hyatt Regency across the street. Meanwhile a group of supposedly androgynous Borg men had tried to "assimilate" her as soon as she entered the lobby of the Marriott Marquis.

This had to be the strangest gathering she'd ever seen, and when given the fact that she was a Were-Panther who up until three days ago had lived solely among her own preternatural kind, that said something.

"I'm never going to find him," she murmured to herself as an extremely tall, gorgeous Goth man stopped in front of her.

Good glory, the man was sinfully delectable!

And he was the last thing she needed to be staring at, yet she couldn't seem to help herself. He was utterly compelling.

He wore a pair of dark sunglasses even inside the hotel while he scanned the motley crowd as if looking for someone. Something about the man commanded attention and respect. Of course, it didn't help that her hormones were currently elevated by the change going on inside her as she came into full womanhood. Her entire body was humming from hormonal overload which, up until his appearance, she'd been keeping under very careful control.

Now she sizzled for a taste of him and it was all she could do to stay seated.

He had to be at least seven feet tall, augmented by the flame biker boots that added at least three inches to his height. He had long black hair that flowed around his broad shoulders, and wore an old, faded motorcycle jacket with a skull and crossbones painted on the back. The worst part was that he wore *nothing* underneath that jacket and every time he moved, she glimpsed more of his tanned, ripped body.

His black leather pants hugged a perfect bottom that would rival any of her Were brethren. Every part of her wanted to stand up, cross the small distance between them, and pull his tall, lean body against hers until the vicious, needful hunger in her blood was fully sated. But even as she felt that primal sexual hunger, the animal part of herself sensed an air of lethal danger from him.

He wasn't the kind of man a woman approached without an invitation.

"*Akri!*"

The man turned as a woman around his age came running up to him. Cute as she could be, she was dressed like a demon, complete with a set of black wings that looked spookily real as they twitched and flapped. Her skin was red and black, and her hair matched his. She even sported a pair of glowing red horns on her head. Her short purple skirt was flared and she wore a black leather bustier with three large silver buckles on the front. Black and purple striped leggings and a pair of six-inch platform combat boots completed her odd outfit.

The tall "demon" handed the man a credit card. "It's broke again, *akri,*" she said, pouting around a pair of vampirelike fangs. "The man downstairs done said that the Simi can't charge nothing else until I'm not over my limit no more. I don't know what that means, but I don't like it. Fix it, *akri,* or else I might eat him. The Simi gots needs and I needs my plastic to work."

The man laughed as he took it from her and pulled out his wallet. He handed her three more credit cards.

The "demon" squealed in delight and pulled him into a hug. She put the credit cards into her coffin-shaped purse, then handed him a small shiny red nylon bag. "By the way, I boughts those for you before I broke my plastic. Since you don't got your real hornays, these are some fake ones to tide you over until we go home."

"Thanks, Sim," he said in an incredibly deep, evocative voice as he took the bag from her.

She smiled, kissed his cheek, then dashed off into the crowd with her wings flapping behind her.

The man looked at Pandora then and gave her a half-grin that could only be called wicked, and yet it seemed somehow knowing. He inclined his head to her, then headed off after the woman who'd just left him.

Every instinct in her body told her to follow him, but she didn't listen.

She was here to find the legendary Acheron Parthenopaeus—an ancient, immortal Atlantean her sister had hoped would help hide Pandora from those who were hunting her. Not chase after some hot, young human who looked stunning in leather.

Acheron was her last hope.

Unfortunately, neither she nor her sister had any idea what he looked like. All they knew was that he came to Dragon*Con every year with his daughter.

He was older than time and more powerful than any other of his kind. She scanned the older men in the crowd who were dressed as wizards, warriors, or other creatures, but none of them seemed to be particularly wise or powerful, nor were they with a daughter.

Just what would an eleven-thousand-year-old man look like anyway?

Sighing, Pandora stood up and went to the bannister so that she could look down to the lower levels of the hotel and scan the crowd.

He had to be here.

But where? How could she find anyone in this thronging mass of people . . . er, aliens.

Chewing her lip, she debated where to go look for him. Suddenly, a tall man in an elegant black suit caught her eye. He wasn't particularly old, probably in his mid-thirties, but she sensed an unmistakable air of power from him.

Maybe he was the mysterious Acheron. And he was heading for the bank of elevators.

Pandora rushed after him, and barely made it before the door closed them inside the small compartment with a Renaissance drummer, a green-fleshed alien, and Darth Vader.

But that wasn't what made her heart stop. As she

glanced out through the glass wall of the elevator, she saw four things that terrified her.

It was a group of devastatingly gorgeous men. The two shortest of the group were identical in looks and they had to be at least six feet four. They all had jet-black hair and were dressed in black Goth clothes.

The four men stood in a specific formation that she knew all too well, with their backs to each other as they scanned the crowd hungrily, intently, as if seeking something in particular. They were fierce. Animalistic.

It was as if they had literally caught wind of something, and in one heartbeat she knew what that something was.

Her.

"Oh no," she said under her breath. By their build and beauty and actions, she would know their breed anywhere. No group of humans could be that handsome or that intense. Nor would any other species be so alerted by her scent.

They, like her, were Were-Panthers, and by the look of them, they were young and virile.

And she was in heat . . .

CHAPTER 1

Dante Pontis wasn't the most patient of creatures. And his patience was quickly running out.

He'd been trapped in a limo from Hartsfield Airport to the hotel with his brothers, Mike and Leo, as they bitched and moaned over the fact that Dante had forced the two young panthers to fly coach from Minnesota to Atlanta while he and Romeo had simply "flashed" themselves here.

And all because the last time he and Romeo had psychically transported the twins somewhere, they had caused such a scene on arrival that they'd almost gotten busted by the humans.

Dragon*Con was far too crowded to take a chance on the four of them "appearing" before so many witnesses.

The key to Were-Hunter survival was to blend in with the humans, not scare the shit out of them.

"You know," Romeo said to them, "you're both lucky I wouldn't let Dante trank you and send you over in a cage. It's what he wanted to do."

"You dick," Leo snarled at Dante as he raked him with a repugnant glare. At six feet four, the panther was still growing and would probably equal Dante's height of six feet six in the next decade or so.

Leo and Mike were identical twins whom Dante had raised after their mother had abandoned them on their father's doorstep. It was typical Were-Panther behavior.

The women would mate with the men, get pregnant, then leave the cubs for the men to raise while the women prowled around unfettered.

If the cubs were daughters, they would remain in the male-dominated pack until puberty, which struck them around the age of twenty-four. Then all the "seasoning" female cubs would form their own group and leave to search for mates.

In the last two hundred years, Dante and Romeo had raised a large number of cubs, since their father was famous for dumping his litters on them and heading for the hills.

Like Dante, the twins had wavy black hair and tawny Italian skin when in human form.

Unlike him, they were only sixty years old, which in their life span made them practically children.

And they acted it.

It was time to either kill them or get away from them. Since Romeo was still rather bent over the fact that Dante had killed off their brother Salvatore for betraying them, Dante decided it would be best to get to his room before Leo and Mike joined Salvatore as skins on the wall at his club.

"I don't understand why I have to share a room with Leo," Mike snarled. "He snores."

"I do not. Besides, you whistle when you sleep."

"No I don't."

Dante passed an irritated look at Romeo. "Why are they here?"

"To get women," Mike said.

Romeo ignored him. "You were afraid to leave them alone at the Inferno without me. The last time you did that, they damn near burned the place down."

Dante expelled a disgusted breath. "And why can't I kill them again?"

"You would miss them."

Yeah, right. Dante snorted at that as he handed off the card key to Leo and Mike.

"Wait, wait, wait, wait," Leo said as he examined it. "These aren't concierge level."

Dante gave him a bored stare.

"Are you concierge?" Leo asked Romeo.

"Yes."

"Why aren't we concierge?" Mike asked Dante.

Dante crossed his arms over his chest. "Because you're unworthy."

Mike opened his mouth to speak, but before he could, a trace of a scent washed over all three of them instantaneously.

Dante went rigid as every hormone in his body suddenly became activated and sizzled. Against his will, he found himself turning around and scanning the crowd in the hotel lobby.

He smelled a virgin pantheress in heat.

They all did.

The scent was unmistakable. It was warm and sweet. Feminine and innocent. Succulent. Inviting. And it made him salivate for a taste of her. His panther sight dimmed as it scanned the females present and detected none of his kind.

"Where is she?" Leo said, his voice ragged as if he were having a hard time holding himself back.

"Too many humans here to tell," Mike said as he tilted his head back to sniff the air. "They have her scent moving in multiple directions."

Dante passed a look to Romeo, who was staring up at the elevator. He turned to stare as well, and saw no one but Darth Vader.

"Did you see her?" he asked.

Romeo shook his head. "Sorry. I was mesmerized by the naked green alien."

"Arrr," Mike snarled. "You're worthless, Romeo. What kind of panther gets fixed on an alien when there's a virgin pantheress in heat?"

"A mated one," Romeo shot back. "Unlike you losers, my hormones are contained."

Dante sniffed and shook his head to clear it of her scent before his animal hormones relegated him to the same childish antics as his twin brothers. "Yeah, and I want to keep mine that way. Frick and Frack, you're on panther patrol. Find her and keep her far away from me."

Mike and Leo exchanged evil grins before they bolted into the crowd.

Dante rolled his eyes at their haste. There were times when they really were losers.

"Aren't you the least bit interested?" Romeo asked as they headed for the elevators. "It's not every day we run across a virgin panther."

"Hell, no. I'll stick to humans. The last thing I want is a mate who'll cruise into my life once a year, screw my brains out for two days, then run off until she delivers my litter to me to raise without her. No offense, being you and Dad sucks and I've raised enough siblings to never want to raise my own young without the benefit of a mate."

Romeo laughed. "Yeah, but for the record, it's one hell-uva two days."

Dante shook his head at him. "You can have it. I'd rather take my pleasure where and when I find it."

He entered the elevator, then paused as he realized Romeo wasn't joining him.

"I'll catch you later," he said.

"You sure?"

Romeo nodded.

"All right." Dante got in and pushed the button for his floor. He stepped back against the glass and did his best to bring his body back under control.

But it was hard.

Every animal instinct he possessed demanded that he stalk this hotel until he located the female.

Since he was a Katagari Were-Hunter, the need to copulate with her was almost overwhelming. Katagaria were animals who could take human form, but at the end of the day, they were animals and not humans. Their animal half ran roughshod over their human sensibilities and it was the animal heart inside them that ruled them and their actions.

What he needed was some time in his room where he could take his animal form and put the female out of his mind.

He was old enough to be able to curtail his nature. To control it. He wasn't about to let any woman have control over him.

Especially not a pantheress.

Pandora fumbled with her key card as she struggled to open her door.

What was she going to do? The man in her elevator wasn't Acheron. And those had been panther males down there. If they caught another whiff of her . . .

She was doomed. There was no way the animal inside her would refuse a virile male. She was in heat and the need to mate reigned supreme inside her. If any male came near her who her animal self sensed could possibly impregnate her, she would throw herself at him.

Around humans, that impulse was controllable. The chances of a human male being her mate were almost impossible. So the animal inside her might be curious and enticed, but it would stand down to her human rationale.

Around a Were-Panther, that animal need wouldn't listen to reason. It would pounce for a taste of the male.

She would have no control!

A shadow fell over her.

Pandora squeaked and jumped back as she looked up to

see one of the men she'd seen downstairs. This close to him, she couldn't mistake his Panthiras attributes.

His scent was undeniable.

He was lean and powerful in human form. Deadly. His handsomeness would guarantee him any female who caught his interest . . . even her own feminine senses reacted to him, but not so much that she couldn't fight him.

Even more frightening than his innate feral masculinity, his scent was Katagaria—the animal branch of their species—while she was Arcadian, the human branch.

Letting go of her room card, she crouched to attack and was amazed that the animal inside her wasn't leaping out to mate with him.

"It's okay," he said quickly. "I've got good news and bad news for you."

"And that is?"

He held his hand up so that she could see the geometric mark on his palm. At least that explained why she could resist the urge to copulate with him. "I'm mated so you're completely safe from me."

Pandora still wasn't ready to trust him, but at least as a mated panther, he wouldn't be able to have sex with her. Once a Were-Panther male was mated, he was impotent around any female other than his "wife." "I take it that's the good news?"

He nodded.

"And the bad?"

"I'm here with three brothers who aren't."

She started to bolt.

"No, no," he said, reaching out to take her hand. He pulled back before he did. "Don't be afraid of me. I really mean you no harm, okay? I have ten daughters myself and I understand your fear."

She still wasn't ready to trust that he wouldn't take her to his brothers for their enjoyment. That was what the ones seeking her would do and she had no intention of becoming a community toy for every unmated male in their pack. "What do you want?"

"Believe it or not, I'm going to help you."

She chose not to believe that. At least not yet. "Why would you do that?"

"*Because* of my daughters," he said sincerely. "You're just a baby and I don't trust Leo or Mike not to hurt you. They wouldn't do it on purpose, but they're young too and not real good at holding back. No doubt they'd both pounce on you at once and who knows what they might inadvertently do."

And that was exactly what she was afraid of. "That's only two brothers. What of the third?"

"Dante's different. Honestly, you'd be lucky to find someone like him for your first. He's a selfish bastard who doesn't like to share much of anything with anyone and he'd make sure no one else touched you while you were with him."

But his brother was still an animal and she had no interest in taking a Katagari lover.

"Is that supposed to comfort me?" she asked.

He shook his head. "No, but don't worry. Dante's a lot older than they are and, lucky for you, he doesn't want a mate. He plans to stay far away from you so I can keep him off you by simply telling him where you are."

Pandora calmed a degree. He was telling her the truth, she could sense it. One of the good things about being part animal was that she knew whenever someone was lying to her.

"Okay," she said slowly. "Thank you for your offer to help. I don't want a Katagari to touch me."

His nostrils flared at that.

She stiffened. "You said it yourself. You get carried away and you hurt us. My older sister was killed by a pack of Katagaria males who snapped her neck while attempting to mate with her when she was my age. I'm barely twenty-four. I don't want to die. Not like that."

That seemed to calm him down. He bent over and retrieved her card from the floor. "Get me something with your scent on it so I can spread it around and keep Leo and Mike away from you."

Pandora nodded, then opened the door to her room. She went to her suitcase and pulled out the T-shirt she slept in.

"Do you know Acheron Parthenopaeus?" she asked as she handed it to him.

"Yes, why?"

"I was told to find him. My surviving sister said that he could help me get home again."

The panther frowned at her. "I don't understand. Why didn't you go home on your own?"

She sighed as frustration filled her. How she wished it were that simple. If she were an older pantheress, she could easily find her own way home, but her kind didn't get all their psychic abilities until after their first mating.

Even then her powers would have to be trained and honed so that she could wield them. That was something that could take decades, if not centuries, to master.

"I was kidnapped from the future by a group of Katagaria panthers and brought to this time period against my will. Unfortunately, my powers are just starting and I have no control over them or any way home on my own until I master them. The last thing I want is to overshoot my time period or end up with the dinosaurs."

He looked at her suspiciously. "I still don't understand why they took *you*. Why go to the future for a mate when there are plenty of packs here?"

She clenched her fists at that. "It's some stupid pact my pack made with theirs. Since we seem to have an abundance of females, my pack agreed to sacrifice a number of females every generation from certain families so that the Katagaria panthers would leave the rest of the pack alone. Every time one of the winter born females in the chosen families starts to season, the same pack comes to our home and brings us to their time period to mate with them. They don't want Katagaria females since they won't stay and raise their young. They keep us instead and use us as slaves. My one surviving sister helped me to escape after they brought me here before they could induct me into their pack. She sent me to Atlanta to find Acheron. She said he could return me to my time period."

"How does she know Acheron?"

Pandora ached at the thought that she would benefit from her sister's misery. "Before she was mated to one of their males and had her own children, she was trying to escape their pack. One night, she overheard some of the Katagaria talking about a Dark-Hunter named Acheron, and after they went to sleep, she searched for him online. By the time she found out enough information to locate him, she was pregnant and couldn't leave her children behind, so she gave her information to me once they brought me over."

"Hell of a sister you have there."

"Yes," Pandora agreed. "She's the best sister in the world and I would give anything if I could help her too."

The panther stepped back with a sigh, then started for the door.

She took his arm to keep him from leaving as another thought occurred to her. "Could *you* help me get home?"

He shook his head. "My powers aren't quite that strong. If I wanted to take anyone other than myself across time, I would have to wait for the full moon. The only one in my pack who could do it without waiting is Dante and if you get near him—"

"I'll attack him for sex."

He nodded.

Damn.

At least all wasn't lost though. "But you do know Acheron, right? Will he help me?"

"I don't know. He's strange sometimes and no one ever

knows how he's going to react or what he's going to do or say. But you can always ask. The best thing is for you to stay here in your room where Mike and Leo hopefully can't find you—like I said, they're young and aren't as experienced at tracking prey. I'll spread your scent around to keep them off you. Once I've got them occupied, I'll bring Ash to you. Okay?"

It was more than okay. It was great. She'd never thought to find a Katagari male who could be so kind.

"Thank you." As he moved away, Pandora stopped him again. "Really, thank you."

He offered her a kind, fatherly smile and patted her hand. "Animals protect their own. I'm doing this to help my brothers as much as I'm doing it to help you. If they were to hurt you, they'd never forgive themselves, and I'd have to listen to them lament for eternity."

Releasing her, he moved to the door and left the room.

Pandora took a deep breath, and for the first time since she'd been stolen from her people, she began to relax a little.

Now all she had to do was stay put until he returned.

But that wasn't as easy as it would normally be. The female in her that was just entering womanhood was all too aware of the fact that there were three unmated panthers at the hotel.

That alien and new part of her wanted with a vengeance the mating ritual that would induct her into adulthood.

It craved it.

For an Arcadian, the ritual was simple. Had she stayed at home, she would have chosen an elder panther from her pack to gently introduce her to the animal side of herself. Once he unlocked her full powers by copulating with her, he would have taught her how to shift from human to panther and how to protect herself and use her newborn powers.

The Katagaria were completely different. She'd heard

the horror stories directly from her sister Sefia. They took their *nearas*—virgin females who were cresting—and allowed every unmated male of the pack to have sex with her to see if she was the mate to one of them.

They would use her without mercy until all their males were fully sated.

Her sister Sefia had been one of the lucky ones. On the night they had deflowered her, Sefia had been mated to a Katagari panther who had then decided to keep her more as a pet than a mate.

Katagaria females left their mates once they were out of heat, and only returned whenever they were in season. If a male tried to mate with a Katagari female when she wasn't in heat, she would attack and possibly kill him.

Once their season passed, the Katagaria females left their males and stayed with their sisters to travel about until their next fertile cycle. If the female became pregnant, she'd birth her young among her sisters, and as soon as the cubs were weaned, she would take them to the father to raise.

Arcadian pantheresses were much more coveted since they were ruled by human hearts that wouldn't allow them to abandon their children until adulthood. Unlike their Katagaria cousins, the Arcadians stayed with their young and their mates. The male panthers didn't have to wait for an Arcadian female to go into heat. She would be receptive to her mate at any time.

The worst part was that a panther male couldn't rape a panther female when she was in heat. All he had to do was come near her and she would willingly accept him. It was nature and a pantheress had no control over her body at such times. It wouldn't listen to any reason or rationale.

She would beg him to fill her.

The shame of that would come later, after the mating was done. Then, the Arcadian pantheress would feel embarrassed that she had acted like an animal and not a human.

Pandora moaned low in her throat as her desire sparked again and coiled through her. Her breasts were heavy, her body hot and alive with need.

Go . . .

The command was overwhelming, but she refused to heed it. She was a human, not an animal.

The Katagari male would return with Acheron and she would be among her own kind again.

Then everything would be normal.

Dante couldn't get the fire out of his blood. The animal in him was awake and craving.

Needing.

One whiff should not have affected him this much, and yet as he drifted through the dense crowd of people pretending to be aliens and paranormal entities, he couldn't stop himself from trying to find her scent again.

It was all he could do to stay in human form and not revert to his true animal body.

The hunter wasn't listening to him.

Damn it!

He caught a glimpse of Acheron Parthenopaeus across the vendor booths. Oblivious to the humans who paused to gawk at his seven feet of height, the Atlantean Dark-Hunter was reading a Dark Horse *Grendel* comic book.

Seeking the distraction of talking with a friend, Dante headed toward him.

"Ash," he said as he drew near. "You seem remarkably relaxed." Which was true. In all the centuries he'd known the man, Dante had never seen him so at ease.

Acheron looked up from his comic and inclined his head in greeting. "What can I say? This is one of the few places I can take Simi where she doesn't stand out. Hell, she actually looks normal here."

Dante laughed at that. Ash's pixielike demon seldom blended in anywhere. "Where is she?"

"Shopping like a demon."

Dante shook his head at the bad pun; knowing Simi, he figured it was probably quite true. "I tried to call your cell phone when we got in to see if you made it."

Ash immediately tensed as he put his comic down and pulled out another issue. "I turned it off on the day I got here."

"Really?" Dante asked, stunned by Ash's confession. It wasn't like him to be out of touch with his Dark-Hunter charges. "What if one of the Dark-Hunters needed you?"

Ash shrugged. "If they can't survive alone for four days once a year, they deserve to die."

Dante frowned. "That's harsh, for you."

He looked at him dryly. "Harsh? Tell you what, you take my phone and skim through the three thousand phone calls I get every day and night and see how harsh I am. I truly hate modern technology and phones in particular. I haven't had a full four hours of sleep in over fifty years. 'Ash, I broke a toenail, help me. Ash, my head hurts, what should I do?' "

Ash curled his lip in repugnance. "You know, I've never understood it. They make a deal with the devil herself and then expect me to bail them out of every minor scrape. Then when I show up to help them, they cop an attitude and tell me to blow. So if I'm selfish for wanting four days a year to be left alone, then I'm just a selfish bastard. Sue me."

Wow, someone was cranky.

Dante took a step away from the Atlantean. "Well then, I'll make sure I don't bug you."

Ash pulled out another plastic-covered comic from the long white box on the table. "You're not bothering me, Dante. Really. I'm just trying to zen myself out of a bad mood. I made the mistake of turning on my phone ten minutes ago and I had four hundred and eighty-two messages waiting on voice mail. I had it on all of three seconds before it started ringing again. All I want is a little break and no damn phone for a few days." He let out an aggra-vated breath. "Besides, I'm the one who told you to come."

"Yeah, thanks. This is . . ."—he hesitated as a centaur pranced by on what appeared to be modified ski boots that looked eerily like hooves—"interesting."

Ash smiled. "Yeah, just wait until you see the Ms. Klingon Beauty Pageant. It's something else."

Dante laughed. "I'll bet. So what good bands should I check out for my club?"

Ash grabbed three Dark Horse *Tales of the Vampires* comics and added them to his growing pile. "Last Dance is really good. They're playing tonight, and Ghoultown too. But the one band you have to see is the Cruxshadows. They're right up your alley and rule the Darkwave scene. The lead singer Rogue'll be over in the Hyatt later signing autographs at their booth. If you want, I can introduce you."

"That'd be great." The only reason Dante had come to Atlanta was because Acheron had assured him Dragon*Con was one of the best places to see several alternative bands so that he could hire them for gigs at his club in Minnesota.

Simi came running up to them with two male "Kling-ons" trailing behind her. "*Akri*? Can I go to the Klingon homeworld?"

Ash smiled at his demon. "Sure, just don't eat any of them."

The demon pouted. "But why not?"

"Because, Simi, they're not really Klingons. They're people pretending to be Klingons."

"Well, pooh, fine then. No eats. But I'm going to go now. Bye bye." She dashed off with the two young men.

Ash handed the comics to the vendor, then pulled out his wallet.

"Shouldn't you go do a head count on the homeworld population?" Dante asked.

"Nah. She'll do what I said . . ." Ash paused as if something occurred to him. "Then again, I didn't tell her not to eat a Bajoran or Romulan. Damn." He paid for the comics. "You're right, I better go count."

Ash took a step away, then stopped. "By the way, you might want to head upstairs right now and check out your room."

"Why?"

He shrugged. "Make sure it meets with your needs."

Dante frowned. "I've already been there."

"Go there again."

The animal in Dante picked up a weird scent from Acheron, but he wasn't sure what it was.

But as the Atlantean headed off, he felt an inexplicable pull to do what Acheron had suggested.

Dante headed out of the vendors' area, toward the escalator. He'd barely reached it when he smelled the pantheress again. He turned sharply to the left, expecting to see her.

She wasn't there.

Still, he was hard for her. Ready. The animal inside was growling for a taste of her body.

He headed up the escalator to escape the scent.

It seemed to grow stronger.

His head low, he scanned the crowd intently, but none of his people was there.

Closing his eyes, he sniffed the air. Her fragrance was subtle now. And it was . . .

He whirled around.

There was no woman there, only Romeo, and he reeked of the pantheress. Dante couldn't stop himself from sniffing Romeo, who immediately shoved him away.

"Man, you skeeve me when you do that. And don't do it in public. Someone might get the wrong idea about us."

He ignored his brother's reprimanding tone. "Where is she?" Dante demanded.

"Out of reach."

Her scent washed over him, even stronger than before. His body was raw. Needful. Every part of him craved her.

And it wasn't taking no for an answer.

"Where?" he growled.

Romeo shook his head.

But he didn't have to be told. Every hormone in his body sensed her. Against his will, Dante took off at a run as he cut through the crowd toward the elevator.

Without thought, he flashed himself from the lobby to the sixteenth floor.

The scent was even stronger here.

More desirable.

More intense.

Dante stalked his way down the hall until he found her door. He couldn't breathe as her scent filled his entire being. Leaning his head against the wood, he closed his eyes and fought the sudden urge to kick the door in.

That would probably scare her, and besides, he didn't want to have an audience for what he intended to do with her.

He knocked on the door with a clenched fist and waited until a small, petite brunette opened it. She had large, lavender eyes and long hair that curled around an oval face.

His breathing ragged, he stared at her, wanting her with every piece of him.

But for all his sexual hunger, he knew that it was now her move . . .

CHAPTER 2

Pandora couldn't breathe as she stared at the tall, sexy panther in her doorway. He embodied everything that was primal and male. His hands were braced on each side of the frame as he looked at her with an intensity so raw, it shook her. Masculine power and lethal grace bled from every pore of his magnificent body.

He had long black hair pulled back into a queue. His eyes were a clear blue that appeared almost colorless against his tanned skin and long midnight lashes. His face was elegantly carved and yet had a rugged quality that kept him from being pretty.

He was dressed in black jeans and a black poet's shirt. There was something timeless and old about him. Something that reached out to her and set her entire body on fire.

Without her invitation, he stepped into the room and bent his head so that he could rub his face against her hair.

Pandora gasped as that simple action sent chills all through her. His breath scorched her extra-sensitive skin, which wanted only to be touched by him. Her nipples hardened in expectation of what was to come.

"*Gataki*." He murmured the Greek word for "kitten" as he took a deep breath in her hair.

The human half of her wanted to shove him away from her. The animal part refused. It wanted only to cuddle with him. To rip his clothes off and know once and for all what it would be like to have sex with a male.

The door to her room slammed shut of its own volition.

Pandora circled around him, rubbing her body against his as she fought the urge to cry out in pleasure.

"Do you accept me?" he asked rhetorically. It was technically the woman who chose her lover, but when a female was this sexually aware of the male, there was really no way out.

All Pandora could do was nod. Her body would never allow her to deny him. He was too virile. Too consuming.

Too much of what she needed.

He turned on her with a fierce growl as he seized her for a scintillating kiss. Pandora moaned at the taste of him. No one had ever kissed her before. It was forbidden until her first cycle for any male to touch a female not related to him.

Ever since she'd been a teenager, she and her girlfriends had whispered about what they wanted for their first matings and who they would choose.

Pandora had expected Lucas to be her first. Almost four hundred years old, he was legendary among her people for his prowess and ability to teach a young pantheress her passion.

But his handsomeness paled in comparison to the dark stranger before her. This male tasted of wine and decadence. Of mystical, exotic power and knowledge.

His tongue swept against hers as her body heated to a fever pitch.

"Are you Dante?" she asked him as she nibbled his firm lips.

"Yes."

Good. At least he wouldn't share her. It was a small relief to know that.

"What is your name, *gataki*?"

"Pandora Kouti."

He pulled back to smile at her.

"Pandora," he purred as he buried his hands in her hair before inhaling the sensitive flesh of her neck, then licking it slowly. Teasingly. "And what surprises are you hiding from the world in your box, Pandora?"

She couldn't answer as he continued to lick her skin. Her knees buckled. Only the strength of his arms around her kept her from falling.

Dante knew he should leave. He should flash himself into a cold shower somewhere.

But he couldn't.

She was too hypnotic. Too tempting. The animal in him refused to leave until he'd tasted her.

And he would be her first. He could smell her innocent state.

That knowledge alone was enough to make him roar. He'd never taken a virgin before. For that matter, he'd rarely taken any woman of his own species. A pantheress was violent by nature. She had to be held down, and if a male wasn't fast enough, he could be maimed or killed during mating.

Once an orgasm seized a pantheress, the ferocity of it would make her feral. She would turn on her lover with claws and teeth bared. In the case of a Katagari female, she'd turn immediately to her animal form and attack her lover.

The male had to be ready to pull back and flash to his animal form or he wouldn't be able to defend himself from her surging hormonal and psychic overload.

It was a sobering thought.

Dante had never cared much for violent mating. He preferred to take his time pleasing his lover. To sample every single inch of her body at his leisure.

He'd always loved the taste of a woman. The scent of her. The feel of her soft limbs rubbing against his rougher ones. Always liked to hear the sounds of her ecstasy echoing in his ears as he brought her to climax over and over again.

And Pandora . . .

She would be unlike any lover he'd ever known. His first Arcadian.

His first virgin.

Kissing her deeply, he dissolved the clothes from their bodies so that there was nothing between his hands and her sweet, succulent flesh.

She shivered in his arms.

"It's okay, *gataki*," he said as he skimmed his hand down her supple back. "I won't hurt you."

His words seemed to make her panic. "You're a Katagari male."

He nibbled her shoulder, reveling in the taste of her soft, salty-sweet skin. She was truly decadent. A mouthwatering treat to sate the beast inside him.

"And I won't hurt you," he reiterated as he nibbled his way around her shoulder blade, down her back, and then around front so that he could taste her breast.

Pandora cried out the instant his mouth closed around her hard, sensitive nipple. Her body jerked and sizzled.

What was this? All she could think of was having him inside her. Of having all that hard, tawny skin lying over her as he showed her exactly what it meant to be loved by a man.

He was all sinewy muscle.

All strength. Power.

Wickedness.

And for the moment, he was *all* hers . . .

He pulled back from her with a growl before he scooped her up in his arms and carried her to the bed. She felt so dainty in his arms, so coveted.

The covers pulled themselves back so that he could set her in the center of it. Pandora's nervousness returned as the chill of the covers brushed her fevered skin.

She'd waited a lifetime for this moment. What would happen to her? Would she be changed?

Would he?

Dante gave her a fierce, ragged kiss as he spread her arms out above her head. Two seconds later, something wrapped itself around her wrists and held them there.

"What are you doing?" she asked, even more nervous than before.

His gentle touch soothed her as he massaged her tense shoulders. "I want to make sure neither of us is hurt, *gataki*. You've never had an orgasm before and you have no idea what it's going to do to you."

"Will it hurt?"

He laughed at that as his large, masculine hand cupped her breast. "No, it won't hurt at all."

She wanted to believe him. The animal in her didn't detect a lie so she relaxed. Dante might not be the man she would have chosen first, but he was proving to be gentle enough to soothe the human part of her.

He laid himself beside her so that he could study her body. He skimmed a callused hand over her breasts, then moved it lower so that he could toy with the short, crisp hairs at the juncture of her thighs.

She clenched her teeth as fire consumed her body. She ached for that hand to move lower. For it to caress the burning ache between her legs until she could think straight again.

"Tell me what you dream of, Pandora," he said quietly as his thumb teased her sensitive nub.

She licked her lips as pleasure tore through her. But it did nothing to ebb the vicious bittersweet pain inside her.

Dante blew a fiery breath across her erect nipple. "How does an Arcadian take a male inside her body?"

"Don't you know?"

He moved so that he was draped on top of her. She moaned at the delicious feel of his naked body pressing down on hers. In that moment, she wanted to see his hair unbound.

"Untie your hair," she said.

The tie came loose immediately.

It was rare among the Arcadians to find a male so at ease with his psychic abilities. They were taught to hide them unless they were fighting their animal cousins.

Dante didn't appear to have such hang-ups and she wondered if all Katagaria were like him.

"You are powerful, aren't you?" she asked.

He nodded as he stared at her in a way that reminded her so much of a panther that it was almost scary.

Pandora watched his light eyes carefully, seeking any sign that he would turn feral on her and hurt her. "Are you going to devour me?"

His smile was wicked. "Until you beg me to stop."

Dante leaned forward so that he could press his cheek to hers and savor the feel of her delicate skin. She was totally enjoyable.

With humans, he had to hide what he was from them. But Pandora knew exactly what he was and, unlike a Katagari female, she wasn't fighting him. She responded to his caresses just as a human would. With delight and innocent trust.

It was refreshing and touched a foreign part of him deeply.

He wanted to please her in a way he'd never wanted to please anyone else.

Reaching down between them, he gently separated the tender folds of her body so that he could touch her intimately.

She cried out in ecstasy.

Her response delighted him. Dante used his powers to shield the sounds from escaping the room as he kissed his way down her body to where his hand played.

Pandora could barely think as she felt Dante spread her

legs wide. It was as if every part of her was burning. Her head spun with pleasure.

And then she felt the most incredible thing of all. Dante's mouth teasing her. Hissing, she threw her head back and arched her spine as his tongue worked incredible magic on her. He sank one long, lean finger deep inside her as his tongue continued to explore every tender fold with a thoroughness that was blinding in its intensity.

Dante couldn't take his eyes off her as he watched her head rolling back and forth on the pillow. There was nothing a male of his species valued more than the taste of a virgin's climax.

His kind was known to kill for the privilege of taking a virgin, and for the first time in his life, he understood that primal desire.

The revelation shocked him. He'd always told himself that a female wasn't worth another panther's life. But as he watched her innocent, unabashed reaction to his touch, he was no longer so sure.

There was no artifice in her response. She was reacting honestly to him. Openly. And he loved it.

When she came, crying out his name, he felt something deep inside him shatter with pride and satisfaction.

Dante held her hips still, expecting to have to pull away from her.

He didn't. She lacked the violent tendencies of his kind. Instead of attacking him, she stayed on the bed, panting and purring as she continued to let her climax flow.

Pandora wasn't sure what had just happened to her. But it had been incredible. Wonderful. And it left her wanting even more from him. She still felt her body spasming as Dante continued to stroke and tease until she was weak from it.

Her hands suddenly free, she reached down and sank her hand into his long, silken hair as he gently rolled her onto her stomach.

He lightly nipped her buttocks.

"What are you doing?" she asked as he placed a pillow underneath her stomach.

"I'm going to show you what it feels like to have a male inside you, Pandora."

She shivered at the erotic image that played through her mind of Dante thrusting against her. "Please don't break my neck."

He brushed her hair aside and placed a gentle kiss on her nape. "I would never hurt you, *gataki*."

She shivered at his whispered words.

He lifted one of her legs up, then drove himself deep inside her. Pandora cried out as he filled her to capacity. He was long and hard, and so deep that she couldn't draw a breath.

Never had she felt anything like his fullness inside her. Of the intimacy of him touching her in a place no one ever had before.

More than that, she felt something breaking as electrical energy surged through her. Every inch of her body sizzled and hummed.

Dante ground his teeth as pleasure tore through him. He'd never felt anything better than her tight, wet heat around him. It was all he could do not to thrust himself into her hard and furiously until he was fully sated.

But he didn't want to scare or hurt her in any way.

Holding himself up on one arm, he ran his tongue over the sensitive skin of her ear and breathed lightly into it. She shivered under him.

He smiled at that as he trailed his hand over her skin so that he could again sink his fingers down her swollen clit.

Pandora groaned at the sensation of his hand moving in time to his long, gentle strokes. No man, Arcadian or otherwise, could be more tender. She would never have believed this was possible from an animal.

Only this wasn't an animal who was holding her. He was more human than anyone she'd ever known.

And kind. There was no pain and she wondered if he were using his powers to heighten the pleasure his touch delivered. She only wished she knew enough about her new powers to return the favor to him.

He began moving slowly against her, then faster. Faster. And faster still.

Pandora gasped at the speed of his thrusts as they continued to crescendo. Growling from the pleasure of it, she rocked her hips against his, driving him in even deeper until it was all she could do not to scream.

Dante ground his teeth as she moved in sync with him. She was exquisitely demanding. And when she came again, he laughed until the sensation of her body gripping his sent him over the edge and he too climaxed.

He roared out loud as ecstasy tore through him with waves and waves of pleasure.

She collapsed under him an instant before she rolled over onto her back.

Expecting her to attack, Dante almost leaped from the bed. But she reached one tender arm up and wrapped it around his shoulders to hold him close to her.

The smile on her face warmed his heart. "Thank you," she breathed. "It's the first time in days that my body feels like it belongs to me again."

He inclined his head to her, then reached down to take her small hand into his so that he could plant a kiss on her knuckles. No wonder Katagaria males took Arcadian females. It was so nice to lie like this with her.

If she were Katagaria, he'd most likely be bleeding in the aftermath of their encounter. Instead, she toyed with his hair and stroked him.

At least until she groaned.

Dante smiled in anticipation. It was her cycle heating up again.

She purred as her hand tightened in his hair and she eagerly rubbed herself against him.

His body hardened again instantly.

He was as ready for her as she was for him. The animal in him could smell her need and it answered accordingly.

This was going to be a long afternoon and he was going to relish every part of it.

And every part of her . . .

Pandora lay quietly in bed while Dante showered in her bathroom. She should be horrified by how many hours they had spent in her bed. He had bent her in more positions than she would have thought possible.

And she had loved every one of them.

He was incredible . . . and extremely limber.

She was sated to a level that defied her imagination. Normally, a pantheress would need days for a male to satiate her.

But Dante had been so thorough, so exhausting, that she felt an incredible sense of peace.

Who would have thought it possible?

She heard the water turn off. A few seconds later, Dante returned to the bed with his hair damp and curling around his shoulders.

He was completely naked and unabashed about it. She stared in awe at that tawny body liberally dusted with short, black hairs.

"Feeling better?" she asked.

He gifted her with a smile that made her stomach flutter. "I would have felt better had you joined me for a bath."

She blushed at that. He'd made the offer and she had declined, though why she couldn't imagine. It wasn't like he hadn't caressed and studied every inch of her in the last few hours. But somehow the thought of showering with him had seemed too personal.

Too strange.

He lay down beside her and pulled her into his arms.

Pandora sighed contentedly. It was so nice to be held by him.

One minute he had a long, masculine arm draped over her waist, and in the next, it was the limb of a panther.

She bolted out of the bed with a shriek.

Dante flashed instantly back into human form. "What's wrong?" he asked.

"Don't do the panther thing around me, okay? It really creeps me."

He frowned at her. "Why?"

"I . . . I just can't stand the sight of them."

He gave her a harsh, condemning stare that set her ire off. "You're one of us, baby. Get used to it."

She cringed at the thought. She was not in the same category as a Katagari female. They were crude and mean, and had no care whatsoever for anyone other than themselves.

"Oh, no I'm not," she said, growling the words at him. "I'm a human being, not an animal like you."

Dante narrowed his eyes at words that shouldn't hurt him and yet for some unfathomable reason did. He'd gone out of his way to be tender with her.

And what had it accomplished?

Not a damn thing except to have her disdain him over something he couldn't help any more than she could help being human.

There was nothing wrong with being a Katagari. He took a lot of pride in his heritage.

His kind was definitely superior to hers. At least they didn't lie, cheat, and steal for no reason.

Curling his lip, he climbed out of bed and flashed his clothes back on.

"Fine. Have a nice life."

Pandora jumped as he slammed out of her room.

"You too!" she called childishly, knowing he couldn't hear her.

What did she care anyway?

He was an animal. But as she headed for the bathroom,

she missed the warm feeling she'd had when he held her. The sweet sound of her name on his lips as he carefully made love to her.

The way his tongue had stroked and soothed her.

Grinding her teeth, she forced the image away and went to shower. And as the water came on, she thought of Dante's brother who had yet to bring Acheron to her. He must have sent Dante to her instead.

How dare he!

She should have known better than to trust an animal. Why would one of them help her anyway?

Angry at both of them, and at herself for being so stupid as to trust them, Pandora regulated the water and started scrubbing with a vengeance.

Suddenly, the bathroom curtain was whisked open.

Pandora gasped as she spun about to find Dante standing there, blue eyes glaring at her.

"You never answered my question."

She sputtered at him. "Excuse me, I'm in the middle of a bath here."

"Yeah, I know, and I'll let you get back to it once you tell me why panthers bother you."

That was none of his business!

Tears burned in her eyes as her ordeal over the last two weeks overwhelmed her. Her unbalanced hormones didn't help matters any and neither did the fact that all she really wanted to do was go home.

Before she could stop herself, the truth came pouring out in wrenching sobs. "Because every time I see one of your people, you steal someone away from me whom I love and I hate all of you for it. Now your kind has taken me away from my home and my family so that I can either be a whore to the entire pack or a slave to one of you."

Dante felt an odd sensation in his chest as she started weeping. Not once in almost three hundred years had he felt such a sense of helplessness.

Such a desire to help someone.

"And what's worse," she said, her voice cracking, "I know I can't really go home because they'll just send me back here to the Katagaria pack that stole me. Panthers have taken everything from me. Even my virginity."

Dante turned the water off with his thoughts and pulled a towel off the rack before wrapping it around her.

"I don't know what I was thinking when I ran away," she sobbed. "Acheron won't help me. Why should he? And even if he wanted to, what could he really do? Dark-Hunters can't interfere in our business. I just wanted some hope. Something other than what is meant for me. I don't want to be a panther whore. I just want to have my own life where no one hurts or uses me. Is that so wrong?"

"No, Pandora," Dante said as he pulled her sodden body into his arms and held her tight. "It's not wrong."

He kissed the top of her head as he pulled another towel down to dry her hair.

Pandora hated herself for falling apart like this. She was normally calm and collected. But it was beyond her ability to cope now.

All she wanted was her life back. One day where she was again in charge of her body and her destiny.

One day of clarity.

What her people had done was wrong and she knew it. She hated all of them, Arcadian and Katagaria, for forcing this on her.

No woman should ever have her choice taken away from her.

She tried to stop crying as Dante rocked her gently in his arms. He was being much kinder than she deserved. Not even her own father would be so understanding of this breakdown. He'd never been the kind of man to tolerate emotional outbursts well and he'd trained all his daughters to suffer in silence.

Yet Dante didn't say anything. He just held her quietly while she cried.

"I don't know what to do," she said, stunned when the words came out of her mouth. It wasn't like her to confide in someone and to admit that she was in over her head . . .

She couldn't believe what she was doing.

Maybe it was because she didn't know where else to turn.

Or maybe it was just after the time they had shared where he hadn't hurt her that she was willing to almost trust him with the truth of her situation and feelings.

"We'll figure something out for you," Dante said as he rubbed her back. "Don't worry."

"Why would you help me? Your brother said you were a selfish bastard."

He gave half a laugh at that. "I am selfish. I'm cold and vicious. I don't have any friends and I spend all my time looking for Arcadians who bother me so I can pick a fight and hurt them. Hell, I even killed my own brother when he sold my pack out to the Daimons. Truly, I am every bad thing you think of when you hear the term 'Katagaria.'"

And still he hadn't hurt her.

He gently laid his hand against her cold cheek to wipe away her tears. "Yet I don't want to see you cry."

She shivered at his hypnotic words.

"Get dressed, Pandora, and we'll go find something to eat and talk about what we can do to help you."

"Really?"

"Really."

She pulled him down so that she could give him a scorching kiss. "I'm sorry I called you an animal, Dante."

"It's okay. I am one."

No he wasn't. In that moment, he was her hero. Her champion. She would never insult anyone so kind.

As soon as she pulled on her jeans and a red shirt, he led

her from the room, downstairs to the lobby that was packed with even more people than earlier.

"This is some party, huh?" she asked as she saw a group of four women dressed only in warning tape wrapped around their bodies surrounded by a group of Storm Troopers, cross the lobby.

"It's definitely something," he said, holding her hand as they passed a woman who was leading a man around on a leash.

"Do you come here often?"

He shook his head. "First time."

Before she could speak again, Pandora felt a vicious pain sear across her palm. Hissing, she jerked her hand back at the same time Dante started shaking his own hand as if he'd burned it.

Pandora frowned as a bad sense of foreboding went through her.

She looked at her hand and watched as an attractive geometrical design formed over her palm, confirming her worst fear.

She was mated.

And there was only one male it could be . . .

CHAPTER 3

Dante stared in horror at the sight of his mating mark.
No. This couldn't be real and it damn sure couldn't
be happening. Not to him.

He took Pandora's hand and held it up against his so
that he could compare their palms.

There was no denying it. The marks were identical.

She was his.

Damn.

"You bastard!" she snarled angrily. "How could you be
the one meant for me?"

"Excuse me?" Dante asked, baffled by her rage. If anyone had a right to be angry it was him. After all, he'd been
minding his own business when she traipsed into his sen-
sory circle. Had she just stayed put, neither one of them
would be in this situation.

"In case you didn't notice, sweetheart, I'm not exactly
thrilled by this either."

She glared at him for two seconds before she whirled on
her heel and headed off into the crowd.

Part of him was tempted to let her go, but that wouldn't
accomplish anything. Neither Katagaria nor Arcadian had
any say in who the Fates chose as their mates. Any more
than they knew when or where they'd find the one person
who was designated for them.

The only way to find a mate was to sleep with him or her and to wait for the mark to appear.

Whenever it did, they only had three weeks to perform their mating ritual or they would spend the rest of their lives sterile. For a female, it wasn't such a bad thing since she could continue to have sex with any man who caught her attention; she just couldn't have children with any male other than her designated mate. But for a male . . .

It was worse than death. The male was left completely impotent until the day his mate died.

Dante shivered at the thought. Him, impotent? Those were two words that would never be said together.

He would die first.

He headed through the lobby in hot pursuit of his "mate."

Pandora was seething as she headed blindly through the crowd. All she wanted was to put some significant distance between her and Dante.

This was awful.

Terrible!

Wasn't it?

Most Arcadians dreamed of finding their mate as their first lover. That way, they wouldn't have to fear their prowling instinct, which would debase them as they hopped from male to male, trying to find the one who could breed with them.

It was a dream come true to find a mate so early and so easily. Most of her kind spent centuries looking. And many died without ever being mated at all.

Technically, she'd been lucky, and yet she was angry because she was bound to a *Katagari* male. Talk about jumping from the frying pan into the fire! This morning her worst fear was being enslaved to a Katagaria pack.

Now she was captured even more fully than before. If

she left Dante, she would never be able to have children. He was the only one who could give her that.

"Damn these hormones," she snarled as more tears gathered in her eyes. It was hard to think straight.

Someone grabbed her from behind.

"Gotcha," a deep, masculine voice said in her ear.

It wasn't Dante.

The panther inside her roared to life, rejecting any male not her mate. She whirled about and struck without thought, making contact with the stranger's groin.

Doubling over, he hissed in pain. But before she could escape, another male took her arm.

She froze as she realized he was an exact, equally handsome copy of the man she had just racked.

"Leo." The lethal growl cut across the tense air and shivered down her spine. Dante's voice threatened violence and death. "Let go my mate, boy."

The panther holding her let go instantly and cursed. "You've got to be kidding me."

Dante shook his head as he joined them. "I wish I were." He scowled at the other male, who was still cupping himself. "You okay, Mikey?"

"Yeah," he said, grimacing as he forced himself to straighten. His face was still an awful shade of red and he was panting. "Just my luck that you would find a mate who is as pissy as you are."

"I take offense to that," Pandora said.

Mike gave her a menacing scowl. "And I take offense to my sudden need for testicle retrieval. You know, I would have liked to have fathered some children one day."

Leo laughed at his twin brother's discomfort. "I'm just glad you got to her first."

Mike curled his lip. "Shut up."

Dante rolled his eyes before introducing his brothers. "Pandora, meet my brothers, Leonardo and Michelangelo."

"Like the Teenage Mutant Ninja Turtles?" she couldn't resist asking.

"Like the Renaissance painters," Leo snapped. He exchanged a snarl with his twin brother. "I seriously hate those damned turtles."

As if on cue, four people dressed as said turtles walked by and frowned at them.

"I swear the gods are mocking us," Mike said as he saw the green-foam-covered humans.

"I know the feeling," Pandora said, sighing. There were no better words to describe her present predicament.

She had no idea what kind of . . . creature the Fates had joined her to.

Then again, Dante wasn't the one acting so bizarrely. She was the one with hormonal overload poisoning. She honestly couldn't blame Dante if he started choking her.

She just wished she could be herself for a few hours so that she could sort through all this better.

"Well, I see all of you found her."

Pandora looked past Leo to see the first one of the brothers she'd met. Ironically, he was the only one whose name she didn't know.

"Shut up, Romeo," Leo said irritably. "Don't think we don't know it was you who spread her scent around this hotel to drive us crazy. You almost got me killed when I grabbed Simi by mistake and she pulled out a bottle of barbecue sauce to sprinkle on me. If Ash hadn't come up when he did, that damn demon would have gladly eaten me."

Romeo laughed for only an instant before he sobered. He sniffed the air.

"Oh shit," he breathed as he looked from her to Dante. "You're mated?"

"Yeah," Dante said. "Thanks, Romeo. Had you not had her scent all over *you,* I wouldn't have been able to pinpoint her so easily. I really appreciate the road map."

Pandora stiffened at Dante's sarcasm. "Thank you for

making me feel really bad. You know, you could try and be a little more positive about this."

"True," Romeo said. "She is Arcadian and not nearly as likely to roam."

It was Pandora's turn to be "thrilled." "Just think, now all of you have a babysitter for your litters and someone a lot weaker to knock around whenever you get angry at your enemies."

All four of the panthers scowled at her.

"What are you talking about?" Dante asked.

"It's all you want me for, right?"

He looked at her aghast. "You're my mate, Pandora, not my servant. Anyone in my pack, including my brothers, who disrespects you disrespects me. And believe me, that's one thing no one will *ever* do."

The sincerity of that tore through her.

He really meant it.

Gratitude and happiness welled inside her, and for the first time since her father had handed her over to their enemies, she had some real, true hope. "Really?"

"You may be Arcadian," Romeo said, "but you're a member of our pack now and we'll treat you as such."

"But what of the children you told me about?" Pandora asked Romeo. "Won't you make me watch them?"

"They're *my* offspring," Romeo said. "I've been raising cubs and siblings for more than three hundred years, even Dante. Why would that change now?"

But she had assumed . . .

"Who watches them while you're gone?" she asked.

It was Mike who answered. "Our brother Gabriel and our cousin Angel."

"Yeah," Dante said. "They do fine with cubs. It's Frick and Frack here who screw them up and get all of them into trouble."

Mike gave him a droll stare. "I really wish you'd stop calling us that."

"When you grow out of your awkward pubescent stage, I will." Dante checked his watch. "That should be, what? Another fifty, sixty years?"

"We're older than her," Leo said, pointing to Pandora.

"Yeah, but she's got something neither of you do."

"And that is?"

Dante rubbed his eyes as if his head were beginning to hurt. "If you can't see what she has that neither of you do, you, need even more help than I thought."

Leo made a disgusted noise at him. "I'm not going to stand here and be insulted. Since I can't touch your pantheress without losing a limb or my balls, I'm going to pursue something a little less dangerous."

Dante and Romeo exchanged an amused look that was completely mischievous.

"Why don't you try one of the filking rooms?" Dante asked. "I heard from Acheron that a lot of wild things go on in there. Women taking off their clothes. Wine being passed around to anyone who wants some."

Both of the twins' faces lighted up.

"That sounds good and dirty to me," Mike said. "Perfect. Later."

Pandora laughed as the twins bolted away from them. "You do realize that filking is just science fiction folk singing, right?"

Dante gave an evil laugh. "I know. I just wish I could be there when they realize it too."

Romeo shook his head. "You are so mean to them. It's a wonder they don't kill you while you sleep."

Dante scoffed. "Yeah, right. Those goofs are lucky I tolerate them."

"And yet you do," Pandora said, smiling at the knowledge. "Why is that, Dante?"

Romeo returned her smile. "Because my brother has a heart that he hates to own up to."

"Shut up, Romeo."

"She's your mate, Dante. Be honest with her. Don't let the past sour you for eternity. She's not Bonita, you know?"

Dante growled and lunged for Romeo, who stepped back lightning fast.

"Later," Romeo said before he left them.

"Bonita?" Pandora asked as soon as they were alone . . . or at least as alone as a couple in a crowd of thousands could be.

Dante didn't answer. From his expression she could tell he was thinking of something very painful.

Her heart wrenched at the thought. Was she an old lover? "Who was she?"

He let out a long, tired breath before he answered. "She was the bonded mate to one of my older brothers, Donatello. He was the pack leader before me and he loved his mate more than his life."

Pandora felt for the panther. "Let me guess. She betrayed him."

"No," he said to her surprise. "They were bonded together, and one night while she was home from her journeys, she lashed out at him while they were having sex and ripped into his jugular. They both died before he could get help."

Pandora covered her mouth as she envisioned the horror. Once Were-Panthers bonded their life forces together, neither of them could live without the other. If one died, they both died.

How terrible that Bonita had killed them in one act of thoughtless passion.

"I'm so sorry," she whispered.

"Thanks," he said quietly. "It was a damn waste of two decent panthers." His gaze penetrated her. "It's why I never wanted a pantheress for a mate or even a lover. I don't want my cubs orphaned because I let my guard drop and left myself open to a female's attack."

"I would never rip at you."

"How do you know?"

"Well," she said as they started moving through the lobby, "right now I don't even know how to turn into a panther. So that alone makes you safe. I tried to do it a couple of days ago and all I got was a tail that was very hard to hide until I went to sleep and it left me."

Dante laughed, and though she ought to be offended that he was laughing at her misfortune, she wasn't. There was something about him that was truly charming.

"I've never heard of that happening before," he said.

"Stick around. All kinds of weird things have been happening to me lately."

He brushed the hair back from her face. "I think I might like to do that. If you don't mind."

For some reason, the thought warmed her. Dante was a lot of fun to be with.

When they weren't fighting.

"What do you expect of your mate, Dante?"

He shrugged, then put his arm around her as they cruised by the banquet tables that were lined with fliers and giveaway items. "Nothing more than any other panther, I guess. I expect you to come home when you're in season and leave when you're not."

It was too good to be true.

"You would let me leave if I wanted to?"

He frowned. "It's the nature of our species, Pandora. Why would I stop you?"

"But the other pack—"

"Ain't right in the head," he said, interrupting her. "There's something profoundly wrong with anyone who would try to get a panther to act against his or her nature. That's something I'd expect an Arcadian to do, not a Katagari."

She smiled up at him as she felt another hormonal surge go through her.

By the sudden feral look on Dante's face she could tell he sensed it too.

His arm tightened around her.

"Can we wait?" she asked quickly. "I don't want to rush mating with you again until we get a few things straight between us."

Even though sex with him would clear her head, her human heart wanted more between them than just a physical relationship. She wanted to know the human part of her mate.

"Such as?" Dante asked.

"I don't know," she answered honestly. "I know in my heart that committing myself to you is the best thing for both of us. It's probably the only thing since I no longer have a pack to shelter me. But the human in me wants to know you better before I take such a permanent step."

To her relief, he didn't try to balk or force her.

"What do you need from me?"

"Just be with me as a human for a little while and let me get to know you, okay?"

Dante nodded even though what he really wanted to do was take her back upstairs and give her what both their bodies craved.

But she was young and scared. This was a momentous step for both of them. Bonding was eternal and it wasn't something to be taken lightly.

True kindness to someone else was all but alien to him. He understood loyalty. Obligation.

But love and tenderness . . .

Panthers didn't dream of such things. They only understood immediate needs. The ones for food, shelter, sex.

Offspring.

And yet he wanted something more from her. Something deeper.

He wanted her acceptance.

Her touch.

It was stupid. What did he need with such things? He had money. Power. Magic.

He could force her to do anything he wanted her to. But it still wouldn't give him what he wanted.

Her heart.

Damn him for his human half.

Sighing, he led her toward the Marquis Steakhouse where they could get something to eat.

The night went by quickly as Pandora followed Dante around to various booths and concerts where alternative bands were displaying their wares and talents. Dante seemed to have a knack for finding really good performers who were excited about being offered money to play in his club in Minnesota.

"How long have you had your club?" she asked as he bought three CDs from a band called Emerald Rose who had been playing earlier outside the conference rooms at the Hyatt.

"Almost thirty years now."

Wow, that was a long time. Dante looked good for a man who was more than two hundred years old.

Really good.

"And the humans don't realize that you're always there and that you never age?"

He shook his head. "When they leave the Inferno, we tamper with their minds a bit. Even if they come in every night, they never remember those of us who don't age or change."

"That must be nice. In my . . ." She hesitated to say "pack" since they had thrown her out. "In my world, we stay away from the humans as much as possible."

"So what's the future like where you live, anyway?"

"Not that much different from this. Haven't you ever been?"

"Not since I was a cub. When I first got control of my time-travel powers, I hopped around quite a bit. But after a while, it got boring. Things and places changed, but the people didn't. So I decided to stay with my pack in Minnesota and not worry about the past or the future."

She would love to be able to time-jump like that. It was true freedom and that was one thing she'd never known.

"Can you teach me how to use my powers like that?" she asked.

"Of course."

She smiled. None of her sisters who had been sent into this time period had been taught anything. The Katagaria hadn't allowed them to develop their powers for fear they would leave. Some of them had even been forced by the Katagaria to wear *metriazo* collars to ensure that none of them would ever be able to use their magic.

It was harsh and cruel.

"Is it hard to time-travel?" she asked.

"Not now, it's not for me. But I've had centuries to perfect my powers. When you first start it can be . . . surprising. Last time I left Leo and Mike at home, they time-jumped from Minnesota 2002 to the Aleutian Islands 1432 instead of New York 2065. It was a bitch trying to find them and get them home again."

"I'm surprised you went after them."

"Yeah, well, they annoy me, but I understand they're just cubs who will eventually grow up . . . probably to annoy me even more."

She laughed at his offbeat humor as they drifted through the strangely garbed crowd. She had to admit that Dante was a lot of fun once he got used to you and stopped being so feral and snarling.

"You do have a heart, don't you?"

"No, Pandora," he said, his blue eyes scorching her with their intensity. "I don't. I only have responsibility. And I have a shitload of it."

Maybe, but she wasn't quite so sure. For one thing the arm he had draped around her shoulders didn't say "burden," it said "protective."

And she wanted to pretend it said something even more. Something like friendship.

Maybe even love.

Dante paused at a dealer's display case. A tiny smile hovered at the edges of his lips as something caught his eye. He motioned for the dealer to come over.

"Can I help you?" the older woman asked as she approached them.

Dante pointed to something under the glass. "I'd like to see that."

Pandora didn't know what it was until the woman handed it to Dante and he turned toward her. She couldn't help laughing at the gold pendant in the form of a panther wrapped around a sapphire as he fastened it around her neck.

Pandora held the pendant in her hand so that she could examine it. "How unusual."

"Yes, it is," the woman said. "That's a shaman designer I met out West. He takes vision quests and then makes a necklace based on what animal guides him. That one there he said was a panther that led him through a nightmare and saved him."

How oddly apropos.

She looked up at Dante and smiled.

"I'll take it," Dante said, pulling out his wallet.

Pandora stared down at the exquisitely crafted piece while he paid. She was so warmed by the gesture, especially since Romeo had told her how selfish Dante was.

"Thank you," she said when he returned to her side.

"My pleasure."

Smiling even more, she lifted herself up on tiptoe and placed a chaste kiss to his cheek.

"You keep doing that," he whispered in her ear, "and I'll have you upstairs and naked in a heartbeat."

An overwhelming wave of desire tore through her body. It was the pantheress in her that needed to feel him inside her. They'd done enough talking and the wild part of her personality now wanted appeasement too.

"I wouldn't mind it one bit," she whispered back.

That was all it took. One second they were in the crowd and the next, he'd pulled them off into an alcove where no one could see them and poofed them into a suite.

"Is this your room?" she asked as she glanced around the elegant accommodations.

"It's *our* room," he said as he stalked her like the hungry predator he was.

She stiffened at his tone. "Is that an order?"

"No, Pandora. But so long as we are mates, what is mine is yours."

"You're being strangely accommodating for a selfish panther Romeo said held no interest in a mate."

Dante paused at that. It was true. He'd never wanted to be bound by anything, especially not a mate. Yet for some reason, he didn't mind Pandora in the least.

"The Fates didn't ask me who or what I wanted for my own." He held her marked palm up for both of them to see. "But they have chosen you as mine and I take care of what belongs to me."

"And if I don't want to belong to you?"

"I can't force you to mate with me, Pandora, you know that. You are free to leave my protection at any time and go wherever you want."

Pandora swallowed at the thought. Yes, she could. But where would she go? The journey to Atlanta had been scary and fraught with the fear of having a pack find her and abuse her or the humans learning that she was a Were-Panther and locking her up.

Many ordinary things had baffled her.

How to buy a bus ticket. How to order food. Those things were all different in her time period. Everything there was done with universal credits. There was no money in her world. No fuel-burning vehicles.

The transports in her century were more akin to monorails and you paid your way with your palm print. Everything at home was automated and clinical.

She didn't know how to survive in the current human world. Didn't know how to use her powers.

It was terrifying here.

Except for Dante. He offered her more than anyone ever had. Protection and education.

He was her safety.

And he was her designated mate. Mating with a male was a physical act. It was the bonding ceremony that was emotional. She could easily mate and then have his protection.

Her heart would still belong solely to herself.

But if she refused to mate with Dante, he would have no reason to protect or educate her. And why would he? Her refusal would leave him impotent. Something she was sure wouldn't endear her to him.

"You will give me total freedom without any limitations on it?" she asked.

"I know no other way."

In that moment, she realized that she could learn to love this panther standing in front of her. He didn't have to give her anything. He could theoretically take anything from her that he wanted. The other panthers did.

If a woman wasn't mated to one of the Katagaria pack, they kept her anyway and used her as a whore for all of them.

But Dante offered her the world and asked for nothing in return. Nothing except a few words that would unite their physical bodies.

"And our children?" she asked him.

"We have a large nursery for them in Minnesota."

She cocked her head. "You realize they'll most likely be human and not cubs."

He looked perplexed by that. "Then I'll read Mr. Spock."

Pandora laughed. "He's the character from *Star Trek,* not the child expert. No wonder you're here."

He brushed the hair back from her face and gave her a sincere, heated look that melted her. "I will do whatever I have to to take care of them. I promise you. Human or cub, they will be protected as my offspring and they will have whatever they need to grow strong and healthy."

She pressed her marked palm against his. "Then I will mate with you, Dante Pontis."

Dante couldn't breathe as he stared down at her and those blessed words rang in his ears. He should be running for the door. But if he did that, he'd never have sex again.

Sex with only one woman. He was really paying the piper for all the years he'd been tormenting Romeo about being mated.

And yet he couldn't quite muster up true fear. Some hidden part of him liked the idea of Pandora being his.

Lacing his fingers with hers, he walked backward toward the bed, pulling her with him.

He used his powers to turn down the bed and strip their clothes from them before he lay on his back and pulled her over him.

The mating ritual was older than time. It was instinctive to their species and it would bind them for the rest of their lives. The only way to break it would be for one of them to die. Whoever survived the union would then be free to try and find another mate . . . if there was another one out there.

It was extremely rare for any Were-Hunter, Katagaria or Arcadian, to find a second mate.

Pandora bit her lip in nervous trepidation. All her life, her thoughts and energy had been spent on worrying about the actual act of sex. Since she was promised to a Katagaria pack, she'd never really thought much about ritual mating.

Now she was almost scared as she tried to take Dante into her body. This was a lot more difficult than she would have guessed. Every time she tried to straddle him, his cock went astray.

Dante smiled gently. "Can I help?"

She nodded.

He shifted his hips, then guided her onto him. They both moaned in pleasure as her body took him in all the way to his hilt.

This was it. A man who ought to terrify and repulse her was about to become her mate.

She would have children with him and somehow they would bridge the differences between their cultures and personalities and become the sole physical comfort for each other.

If she had to have a Katagaria lover, she couldn't imagine a better panther to have as her own than Dante.

Pandora could barely think as she felt heat coming from their joined hands that held the mating mark. She moved against him slowly, then spoke the words that would unite them. "I accept you as you are, and I will always hold you close in my heart. I will walk beside you forever."

Dante watched her intently as he felt every inch of her body with his. He'd never thought to have a mate at all and had relegated himself to a future bereft of children. Now the thought of having his own cubs warmed him.

She was his.

A hot, demanding possessiveness unlike anything he'd ever known before tore through him as he watched her ride him slow and easy. Not feral like a pantheress.

Human and yet not. Who would have thought that Dante Pontis could be tamed by such a small creature? And yet her tender touch seared him with a humanity he wouldn't have thought possible.

The beast inside him was calm. No longer searching, it

lay at peace as if she fit some part of him he'd never known was missing.

Smiling up at her, he cupped her face with his free hand and repeated the vow back to her.

Pandora moaned at the deepness of his voice until an unexpected pain sliced through her as her canine teeth started to grow.

Pandora hissed. This was the *thirio,* a need inside both their races that wanted them to bite each other and combine their life forces so that if one died, they both did.

Like the mating ritual itself, the choice of bonding was hers alone to make. Dante could never force it on her.

Nor did he ask it of her now.

True to his words, he left it entirely up to her and only watched her as she rode him.

Pandora kissed the hand that held his mark, then led it to her breast as her orgasm pierced her.

Dante couldn't breathe as his own climax blazed. He roared in satisfaction as his teeth finally began to recede.

It was done now. There was no going back.

They were joined, but not bonded.

Still, she was his.

He reached up to touch the necklace he'd bought for her. She looked beautiful naked in his arms. Her spent body was still wrapped around his.

"Pandora Pontis," he breathed. "Welcome to my pack." With that thought in mind, he pulled the small signet ring off his little finger, wished a spell onto it, then handed it to her.

Pandora studied the antique piece. It was beautiful, with gold filigree surrounding a large sapphire stone where an ornate *"DP"* was engraved. "What is this?"

"A homing beacon so that wherever you find yourself, you can always come back to me simply by thinking of me."

She scowled at his words. "I don't have those powers."

"I know. It's why I'm giving you the ring. The spell works from my powers and it's unbreakable."

Her lips trembled at his kindness. He'd really meant it when he said she had her freedom. Swallowing against the lump in her throat, she slid the ring onto her left hand. It was a perfect fit. "Thank you."

He inclined his head to her, then pulled her lips to his so that he could give her a passionate kiss.

A bright flash filled the room.

Pandora pulled back with a cry as someone grabbed her from behind.

Two seconds later, all hell broke loose.

CHAPTER 4

Pandora cried out as she realized that eight panthers from the pack that had originally snatched her from her time period had suddenly appeared in Dante's suite.

"How dare you run from us?" their *tessera* leader snarled as he slung her away from the bed and Dante, into the hands of two of his cronies.

Pandora fought their hold as Dante threw his hand out and blasted the man who had grabbed her. The leader recoiled into the wall, but came right back on his feet.

Dante crouched low, ready to pounce on them. "Don't you dare touch her."

The leader straightened to give Dante a murderous glare. "Stay out of this, *panthiras*. She belongs to us."

Dante came off the bed with a snarl. "The hell you say." He turned to panther form as he attacked.

With the exception of the two holding her, all the men in the room transformed into panthers to fight. Pandora cringed at the growls and roars as the animals slashed and clawed each other in a primal battle.

Terrified that they might hurt Dante, she bit the man to her right, then stomped the foot of the one to her left. They let go of her, then reached for her again.

She spun away from them. Clothes appeared instantly on her body.

"*Run*, gataki," Dante said in her mind. "*They won't be able to find you in the crowd.*"

The next thing she knew, she was downstairs in a women's bathroom stall.

"Dammit, Dante!" she snarled as she left the stall and almost ran into a human woman dressed in an ornate burgundy and gold Renaissance gown who appeared to have just left the stall before her.

The woman gave her a fierce scowl that Pandora ignored as she brushed past her.

She had to get back upstairs with some reinforcements.

Dante couldn't fight that many panthers on his own. They'd kill him.

Her heart hammering, she ran out of the bathroom to find herself inside a roomful of dealers. She scanned the booths hoping to find one of Dante's brothers.

Instead her gaze landed on a medieval weapons booth that was lined with every kind of weapon imaginable.

Pandora headed for it. She skimmed through the weapons. They had poleaxes and swords, which would be too awkward for her. She had no idea how to skillfully wield one, and the daggers would force her to get too close to the panthers.

But the double-sided handaxe . . .

She seized it without hesitation, then closed her eyes, conjured up an image of Dante, and prayed his spell actually worked. Her head swam as she was whirled back into the room in the middle of the fight.

Pandora tightened her grip on the axe, then realized she wasn't sure which panther was Dante.

Not until one attacked her. Assuming her mate wouldn't do such a thing, she swung the axe with every ounce of strength she possessed.

It made contact with the beast's shoulder.

The panther howled as he limped away.

"*Pandora!*" Dante snapped in her mind. "*What are you doing?*"

"I'm saving my mate," she said between clenched teeth as she went after another panther. "You're not Dante, are you?"

"*I'm behind you.*"

"Good." She swung at the panther in front of her who dodged her first blow but was caught by her second one.

Before she could swing again, she found herself back in the handicapped bathroom stall, this time with two women who were trying to unlace a female Klingon costume.

They both gaped at her as they stared at her bloodied axe.

Too worried over her mate, Pandora paid them no attention.

"I'm getting tired of this!" she said, then wished herself back to Dante.

Dante cursed in her head as she reappeared in his room. "*I'm going to take that damned ring from you.*"

A panther leaped at her.

Pandora started to swing, but caught herself as the panther flashed to Dante's naked, human form. He wrapped his arms around her and flashed her into her hotel room.

"Dante?" she said, her voice shaking as she realized he was covered in blood from the fighting. He looked terrible. There were bite wounds and scratches all over him.

Dante wanted to speak, but in truth it was taking way too much of his powers to assume human form while injured. His human body ached and throbbed.

He had to protect Pandora.

Closing his eyes, he summoned Romeo.

But no sooner had he sent out the call, than his human legs buckled.

"Dante?" Pandora asked as she pulled him into her arms.

He had no choice except to return to his panther's body.

To his surprise, she didn't release him or flee in fear of his animal form. She held him tight and stroked his fur.

He licked her chin, but couldn't muster any more strength. He was in way too much pain.

Pandora's heart stilled at the way Dante was acting. He had to be hurt badly to not even move.

A flash of light startled her. She reached for her axe, then hesitated as she saw Romeo in human form by the bed.

His gaze narrowed on her as he saw his brother's limp form and the bloody axe. "What did you do to him?"

"Nothing. The other panthers came for me and I tried to help Dante fight them off."

Something hit the door, then flashed into the room. Romeo whirled as a panther rushed them.

Dante leaped out of her arms so fast that she shrieked. He went straight for the panther's throat as Romeo changed form.

Pandora grabbed the axe from the floor and scrambled to a corner.

One by one, four more panthers appeared in the room. There was no way to tell them apart as they fought with Romeo and Dante. Roars and growls echoed in her ears and the scent of blood filled her nostrils.

Two more panthers appeared.

How she wished she knew if they were friend or foe. All she could do was grip her axe and pray.

The one panther she thought was Dante appeared to maim the one he was fighting by snapping the hind leg of his opponent. A baleful whine filled the air as the panther evaporated from the room.

The victorious panther turned to another that was fighting with the two new panthers. With his powerful jaws, he grabbed it by the neck and slung it away from the two.

He charged the downed panther, using his shoulder to

drive it farther away from her and from the other two who snapped behind him.

His enemy tried to claw at his head, but the panther ducked his head and bit into his opponent's throat.

The opponent became wild, thrashing before she heard something break. It went limp.

Two more panthers vanished instantly.

The remaining four turned on the one panther that had been left behind and cornered it. It roared fiercely, then poofed out as well.

Terrified of what that meant, Pandora tensed as the four panthers turned to face her.

She watched them, determined to fight to the bitter end as they stalked nearer.

Three of them fell back while the fourth approached her.

"Dante?" she asked hesitantly, hoping it was him.

He collapsed at her feet before he placed one large paw on her foot and licked her ankle.

She sobbed in relief as she slid down the wall to pull his head into her lap.

The other three flashed into Romeo, Leo, and Mike.

"How badly are you hurt?" Romeo asked the twins.

They were a bit scuffed up, with bruises and bloodied lips and noses, but weren't hurt nearly as badly as Dante had been.

"We're okay, thanks to Dante."

Romeo approached her slowly.

"He's unconscious," she said quietly as she kept her hand on Dante's ribs to make sure he was still breathing. "There were eight of them in the beginning. He fought them alone."

"Dammit, Dante," Romeo snarled as he picked the panther up in his arms. "Why didn't you call us sooner?"

"Put him in my bed," Pandora said, moving to pull back the covers.

"Are you sure?"

She nodded.

Romeo set him down, then ordered Leo to keep watch at the door in case the others came back.

"Mike," he said to the other twin. "Go grab Acheron and tell him I need a favor."

Pandora crawled into the bed beside Dante. Part of her was terrified to be so close to him in his animal state and yet the other part of her wanted only to comfort her mate.

She'd never been this close to a panther before. It was scary and yet not.

Somehow it seemed right to be here.

His black fur was so dark, it reminded her of midnight velvet. She carefully brushed the whiskers of his muzzle back, then sank her hand in the soft fur of his neck.

Even though she knew it was true, it was hard to believe this was the same gorgeous man who had made the tenderest love to her.

And he had risked his life to protect her.

Her heart swelled with joy and with something she thought might be the first stirrings of love. No one had ever protected her. Not like this.

Pandora placed her hand near one of the vicious bite wounds above Dante's shoulder. "Will he be okay?" she asked Romeo.

If she didn't know better, she'd swear she saw pride in his eyes as he watched her.

"He's had worse."

"Really?"

"Really."

Romeo reached out and took her left hand so that he could see Dante's ring. His grip tightened on her hand. "That belonged to our brother Donatello," he said quietly. "I've never known Dante to take it off."

"He put a spell on it so that I could come back to him any time I wanted to."

Romeo smiled at that. "You have no idea just what a completely unbelievable feat that was for him."

"No, I think I do know." It ranked right up there with her lying beside him right now when she was terrified of panthers. This wasn't something she would have done even a few hours ago—and now . . .

Now she accepted the fact that this was her eternal mate. And for the first time in her life, she was beginning to understand exactly what that really meant.

Someone knocked on the door.

Pandora jumped.

"Relax," Romeo said as he moved to answer it while Mike stood aside. "The bad guys don't knock."

Pandora frowned as Romeo let in Leo and the gorgeous Goth man she'd seen downstairs. Leo went to stand beside Mike while the Goth came toward the bed.

"Pandora," Romeo said, "meet Acheron Parthenopaeus."

Acheron inclined his head to her.

She gaped. "You're the ancient Dark-Hunter?"

Acheron gave her that same wicked grin he had given her earlier. "The one and only."

A weird ripple went through her. "You knew me downstairs when our gazes met, didn't you?"

He nodded.

"If you knew I was looking for you, why didn't you say something?"

His gaze went to Dante. "Because it wasn't time for you to meet me yet." He glanced to Romeo. "And it's not time for you to lose another brother."

Pandora watched as the wounds on Dante healed instantly.

Romeo smiled in relief. "What do we owe you for that, Ash?"

Acheron shrugged. "Don't worry about it. I'll call the favor in at a later date."

Dante flashed into human form. He looked up at her with a tender expression that melted her.

"Ash," he said, without looking at the Dark-Hunter. "Could I trade another favor for you to watch my mate for me while my brothers and I take care of something?"

"Absolutely."

Dante placed one large, warm hand against her cheek, then chastely kissed the side of her face. He got up and gathered his brothers to him.

"We'll be back in a minute."

Before she could ask him where he was going, they vanished.

"What is he doing?" she asked Ash.

"Knowing Dante, I'm confident he's going to guarantee that your 'friends' never return to threaten you or anyone from your pack again."

It didn't take Dante long to find the rogue pack of Katagaria panthers. They were camped in a small, isolated commune just outside of Charleston.

Ironically, they even had a sign up declaring the area a wildlife preserve.

With his three brothers behind him, he walked through the wooded area until he found the first panther he'd fought. The panther was lying wounded with a human woman tending him.

"Who leads this pack?" he asked the pair.

The panther didn't answer, but when the petite, blond woman did, Dante recognized a voice that was almost identical in tone, accent, and cadence to Pandora's. "Aristotle is the *regis*. He's sleeping over there." She pointed to a tree.

Dante inclined his head respectfully to her, then went to the tree to call down their leader.

Aristotle responded by only opening one bored eye. *"Who are you?"*

"Take human form when you address me, you bastard,"

Dante said harshly. "Or there won't be enough left of your pack to even start a new one."

The panther flashed into human form, then moved to stand before Dante in a stance that said he was ready to fight. He was four inches shorter than Dante and had short black hair that matched his black soulless eyes.

"Who the hell are you?" he snarled.

"Dante Pontis."

Aristotle's eyes widened as he took an immediate step back.

Dante's brutal, take-no-prisoners reputation was known far and wide, and it was respected or feared by all their kind.

"To what do I owe this honor?" Aristotle asked.

"A group of your *strati* tried to take my mate from me. Now I'm here for blood."

Aristotle sputtered. "There was some misunderstanding. My men went after an Arcadian whor—"

Dante slugged him before he could finish the insult. "Pandora Kouti-Pontis is my mate. If you speak of her with anything other than extreme reverence in your tone, you piss me off."

Aristotle turned pale. "I had no idea she belonged to you. Believe me."

"Now you do, and if I ever see any of you near her again, I'll end all your problems. Permanently."

Pandora was sitting in the Grandstand Lounge with Acheron, his daughter demon Simi, and two gods while they waited for Dante's return.

This had to be the oddest moment of her life. The demon was busy eating an extremely rare hamburger drenched in barbecue sauce while the gods and Acheron were telling Pandora stories about how they'd all met Dante.

Apparently her mate had quite a rambunctious club that catered to all manner of bizarre clientele. The gods and Acheron made routine visits there.

Zurvan, who went by the name Cas, was the ancient Persian god of time and space. He was the elegantly dressed man she had followed earlier toward the elevators, thinking he was Acheron.

Ariman—not to be confused with the Persian god Ariman—had been an ancient Phoenician god who had had the misfortune of visiting Atlantis at the time the continent was destroyed. He'd been in human form, trying to seduce a young woman, and as a result, he was now trapped in human form with no god powers except immortality.

He wasn't happy about it either.

"I really wish one of you would take mercy on me and fix me or kill me," Ariman said for the fifth time since he had joined them at their table.

Cas rolled his eyes, then turned toward Acheron. "I think we ought to banish him from our presence so we can't hear him bitch anymore."

Ash laughed.

"You're such—" Ariman's words broke off as he spotted the women who weren't wearing anything except warning tape. "Later." He bolted after the women.

Cas shook his head. "He is never going to learn, is he?"

Ash took a drink of beer before he responded. "Be grateful he doesn't. It gives us endless hours of amusement watching him screw his life up."

Cas snorted. "Considering how screwed up yours is, that says something."

"Let's not go there," Ash said, his eyes flashing red before they returned to their spooky swirling silver shade.

Sometimes it was very scary to hang out with supernatural beings.

"Pandora?"

She froze at the sound of a voice she never thought to hear again. Afraid she was hearing things, she turned to see her sister Sefia running up to her.

Pandora shot to her feet to throw her arms around her

sister. Oh, it was too good to be real! "What are you doing here, Sef?"

"Your mate brought me," she said as tears poured down her cheeks. "He made them let us all go. Now it's up to us if we want to return to our mates or not."

Pandora was stunned as she looked past her sister to see Dante and his brothers approaching at a much more sedate pace.

"Dante?" she asked as he stopped by her side.

He shrugged nonchalantly as if he hadn't just given her the impossible. "It wasn't right what they were doing to their females and I figured you'd rather travel with your own female kind than with mine."

She still couldn't believe he'd done this. He had formed a new pack of female panthers for her to roam with. "What about the pact they made with our pack?"

"It's dissolved," Dante said. "If they pull any more of your kin out of their time period, I'm going to send them a special welcoming committee."

"Damn, Dante," Cas said from behind her. "That's harsh. Last time you turned your brothers loose on a pack, they left no male standing."

"I know." Dante looked back to her. "And so do they. Your sister and her friends are all safe now."

Pandora threw her arms around his shoulders and held him close. "Thank you!"

He hugged her back, then kissed her gently.

Pandora turned back to Sefia as another thought occurred to her. "What about your children?"

"Their father is raising them, per Dante's orders." Sefia looked at Dante with glowing eyes. "Your mate took all of the women to La Costa and is paying for us to stay and be pampered there for as long as we like."

"And we volunteered to guard them," Mike said, indicating himself and Leo.

"Is that a good idea?" Pandora asked Dante. After all he

and Romeo had said about the twins, she wasn't sure whether having them as guards would be a help or a hindrance.

Dante's face mirrored her skepticism. "I personally don't think so, but Romeo talked me into it. There's a large number of the females who aren't mated."

"And Dante owes us big after the filking fiasco," Leo said irritably. "There weren't any naked women there, just some guy singing about *Star Trek* and Romulan brew. It really pissed us off."

Pandora had to stifle her laughter.

"Are you going to come with us?" Sefia asked.

Pandora felt a lot more torn than she should have. Spending time with her sister at a resort or staying with a Katagari panther at Dragon*Con . . .

There shouldn't be a choice.

So why did she feel this way?

"It's entirely up to you," Dante said quietly. "I told you I wouldn't interfere with your freedom."

"C'mon, Dora," Sefia said, taking her hand. "We're going to have a lot of fun."

Dante's face was completely stoic and yet she sensed his sadness.

"I'll be back soon," Pandora promised him.

He nodded.

"I'll take them upstairs to my room to flash them to the resort," Romeo said.

Dante didn't speak as he watched his brothers disappear into the crowd with Pandora and Sefia.

He'd done a good deed and now he knew why he hated doing good deeds.

They were painful.

What did he get out of it? Not a damn thing except a pain so profound that he felt as if something were shredding his heart.

"Here," Ash said, handing him a beer. "Have a seat."

Sighing, Dante took the beer and grabbed the chair where Pandora had been sitting on his arrival. "I did the right thing, right?"

"No," Simi said as she wiped barbecue sauce off her chin. "The panther woman didn't want you to leave her and now you made her go away. That was just stupid if you ask the Simi. Not that anyone ever does, 'cause if they did, then they would be smart. Some people are smart. But many, like you, are too stupid to ask me what I think. See?"

"It's not that simple, Simi," Dante said, wondering why he was trying to explain himself to a demon who had no understanding of human emotions or animal relationships. "She doesn't want me to own her."

"Well, the Simi doesn't understand that. Owning's not so bad. I own *akri* and he kind of fun."

Dante arched a brow at Ash who didn't bother to correct his demon.

Whatever. Those two were far beyond his understanding anyway.

"I'm telling you, Faith," a woman said as she and a friend walked by them. "There's a portal in the handicap stall downstairs that allows people to drop in from alternate universes. I was in there with Amanda helping her with her costume when this woman popped in, holding an axe. She immediately popped back out."

Dante laughed at that, even though a fierce pain cut through him at the memory.

Only his pantheress would be so bold as to defy his orders.

"I better go pay for that axe before someone puts out an APB on my mate," he said to Ash, Cas, and Simi.

But as he got up and headed down to the dealers' room, he couldn't squelch the need he felt to find Pandora and bring her back.

He wouldn't do that to her.

Dante was nothing if not a panther of his word.

CHAPTER 5

Pandora spent two days in La Costa with her sister and the other females while Leo and Mike tutored them well on how to use their powers. They also tutored some of the unmated females on things she didn't even want to think about.

But none of her newfound freedom made her happy.

In fact, the longer she stayed here, the more her heart ached. Every time her gaze fell to her marked hand, she thought about the panther she'd left behind.

No, she thought about the man. The one who had given her so much.

"How's Dante doing?"

She paused outside the sliding glass door that led to Mike and Leo's room. The two panthers were in there alone and she wasn't sure which one was which. One of them was resting in a blue recliner, while the other appeared to have just ended a phone call.

That one tossed a cell phone to the dresser before he shrugged. "Romeo said he's still screwed up."

The one in the chair sighed heavily. "Yeah. I can't believe he didn't tell Pandora about his phobia."

"What phobia?" Pandora asked as she came through the door to confront them.

The twins looked at her sheepishly.

"It's not nice to eavesdrop," the one in front of the dresser said in a reprimanding tone.

She was in no mood to take that from him. "And it's not nice to talk about people either, but since you're talking about my mate, I'd like to know what you mean."

The twins exchanged a pained look.

"What do you think, Mike?" Leo was the one who'd had the cell phone.

Mike leaned back in his recliner as he silently debated for a few seconds more. "Might as well tell her, I guess. I don't see what it would hurt."

Leo let out a loud breath before he spoke again.

He looked at her. "When Dante was a cub, he and his litter and a group of our cousins escaped their babysitter and went out prowling on their own. After a few hours, they got lost and one of the females with them got really scared because it was getting dark. She didn't want to try and find her way back until morning so Dante agreed to stay with her and keep her safe. Our brother Sal told Dante he'd be back with help and then led the others off."

Pandora frowned at his story. "Why would that make him phobic?"

"Because it was a cruel prank," Mike said bitterly. "As soon as Dante went to sleep, Tyla snuck out and they all headed back home without him. Dante woke up alone and had no idea what had happened to her or how to get home. He was terrified."

Pandora was appalled at how mean his siblings and cousins had been to leave him behind. A cub on its own could be picked up by humans and put in a zoo or, worse, killed by any adult wild animal that came across it.

"They left him there by himself for a solid week," Leo continued with the story. "Every time someone asked about Dante, they made up some lie about where he was. When Donatello found out what they'd done, he went back to the woods to get him. He found Dante practically starved to death. He'd been living off scraps and having to keep predators away with no help. He was weak from exposure, but still he'd kept searching for Tyla, afraid something had happened to her."

His face sad, Mike shook his head. "Romeo has always said that that was what made Dante so damned selfish. After they returned, Dante was freaky about ever running out of food or trying to help someone. He started hoarding things and turning on anyone who threatened him."

Her heart ached for her mate. It must have been horrible for him to be afraid for his life while trying to find Tyla. And all because of a joke.

"I hope Donatello punished them for what they did."

Mike sighed. "He did, but the damage had already been done. Like Acheron so often says, there are a lot of things in life that 'sorry' doesn't fix and that was one of them."

"Ever since then," Leo said, "Dante can't stand for anyone to leave him. He practically climbs the walls if he can't account for his family."

"That's why he went to find you two when you were lost, isn't it?" she asked.

Leo nodded. "His worst fear is to have someone he loves not be able to find their way home again."

Tears filled her eyes as she looked down at the ring Dante had given her when they mated.

Now it all made perfect sense.

Why he didn't want a wandering Katagari female for a mate . . .

Why he tolerated his brothers even when they drove him insane . . .

Why he had freed her sister and the other women to travel with her . . .

And why he had given her Donatello's ring.

Closing her eyes, Pandora conjured up an image of Dante.

* * *

Dante was watching the acid metal band on a TV monitor. But his mind wasn't really on the act or the handouts and CDs on the table in front of him.

It was on the fact that he should never have let Pandora go.

You can't keep her . . .

He should have at least tried.

But at least she wasn't out there alone. He'd made sure that she would have her sister with her.

A warm hand touched his arm.

Grinding his teeth, Dante turned, ready to rebuff yet another woman coming on to him. He was really getting tired of telling them he wasn't interested.

But as he opened his mouth and his eyes focused on the beautiful face of his latest admirer, all thoughts scattered.

It couldn't be.

Not this soon.

"Pandora?"

"Hi," she said with a smile that made him feel sucker-punched. "I missed you."

This had to be a dream. His pantheress couldn't be back.

He wanted to tell her that he'd missed her too, but the words wouldn't come. All he could do was react.

He pulled her into his arms and kissed her fiercely, letting her feel that every part of him wanted her never to leave him again.

Pandora laughed at his heated welcome. "I think you missed me too."

Dante left her lips to take a deep whiff of her hair so that he could memorize and savor it. "You have no idea."

Actually, she did. She hadn't doubted the twins before, but this thoroughly confirmed their story.

She nuzzled his neck, inhaling the warm spicy scent of his masculine skin. "Want to get naked?"

He laughed. "Yeah, but not here."

Pulling back from her, he took her hand and led her to a secluded corner so that he could flash them into his room.

They were both naked and in his bed three blinks later.

Dante couldn't breathe as he felt the impossible softness of Pandora lying beneath him.

Nothing felt better than her caresses. The fact that she was warm and welcoming. He slid himself inside her, and groaned at just how good she felt.

Pandora savored his hardness inside her and now more than ever she was glad she was human and not a real panther. Her Katagaria cousins only sought sex when they were in heat.

She could seek it anytime she wanted and she wanted Dante right now. Needed to feel his strong, powerful thrusts.

But the human in her wanted even more.

It wanted him with her forever.

"Will you bond with me, Dante?"

Dante froze as her whispered words went through him. "What?"

She held her marked palm up. "I don't ever want to leave you and I don't want to live without you. Not for one minute. Bond with me, Dante, so that neither one of us is ever abandoned again."

He took her hand into his and kissed her as love for her overwhelmed him.

He thrust against her hard and furiously as she repeated her vows to him and he returned them to her.

This time when his teeth grew, he pulled back to stare down at her an instant before he sank his fangs into her neck.

Pandora arched her back as the pain of his bite quickly turned to pleasure. Her head spinning, she sank her own teeth into his shoulder.

For that one instant in time, every thought and emotion Dante felt coursed through her.

Any doubt she'd ever had about him fled as she felt his love for her, and it ignited her own.

This was what was meant to be.

He was hers and she was his.

She cried out as she came in a fierce wave of pleasure. Dante's own growl of pleasure filled her ears.

Joined together, they drifted through the ribbons of ecstasy until they were fully drained and spent.

Dante collapsed on top of her and she cuddled him in her arms. "I love you, Dante," she breathed. "And I promise I'll never again leave you."

He smiled languidly as he stared at her. "I love you, too, Pandora, and anytime you want to leave, I'll gladly go with you."

EPILOGUE

In the Marriott's lobby, Dante stood off to the side with Acheron while everyone at the hotel was packing up to leave. All the Klingons, Storm Troopers, fairies, and so on were now in normal dress with only scattered parts of their costumes evident as, one by one, they returned to real life.

Dragon*Con was over.

Just like Ash had promised him a year ago when he told him to come to Atlanta, it had been a remarkable weekend that would stay with him forever.

"You knew Pandora would be here when you told me to come, didn't you?" he asked the Atlantean.

Ash shrugged. "There's always room for error, but yeah. I did."

"You're a scary SOB."

Ash laughed.

Dante felt Pandora's presence behind him.

Turning, he saw her and Simi coming over to them.

Simi was beaming as she carried a wide collection of bags. "I gots my last bit of shopping done," she announced proudly. "You should be glad, Dante, your panther-woman don't buy much."

"You know you could have spent whatever you wanted," he said to Pandora.

"I know, but all I wanted was this."

He frowned as she handed him a small wooden box. "What is it?"

"Open it and see. I bought it just for you."

Dante opened it to find what appeared to be a bell-shaped necklace. "I don't get it," he said.

Pandora took the necklace out and placed it around his neck. "This is just in case you ever again have to fight someone else. Next time, I'll know which panther you are and I won't accidentally cut your head off. I plan on living a long, long life with you, Mr. Pontis. And no one, not even you, is going to stop me."

BORN OF THE NIGHT

AMANDA ASHLEY

For all those who adore dark and dangerous men and
are intrigued by things that go bump in the night

Save me from this darkness
I know you are a creature of light
I was born to shadow
but I rebel, do not accept
this cursed, haunted life.

I have seen the hope that you represent
the future that you dangle before me
give me the strength to reach above the tide
to grab hold and drag my drowning self
from this inner, bitter sea . . .

CHAPTER 1

Death carried a sword and rode a tall black stallion. Shanara stared up at the figure on the horse, unable to stop the tremors that wracked her from head to foot. The rider's clothing matched the color of his mount—black boots, black trousers, black shirt, a black hooded cloak that hid most of his face. She glanced at the sword in his hand, the wicked-looking blade stained crimson with the blood of her kinfolk, and felt the bile rise in her throat. Would he now add her blood to that of her slain family?

With a choked cry, she scrambled to her feet and shook off her fear. She would not die in the dirt like some sniveling coward. She was Lady Shanara of the House of Montiori and she would die in a manner befitting her station.

"Do it!" she said defiantly. "Strike me down and be done with it."

"Eager to die, are you?" His voice was low and deep, tinged with a hint of wry humor.

She stared at him. How, in the name of Astur and Caleron, could he find amusement at a time like this? She glanced at the field of battle, the greening grass of spring made dark and ugly with the blood that had been spilled only moments before. There were bodies everywhere, limp, lifeless, like broken dolls cast aside by a careless hand. And somewhere, lying among the dead, were the bodies of her uncle and two of her cousins. For all she knew, the hooded man had killed them. If only she had stayed home where she belonged instead of coming here! But she'd had to get away from her father and her future, if only for a little while.

Death threw back his hood and ran a hand through his hair, hair as black as ten feet down. He studied her through eyes that were the cool deep blue of a midnight sea. His brows were straight and black, his jaw roughened by thick black bristles. A thin white scar ran from the outer edge of his right eye to the curve of his jaw. With the sun setting behind him, he reminded her of a demon rising from the smoldering pit of Hel.

In a lithe motion, he swung out of the saddle and walked toward her, arrogance in every step.

With no thought save to escape, she turned and ran.

It was a foolish thing to do. Far better to stand her ground than to give him a reason to chase her, something no true predator could resist. Fear gave wings to her feet and she flew over the ground, her heart pounding in her chest, her breathing labored.

She gasped when she heard a noise behind her. It might have been a harsh laugh. It might have been a howl. Whatever it was, it fueled her fear and added impetus to her flight.

But like a hare trying to outrun a winter-starved wolf, there was no way to escape.

She screamed in fear and defiance when his arm snaked around her waist. His momentum carried them both to the ground, his body turning in midair and sliding under hers so that he took the brunt of the fall against his back. She landed on top of him, the air whooshing out of his lungs and hers.

His arms circled her body, as unyielding and confining as prison bars. Well and truly caught, she glared down at him.

"Unhand me this instant!" she demanded, her voice

filled with a bravado she was far from feeling. "I am Lady Shanara of the House of Montiori."

An emotion she could not fathom showed in his eyes. A muscle clenched in his jaw. The arms imprisoning her grew tighter until she feared he might break her in two.

Breathless, she gazed down at him, all bravado gone as she prayed that her death would be swift, painless.

"Why were you at Castle Dunhaven?" Death demanded, his voice harsh.

"Why did you attack us?" She thought of her uncle's keep now lying in ruins, spoiled by this man and his barbarians. She wondered if her aunt Eugenia had survived the attack.

"Why did your father kill mine?"

She stared at him, her fear growing as his cold blue eyes raked over her. "He . . . he didn't," she replied tremulously, though, for all she knew, it could be true. Her father was an austere, cruel man, one who loved and lived for the heat of battle, the clash of swords, the bloody smell of victory.

"Did he not?" Death asked, his expression as cold as winter in the high country. He shook her until her head snapped back. "Did he not?" he asked again, a tremor in his voice. "He wears my father's pelt to warm him."

She looked at her captor in horror, realizing, too late, who it was who had seized her. Dread uncoiled deep within her. Now that she knew who he was, death in any form would have been a blessing. She knew her father would avenge her, not because of any great love for his youngest daughter, but because it would give him just cause for another war.

Reyes drew in a deep breath, his rage dwindling as he grew increasingly aware of the slim female form pressing against his. Lifting his head, he sniffed her skin, his senses filling with the flowery scent of her perfume, the acrid stink of her fear. Her hair was not red and not brown, but something in between, reminding him of the rich earthy color of autumn leaves. Her eyes were the green of new grass, her skin a soft golden brown. She squirmed beneath his regard, making him acutely aware of her full breasts, of the fact that her body was cradled between his thighs.

He could have taken her there and then. It was his right. No one would dare dispute it. He had wrought the victory. It was his right to claim whatever or whoever he wished. But he did not want her writhing beneath him in fright, only in ecstasy. To his surprise, he discovered that he didn't want to take her by force or fear, not here, on the fringes of a bloody battlefield. Nay, far better to seduce her slowly and gently on a bed of soft furs by candlelight.

It amazed him that he wanted her at all, knowing that it had been her father who had butchered his. Rage burned anew when Reyes recalled how Luis Montiori had taken his father's rich black pelt and then had the gall not only to line a cloak with it, but to boast to any and all who would listen of what he had done. The memory of Montiori's treachery cooled his desire as effectively as if he had plunged into an icy lake, leaving only the simmering coals of hatred and the ashes of revenge.

Putting the woman away from him, he took a deep breath. Rising, he grabbed her by the arm and lifted her onto his horse's back. Heedless of the fear in the woman's eyes, ignoring the tears trickling down her cheeks, he vaulted up behind her, took up the reins, and turned his horse toward the misty mountains of home. His men, drunk with the wine of victory, gathered up the last of the spoils and fell in behind him, eager to return home to bed their wives and boast of their victory.

CHAPTER 2

Shanara had never been so afraid in her whole life. The arm around her waist was thick with muscle, unmoving, unyielding. Her back bumped against his chest from time to time. It, too, was hard and unyielding.

What was he going to do with her?

It was a question that plagued her on the long ride to his keep until, weary with fear and exhaustion, sleep claimed her.

Reyes felt the woman slump in his grasp. His arm tightened around her and he drew her closer, cradling her head against his chest, all too aware of her hips and thighs cradled between his. She was warm and soft in sleep. Once, she whimpered softly. He refused to be moved by it. Hardening his heart against her, he reminded himself that she was his prisoner and nothing more, a pawn in a dangerous game. He had sworn a blood oath to avenge his father's cruel death. It was a vow he would honor no matter what the cost. If her father refused to take her place in the dungeon, then Reyes would kill the girl and send her body back to Montiori a piece at a time.

The girl was still asleep when he drew rein for the night.

Holding her in his arms, he swung his right leg over his mount's withers and slid to the ground. Cradling her against him with one hand, he untied his bedroll from

behind his saddle and spread the blankets on the ground for
the girl. She murmured in her sleep when he put her down,
but didn't awaken. He stared at her for a moment, then
drew the covers up to her chin.

In a short time, fires were laid and food was being prepared. His men sat in small groups, sharing tales of old
battles, or refighting the battle they had just won.

Reyes moved through the camp, taking time to speak to
each of his men, commending them for their bravery, con-
soling the wounded, stopping to spend time with two of the
men who he knew would not survive the night.

A short time later, the women arrived—a dozen whores
and camp followers who made their living the best way
they knew how. They followed him and his men whenever
they rode out of the keep, setting up their gypsylike wagons on the outskirts of the camp.

Reyes allowed it because his men were, after all, red-
blooded fighting men. Warriors all, after facing a day of
battle where death might find them at any time, they had a
need for a woman. It was more than the pleasures of the
flesh that they sought. It was a reaffirmation of life. Sometimes he envied his men. Though tempted, he had never
bedded any of the camp followers. He knew his men wondered why he never visited any of the wagons. Some
thought he must be a eunuch, but he shrugged off such
speculation as idle talk. He was not a man to indulge in
meaningless copulation with a woman who was available
to any man for the right price. If he mated, it would be for
life. Cursed as he was, he dared not spill his seed wantonly.

He sought his bed when the fires burned low. The girl
was sleeping soundly, one small hand tucked beneath her
cheek, her lips slightly parted. He could see the shapely
outline of her form beneath the thin blanket. He took a
deep breath, drawing in the sweet scent of her skin and
hair.

She is here. She is mine for the taking . . .

His body responded to the words moving through his mind.

Muttering an oath, he stalked into the darkness.

Shanara woke to the sound of rough male laughter and the smell of food cooking. Disoriented, she sat up, her gaze darting right and left. Where was she? And then it all came rushing back to her—the battle, the stink of blood and death borne on the early morning air, being captured by Reyes, who was known among her people as the Lord of Black Dragon Keep.

Where was he?

She saw no sign of him. Many of his men were gathered around a large campfire. She saw others moving back and forth between the wagons that surrounded the camp. No one seemed to be paying her any attention.

Taking a deep, calming breath, she threw back the covers, then gained her feet.

No one noticed.

As causally as she could, she walked toward the water wagon and took a drink.

No one paid her any heed. Nor did anyone seem to notice when she took a knife from a sheath someone had carelessly left lying on the ground. Tucking the weapon into the pocket of her skirt, she turned away from the wagon and headed for the darkness beyond the camp, hoping that anyone who saw her would think she was one of the camp followers seeking a momentary bit of privacy.

Had anyone noticed her departure? She didn't dare look around, only kept walking, moving deeper into the shadowy darkness beneath the trees.

A capricious wind stirred the leaves.

Far off in the distance, she heard the melancholy howl of a wolf.

Glancing upward, she reckoned her direction by the position of the moon. All she had to do was keep heading west. With any luck at all, she would make it to her brother's estate. Thomas was her oldest brother, and her favorite. He would take her in and give her shelter until her father came for her.

She ducked under a low branch, wondering how long it would take her to reach her brother's estate. She was hungry and weary and not at all certain how much farther she had to go.

With a sigh, she increased her stride. She could rest later. For now, she needed to put as much distance as possible between herself and the camp she had left behind. She had gone only a short way when she paused, a shiver of unease prickling her spine. Someone was watching her.

"Who's there?" she called softly. "Show yourself." Delving into her pocket, she withdrew the knife and held it close to her side, hidden in the folds of her skirt.

A rustle to the left drew her attention. Heart pounding with fear, she turned to see a giant of a man striding toward her.

"So, missy," he said in a voice like rumbling thunder, "what are you doing out here all by yourself?"

She shook her head, her hand tightening on the knife even as she wondered if the weapon would do her any good against a man of his size.

"Are you lost, girl?"

She shook her head again.

"Are you deaf, then?" he asked, moving closer. "Mute, perhaps?"

She took a step backward, her eyes widening as he began to unfasten his belt.

"Lucky I am that I followed you out here," he said with a leer. "I was getting tired of waiting my turn."

Shanara's heart plummeted to her toes. She had hoped anyone seeing her leave the camp would think she was one of the camp girls. Now she saw the error in her thinking.

She turned to run, but he was too fast for her. One beefy hand closed on her shoulder. With a cry, she twisted in his grasp, the blade glinting in the moonlight as she raised her arm to strike.

Muttering an oath, he grabbed her wrist, his hand squeezing it until her fingers went numb and the knife tumbled from her grasp. In the next instant, she was flat on her back, held in place by his knee while he unfastened his trousers, then tossed her skirt over her head.

She screamed in terror and revulsion as he parted her thighs and she felt his skin against hers. Desperate to stop him, she pounded her fists against his head and shoulders, but he only laughed, one meaty hand holding both of hers over her head.

It was difficult to breathe with her heavy skirt covering her face. Her heart was pounding so rapidly she was certain she was going to faint. She prayed that she would faint before he defiled her.

Abruptly, his weight was gone.

She heard a horrible shriek followed by an even more horrible gurgling sound, and then silence.

Afraid to look, afraid not to, she pulled her skirt away from her face and peered into the darkness.

A huge black wolf stood over the man's body. As if sensing her watching him, the wolf lifted its head. It stared at her through midnight-blue eyes. Blood dripped from its fangs and its tongue. The man's blood.

The wolf lifted its head. A howl rent the stillness of the night and then, amid a shimmer of moonlight, the wolf's form began to change, its thick pelt undulating, changing, until the wolf was gone and a tall man stood naked before her, his long black hair awash in the light of the moon, the scar on his cheek like a ribbon of silver.

It was the last thing she remembered before slipping into unconsciousness.

* * *

When she woke again, it was morning and she was lying on his blankets back at camp with no recollection of how she had got there.

The wagons were gone. Some of the men were eating breakfast, others were saddling their horses. There was no sign of Reyes.

She sat up as the memory of what had happened the night before returned. Surely she hadn't seen what she thought she had seen! She had heard the stories of the Reyes family, how they had been cursed by a witch to run with the wolves when the moon was full, but she had never believed such ludicrous tales. Men could not transform into wolves. It was impossible . . . yet how else to explain what she had seen last night, when the moon was full?

"A dream," she murmured. "It was naught but a bad dream."

And even as she spoke the words, she saw Reyes striding toward her, his long black hair falling over his shoulders, his dark blue eyes fixed on her face.

She suddenly recalled that the wolf's eyes had also been blue . . .

"Get up, woman," he said gruffly. "We ride at once."

When he reached for her arm, she scrambled to her feet and backed away. "Touch me not!"

"I've no time for your nonsense," he said impatiently. "We're leaving."

"Please, let me go home."

"All in good time," he replied, and taking hold of her hand, he dragged her to his horse, lifted her into the saddle, and vaulted up behind her.

They traveled all that day. She was grateful, at least, that they rode at the head of the column as the horses behind them stirred great clouds of dust.

They stopped once at noon to rest and water the horses and again a few hours later. She had expected they would make camp at dusk, but night fell and there was no sign that they were going to stop.

She sagged against Reyes, too exhausted to care that he was her enemy.

She didn't remember falling asleep, but she woke abruptly, a huge castle rising before her eyes. Reyes guided his horse across a narrow stone bridge that spanned a moat, and then under a portcullis. They passed through the main gate and then they were inside the inner courtyard. Servants ran to and fro, offering water and wine to the trail-weary warriors. Youths led the warhorses into the barns to look after them. Wives and children filled the yard, welcoming their husbands and fathers home.

Reyes took Shanara by the arm and led her up a winding staircase to the first floor and into the banqueting hall. Inside, he bade her sit down at one of the tables. At any other time, she would have argued, but she was too tired to offer any resistance, and too hungry.

She watched through heavy-lidded eyes as serving women hurried into the hall, laying out trays laden with meat and vegetables and baskets of crusty brown bread. Tankards filled with ale were set on the tables.

Stomach growling, Shanara filled a trencher with food, acutely conscious of Reyes sitting at the head of the table.

The room was soon filled with hungry men. Laughter and conversation rose on all sides as the women joined their men.

With the edge taken from her hunger, Shanara looked around the hall. It was an enormous room. A dozen long trestle tables were scattered down its center. A huge fireplace took up most of one wall, with a pair of crossed swords hanging over the mantel. A chandelier hung from the ceiling, and fresh rushes covered the floor. On the walls were tapestries depicting a variety of hunting and battle scenes.

But it was Reyes who drew her attention again and again. Clad all in black, he sat alone at the head of the table absently picking at his dinner while he watched the goings-on in the hall. He smiled as his men toasted him again and again, sharing stories of his bravery in battle, telling how he had ridden into the midst of a fierce skirmish to save one of his men.

She found it curious that he sat at the head of the table without female companionship.

She had no sooner finished her meal than a young woman clad in a long gray gown appeared at her side. "Please come with me, my lady."

Shanara sent a glance in Reyes's direction, but he was paying her no attention. When the girl gave a gentle tug on the sleeve of Shanara's gown, Shanara rose and followed her from the hall.

The maid led her up a narrow winding stairway, down a long dark corridor, and into a large room where another, older woman, also clad in gray, waited.

Before she knew what was happening, Shanara found herself being undressed and urged into a large wooden tub filled with hot water. In spite of her protests that she was perfectly able to bathe herself, the women bathed her and washed her hair, then helped her out of the tub. They dried her off, anointed her with fragrant oil, wrapped a bit of toweling around her hair, then helped her into a long, loose-fitting gown of ice-blue velvet.

"Sit here, my lady," the older one said, indicating she should sit on a low stool.

Knowing it was useless to argue, Shanara did as she was told.

"Such beautiful hair," the woman said, removing the toweling. "Like auburn silk."

"Indeed," murmured her companion, a note of envy in her voice.

Shanara closed her eyes. She had always enjoyed hav-

ing someone else brush her hair. The woman had gentle
hands, and for a few moments, Shanara gave herself up to
the luxury of being pampered, something she had sorely
missed since her mother passed away.

"Will there be anything else, my lady?" the older
woman asked.

"Thank you, no."

Looking pleased with themselves, the two women
bowed in her direction and then left the room.

Sitting there, Shanara took a good look at her surroundings. A large bed covered with furs stood between two
arched windows that overlooked the courtyard. There was a
large wooden chest at the foot of the bed, a square table
and two chairs in one corner. A fire burned in the raised
hearth, providing the room with heat and light. Another,
smaller round table held a flagon of wine, a pair of goblets,
a bowl of fruit, and a platter of assorted meats and cheeses.

She was thinking of pouring herself a glass of wine
when she heard the sound of heavy footsteps outside the
door.

CHAPTER 3

Reyes paused at the door to his bedchamber, his hand on the latch. Why had he sent the girl to his room? He had no intention of treating his captive as a guest or using her as a whore. She was only a pawn in a dangerous game of cat and mouse.

He closed his eyes, picturing Shanara Montiori in his mind: defiant green eyes set beneath soft brown brows, a fall of reddish-brown hair as thick as his own, skin smooth and unblemished.

Reyes swore a vile oath, annoyed by the turn of his thoughts. She was the daughter of his enemy and he would do what he had vowed to do. He would keep her imprisoned while he waited to hear from Montiori, and when her father refused to take her place, as Reyes knew he surely would, Reyes would send her back to her father a piece at a time, until the coward agreed to surrender or to face him, one on one, in a battle to the death. No armies. No spectators. Just the two of them, alone.

He had ordered that she be bathed and attired in clean clothes because he could not, in good conscience, do otherwise. Now it was time to remember that she was his prisoner and treat her as such. He would personally escort her to the dungeon. He would demand that she write a letter to her father, telling Montiori of his terms, and then it was up to Montiori.

Filled with new resolve, Reyes opened the door and stepped inside, felt his breath catch in his throat as she turned away from the hearth to look at him, her eyes wide and startled, like a doe sensing danger. The velvet gown hugged a figure any man would kill to possess. The light from the fire danced in her hair and caressed her cheek.

Clearing his throat, he closed the door behind him.

She took a step backward and then, as though thinking better of it, she drew herself up to her full height. And waited.

And he did what he had been wanting to do from the moment he first saw her. Walking purposefully across the room, he pulled her into his arms and kissed her. He had expected her lips to be sweet, but he hadn't expected the sudden heat that flowed through him. It wasn't just the heat of desire, or the normal longing of a man for a woman. No, it was more than that, a feeling he didn't understand, one he had never known before.

Forcing himself to let her go, she stared up at him, her eyes filled with confusion. He had to get her out of here, now, he thought, before he drew her down on the bed, removed her gown, and explored the lush curves that lay beneath.

"Follow me," he said curtly, and before he could change his mind, he opened the door and stepped into the corridor.

After a moment's hesitation, she followed him.

Wordlessly, he led her through the keep and down the winding stone steps that led to the dungeon.

It was a cold and dismal place, lit by torches. He heard the scurrying of rats as he opened the door to the first cell and motioned the girl inside.

Without looking at him, she entered the cell, her head high.

He locked the door and pocketed the key. "My steward will bring you paper and quill in the morning. You are to write to your father and tell him of your circumstances.

Tell him if he wishes to see you again, he will take your place here. If not . . ." He almost choked on the words. "Your life will be forfeit."

"He will never agree," she said.

"You had best hope he does," Reyes replied. And then, unable to face her any longer, he turned and left the dungeon.

Shoulders slumping in defeat, Shanara looked at her surroundings. The floor and the walls were of damp gray stone. There was a straw tick and a ragged blanket on the floor in the corner, both of which were no doubt crawling with vermin. A vile odor rose from the slop jar in the corner.

Despite her determination not to cry, hot tears burned her eyes and dripped down her cheeks. Her father would never sacrifice himself for her. He had five strong sons and three other daughters. His youngest daughter was of little value. She doubted he even remembered her name or was aware of her absence from the keep.

If only her mother were still alive, but Elene had died last year, struggling to give her husband yet another child.

Shanara whirled around as she heard a scrabbling noise behind her, a cry of alarm rising in her throat as a large black rat crawled out from under the straw tick. Picking up her skirts, Shanara retreated to the far corner of the small cell, her back pressed against the damp wall.

Despair settled on her shoulders like a shroud. She was going to die here, in this horrid little cell. The rats would eat her flesh, and no one would care . . .

She pressed her fingertips to her lips. Why had Reyes kissed her, then thrust her aside? She would not have been surprised if he had forced himself upon her, but the fact that he had pushed her away surprised her a great deal.

But it didn't matter now. Nothing mattered now.

* * *

Reyes sat in front of the hearth, his fingers drumming on the arm of his chair. Six days had passed since he had locked Montiori's daughter in the dungeon. He hadn't had a decent night's sleep since. Every time he closed his eyes, he imagined her sitting in that damned dismal cell with nothing to do but stare at the bars that imprisoned her. He imagined her horror at sleeping on a stained tick on the cold floor. He shied away at the thought of rats sharing her cell. His only concession had been to see that she received nourishing meals. Meals she had, thus far, refused to eat. Perhaps he was being too cruel. Perhaps he would tell Rolf to put a bed in her cell . . .

"No!" She was the enemy. No matter that she was young and more beautiful than any woman he had ever seen. He could not think of her as a woman. She was a means to an end, no more, no less.

He looked up as his steward entered the room. "Did she write the letter?"

"Yes, sire." Rolf handed him a piece of rolled parchment.

Reyes read it quickly. As he had instructed, she told her father that she had been taken captive by Lord Reyes and that her life would be forfeit if Montiori did not comply with his wishes before the next full moon.

"Shall I send the missive?"

"Yes. Have Mergrid take it. Tell him to wait for an answer."

"Yes, my lord."

"Is there something else?" Reyes asked.

"She still refuses to eat."

Reyes nodded, then dismissed Rolf with a wave of his hand.

Rolf bowed from the waist, then left the hall.

Reyes swore. He had ordered his cooks to prepare dishes to tempt a lady's taste, but to no avail. For the last six days, every tray had been returned, untouched. He took small comfort in the fact that she drank the water if not the wine.

Gaining his feet, Reyes paced the floor. She was the enemy. It should make no difference whether she supped or not. He swore under his breath. She was only a woman. When she got hungry enough, she would eat.

It was the same thought that crossed his mind later that night when he sat at the table, his plate piled high with fresh venison and an assortment of side dishes.

Muttering an oath, he grabbed a plate, filled it with meat and vegetables, and then made his way to the dungeon. She would be of no use in a trade if she starved herself to death. A harsh laugh escaped his lips. No doubt that was her intent.

He opened the door that led to the dungeon, grimaced at the stink of waste and decay that fouled his nostrils. Who could eat in a place like this? He thrust the thought from his mind as he descended the stairs and walked down the corridor that led to her cell.

She was standing in the corner farthest away from the straw tick.

His heart clenched when she turned to look at him. There were dark shadows under her eyes, her cheeks looked sunken, her skin pale. Her eyes were dull and filled with resignation.

"I've brought your supper," he said, his voice gruff.

She gestured at the straw tick. A large gray rat with beady black eyes looked up at him, a bit of potato in its jaws.

A vile oath erupted from Reyes's throat. Tossing the tray in his hands aside, he pulled a key from his pocket and unlocked the cell door. The girl let out a wordless cry as he grabbed her by the arm and dragged her out of the dungeon and up the stairs to the second floor. He opened the door to one of the vacant bedchambers, pushed her inside, and locked the door.

Striding to the head of the stairs, he looked over the railing at the servants milling below.

"Alyce! Beatrice! Attend me immediately."

In moments, the two maids were there, awaiting his orders.

"There is a woman in the room next to mine," he said, thrusting the key into Beatrice's hand. "Clean her up and bring her something to eat."

Beatrice curtsied. "Yes, my lord," she said, and hurried away.

"As you wish, my lord," the younger one replied with a saucy smile.

She was a pretty thing, was Alyce, with her curly brown hair and guileless blue eyes. He dismissed her with a wave of his hand, then returned to the hall and his own dinner, but food no longer held any appeal.

Late that night, he prowled the castle until, too restless to remain inside its walls, he left the keep by way of a secret passageway that emerged in the side yard. Under cover of darkness he shed his clothing, then surrendered to the beast within him, his body shifting, his bones popping and cracking as they took on a new shape.

Shanara stood at the window, her heart pounding. Surely she could not be seeing what she was seeing. But even as she watched, the man in the yard below cast off his clothing, and his body began changing, stretching, until, impossible as it was to believe, a large black wolf stood in his place.

She jerked away from the window when the wolf lifted its head. Had he seen her? She shivered as a howl rose on the midnight wind.

When she looked out the window again, the wolf was gone.

So, she had not been dreaming the last time. All the stories were true. Everything she had heard about Reyes was true. She had been afraid of him before, but not like this. It was one thing to be held prisoner by one's enemy, something else entirely when your enemy wasn't human.

She couldn't stay here any longer, clinging to the slim hope that her father would rescue her. Montiori would never agree to take her place. Still, he might consider the killing of his brother and the abduction of one of his daughters reason enough to attack Reyes.

But whether her father came for her or not, her life would be lost one way or another. If her father refused to take her place, she would be killed. If war came, her fate would be the same. Her father would not barter for her life. Alive or dead, she would be nothing but an excuse for another battle, another war.

She moved around the room, looking for anything she could use, either as a weapon or as a way to break the lock on the door.

She was about to give up hope when she saw the handle of a knife protruding from under the napkin on her dinner tray. A tray that should have been picked up hours ago. Using the tip of the blade, she pried at the lock on the door.

It gave with a soft click. Slipping the knife into the pocket of her gown, she tiptoed out of the room.

CHAPTER 4

He ran through the night, every sense aware of his surroundings. He knew there was a deer hiding in the trees behind him, that another wolf had made a kill. He smelled the blood in the air. The earth was damp beneath the sensitive pads of his feet as he ran tirelessly through the darkness.

Freedom. It sang through his veins. He was no longer the lord of a great castle, no longer responsible for hundreds of lives. The woes and wars of mankind meant nothing to the wolf.

There was only freedom and the urge to hunt.

A rabbit sprang out from behind a bush. He chased it down; grabbing it in his jaws, he devoured it in a few bites.

The kill satisfied the urge to hunt, stilled the restlessness in his soul. What would it be like to succumb fully to the wolf, to turn his back on mankind and live in the wild? Even as the thought tempted him, the image of a green-eyed woman rose in his mind, luring him back toward the keep.

He had to see her one more time.

He was halfway back to the castle when a dark gray shape materialized out of the shadows and padded silently toward him.

Reyes came to an abrupt halt when the other wolf growled, its hackles rising as it bared its teeth.

Reyes sniffed the air and immediately recognized the

scent of the other wolf. They had met before. On other
occasions, Reyes had backed down. But not tonight. Tonight, the image of a green-eyed woman tormented him, a
woman who filled him with a yearning he dared not
indulge. Tonight a fight was just what he needed to ease his
frustration.

He bared his own teeth as the gray wolf walked stiff-
legged toward him. Reyes was aware of other wolves
nearby. He felt the weight of their eyes watching him.

The gray wolf attacked without warning, burying its
fangs deep in Reyes's shoulder. Reyes howled, the pain
slicing through him like the cut of a knife.

Shaking off the gray, Reyes whirled around and
charged, his own teeth leaving bloody furrows along the
other wolf's hindquarters.

Backing off, they faced each other and then the gray
wolf lunged forward. Reyes dodged his attack, his teeth
savaging the gray's neck.

They met again, and yet again. Reyes was confident of
victory until he lost his footing on the damp leaves. The
gray wolf was on him in an instant, his teeth slashing at
Reyes's neck and shoulder.

Knowing it was only a matter of time before the rest of
the pack came to finish him off, Reyes fought back as best
he could. And then, abruptly, the gray wolf let him go and
backed off. Moments later, the pack had disappeared into
the darkness.

Reyes lay there, panting heavily, wondering why the
other wolf had broken off the attack.

And then he heard the sound of footsteps moving in the
underbrush. Had it been a deer, the wolves would have
attacked, but in spite of tales to the contrary, wolves rarely
attacked humans.

Shanara darted behind a tree, one hand covering her
mouth to stifle a gasp. The foolhardiness of leaving the
castle struck home as she watched half a dozen dark shapes

disappear into the underbrush. What was she doing out here, armed with nothing but a knife?

She shook off her fears. Better to die trying to escape than wait like a lamb for the slaughter! She was about to continue when she realized that what she thought was a shadow on the ground was, in reality, another wolf. Was it dead? Wounded wolves were doubly dangerous.

Just when she was certain she had nothing to fear, it struggled to its feet, whining softly.

Pity welled in her heart as the beast stood there, head hanging, tongue lolling. Blood soaked its shoulder, dripped from its neck.

Her heart seemed to stop beating when it lifted its head and looked at her through eyes dark with pain. Midnight-blue eyes.

"Reyes." His name whispered past her lips. Hardly aware of what she was doing, she moved toward him, stopping only when he bared his teeth. "You need help." Even as she spoke the words, she wondered if he understood her. "You're bleeding."

He growled softly and she took a step backward. Would he kill her for trying to help him? She felt a bubble of hysterical laughter rise inside her. What difference did it make if he drove a sword through her heart or savaged her with his teeth? One way or another, he intended to kill her, making her wonder why she had ever thought to help him. He was her enemy, as she was his.

He took a step forward, fell heavily as his wounded leg refused to support him.

More fool she, she had always had a soft spot for wounded animals . . . but this was no animal. "Can you walk if I help you?"

He let out a soft bark which she took to mean "yes." Slipping her arm under him, she helped him stand.

"What shall we do now?" she wondered aloud. " 'Tis a long walk back to the castle."

The wolf shook his head and started walking, not toward the castle, but deeper into the woods. Stooped over, she walked beside him, supporting him as best she could. No easy task, as heavy as he was.

Finally, after what seemed like hours, she saw a small stone cottage through a clearing in the trees.

The wolf was panting heavily by the time they reached the cottage. Shanara opened the door, waited for him to enter, then stepped inside and closed the door behind her.

When she looked at the wolf again, she saw that he had collapsed on the floor.

She searched the darkened room until she found a candle and a flint on the mantel. Lighting the candle, she glanced around the one-room cottage. Did it belong to Reyes? She moved about the room, looking into the cupboards, which were stocked with a few foodstuffs—sugar, flour, salt, a box of dried venison, as well as pots and pans, pewter plates and goblets and cutlery. A square table and three chairs stood against one wall, a narrow bed against another. A small box held an assortment of bandages and liniment, as well as a sharp knife, a needle, and sturdy thread.

After laying out the supplies on the table, she went outside and filled a bucket with water from the well, then went back into the cottage, hoping the wolf hadn't bled to death in her absence.

Reyes lay on his side, his eyes closed, his nostrils filling with the scent of his own blood. He had been injured in the past, but never this badly. Blood leaked from the cut in his neck, the deep gash in his shoulder, leaching away his strength.

He opened his eyes when he heard the woman approach, watched warily as she knelt beside him. Dipping a bit of cloth in a bucket, she washed the blood from his neck and shoulder. She threaded a needle with a long piece of thread and then, biting down on a corner of her lower lip, she began to stitch his wounds.

He whined softly as the needle pierced his flesh. If he'd had the strength to regain his human form, he could have dulled the pain with a glass of ale. In his wolf form, all he could do was endure it.

She worked quickly. From time to time she spoke to him, soft words of reassurance. Steeped in pain, he clung to the sound of her voice.

"There." Laying the needle aside, she stroked his head. "'Tis done."

He licked her hand, then closed his eyes and slept.

Shanara stared at her hand, startled, and then laughed softly. No doubt it was just the wolf's way of saying thank you.

Still bemused by her reasons for helping him, she put the needle in the box and replaced it in the cupboard. Finding an old rag, she wiped the blood from the floor, then pulled a blanket from the cot and spread it over the wolf.

Feeling suddenly weak from all that had transpired that night, she dropped into one of the chairs and wrapped her arms around her waist. She was hungry and tired, so tired. She glanced at the cot against the wall, thinking how good it would feel to lie down and sleep for a few hours. And then she looked at the door. This would be the perfect time to get away from him.

And that was just what she would do. Going to the cupboard, she pulled out several pieces of dried venison. She put all but one in her skirt pocket and moved toward the door.

She stood there with her hand on the latch, unable to make herself walk out the door. It was true that Reyes had killed her uncle and her cousins and kidnapped her, but it was also true that he had saved her from being ravished by one of his own men. She couldn't leave him, not now, when he was hurt.

Turning away from the door, she went to the cot and sat down, her gaze resting on the wolf while she ate the dried venison. Then, with a sigh, she slid beneath the blankets, asleep as soon as her head touched the pillow.

Reyes opened his eyes, awakened by a shaft of golden sunlight filtering through the cottage's single window. He drew a deep breath and his nostrils filled with the scent of the woman. Was she still here?

Turning his head, he saw her curled up on the cot. She had tended his wounds last night. Even now, he found it hard to believe, not only because they were enemies, but because he had been in his wolf form. Why had she helped him? He had done nothing to incur either her friendship or her concern, yet she had stitched his cuts and covered him with a blanket. He grinned wryly, wondering which of them would be the most grateful for that this morning.

Sitting up, he ran a hand over his neck and shoulder, remembering how gently she had washed the blood from his wounds, the compassion in her voice as she sewed the gash in his neck and shoulder.

His stomach growled, reminding him that he had not eaten since the night before, and not much then, since his mind had been on the woman instead of the meal.

Rising, he wrapped the blanket around his waist, then rummaged through the cupboard until he found a few strips of dried venison. He ate three pieces, then, grabbing a cast-iron pot, he went outside to fill the container. Returning to the cottage, he lit a fire in the hearth, hung the pot from the tripod to heat.

His gaze returned to the woman. Her hair fell over her shoulders like a waterfall of auburn silk. He sucked in a deep breath as he remembered the feel of it against his cheek, the flowery fragrance that clung to each strand.

Why hadn't she left last night?

He noticed the soft curve of her cheek, the slender line of her throat, the arch of her brows, the swell of her breasts beneath the blanket.

The woman stirred, but didn't awaken.

Desire stirred within him. She was here. She was his to do with as he pleased. The words whispered through his mind, urging him to take her, willing or not.

It was tempting, so very tempting. Had she not come to his aid the night before, he might have surrendered to the longing that burned through him, but she had not only helped him, she had stayed with him through the night. He could not repay her kindness by forcing himself on her.

Lost in thought, it took him a moment to realize she was awake and staring at him, the look in her eyes telling him that she knew every lustful thought that had crossed his mind.

"Good morrow," he said, his voice gruff.

She nodded, her gaze moving over his bare chest and the blanket tightly wrapped around his waist.

"Thank you for tending my wounds."

"You're welcome," she murmured.

"How did you get past the gates last night?"

She stared at him. Was he so foolish as to think she would tell him?

Reyes nodded. "Why did you not leave here when you had the chance?"

Her gaze slid away from his. "I know not."

"You should have gone when you had the chance," he said curtly.

She looked up at him, a glimmer of hope in her eyes. "You could let me go now."

"No, I cannot." He gestured toward the hearth. "There is hot water if you wish to bathe."

She nodded, but made no move to get up.

Grunting softly, Reyes left the cottage.

* * *

Throwing back the covers, Shanara slid her legs over the edge of the cot. Did she dare bathe with him prowling the grounds outside?

Keeping one eye on the door, she found a chunk of soap and a piece of toweling. Moving quickly, she washed her hands and face, then removed her stockings to wash her legs. She was drying her feet when he knocked on the door.

"Nay, do not enter!" she cried, her heart pounding at the thought of him seeing her bare legs.

Moving quickly, she finished drying her feet, then drew on her stockings and shoes, smoothed her skirt, ran a hand through her hair.

He knocked on the door again.

Shanara took a deep, calming breath, then called, "Enter."

Reyes stepped into the room and moved toward the hearth.

Shanara's eyes widened as he reached for the cloth she had used. "Do you mean to bathe?"

"Aye."

"I will wait outside."

"No."

She stared at him, speechless. "You cannot expect me to stay while you wash!" she exclaimed in horror.

"And how long would you remain if I let you out of my sight?"

The rush of color in her cheeks was all the answer he needed.

When he reached for the soap, she quickly turned her back to him, her arms crossed over her breasts.

Grinning, Reyes dropped the blanket.

Shanara stared at the wall, trying not to listen as he washed, trying not to imagine how he looked without the blanket. She knew it was shameless of her, but she couldn't seem to help herself. Having five brothers, she was no stranger to naked men or the male body, but Reyes was not kin and, truth be told, none of her brothers was as tall as her captor, nor did any of them have shoulders as broad. Certainly none were as handsome . . .

She shook the thought aside. The man was her enemy. He was keeping her against her will, hoping to trade her life for her father's, and though she had little love for her father, he deserved her loyalty.

"Let's go, lass."

"Are you decent?"

"Not always, but I am covered."

She turned to find he had wrapped the blanket around his waist and tied it in place with a leather thong.

"Do you often find yourself naked in the woods?" she asked, then clapped her hand over her mouth, her cheeks burning with embarrassment.

"Not often." Opening the door, he waited for her to cross the threshold, then followed her outside, closing the door behind him.

They walked for a time in silence. Shanara was acutely conscious of the man at her side. He towered over her. Bare-chested and barefooted, he looked more like a barbarian than ever. His skin was very brown. Dark bristles shadowed his jaw. His wounds looked red and painful. In truth, she was surprised that he was on his feet at all.

From time to time she could feel his eyes on her, as tangible as a touch. What was he thinking? She shivered, wondering what he would do to her when her father refused to take her place.

She slid a furtive glance in his direction, her mind filling with questions.

"What is it?" he asked gruffly.

"Nothing."

He made a dismissive gesture with his hand. "'Tis obvious you want to ask me something. Ask it."

"How long have you been cursed?"

"Since I reached manhood."

"Were you frightened, the first time it came upon you?"

"Aye."

"Does it hurt? I saw you one night, from the window. It looked . . ." She shivered, unable to find the words to describe what she had seen.

"It hurts," he admitted quietly. "Every time."

"And you have no control over it?"

"Some, but very little when the moon is full."

"What does it feel like, to be a wolf?"

He looked down at her. "Like nothing you can imagine. Everything is magnified. Sounds. Smells. I can hear a leaf falling from a tree, see clearly in the darkness, run for miles and miles . . ."

"It rather sounds as if you like it."

"In some ways, I do."

"Can you change at will?"

"Aye."

"And if you have a son, will he be accursed, as well?"

He nodded curtly.

"Why was your father cursed in this way?"

"He angered your father's witch," he said, his voice bitter.

"Do you mean Melena?"

Reyes nodded. "In return, she decreed that all males in my father's line would be cursed to run with the wolves when the moon is full."

"I find that hard to believe. She has ever been kind to me. What did your father do that made her so angry?"

"He was a handsome man, my father. She wanted a son and wished for him to sire it. When he refused to betray my mother, Melena set a curse upon him."

"Did your father try to break the spell?"

"Aye. My father went to Melena and pleaded with her to release him. But she refused. A year later, after my mother had conceived, my father went to Montiori and begged him to order Melena to break the spell. Your father promised he would do so, but first he wanted to see my father undergo the change. My father agreed. During the next full moon, he went to your father's keep, and when the moon rose, he transformed into a wolf. And your father killed him."

She fell silent, thinking of what Reyes had told her. It explained why he was not married. What woman would marry a man knowing that her sons would inherit the same dreadful affliction?

"Why did your father have to wait for the full moon? Could he not change at will?"

"No, though I do not know why." He shrugged. "Perhaps the curse gets stronger with time."

Though the day was cool, a fine sheen of sweat covered Reyes's face and chest. His steps had slowed. His skin was hot when her arm brushed against his.

"You've a fever," she said.

He nodded.

"You should rest."

He glanced at her, bemused by her concern. Would she care whether he lived or died if she knew what he had planned for her? "The keep is just over that rise," he said. "I'll rest there."

She didn't argue. If he fainted along the way, so much the better for her. It would give her yet another chance to try to escape.

But he didn't faint.

They were nearing the crest of the hill when a dozen riders appeared. The men halted a short distance away.

"My lord!" one of them called. "We have been searching for you since daybreak."

The man closest to them dismounted. "Here, my lord, take my horse."

With a nod, Reyes put his foot in the stirrup. He took a deep breath, then swung his leg over the saddle. "Bring the woman." Clucking to the horse, he rode toward the castle.

The rider who had given Reyes his mount lifted Shanara onto the back of one of the other horses. The knights followed their lord back to the castle. The riderless knight ran behind them.

Shanara let out a sigh as they rode through the gates into the keep. She was his prisoner yet again.

CHAPTER 5

Shanara followed one of Reyes's men up the stairs. He showed her to a room where the two gray-clad women who had looked after her before awaited. She frowned, trying to remember their names. Beatrice and Alyce, if she recalled aright. In less time than she would have thought possible, the maids had removed her clothing, washed her from neck to heel, and then wrapped her in a towel.

"Now," said Beatrice, tapping her foot. "What shall she wear?"

"The mauve velvet," said Alyce.

Beatrice shook her head. She was the elder of the two, with brown hair, gray eyes, and a sweet, motherly face. "Nay, Alyce, the green silk. It matches her eyes, and you know it is Lord Reyes's favorite color."

"Then I shall wear the mauve," Shanara decided. She had not missed the smirk on Alyce's face.

"Will you not reconsider?" Beatrice asked hopefully. She ran her hand over the green silk. "Tis a lovely gown."

Shanara shook her head. "The mauve."

With a sigh of resignation, Beatrice helped Shanara into the mauve gown. She brushed Shanara's hair until it gleamed, then swept it away from her face with a pair of jeweled combs.

"You look lovely," Beatrice declared. "Does she not, Alyce?"

The younger woman nodded sullenly.

"Come along," Beatrice said, and Shanara followed her down the corridor to a door she recognized all too well. It led to his bedchamber.

With a smile, Beatrice opened the door. When Shanara didn't move, the woman gave her a little push, then shut the door behind her.

The room was dark and smelled of candle wax and herbs. A fire blazed in the hearth. She took a step toward the huge four-poster bed in the center of the room.

Reyes lay under a mound of heavy blankets. As she drew nearer, she could hear the sound of his labored breathing. His brow was covered with perspiration.

Moving to his bedside, she called his name.

He stirred restlessly at the sound of her voice.

Shanara laid her hand on his shoulder. His skin was hot. Now that she was close, she could see that the wound in his arm was discolored and swollen. He groaned when she ran her fingertips over the wound.

Leaving the room, she went down to the kitchen. The cook looked up, startled to find a stranger in her domain.

"I need some hot water," Shanara said, "and a pot of strong willowbark tea. I also need a poultice to draw poison from a wound, a sharp knife, and a needle and thread."

"Who are you to give me orders in my own kitchen?" the cook demanded, waving a big wooden spoon in Shanara's face. "Begone from my kitchen this instant!"

Holding her ground, Shanara drew herself up to her full height. "If you refuse to do as I ask and Lord Reyes surrenders to the fever burning within him, his death will be upon your head."

The cook's eyes widened, then, without another word, she began to fill a clean pot with water.

Certain her orders would be obeyed, Shanara returned to Reyes's bedchamber. Crossing the room, she threw open one of the windows, then dragged all but one of the blankets off the bed.

It took her a moment to realize he was awake and watching her through narrowed eyes.

Filling a glass with water, Shanara lifted Reyes's head and offered him a drink. "Slowly, now," she admonished.

He drained the glass and asked for more.

"Why is there no one here to tend you?" she asked, surprised that the lord of the keep would be left alone when he was obviously ill. "Why do you not call your physician?"

"I sent him away."

"Why?"

He glanced at the open window. "The moon will be full tonight."

She nodded her understanding. "But surely, when you're so ill, the curse will not come upon you."

"I do not know. It is a chance I cannot take. There are but few who know that the curse is more than just a fable told to frighten children."

Frowning, she looked at him closely. His face seemed hairy, but it was only because he had not shaved. Wasn't it? "Why did you summon me?"

"I may have need of your help later."

"You have need of help *now*," she muttered.

A knock at the door drew her attention. When she opened it, she saw Alyce standing in the corridor. The maid's eyes widened when she saw Shanara. When Shanara reached for the tray in Alyce's hands, the girl stepped back, pulling it out of reach.

"Give me the tray," Shanara said, irritated by the maid's behavior.

"Nay. I have come to look after my Lord Reyes."

Shanara did not miss the possessive tone in the girl's voice. "I shall attend him," she said imperiously.

"'Tis not a job for a lady," Alyce retorted, the word

"lady" dripping with disdain. She leaned to one side, trying to see past Shanara and into the room beyond.

"Perhaps not," Shanara said. She fixed the girl with a hard gaze. She was Lord Montiori's daughter. If there was one thing she knew, it was how to give orders and have them obeyed. "Give me the tray and be gone."

For a moment, it seemed the girl might refuse; then, lips pursed in silent mutiny, she handed Shanara the tray.

Using her heel, Shanara shut the door in the maid's face.

Reyes eyed her balefully as she set the tray on the table beside the bed. She drew the blade through the fire to clean it, then she cut the old stitches from his shoulder. Taking a deep breath, she pierced the edge of the wound with the tip of the knife. Thick yellow pus mixed with blood that looked almost black oozed out in the wake of the blade. Taking the poultice, she placed it over the wound to draw out the last of the poison.

An oath hissed from between Reyes's clenched teeth as the hot poultice touched his skin.

While the poultice did its work, Shanara poured a cup of willowbark tea, then, lifting his head, she held the cup to his lips. "Drink."

He shook his head.

"Drink, you stubborn man. 'Tis good for what ails you."

When he still refused, she tugged on a lock of his hair. "Drink, I say!"

"Shrew," he muttered, but he drank the tea, grimacing at the bitter taste.

Lowering his head to the pillow once more, Shanara lifted the poultice, surprised to see that the wound looked much better already. She had intended to leave it in place through the night, but that no longer seemed necessary. Was he by nature a man who healed quickly, she wondered, or was it a by-product of the curse?

Threading the needle with a length of silk thread, she

endeavored to put everything from her mind but the task at hand. She tried to ignore the whisper of the needle passing through flesh, tried to pretend it was no different from sewing a piece of cloth, but cloth did not bleed. She paused frequently to wipe away the blood that oozed from the edges of the wound as her needle moved in and out, drawing the ragged edges together.

As he had before, Reyes endured her stitching in silence. Sweat beaded his brow. Using a corner of the sheet, she wiped it away.

She didn't know who was more relieved when she took the last stitch and put the needle aside. After wiping her hands on a scrap of cloth, she sat down in the chair beside the bed and blew out a sigh of relief.

Reyes looked at her, one brow arched. "Want to change places?" he asked with a wry grin.

She wrinkled her nose at him. " 'Tis not so easy, putting a needle to a man's flesh."

" 'Tis not so easy to be the man whose flesh you are sticking, either."

She laid her hand on his brow. "We need to bring your fever down."

He nodded.

"Perhaps I should call your steward . . ."

"No."

She glanced at the blanket where it covered his hips. "Are you . . . ?"

In spite of the pain of his wounds and the fever burning through him, he grinned roguishly. "As the day my mother bore me."

With a nod, she carefully folded the blanket down to his waist, then folded the other end up to mid-thigh. She felt herself blushing under his regard.

She found a length of cloth, poured water from the pitcher into a basin, and began to draw the cool cloth over his heated flesh. The task should not have caused her any embarrassment. He was sick and she was caring for him. It was no more than that, and yet it was much more than that. She was acutely aware of his every breath, of the way his eyes followed her every movement. She couldn't help but admire the spread of his shoulders, his flat belly ridged with muscle earned from long hours of battle practice. His arms were well muscled from years of wielding a heavy sword, his legs from years of hard riding. When she ran the cloth over his neck, his hair brushed against her hand. It was softer than she had thought it would be.

She wet the cloth again and again, drawing it over his chest and belly, down his arms and legs. She wiped the sweat from his face, offered him another drink of cool water.

The room gradually grew darker, making her acutely aware of time passing. She lit the candles on the mantel, added wood to the fire. She glanced at the window, her heart pounding.

A startled cry erupted from her throat when Reyes laid his hand on hers. "I need to go outside."

"What foolishness is this? You've a fever."

His gaze captured hers. "I cannot stay inside any longer. I need your help."

"Wh-what do you want me to do?"

"Help me down the stairs. Later tonight, when the servants have gone to bed, I want you to leave my robe by the back door. Will you do that for me?"

She nodded, wondering at her willingness to help him. She turned her back when he started to sit up, listened to the sound of his body sliding over the bedding, the soft thud of his feet on the floor, the whisper of the blanket as he wrapped it around his hips.

She wondered how he had kept his secret so long and then realized that it would be an easy thing for the lord to leave the keep whenever he wished. He didn't have to answer to anyone or explain where he might be going in the middle of the night should someone see him. Most likely, anyone seeing him would assume he had a midnight tryst.

She turned when he took her hand. "Let's go."

With her arm around his waist, they made their way down the steps, through the keep, to the back door located in the kitchen. He opened the door, then paused to look back at her.

"Be careful," Shanara said.

"Do not run away again," he warned. " 'Tis not safe beyond the walls. Promise me you will be here when I return."

She glanced past Reyes to the yard beyond, her need to go home burning within her, though she couldn't say why. There was nothing for her there, no one who wanted her. No one who needed her.

Reyes took hold of her arm. "Promise me!" he said again, his voice almost a growl.

She looked up at him. The change was almost upon him. She could see it in his eyes, feel it in the air around them. "I promise."

As soon as the words were spoken, he was moving away from her, loping toward the shadows beneath the trees.

She watched until he was out of sight, wondering what had prompted her to promise him that she would be there when he returned. She owed him nothing. He was the enemy. Lying to the enemy was not the same as lying to a friend. She glanced at the wall in the distance. Freedom was just a short distance away. There, behind one of the shrubs, she had found a hole in the wall just big enough for her to squeeze through.

She stared across the yard for a long time; then, with a sigh she closed the door and went up the stairs to wait for Reyes to return.

CHAPTER 6

Montiori leaned back in his chair, his eyes narrowed, as he read the missive from his daughter, sent at the order of Reyes, the Lord of Black Dragon Keep:

> *Father*
> *I am being held hostage by Lord Reyes. It is his command*
> *that you present yourself at Black Dragon Keep before the*
> *next full moon and surrender yourself and your arms. If*
> *you refuse, my life will be forfeit.*
> > *Your obedient daughter, Shanara.*

He read the note again, then crumpled the parchment in his fist. Did Reyes think him a fool, that he would give up his own life in exchange for that of his youngest whelp? It was nothing to him if the girl lived or died. He had five sons to carry on the family line, and more daughters than any man needed.

Montiori turned his attention to the man who awaited his answer. "How do I know my daughter is still alive?"

"You have my lord's word on it."

Montiori snorted derisively. "As if I would believe anything that wretched beast has to say."

Mergrid took a step forward. "My Lord Reyes says he will send the girl back a piece at a time until you surrender, or she dies." He withdrew a small bundle wrapped in cloth from his pocket. "This is so you will know that my Lord Reyes means what he says."

Taking the bundle, Montiori removed the wrappings. Inside, he found the first knuckle of a woman's little finger. Grunting softly, he tossed the bloody bit of bone and flesh into the fire. "Return to your lord."

"I was told to wait for your answer."

"He will know it when he sees it."

"As you wish," Mergrid said. Bowing, he turned and left the hall.

Montiori waited until Reyes's servant was out of the room, then motioned for one of his knights to follow the man.

With a nod of understanding, the knight drew his sword and followed Mergrid from the hall.

CHAPTER 7

Shanara stood at the window staring out into the darkness, waiting and wondering. Where was he? What was he doing? Was he running through the deep shadows of the night in search of prey, or running just for the sheer joy of it? She knew he remembered being a wolf when he was a man, but when he was clothed in the skin of the wolf, did he remember being a man? What a sad and lonely life it must be for him. She knew now why he remained apart from the others in the keep, why he had never married. Why he would never marry. A pity, when he was such a handsome man!

She thrust the thought from her mind. He was the enemy! Why did it grow ever harder to remember that?

She dozed, then woke abruptly, wondering what had awakened her. And then she knew. The moon was setting. He was near.

Rising, she grabbed a long hooded robe and hurried down the stairs to the kitchen. But she didn't leave the garment by the door. Instead, she carried it outside and walked across the yard, following the path he had taken earlier.

She looked up at the moon, so beautiful against the black velvet sky. She wondered if Reyes saw the beauty of it anymore, or if it was a constant reminder of the curse that plagued him.

Frowning, she paused under a tree. If his affliction had

been caused by a curse, then there must also be a way to undo it. But how?

A rustle in the underbrush drew her attention. She held her breath as a dark shape materialized out of the shadows. If it wasn't Reyes . . . but it was. She recognized him immediately.

He trotted to her side, stood there looking up at her. If she had thought it possible, she would have said he was grinning at her.

She held up the robe. "Are you ready to change back?"

He whined softly, his body convulsing, muscles rippling beneath the thick black fur as his body transformed, paws becoming hands and feet, fur receding to become human skin.

It was fascinating and yet frightening to watch as bones and muscle and sinew rearranged themselves until Reyes stood before her, his body sheened with perspiration. She looked at him standing there and thought him the most beautiful thing she had ever seen.

It was only when he reached for the robe draped over her arm that she remembered to be embarrassed by his nudity. With a gasp, she put her back to him, but by then it was too late. She had seen all there was to see.

"Why did you come here?" he asked, his voice sharp with disapproval.

"I . . . because . . ." She frowned. Why had she come?

"Because you wanted to see the monster?" he asked quietly, but she heard the bitterness in his voice.

"Is that how you see yourself?" she asked, her back still toward him. "As a monster?"

"Do you not?"

She turned to face him. "I see only a man who is being made to suffer for something that happened before he was born."

His gaze searched hers as if seeking to know the truth of her words. Unable to help himself, he took a step forward, his hand stroking her cheek. When she didn't recoil from his touch, he moved closer. And then he lowered his head and claimed her lips with his. As he had the first time he kissed her, he expected her to resist, but once again her response took him by surprise. Her eyelids fluttered down and then she was kissing him back, her innocence and her eagerness more powerful than any aphrodisiac. Her lips were sweeter than a honeycomb, more intoxicating than spring wine. Putting his arms around her, he drank from her lips like a man dying for sustenance. He plunged one hand into her hair, his fingers delving into the thick mass. Her scent filled his nostrils, the heat of her body turned away the chill of the night. She was the reason he had never married, he thought, the reason he had shunned the wagons of the camp followers.

He kissed her again, reveling in her sweet response. For a moment, he let himself pretend he was a normal man, let himself believe that she could be his, that he could take her as his wife and safely spill his seed within her womb. He imagined children born of their joining—strong sons and beautiful daughters, imagined the sound of their laughter filling his dreary keep. He would stop seeking battles to fight and spend his days in peaceful pursuits, and his nights . . . ah, his nights would be spent in Shanara's arms . . . Shanara. She was here, in his arms, and yet forever out of reach.

With a low growl, he released her and turned away.

Shanara stared at his back. "Reyes?"

"Go back to the keep."

"Have I displeased you?"

"Displeased me?" An anguished laugh rose in his throat. "Go from me, Shanara, now, before it is too late for both of us."

She started to reach out for him, needing to comfort him, and then lowered her arm. She didn't know what madness possessed her to let him kiss her but there could never be anything between them. He was going to kill her or her father. How could she have forgotten that?

Wrapping her arms around her waist, she ran back to the keep, grateful for the darkness that hid her tears.

She woke to the sound of shouts and harsh curses. Rising, she went to the window overlooking the courtyard. A number of men surrounded a horse. Reyes was easy to pick from the crowd. He stood head and shoulders above the others.

Curious to know what had caused such a tumult at such an early hour, she donned a robe and hurried down the stairs and out the door.

As though sensing her approach, Reyes turned to face her, his expression grim, his eyes hard.

She slowed her steps as she drew near, then came to an abrupt halt when she saw the source of the commotion. The horse she had seen from her window carried a burden on its back. She stopped, one hand covering her mouth, when she saw the headless body draped across the saddle.

She looked up at Reyes. "Who . . . who was he?"

"The messenger I sent to your father."

His words sent a shiver through her. Caught up in the horror of what she was seeing, she hadn't realized that Reyes had come to stand beside her.

She looked up at him. He had sent her plea for help to her father and this was her father's reply. Coldness settled over her, leaving her numb. Her father would not save her. She had known all along that he would not, yet she had clung to some small scrap of hope, and now that, too, was gone.

As he had been the first time she had seen him, Reyes was clad all in black. He had reminded her of Death on that day not so long ago. And now that her father had abandoned her, Reyes would, indeed, be her death. Because her father would not take her place, her life would be forfeit, and then there would be another war, with more death and more killing.

"How soon?" she asked, her voice a choked whisper. She didn't want to die. She wanted to live, to marry and bear children, to watch them grow, to hear their laughter and dry their tears.

He frowned at her. "How soon? How soon for what?"

"Until you . . . until you . . ."

"Speak, woman, what are you trying to say?"

"How soon until you . . . you take my head in exchange for his?"

Reyes blinked at her. "Is that what you think I'm going to do?"

"Are you not? You said my life would be forfeit if my father did not surrender to you."

Reyes snorted. "I may be a monster but it is not my habit to slay women or children."

She stared at him, feeling suddenly dizzy with relief.

Reyes pulled her into his arms to steady her. Had she truly thought he would take her life if her miserable cur of a father refused to surrender? Reyes knew he would as soon cut off his own hand before he raised it in violence against her. He spat into the dirt. He had known all along that Montiori would never sacrifice his own life for that of his daughter, or for any of his children. Still, he had hoped that Montiori would fall for his bluff, that some spark of fatherly devotion existed in the man. He should have known better. His bluff had failed. To his regret, the finger that his physician had amputated from the diseased hand of one of the serving women had not fooled Shanara's father.

He frowned thoughtfully, his mind forming and dismissing a dozen ploys, and then he smiled. Of course! He knew exactly how to avenge himself on his enemy. Why had he not thought of it sooner?

Shanara looked up at him, obviously confused by his sudden change of mood.

"I have a better way to avenge myself on my enemy," he remarked. "A way that cannot fail."

"You mean to go to war against him?" she asked in alarm.

"No," he said quietly. "I mean to marry his daughter."

CHAPTER 8

Shanara stared up at him. "And which of my father's daughters do you intend to marry, my lord?"

A slow smile curved Reyes's lips. "The one in my arms, of course."

Numbness gave way to trepidation. She could not deny that she was attracted to Reyes, or deny that the prospect of staying here, as his wife, was far more appealing than returning to her father's keep. But in the next heartbeat, trepidation turned to despair. She could not marry Reyes, could not conceive a child that would carry the same curse as its father. Not so long ago, she had been certain he would never marry.

She twisted out of his grasp. "Nay."

"Aye. You will be my bride within a fortnight."

"But why? You do not love me!"

"Your father's witch cursed me. Perhaps your father will reconsider his offer when he realizes the curse will now fall on his own kin."

"And on your own!" she exclaimed in horror. "Would you be so cruel as to condemn your own son to the kind of life you lead?"

He recoiled as if she had slapped him. Did she truly think he would get her with child, that he would condemn a son of his to the life he led? If so, so be it. Let her think what she would.

"My life is not as bad as it once was." His gaze slid over her body, his eyes dark, hot, and hungry, and filled with yearning.

"Nay!" she exclaimed. "I will not marry you. I will not allow you to use me or any son we might have to avenge yourself on my father."

"You will be my wife or my enemy," he said coldly. "The choice is yours."

She squared her shoulders, her eyes flashing defiance. "I am already your enemy!"

"Are you?" he asked.

His voice, no longer cold, was as warm and seductive as honeyed wine.

She lifted her chin defiantly. "I will take my own life rather than marry you."

"We shall see. Make whatever preparations you need. We wed in a fortnight."

And with those words ringing in her ears, he took her by the arm and led her into the keep.

Shanara paced her chamber, her mind in turmoil. She had to get away from here before it was too late. Save for the witch's curse, marriage to Reyes would have been far more appealing than returning to her father's keep, but she would not bear a child knowing that it would be cursed to run with the wolves at the full moon. How could Reyes expect it of her? How could he consider it himself?

Too upset to eat, she refused the tray that Beatrice brought her later that evening, flinched when she heard Beatrice turn the key in the lock. One way or another, she had been naught but a prisoner since Reyes had defeated her uncle in battle. Nay, even before that, she mused. Being a woman, she had never truly known the kind of freedom her brothers enjoyed.

With a sigh, Shanara went to the window and stared down at the yard below. She had to find a way out of here or, at the very least, get word to her father. Surely he would come to her rescue rather than see her wed to his enemy!

Dropping down onto the window seat, she rested her chin in her hands and stared into the gathering darkness. She wouldn't be here now if she hadn't gone to visit her uncle.

Rising, she began to pace the floor once again. She was still pacing when Alyce came in to light the fire and turn down her bed.

Alyce helped her out of her dress and undergarments, helped her into a long white sleeping gown, and then glared at her. "Why did you have to come here?"

"I assure you, it was not my wish," Shanara replied, startled by the girl's insolent tone and sullen expression.

"Then why are you marrying Lord Reyes?"

Shanara sighed. It came as no surprise that the news had already spread throughout the keep. Did his servants also know that she had refused his offer?

Alyce reached for Shanara's brush. "Lord Reyes deserves a woman who loves him." She brushed out Shanara's hair, her touch far less gentle than Beatrice's. Laying the brush aside, she began plaiting Shanara's hair. "If you had not come here, perhaps . . ."

Shanara glanced over her shoulder. "Perhaps what?"

Alyce shook her head. "Nothing."

"Tell me, Alyce. It may be that I can help."

A single tear slid down the maid's cheek. "No one can help me."

"I cannot help you if you will not confide in me."

"I love him!" Alyce spoke the words in a rush, then clapped her hand over her mouth, her eyes widening in horror. "Forgive me, my lady. Please do not tell him what I said!"

"Alyce, there may be hope for you yet."

"How so? You are to wed in a fortnight."

"I have no wish to marry Lord Reyes, only to return to my father." Strange how, having said the words, she knew them for lies. "Can you help me?"

"There is a little chapel in a copse of trees behind the mews. Meet me there in three hours."

"But the door to my room . . ."

"I shall unlock it when it is time to go. Do not be late."

Reyes paced the floor of the great hall, wondering what madness had possessed him to tell Shanara that they would be wed. He had vowed that he would never marry, thus putting an end to the curse that plagued him. But he had looked into Shanara's eyes, felt her warm breath upon his face, tasted the sweetness of her kisses, and selfishly wanted more. He could not kill her and he could not let her go. At the time, his impulsive decision to marry her had seemed like the only sensible thing to do.

He turned at the sound of footsteps, surprised to see the young serving maid Alyce up so late.

"Is something amiss?" he asked.

"No, my lord," she replied softly. She filled a goblet with wine and carried it to him. "You look troubled."

He nodded as he accepted the drink. She was a pretty girl. It occurred to him that he had seen a good deal of her of late, and then he grinned inwardly. She was young and impressionable. No doubt she was infatuated with the lord of the keep. It had happened before.

"Is there anything else I can do for you, my lord?" She stood near at hand, her gaze on his face. The throaty purr in her voice and the look in her eyes told him she was only too willing to do anything he asked.

For a moment, he was sorely tempted to take what she was offering so brazenly. Perhaps satisfying his lust would enable him to think more clearly, but even as he considered it, he knew he would not touch the girl. He wanted no woman in his bed but Shanara, and if he could not have her, then he would continue to remain celibate, unpleasant as that might be.

Placing her hand on his forearm, Alyce looked up at him through the veil of her lashes. "Perhaps you would like a warm bath," she suggested. "It would help you sleep."

He took a deep, calming breath, certain that, after accepting what she was offering, he would sleep like a newborn babe. Again, he shook off the temptation.

"Go along with you now, girl," he said, dismissing her with a wave of his hand.

She lingered a moment more, then turned and flounced from the room. Reyes watched the enticing sway of her hips, then, muttering an oath, he left the hall for the room he planned to occupy until Shanara was his bride. Unfortunately, since he knew he would not be able to share her bed without possessing her, it was the room he would be occupying after the wedding as well.

On that dreary note, he stripped off his boots and shirt and sought his rest, grateful that tonight there was no full moon.

Wearing a dark cloak over her gown, Shanara crept out of her room, down the stairs, and out the back door of the keep. She cast a wary eye behind her, giving thanks for the lowering clouds that hid the moon and the stars and, hopefully, her progress across the yard toward the mews.

Once, certain that someone was watching her, she glanced up at the windows overlooking the yard. No lights shone. No moving shadows betrayed a watchful eye. Telling herself there was nothing to fear, she hurried onward.

The small whitewashed chapel, topped by a carved wooden cross, stood in a copse of ancient oaks and elms. Opening the door, she paused at the threshold. Hearing nothing, she stepped inside the dark building.

"Alyce," she whispered. "Are you here?"

Silence was her only answer.

Heart pounding, Shanara took a step backward and then, hearing a noise off to her left, she whirled around, reaching blindly for the door. Her hand was on the latch when she felt a sharp pain on the back of her head, and then she felt nothing at all.

He woke suddenly, not knowing what had roused him. Sitting up, he stared into the darkness that surrounded him, his head cocked as he listened to the sounds of the night. He could discern nothing amiss, yet he couldn't shake the feeling that something was wrong.

Swinging his legs over the edge of the bed, he reached for his boots, then changed his mind. Padding barefoot across the floor, he left the room and walked quickly down the corridor to his bedchamber. He pressed his ear to the door, listening. There was no sound from within.

He was about to return to his own room when some inner voice urged him to try the latch. The door opened at his touch. Without stepping inside, he knew the chamber was empty.

Muttering a vile oath, he stalked down the stairs and out the kitchen door. Once he was safely in the shadows, he removed his trousers and summoned the wolf. Ah, the pain of it, the wonder of it. He dropped to his hands and knees, stared at his hands as they turned into paws. He groaned as muscles and tendons stretched and changed shape, his body contracting here, expanding there, the whole of it sprouting a thick black pelt.

When the transformation was complete, he shook himself all over, let out a low whine as her scent filled his nostrils. She had been here not long ago, and she had not been alone. Alyce's scent also hung in the air.

He broke into a trot, his nose to the ground. Alyce's scent was soon left behind, but Shanara's led him to the small chapel behind the mews.

His hackles rose when he reached the door. Her scent was strong here, and overlaying it, he detected the scent of a man. A scent he recognized. Ragan. He growled low in his throat at the thought of her sneaking out of the keep to meet another man. A man who had sealed his doom the moment he laid his hand on Shanara.

Reyes intended to have Shanara for his mate, and wolves mated for life.

She was afraid, so afraid. Her head throbbed with every breath. She could feel the sticky warmth of her own blood trickling down the back of her neck. She glanced from side to side, though there was nothing to see but blackness. She had no idea who had struck her or where she was now. She knew she was lying on her side. There was dirt beneath her cheek. When she tried to lift a hand to her head, she discovered that her hands were tied behind her back. When she tried to sit up, she realized her feet were also bound.

Willing herself to be calm, she began to twist her hands back and forth in an effort to loosen the ropes that bound her wrists. She had to get out of here, wherever *here* was. Tears burned her eyes and she blinked them back. She would cry later. Shaking off her self-pity, she thought of Alyce, the lying wench. It was Alyce who had done this to her. But why?

Because of Reyes, of course. The girl had declared she was in love with the lord of the keep. Had Alyce thought that by getting rid of her lord's intended bride, she might be able to win his love?

Shanara frowned. There had been no need for Alyce to do her harm. She had told the maid she didn't want to marry Reyes, that all she wanted was to return to her father. Either Alyce had not believed her, or she had decided to make certain that Shanara would never return to Black Dragon Keep. Deep in her heart, Shanara knew that should Fate decree that she never see Reyes again, she would miss

him far more than she would ever admit to herself or anyone else.

Shanara winced as the thick rope cut into the tender
skin of her wrists. There was no time to worry about the
maid's motives now. She had to get away before it was too
late. Had to find her way home . . .

Home. She thought of her father's keep and the people
in it. His knights were taciturn and sullen. The servants
were the same. Her brothers spent their days honing their
battle skills and their nights whoring, seemingly happy
only when they were on the battlefield, or preparing for
war. Her sisters had little time for her, preferring to spend
their days pampering themselves behind closed doors or
gossiping about their neighbors when they weren't simper-
ing over one man or another. Shanara had spent most of
her days in her chambers learning the fine arts from her old
nursemaid. She saw her father only at meals, considered
herself fortunate if he deigned to notice her presence at the
table.

As she did so often, she wished her mother was still
alive. Her mother had been the only one who cared what
happened to her youngest daughter, the only one who took
time to speak to Shanara, to cheer her when she was down,
to assure her that in spite of her father's indifference, he
loved her. Shanara had never believed it, but she had loved
her mother the more for trying to spare her feelings.

A sound from above drew her attention. Looking up,
she saw a narrow bit of moonlight shining through the
clouds. She froze as she heard movement overhead again,
a low snuffling sound followed by a low growl.

Panic surged through her. With a grunt, she freed one
hand and then the other. A million pinpricks rushed
through her fingers as blood flowed into her hands again.
Sitting up, she massaged her wrists for several moments
and then reached for the rope that bound her ankles. As she
did so, her hand brushed against something cold and slip-

pery. At first she couldn't tell what it was, and then she realized it was a chunk of raw meat.

Terror clogged her throat as she scrambled to her feet. She knew where she was now.

She was out in the woods, in one of the pits that were used to trap wild animals. And she was now part of the bait.

CHAPTER 9

Lifting his head, Reyes sniffed the air, sorting Shanara's scent from the hundreds of others that assailed him—the scent of damp earth and trees and rotting foliage. He detected the fear rising from rabbits and mice and other small creatures that cowered in their dens and holes, hiding from the fierce predator that stalked the night.

He howled as he honed in on Shanara's scent, growled when her spoor led him to a wolf trap. Anger twisted through him. Fearful that he might accidentally stumble into one of the pits some dark night, he had long ago declared that all such traps be filled in.

Hackles raised, he padded closer to the edge of the pit. In spite of the depth and the darkness, he had no trouble seeing the bottom of the chasm, or the woman who crouched there, looking up at him through frightened green eyes.

Giving what he hoped was a reassuring bark, Reyes backed away from the edge of the pit. Sitting on his haunches, he closed his eyes and pictured his human image in his mind, visualizing the transformation. He howled in protest as his body began to change, the man overtaking the wolf, humanity overtaking the wildness.

When the change was complete, he crawled back to the pit and peered over the side. "Shanara?"

"Reyes!"

"I will have you out of there soon."

Rising, he cast around for something he could use to pull her out of the pit. Spying several long vines, he twisted them together, then tossed one end over the side.

"Catch hold," he said. "I will pull you up."

Moments later, she was standing beside him brushing dirt from her gown and her hands. "How did you find me?"

"I followed your scent. There was a man with you. Where is he?"

She shook her head. "I know not. He dumped me in the pit and . . ." She shrugged.

"And Alyce?" he asked curtly. "What part did she have in all this?"

Shanara stared at him, mute.

"Answer me!"

"She said she would help me get back to my father."

Reyes swore a vile oath. He would kill Alyce for this, and Ragan as well!

He blew out a deep breath, then took Shanara's hand. "Is the thought of being my bride so repulsive to you that you would rather risk death than take your vows?"

She looked up at him, not knowing what to say, afraid to admit to him, or to herself, the depths of her feelings for him, feelings she could not begin to understand. No matter how hard she tried to hate him, no matter how often she reminded herself that he was her enemy, she could not hate him.

She gasped as he drew her into his arms. She placed her hands on his chest, intending to push him away. Only then did she remember that he was naked. The warmth of his body quickly penetrated her clothing, the heat in his eyes seared her soul.

"Shanara . . ." His hand brushed her cheek, slid down her back to cup her buttocks, drawing her closer, letting her feel the visible evidence of his desire.

"Please, do not . . ."

"What?" he asked gruffly. "Do not touch you? Do not kiss you . . ." His gaze moved over her face. "How can I resist? Your hair is like silk beneath my hands. Your skin smells of lavender. Your body is a temptation no man could resist. Shanara . . . accept your fate and be my bride."

In her heart, it was what she wanted, but how could she wed him now, when she knew about the curse that awaited his offspring?

His hands caressed her and then, murmuring an oath, he lowered his head and kissed her.

For the space of a heartbeat, she resisted. And then, with a sigh, she surrendered to her heart's desire. Slipping her arms around his neck, she closed her eyes and returned his kiss, reveling in the pleasure that flowed through her, the excitement that fluttered deep in the core of her being, urging her to give him everything he wanted, to surrender everything his body and her own heart were urging her to give.

Her hand slid down his back, exploring the deep vee between his shoulder blades, the indentation of his lean waist.

He groaned softly and then, with a cry that was almost a growl, he gently pushed her away.

She blinked up at him, her whole body aching and on fire for his touch.

"Not now," he said tersely. "Not here. I will not take you like a wild beast in heat." Tenderly, he drew her back into his arms. "When I take you, it will not be in the dirt, but upon silk sheets. And you shall be my bride."

He gazed deep into her eyes, wondering at his sudden change of heart. Only days ago, he had vowed never to marry. Now he was equally determined to make Shanara his woman, in name only if nothing else. Right or wrong, he could not let her go. Should Montiori arrive on the morrow to take his daughter's place, Reyes knew he would turn his enemy away rather than lose the woman in his arms.

It was near morning when they reached the keep. He quickly retrieved his trousers, then headed for the kitchen door. Under other circumstances, he would have taken the secret passage to his chamber, but he didn't want Shanara to know of its existence. By a stroke of luck, they met no one when they entered the castle. Reyes saw Shanara to her room. Inside, he searched for anything she might find useful should she try to escape. He confiscated the knife from her dinner tray, kissed her long and hard, then locked her in her room.

Going to his own chambers, he rang for Rolf and ordered baths to be drawn for himself and Shanara, then added that he wanted a morning meal for two sent to his room in an hour.

Rolf was about to leave the room when Reyes called to him.

"Yes, my lord?"

"Where is Alyce?"

"Belowstairs, my lord."

"Send her to me immediately."

With a nod, Rolf went to carry out his lord's bidding. Reyes paced the floor, his anger building with each step he took. He was in a fine rage when she knocked on his door. "Enter."

She stepped into his room, a smile of anticipation on her face. "You summoned me, my lord?"

"Shut the door."

She did as he asked, her smile not quite so bright when she faced him again.

"Why did you do it?" He held up his hand when she started to speak. "Do not lie to me, Alyce. I know what you did. What I want to know now is why? What did you hope to gain by murdering my future bride?"

She stared at him, her face pale, her lower lip quivering. "My lord, I didn't know . . . I . . ."

"Go on."

"Forgive me, my lord! Please, be merciful. It was only

that I love you so much! She said she wanted to return to her father . . ."

"And you were going to help her?"

"Yes, my lord. I thought if she returned to her father, you might . . . that is, that we—"

"So you had Ragan throw her into a pit?"

"How did you . . . ?" She bit down on her lower lip as she realized she had given herself away.

"You tried to kill Shanara because you love me?" he asked incredulously. He had known the maid was infatuated with him, but love?

Alyce looked at him, her eyes brimming with tears.

Whether she loved him or not, there was no excuse for what she had done. And she had not done it alone. Her accomplice was somewhere within the keep.

"I want you out of the keep by nightfall."

With a sob, she threw herself at his feet, her arms wrapping around his ankles. "No! Please, not that!"

"Count yourself lucky that I'm letting you keep your head!"

"Where will I go? Please, my lord, let me stay!"

"Go where you will. Be gone from my sight! And take Ragan with you."

Sobbing, she gained her feet and moved woodenly toward the door. She paused to look back at him, her eyes begging him for mercy. Finding none, she left the room, closing the door behind her.

Reyes stared after her. He would have no one within the keep whom he couldn't trust. He held loyalty above all else. To betray someone under his roof was the same as betraying him. Alyce had crossed the line and there was no going back.

Later, after he had bathed and dressed, he summoned Shanara.

She arrived a short time later. She was more beautiful

every time he saw her. This morning, she wore a lavender long-sleeved gown. The square neckline revealed a modest amount of golden-brown flesh. Her hair fell over her shoulders, a mass of thick auburn waves that tempted his touch.

He felt his gut clench when he thought of how he had found her in the bottom of the pit. Had he not found her in time, she might have fallen prey to wild beasts, or starved to death.

He took a deep, calming breath, then gestured at the table, now laden with covered dishes. "Sit, Shanara," he invited.

She walked across the room and took a seat at the table. She carried herself like a queen, he thought. Her every movement was regal.

He sat across from her, every fiber of his being aware of her beauty, her nearness. It had been a mistake inviting her to his chambers. She was far too desirable and his bed was far too near at hand for his peace of mind.

He filled her plate with the meal the cook had prepared for them. They ate in silence for a time. Reyes had no interest in food, not with Shanara sitting across from him. All he could think of was carrying Shanara to bed and making slow, sweet love to her, then falling asleep in her arms.

"My lord, you must not stare at me so."

"It displeases you?"

She blushed prettily under his regard. "It is unseemly."

"Unseemly?" he asked, amused. "There is nothing unseemly about a man admiring his bride-to-be."

"I never said I would marry you."

"But you will."

"Nay."

"I will have my way in this, Shanara. Tomorrow, the castle seamstress will attend you. We will be wed on Sunday."

"You said a fortnight!"

"I have changed my mind."

Rising, he rounded the table and drew her into his arms.

"My lord, we must not . . ."

"Just a kiss," he murmured, lowering his head. "One kiss."

One kiss, she thought, and she was lost. What power did he possess that he could so easily make her want him? All thought of right and wrong, friend or foe, fled her mind as his lips captured hers. Her stomach fluttered at his nearness. Her legs grew weak and she leaned against him, gasping as she felt his arousal. Her body grew warm, her heartbeat erratic.

She moaned softly. It was meant to be a protest. Why then, did it sound like a sigh of pleasure? A distant voice in the back of her mind whispered that she should push him away. Instead, one arm slid around his waist while her other hand slid around his nape to bar his escape.

He broke the kiss for a moment, his eyes looking deep into hers, and then he was kissing her again, his lips moving over hers, his tongue dueling with her own in a way that made her think of their bodies joining together.

"No. We mustn't." It took all her willpower to push him away. She could not surrender her maidenhead, not while there was a chance she might still escape. With her virginity gone, no other man would want her.

"You are a wise woman," he said, his voice raw with desire. "Another moment in my arms and you would not have been a maiden on your wedding day."

She stared up at him, her lips bereft, her body trembling. For a moment, she was tempted to return to his arms, but then she remembered that he was supposed to be her enemy, and that, even worse, he was only marrying her to antagonize her father.

Wordlessly, she opened the door and left the room.

She wasn't surprised to find Rolf waiting for her in the corridor. Silent as a shadow, he followed her down the hallway to her chambers. When she went inside, he closed and locked the door behind her.

CHAPTER 10

Sitting upon his throne, Lord Montiori looked down at the girl kneeling on the floor before him.

"How do I know Reyes did not send you?" he asked. "Need I remind you that spies are beheaded?"

Alyce looked up at him, her eyes red and swollen. "I am no spy! I cannot prove otherwise, my lord, but I speak the truth. I tried to help your daughter escape from Lord Reyes and he sent me away in disgrace. I came to beg your indulgence, my lord. I have nowhere else to go."

"My daughter is well then?"

"Yes, my lord."

"The finger that Reyes sent me, was it hers?"

"No, my lord."

Montiori grunted softly. "I thought not." He leaned forward. "So, what news have you from Black Dragon Keep? Is Reyes preparing for war? Is he planning to ride against me?"

"No, my lord. He plans to wed."

"Indeed? And what unfortunate woman will bear his accursed young?"

Alyce took a deep breath. "Your daughter. Shanara."

Montiori sprang to his feet. "What?"

"Aye, my lord, 'tis true."

"When is this loathsome deed to take place?"

"Within a fortnight, if kitchen gossip be true."

Descending the dais, Montiori began to pace the floor. "How dare he mingle his foul blood with mine! My daughter, to wed that beast and bear his young! I will not have it!"

Turning, he almost tripped over the girl. "Be gone!" he roared.

"My lord?"

"Go into the kitchens. Tell Grendal to put you to work."

"Yes, my lord," Alyce said, scrambling to her feet. "Thank you, my lord!"

Montiori scarcely heard her. He was bellowing for the captains of his armies.

CHAPTER 11

For Shanara, the next few days passed in a whirlwind of activity. The dressmaker came, bringing bolts of material in every fabric and color imaginable. It took most of one day for her to choose the color, and when she couldn't decide between pale pink or ice blue, she decided to go with white. She spent most of another day picking out just the right style. Her mood seemed to change from excitement to trepidation and back again from moment to moment.

She saw Reyes each evening. Now, with the moon no longer full, he was more relaxed, and quite charming. Sometimes he took her walking in the gardens in the evening after supper. Sometimes they sat before the hearth listening to the minstrels; other times they were entertained by the court jester, or by wandering jugglers or magicians.

But the best times were when he walked her to her chamber before she retired for the night. There, alone in her room, he wooed her with soft words of love and slow, sweet kisses that made her heart race and her toes curl.

There, alone in the shadowy darkness, she could forget, if only for a little while, that he lived under a curse that could only be broken by her father's witch.

Melena, Shanara mused. She was the answer. The witch had ever been kind to her. If she could find a way to speak to Melena or to send her a message, perhaps she could convince the witch to break the curse.

But no opportunity arose and then, all too soon, her wedding day was upon her.

Shanara stood in the middle of her chamber while Beatrice brushed her hair until it shone. The maid drew the sides back with a pair of jeweled combs, leaving the rest of Shanara's hair to fall down her back in an artless mass of thick auburn waves.

Next, Beatrice helped Shanara into her wedding dress, then arranged her veil with its floor-length train.

"Ah, my lady," Beatrice exclaimed, taking a step back. "You look as beautiful as a princess in a fairy tale."

"Thank you," Shanara murmured. She ran her hands over her gown, loving the feel of the gossamer material beneath her fingertips. Made of the finest white on white silk, it was an exquisite creation, so light it might have been made of angels' wings. She couldn't help wondering what Reyes would think when he saw her. Would he be pleased? Would he think his coin well spent?

A knock at the door sent her heart to fluttering. "I cannot do this," she whispered. "I cannot!"

"Now, now," Beatrice said cheerfully, "'tis only a bad case of nerves, common to all brides on their wedding day."

It was more than mere nerves, Shanara thought. If her husband-to-be had been an ordinary man, she would have been eager to wed him and bed him, but Reyes was not an ordinary man.

Beatrice opened the door and Rolf entered the chamber. He smiled at Shanara. "Your bridegroom awaits," he said.

She wanted to tell Beatrice and Rolf that the wedding was off, that she could not marry Reyes tonight, or any other night, but the words would not come.

As if caught in a trance, Shanara allowed Rolf to take her hand and lead her down the staircase to the small chapel located within the keep. Rolf paused at the door, giving her a chance to peruse her surroundings. There were flowers everywhere, some in white wicker baskets, some in tall glass vases, others in colorful pots. Tall white tapers cast shadows on the walls.

There were no guests other than two of Reyes's most trusted knights who would serve as witnesses.

Shanara felt her breath catch in her throat when she saw Reyes. He stood in front of the altar next to the priest. For once, Reyes had eschewed black. Instead, he wore buff-colored trousers, a white shirt open at the throat, a dark green jerkin trimmed in black velvet, and a pair of soft leather boots.

His gaze settled on her face, the force of it sending a shiver of excitement to the very deepest part of her being.

Rolf gave a gentle tug on her hand. She took a step forward, her gaze locked with that of the man who was going to be her husband. By the time she reached the altar, her heart was pounding so loudly she was surprised the priest could not hear it.

A rush of heat flowed into her fingers and up her arm when Rolf placed her hand in that of his lord. Bowing his head, Rolf took a step back, then sat in the front pew.

The priest looked at Shanara and then at Reyes. "Are you ready, my children?"

"Yes, Father," Reyes said. He smiled at Shanara, then squeezed her hand.

She tried, but she could not summon a smile. What would he do when she refused to be his bride? Would he send her back to the dungeon, or fulfill his vow to send her back to her father a piece at a time?

She felt an unexpected warmth in the region of her heart when Reyes vowed to love, honor, and protect her so long as he lived.

And then the priest settled his somber gaze on her face. She could scarcely breathe as he put the question to her.

"Do you, Shanara Montiori, take Alexandar Reyes to be your husband from this day forward? Will you love and honor him so long as you both shall live?"

Her heart was beating so fast she feared she might faint. She took a deep, calming breath and then, to her utter amazement, she whispered, "I do."

The priest smiled for the first time. "Then, by the power vested in me, I now pronounce you man and wife. What the Lord God hath joined together, let no man put asunder. Lord Reyes, you may kiss your bride."

She trembled as Reyes put his hands on her shoulders and turned her to face him. Lifting her veil, he drew her into his embrace. For a moment, he gazed down at her, his expression enigmatic, and then he kissed her.

Her eyelids fluttered down at the touch of his lips on hers and she forgot everything else, everything but the aching sweetness of his kiss, the faint tremor in the arms that held her. Was it possible that he was as nervous as she?

She blinked up at him when he broke the kiss. Glancing around, she felt a rush of heat flood her cheeks when she saw the indulgent smiles on the faces of the priest and the knights.

Feeling suddenly self-conscious, she started to pull away from Reyes, but his arm around her waist kept her close to his side.

He thanked the priest, Rolf and his knights, then led her out of the chapel and up the stairs to his bedchamber. The maids had laid a fire, there were candles burning on the mantel and in wrought-iron sconces on the walls. Bowls of flowers filled the room with a sweet fragrance. Someone had sprinkled flower petals across the floor and over the bed. A plate of bread and cheese and a bottle of wine awaited them on the table.

When he closed the door, she was trembling so badly that, had it not been for Reyes's arm around her waist, she feared she might have collapsed in a pool of silk at his feet.

"Does the room please you?" he asked.

She nodded, unable to speak for the pounding of her heart, the lump in her throat. She was his wife now, subject to his whim and will. If she cried out for help, no one would come to her aid. She belonged to him, the same as his horse and his sword. He could lock her up for the rest of her life. He could beat her, starve her, order her to spend the rest of her days in a convent, and she would have no recourse but to accept his will, whatever it might be.

He frowned at her. "Is something amiss?"

She shook her head, her eyes widening as his fingertips stroked her cheek.

"Are you afraid of me now?"

She shivered as his fingers traveled down the length of her neck, then, ever so slowly, skimmed the curve of her breast.

"I will not hurt you, wife," he said quietly and then, as if to prove his words, he kissed her gently, tenderly. His mouth was warm on hers, demanding nothing, asking everything.

And because she could not resist his kiss any more than she could cease to breathe, she kissed him back, a long slow kiss that brought all her senses vibrantly alive. Caught up in his kiss, she was scarcely aware that he was undressing her until she stood before him clad in nothing more than her shoes and her petticoat.

She looked up at him, mute, as he knelt before her to remove her shoes, then unfastened the ties of her petticoat and let it fall to the floor.

In the way of maidens since time began, she crossed her arms over her breasts.

Reyes shook his head. "Do not hide your beauty from me, my Shanara," he said, his voice husky with desire.

Biting down on a corner of her lip, she slowly lowered her arms, felt herself blush from the soles of her feet to the crown of her head as his hungry gaze moved over her.

"Beautiful," he whispered. "More beautiful than anything I have ever seen."

Drawing her into his arms once more, he showered her with kisses, his lips like fire as they slid over her breasts and belly, then returned to her lips to drink deeply.

Desire was an ache deep inside, a longing so intense it was painful. She moaned softly, all thought of resistance melting away like morning dew. She wanted him. There was no doubt that he wanted her. Why didn't he carry her to bed?

He kissed her again, his tongue exploring the warmth of her mouth and then, abruptly, he let her go.

"Sweet dreams, my lady wife," he said hoarsely, and he was gone.

She stared after him, unable to believe he had left her alone on her wedding night, or that his going could hurt so much.

Unable to believe that, in spite of everything, she had fallen in love with her father's sworn enemy.

Reyes stood in the darkness, staring up at the window of his bedchamber. Leaving his bride had been the most difficult thing he had ever done, but to stay would have been madness. No matter how desperately he wanted to make love to her, no matter that his entire body ached with the need to possess her, he could not bring himself to bed her, could not condemn any son she might conceive to endure the kind of life he now lived.

Hands clenched at his sides, he paced back and forth beneath the window, his mind filling with images of Shanara's delectable body. Her skin was creamy smooth, unblemished by wart or mole. Her body was lush, neither too plump nor too thin. His body hardened anew at the thought of hers. He groaned low in his throat as he imagined carrying her to his bed, burying himself deep within her warmth, making love to her all through the night, waking in her arms.

Taking shelter behind a bush, he summoned the wolf within him. Muttering an oath, he tore off his clothes, a howl of pain and frustration rising in his throat as his body transformed. With a last look at his chamber window, he ran away from the keep, away from the temptation that was growing ever harder to resist.

He loped through the darkness, finding a measure of solace in the touch of the wind in his face, the feel of damp earth beneath the sensitive pads of his feet. He ran for miles, effortlessly, mindlessly, ran until weariness overtook him and he flopped down on the ground, his tongue lolling out the side of his mouth, his sides heaving.

When his breathing calmed again, he lifted his head and howled at the moon, howled in rage and frustration because even here, miles and miles from Black Dragon Castle, Shanara's image lingered in his mind, and he knew that no matter how far or how long he ran, he would never be able to run away from the fact that he had fallen in love with the daughter of his sworn enemy.

But he wasn't ready to face that revelation now, or ponder the possibilities and problems. For now, he wanted to run with the wolves.

CHAPTER 12

Reyes ran through the night, sometimes alone, sometimes with a pack of friendly wolves. They chased
each other playfully through the darkness, howled their
success when they brought down a deer.

And always, in the back of his mind, was the woman.
Shanara. His bride.

It was just after dawn when Reyes returned to the outer
wall of the keep where he had left his clothing and took on
his own shape.

Had all his senses not been centered on the woman
sleeping in his bed, he might have realized sooner that
something was amiss, but his whole being was focused on
returning to his chambers and slipping under the bedcovers
beside his bride.

Too late, he realized he was not alone.

Feeling the hairs rise along his nape, he turned and
came face-to-face with the man he had sworn to kill.
Instinctively, he reached for his sword, only then remembering it was lying on the ground beneath his clothing.

He lowered his hand as Montiori's laughter filled his ears.

"And so," Montiori said, "you sent for me, and I am
here." Dismounting, he tossed his horse's reins to one of
his men. With his hand resting on the hilt of his blade, he
circled Reyes. "I must confess, your battle attire is not what
I expected."

The hearty laughter of Montiori's men filled the early morning air, then stilled abruptly as Montiori drew his weapon and laid the edge of the blade against Reyes's throat. "Where is my daughter?"

"I am here, Father."

Reyes felt his insides grow cold as Shanara ducked through the hole in the wall, even as the fact that she had come out to meet him upon his return filled him with a wave of tenderness.

"She is no longer your daughter," Reyes retorted, wincing as the blade nicked his skin. "She is my wife."

Montiori's eyes narrowed ominously. "You have defiled my daughter," he said coldly. "And for that you will die, as will she. I'll have no half-human whelps as my kin!"

Reyes looked at Shanara, fully realizing for the first time how much he had come to love her. No matter what fate awaited him at her father's hands, he would not see her killed. Shanara's life was more important than his need for vengeance, more important to him than life itself. His only hope of saving her was to confess that he had not touched her and hope that Montiori would believe him and return Shanara to her family home.

"I have not defiled her," Reyes said quietly. "Kill me if you must, but do no harm to Shanara. She is yet a maid untouched."

"Do you think I would believe one such as you?" Montiori asked scornfully.

"Believe what you will. I speak the truth."

"We shall see. Melena! Attend me!"

There was a restless stirring among the men as they stepped aside to make way for their lord's witch.

Reyes stared at the woman. She was small and spare, hardly bigger than a child. Though she was now old and bent, he could see she had once been a beauty. Her hair, once golden, was now dull and streaked with gray. Her skin was wrinkled and leathery, but her eyes still held the fire of youth.

She stopped in front of Reyes, a cackle rising in her throat. "I know you," she said, poking her finger in his chest. "You look much like your father before you." Her hand curled around his biceps. "Tall and strong, just like him, you are." Her fingernails were long and sharp and she raked them down his chest, then turned and looked up at Montiori. "You summoned me, my lord?"

"Before I take his head, I want to know if he speaks the truth."

With a nod, Melena turned her attention back to Reyes. "The truth," she murmured, "we must have the truth." She placed a gnarled hand over his heart, her eyes burning into his. "Do you speak the truth?"

Reyes clenched his hands as he stared at the witch who had cursed his father. "My words are true," he replied. "I have not defiled Shanara, nor will I."

The earth seemed to hold its breath as Melena stared into his eyes. The horses stood quiet. The birds stilled their songs.

Melena withdrew her hand from Reyes's chest. "It is as he said," she admitted reluctantly. "The girl is as yet untouched."

Montiori's hand tightened on the hilt of his sword. "So it ends," he said, and drew back his arm.

"No!" Shanara's cry rent the stillness that hung in the air. She ran toward Reyes as though her feet had wings, throwing herself between her husband and her father. "You will not hurt him!" she cried. "You will not!"

"Get out of my way," Montiori demanded, his face mottled with rage. "Get out of my way or you will be the first to die!"

Shanara lifted her head, exposing her throat. "Then strike me down. I will not live in a world without him."

Grasping Shanara by the shoulder, Reyes thrust her behind him. "This is between you and me, Montiori. She has nothing to do with it."

"Indeed." Montiori lowered his sword. "Long have I waited to add your pelt to that of your father's. Assume the guise of the wolf now, and I will spare the girl's life."

"Reyes, no!"

"Be still, daughter!" Montiori said.

"First let Shanara return to the keep," Reyes said, an unwanted note of pleading in his voice. "It is hers now, by right of marriage."

With a shake of his head, Montiori laid his sword against Reyes's throat once more. "The girl is mine." He grabbed Shanara by the arm and pushed her toward one of his men. "You have nothing to bargain with, Reyes, only the choice to die as a wolf or as a man."

"Or not at all." The words, softly spoken, were uttered by Melena. With a wave of her hand, the witch conjured a sword from midair and tossed it to Reyes.

Taking a step backward, Reyes caught the sword by the hilt, his gaze never leaving Montiori's face.

Montiori stared at Melena. "Traitor!" he hissed, then, without warning, he lunged toward Reyes.

Shanara ceased struggling against the man who held her, all her attention now centered on the two men crossing swords. It was a strange battle. Considering the fact that her father was attired like a king and Reyes was startlingly nude, it might have appeared comical had it not been so deadly serious.

The clang of metal striking metal filled the air, obscene in the stillness that had settled around them. Her father fought like a fury, the love of battle shining in his eyes as he drew first blood. Confident of victory, he pressed his attack again and again.

Reyes parried every thrust, his movements smooth and unhurried, his rage fueled by the blood oozing from the gash in his arm. For this moment, there was nothing else in all the world but his opponent. It didn't matter that Montiori was Shanara's father, or that Shanara was watching him, her hand pressed to her heart. Nothing mattered but avenging his father's death. It was fitting, somehow, that Montiori had come to battle wearing the cloak lined with the thick black pelt that had belonged to Reyes's father.

With a cry, Reyes carried the attack to Montiori. His blade slashed through the air, slicing Montiori's left arm open to the bone. He struck again and yet again, his sword opening wounds in Montiori's right thigh and side.

Panting heavily, both men fell back.

Montiori staggered toward his daughter and then, to the surprise of all who watched, he grabbed her by the hair and laid the edge of his blade against her throat.

Montiori sneered at Reyes. "You will surrender," he said. "You will lay down your sword now, or she dies."

Without hesitation, Reyes tossed his weapon aside.

A low murmur of disapproval ran through Montiori's army.

A muffled oath emerged from Melena's lips.

Reyes ignored them all. He had eyes only for Shanara.

Smiling triumphantly, Montiori flung Shanara aside. He strutted toward Reyes, then raised his sword in both hands, prepared to strike.

Reyes kept his eyes fixed on Shanara, determined that her face would be the last thing he saw in life.

But the blade did not fall.

Puzzled, Reyes darted a quick glance at his executioner. Montiori stumbled backward, the sword falling from his hands. Blood bubbled from his nose and mouth and then, with a strangled cry, he pitched forward and lay still.

Shanara threw her arms around Reyes's neck, her words incoherent as she showered him with kisses.

"What happened?" Reyes asked, surprised to find himself alive and his enemy dead.

Shanara shook her head, then kissed him again.

Reyes put his arm around her and drew her to his side as Melena made her way toward them.

"Why?" he asked the witch. "Why did you not let Montiori kill me?"

"Because Shanara loves you," the old crone said. "And because I love Shanara." Melena pointed a gnarled finger at Reyes, her dark eyes glittering. "Be good to my girl else a worse fate come upon you than the one you had."

"Had?" Reyes asked, frowning.

"Aye. Shanara's love for you has broken the curse. But beware, Reyes, I will be watching how you treat her."

Reyes smiled at his bride, then looked back at Melena. "Have no fear, old mother. I will spend the rest of my life making Shanara happy, starting now."

And so saying, he swung his bride into his arms and carried her home.

EPILOGUE

Reyes sat on the edge of the bed, watching as his wife slowly disrobed. A month had passed since Montiori's death. For a time, he had regretted the fact that Melena had killed Montiori, thereby robbing Reyes of his chance to avenge his father's death. Later, he realized the witch had done him a favor he could never repay. Though he knew Shanara would have forgiven him had he killed her father, he was grateful that her father's blood was not on his hands, that his death did not stand between them.

Much had happened since then. Montiori's eldest son had assumed leadership of the Montiori clan and there was now peace between their people.

Melena had foretold that Shanara would bear Reyes twin sons within the year. To that end, the witch had moved into Black Dragon Keep to be near the infants and to care for Shanara after the birth.

Reyes felt his breath catch in his throat as Shanara removed the last of her undergarments to stand gloriously naked before him. How beautiful she was, with her hair falling over her shoulders and the lamplight bathing her face with a soft golden glow.

Murmuring her name, he drew her into his lap. "Are you happy here, with me, my beloved?"

She kissed the tip of his nose. "Need you ask, my lord?"

"Indeed, I must. I dare not take a chance on angering

Melena. Who knows what evil might befall me should she find you looking displeased?"

Shanara smiled at him, her eyes twinkling. "Then perhaps you should do this." Her hand caressed his chest. "Or this." She kissed the corner of his mouth. "Or this . . ." Her hand slid down his naked belly, eliciting a groan of pleasure from his lips.

"You have but to command, my lady," he said. And capturing her lips with his, he drew her down on the bed and did his best to make his wife happy that night, and every night for as long as they lived.

Dear Reader:

This is my first foray into the world of werewolves. Granted, Reyes isn't your typical werewolf, but I loved writing his story.

Once again, I'm pleased to thank Joseph Walsh for allowing me to use his poetry. I think we must be connected on some plane of existence, since he always sends me poetry that seems to fit whatever book I happen to be working on at the moment.

I hope you enjoyed "Born of the Night."

Best,

Amanda Ashley, aka Madeline Baker
www.madelinebaker.net

MAKE IT LAST FOREVER

L. A. BANKS

ACKNOWLEDGMENTS

This is for my first love and soul-mate, my husband, who loves me fangs and all . . . the only one after all these years who I want to make it last forever.

CHAPTER 1

OKLAHOMA...1979

Tara took her time boarding the bus, her gaze sweeping the elderly passengers headed for Las Vegas. New Mexico and her grandmother's reservation homestead seemed so far away. So many days, and so many nights away now that the night was something terrible to fear.

But with her dying breath, her mother had told her to go there. It was part of her destiny and her only salvation. One simple mistake had cost her her life, and she was only eighteen. Tara willed away the tears as she clutched her small, square leather suitcase tighter in her grasp, and refused to look back. What was done was done.

The dry, oppressive heat made her feel as if she would crumble into dust. Maybe one day she actually would. The people who were boarding with her smelled like they had already begun to decay, but their vibrant smiles and incessant chatter about a trip to win big and start their lives all over again almost made her weep. If her grandmother's medicine didn't work, there'd be no second chance for her. She wouldn't have a chance to grow old and hopeful. She wouldn't grow old at all.

She found a seat by the window in the middle of the bus and cast her gaze out of it. For as long as she could, she'd savor the beauty of natural light. She'd turn her face up to the clouds and ask the Great Spirit to spare her.

As new tears filled her eyes, she thought of the grave-stones that marked her parents' final resting places side by side. That was the natural order of things. Maybe if she were lucky, she'd have that, too; a marker beside someone who'd loved her for years, where they both could be at peace after a long, joy-filled existence.

Part of her had considered going south to her father's people. The blue calico print of her dress blurred in her peripheral vision as she thought of Nana Wainwright. Each of the women in her family had a piece cut from that cloth; her Southern Nana said this was the way it was done, to bind all in like-mindedness, and she had made the dress, had made her mother and her maternal grandmother aprons from it, and Nana kept the scraps for her leg quilt. After her mother died, Nana had told her repeatedly, "Chile of mine, you never too grown to come home and always gots family wit us. Don't you brave this awful world of woe and evil alone."

But to go to Alabama—the Bible Belt—being what she was, and with a dear Nana who knew nothing about revers-ing curses, would be to visit horror upon those she loved . . . just like she'd visited it upon her mother. Tara banished the invitation, guilt squeezing her heart and mak-ing tears fall in earnest now. Her daddy always said that God-fearing black folks didn't mess with hoodoo. And even though her Cherokee grandmother didn't dabble in "hoodoo," as her father put it, she was a seer. A respected one, at that. And just like her mother had always explained, she would be caught between worlds forever. Perhaps her mother's words were more prophetic than she'd even known. Tara had to get to her grandmother before it was too late, before she didn't wake up with the sun, and before the moonlight would become her dawn.

One bite in the dead of night that hadn't killed her had stolen her life just the same.

MAYFIELD, KENTUCKY . . . 1979

"Jack Rider, you are not going to leave my bed without telling me where you're going, or when you're coming back."

He kissed Marianne's pout away, pushed himself up with a grunt, and sat on the side of the motel bed, allowing his gaze to travel down her curvaceous form. He chuckled as he rubbed his beard and tried to think of an excuse to extricate himself from her temporary hold. Everything had a price, and sleeping with her meant that she thought she had some claim to his time. Not even. His personal freedom wasn't for sale, that's why he'd bought her dinner, first.

"Now, don't be like that," he said, rolling a taut strawberry nipple between his fingers, loving how her pout melted away on a moan. "You know I've gotta go to work. This ride'll bring in a lot of cash."

As she sighed, he filled his hands with both porcelain breasts, and let his caress drag down her torso, past her tiny waist, and then pausing, allowing her shapely hips to warm his palms. Damn, Marianne had been a great roll in the hay, always was. Blondes were indeed more fun, but he had things to do. He kissed her navel and stood. There was no way he was going back to the trailer with his parents, who'd most likely be in the midst of another of their drunken rages. He'd had enough of it all. The road was calling his name. This had just been a pit stop. Marianne had known what this was, going in.

"Well, when are you coming back?" She sat up slowly, thoroughly disappointed, and began twisting a long tendril of corn-silk-colored hair around her finger.

"Soon," he lied, pulling on his jeans, and stalking around the room to find his T-shirt and boots. "I'm just going to ride with the fellas to be their road mechanic, then I'll be back. I'm the best in the business, and if they're gonna do the Arizona races, then I not only get fed and paid, with free drinks along the way, but also get a cut of what they win. Nobody can rebuild a Harley like me. Like I said, I'm the best at what I do."

"You *are* the best," she murmured, sending him a double message with her sad smile as she left the bed and came toward him slowly. "But you promise you'll call from the road?"

"Yeah, baby, of course," he said absently. "Don't I always take good care of you?"

She nodded and melted against him, and leaned up for a kiss. He returned it hard, holding her silken tresses in his hands, and then let her go. Damn it, she was going to make him late.

"I'll call you," he said, pecking her lips one more time, and swiping his wallet off the dresser.

"I wish you could make it last forever," she said quietly.

"Maybe when I come back, I will," he said offhandedly, giving her a sly wink that contained its own double message, and then he was out the door.

Freedom, blessed freedom. He'd broken out of Kentucky's red-clay prison, had money in his pocket, wind in his face, and was riding with the pack. Even the rough riders had respect for his skill and his custom rebuilt bike. She was purring like a kitten between his legs, petting his crotch with her vibrations—a black and chrome beauty, and the sexiest thing he'd ever been with.

He was proud of his pretty woman. She could make love to the asphalt at a hundred and ten without a shudder, and could go faster than that if he wanted her to. All he had to do was stroke her right and she'd respond. There wasn't another one like her. She was a fingerprint original with his stamp of excellence; a custom-built Easy Rider that would make a man shiver just looking at her.

She had fine Hell's Angels high bars in the front, a

teardrop gas tank, custom painted, with blue and red flames . . . V-twin engine—a hard-tail, with no shocks . . . fishtail stack exhaust, highway pegs that demanded respect, and a sissy bar for those times when he needed to pick up a stray babe and ride a little female companionship toward a motel. When the women got off his chopper, they were already wet. She was the hottest thing on two wheels, and the only thing he needed to make a commitment to. No, he wasn't coming back. Unfortunately, Marianne's sweet charms couldn't compare.

He pulled fourth position in the convoy, just behind Snake, Crazy Pete, and Razor, and had moved up a notch in front of Bull's Eye, loving the way the vibrations traveled up his arms, quaked his legs, and jarred his spine. Motion was an aphrodisiac. Speed was a rush. He had no plans to take a job he hated, like his father, and then come home to beat his wife. The old man should have gotten out before he'd lost his mind in a bottle. He should have done what Rider was doing now. Just got out. But roaming probably wouldn't have helped his dad. From northwest Kentucky near the strip mines, to Mayfield in the southwest parts near the Mississippi, it was all the same nonsense.

Where he'd been didn't allow for the individual soul to explore. They said music was a waste of time. Playing the guitar was a fool's dream. Trying to get some of Johnny Cash's and Willie Nelson's riffs under his belt had mollified them. He could do that on a plaid nylon lawn chair out back without protest being hurled out the window at him. But he had to tinker with B. B. King, Eric Clapton, Muddy Waters, Bo Diddley, Led Zeppelin, and the other masters in private, at the garage. Messin' 'round with Hendrix had made his father threaten to break his arm. Had put his other lover, his guitar, at risk. Had to pet her like that on the sly. Didn't his father know some things just transcended race? Music, like knowing how to rebuild an engine, was another one of those things.

L.A. was his destination. After he made some money, he was never coming back. He was twenty-one and there was just too much of the world to see.

His guitar was slung over his back, his tools, a bottle of Jack Daniel's and a roll of jeans, concealing a Smith and Wesson model 19 revolver, were in his side saddlebags—just in case life got crazy, as he headed toward the Wild West. Black tires set in gleaming wire rims eating up Route 66 blacktop.

And they said Paradise was lost. Well, he was living testimony. Being a nomad was in his genes; this was the only thing he wanted to make last forever.

Words weren't even necessary to communicate with these guys he was with. One of them would simply ride down the line, offer a nod, and it meant "pull over; bar stop." Time to leave highway civilization and do the back roads.

Rider squinted at the setting sun, loving how it turned burnt orange and fired his bike with a supernatural glow. There was just something about sunset going down on a man's chrome. It was almost a religious experience, if there was such a thing.

Kicking the stand and stopping the motor's purr in one deft motion, he stretched as soon as he dismounted. All of them did, just as they all glimpsed the smoking bus that stuck out like a sore thumb in the dirt lot a hundred yards away. Its front sign read, "Las Vegas." Rider just shook his head. Tourists.

"Check it out," his buddy Snake said, nodding toward the bus. "Think they've got balls enough to come in?"

"Nah," Jack said, laughing, and slung an arm over Snake's thick shoulders without breaking stride. But his laughter slowly trailed off as he glanced back and appraised the passengers through his dark aviator shades. A pair of eyes held him for a moment and his stomach clenched. Her large liquid-brown irises were mesmerizing;

had the startled quality of a deer. He shook it off. "But leave the old ladies alone."

"You going soft on us, Rider?" Razor asked, punching his arm. "Or you just miss your momma?"

"Or did something real different on the bus catch your eye?" Bull's Eye asked with a knowing smirk.

"Neither," Rider said, his smile wide as he glanced at Crazy Pete. "I just don't want him to get tangled up in girdles and garter belts. I'm just trying to help the man."

It had happened so fast that she almost couldn't catch her breath, and then time stood still. A long, lanky biker had paused, tilted his head to the side, and she saw it. The thin blue-white light around him that the old ones said all seers could see. His back was straight, and behind his dark sunglasses she was almost sure she'd seen a pair of kind eyes. It was in the crinkles around them that made her know. It was also in the regal way he lifted his strong chin and squared his shoulders, standing with the pack but apart from them in a way she couldn't define. Then he turned away slowly, still glancing over his shoulder at the bus. His laughter boomed rich, deep, and honest. There was just something in his carriage, but it wasn't false pride. Somehow it seemed so natural, dirty blond ponytail and all. Then he was gone.

Her fingers pressed to the window in reflex. The hair stood up on her arms. Danger was near, but where?

Rider laughed as the guys continued to tease him, elbowing and play-boxing with each of them as the rest of the squad straggled into the roadside tavern. Crazy Pete purposely bumped the bus driver, who was anxiously speaking into a black rotary telephone provided by the bartender as they went up to the bar to get a drink. The burly driver looked up, saw Pete's wiry, muscular build, then immediately glanced at the others, nodded an apology, and moved out of the way.

"Leave the man alone, dude," Rider said, shaking his head. "The poor SOB is about to drop a brick in his pants, as it is."

"Just marking our territory as off limits," Crazy Pete argued, accepting his shot of tequila. He downed it hard and set his glass in front of the bartender for another. "Can't have them desecrate sacred lands. Next thing you know this'll be a damned mall."

"Everything's changing around here," Bull's Eye said with a weary sigh, then removed the sweaty black bandana from his bald head to mop his sunburned brow.

"Yeah, well, with change comes progress," Rider said sarcastically, then ordered a Jack Daniel's, as the others around him laughed and slapped Pete's back.

"Progress?" Pete was beyond indignant, but still had to laugh. The tequila helped.

Rider took a deep swig of his drink as soon as the bartender put it in front of him, made a face and shuddered. "No. I stand corrected," he said, holding up his near-empty glass. "*This* is progress."

His cronies laughed and raised their glasses, each mimicking him, and slamming their glasses down hard enough to nearly shatter them.

"But how did we end up in this godforsaken place?" Razor asked. "No women, nuthin' but an old man bartender and old tunes on the juke."

The bikers cast a disparaging glance around the tavern. Rider nodded in agreement. This was piss-poor and pitiful. The establishment seemed like it had had a day, once, a *looong* time ago. It wasn't the mix-match chairs, or the wooden tables that were scored and engraved with names and every profanity known to man that gave it a dead look. Truthfully, that was pretty cool, gave the joint character.

He couldn't put his finger on it. It wasn't the old sawdust on the floor, or the old Elvis tunes skipping and popping vinyl in the ancient jukebox, nor was it the dingy paneled walls and dusty moose head hanging above the bar. He and the fellas weren't picky. It wasn't even the old pool table that couldn't give a good game anymore because it wasn't level and leaned like a dead battleship. To his mind, it was pure evidence that a good brawl had broken out here at some point. Now *that* was life.

What he was feeling had absolutely nothing to do with the fans that only swirled dead, dry air. The long, yellow strips of flypaper that were polka-dotted with insects didn't bother him, no more than the ever-present dank smell around them did. Hell, the guys he was riding with gave BO funk a new definition. Maybe it was the eerie fact that they had the place all to themselves. The guitar on his back suddenly felt too heavy.

Rider pulled out a Marlboro and slowly lit it. He watched the ember fire red on a hard inhale, and tapped the back of his pack, offering the group's leader one. He glanced at the bartender when Snake accepted it and just put it behind his ear, then he glanced over to the bus driver and noted his dejected expression. He could tell by the look on the man's face that the bus was fried and nobody was coming for a tow tonight. It was the way the bus driver slowly hung up the receiver and passed the telephone back to the bartender.

Both men seemed to be in their late forties. Their crew-cut hair was just too neat and conservative, restricted, their faces puffed red from the incessant heat. Their shoulders slumped like life had kicked their butts; their guts hung over too-tight pants. One had on a blue-gray uniform soaked with sweat, the other had on a butcher's apron over a sleeveless T-shirt, sweat making the thin white fabric stick to his portly build. Watching them made the heat in the joint unbearable. They reminded him too much of his father. Trapped. How did men allow crap like this to happen to them? he wondered. Maybe that's what was making the crew edgy, seeing the possible future in these two old

dudes and looking around a place that held only the rem-
nants of its heyday. Maybe it was because one of their own
had recommended it from that memory.

Rider took his time, choosing his words carefully.
Snake was the leader and had to make the decision to
leave, or else it would be taken as a sign of disrespect that
wouldn't be tolerated. He could tell everybody else was
feeling it, too.

They all watched Snake's massive back expand slowly
and contract the same way, stretching his black leather vest
to the limit and making the medallions on his breast pocket
catch the setting sun in prisms. Their leader was leaning on
his forearms, studying his drink like it might divine the
future. His ragged black ponytail attracted gnats, which he
swatted away intermittently like a bored bull, making his
huge bicep flex. No, he wasn't gonna mess with Snake, if
they'd taken a wrong turn.

Crazy Pete's eyes held a quiet desperation. Pete could
never sit still, and his narrow weasel face was almost covered by his greasy, matted brown hair. It irked Rider the
way he kept raking his fingers through it, like that would
solve their problem. They needed food, gas, liquor, and
willing women—not to be trapped in a bar like bugs on
sticky paper. This was no way to run a road trip.

Rider only shook his head, watching Razor whip himself up into what was sure to be a trademark Razor tirade.
It was in his bloodshot blue eyes. But no matter how skinny
the dude was, Razor had him by two inches, was made of
stone, kept a bowie knife on his hip, and had done
prison . . . Bull's Eye was normally cool, but, carried a gun
at all times, and was one cock-strong bastard when provoked. He had to wait it out. This was why he normally
rolled solo; he didn't have to deal with democratic deci-
sions. Rider had a nose for trouble and for tracking opportunity. He smelled both in the offing here. Group
consensus sucked.

The other guys had fallen in and had taken up a post at the bar. Fifteen in all; that was a lot of testosterone to defuse and a lot of bikes to refuel. Rider slowly removed his sunglasses and stuffed them into his vest breast pocket.

"So, Snake, man," Rider said after a while, finally growing impatient, "your boy said this was the place to pull over. I know Oklahoma is a dust bowl, but this is ridiculous. We need fuel and . . ." The fact that Snake hadn't looked up made him let his argument rest.

Snake calmly pulled the cigarette from behind his ear, put it in his mouth, struck a wooden match on the bar, sucked hard on it, and hailed the bartender. "You all got grub here?"

The bartender shook his head and simply refilled Snake's drink. "Just liquor." He glanced at the bus driver who was edging toward the door. "No fuel either."

Snake nodded and stood. An inaudible sigh of relief swept through the group as money was slammed onto the bar and everyone stretched their legs, downed the last of their drinks, and rolled their shoulders.

"We ride," was all Snake said.

Progress.

Then something happened that should never have happened. A fragile female figure entered the doorway, her chin held high and her gaze darting nervously around the tavern. The last of the sun hit her light-blue calico dress, framing her petite form like a halo. The rays fired her caramel skin, warming it with reds and gold, and the hued light shone off her long, dark brunette braids. She moved with the trepidation of a doe that needed water so desperately that she'd take a risk, even though she knew danger was lurking near. Her light lavender scent wafted in on a breeze and was the only life in the place.

When she saw him this time, she couldn't pull her gaze away. Even beneath the grime, this one was different. He was bronzed strength from head to toe in a filthy pair of jeans slung low, no shirt on beneath a black leather vest. But his eyes . . . Liquid hazel set in a ruggedly handsome face. In their depths she saw honor. No, she couldn't let this one die.

Rider immediately cringed. The girl at the door had glanced at him and then gone up to the bar, literally stepped around a pack of wolves, ignoring the fact that the blood had drained from the bus driver's face, and hailed the bartender. The group behind him stopped. Snake stopped and cocked his head to the side like a hunting dog. Oh . . . no . . .

"Sir," she said in a soft but urgent tone, "Mrs. Parker is diabetic, and she needs water and something, anything, to eat to keep from passing out. I know you don't actually serve customers food here . . . but maybe you just have a piece of bread?"

"We got us an Indian Florence Nightingale in the joint," Crazy Pete said, chuckling and rounding Rider. "I got beef jerky she can eat. Ask her—"

Rider's hand hit Crazy Pete's shoulder. Some insane place in his brain made him grab the back of Crazy Pete's vest to keep him from moving forward. Then his brain didn't consult his mouth at all when he looked at Crazy Pete hard and spoke. "Leave the kid alone," Rider said quietly. "Let the man get her some water and something for the old lady on the bus. We got things to do."

Outraged, Pete snatched himself from Rider's hold and spun on him. "Back off, man! What's wrong with you? Nobody touches me. Especially not for some black Indian tail. Are you crazy?"

Razor had already approached the young woman, had reached out and touched her cheek, and laughed as Rider and Pete pushed each other back and squared off. The young woman jerked her head away from the offending touch, fury and fear glittering in her eyes. The pending fist-fight was temporarily defused as Rider and Pete looked at Razor.

The bartender had moved back. He'd apparently seen how quick lightning could strike his establishment. Snake gave him a hard glare that was a warning not to be so foolish as to pull a shotgun from behind the bar. Bull's Eye flanked Snake and shook his head, conveying that to make a sudden move would not be advisable. But that obviously wasn't the man's intention. The bartender kept cleaning the glass that was in his hand, unfazed, simply moving out of harm's way.

However, the bus driver was determined to die a hero. He'd pushed the girl behind him. The others formed an immediate horseshoe circle behind Rider, Pete, Razor, Bull's Eye, and Snake. The bus driver and the girl were huddled against a wall. Nerves were pulled wire-tight, hair trigger. The bus driver had hidden the girl behind his back. One false move and the joint was gonna blow.

"I wasn't tryin' ta hurt her," Razor said, attempting to peek behind the bus driver. "I just wanted to touch her hair to see if it was as soft as it looked, being she's an angel and all. Y'all ever had exotic fare?" he asked the group, glancing at them and laughing.

"We don't want no trouble," the bus driver said, new beads of sweat forming and rolling down his temples. "Our bus just got stuck, and I've got elderly folks who just need to get to Vegas. That's all."

Rider stepped forward and put a hand on Razor's shoulder. "The man needs a mechanic. My rate is twenty-five dollars an hour," he said, making himself smile, which made the men around him relax and chuckle.

"Always got an angle, don't you, Rider? But I like how you think," Razor said, and then grudgingly conceded with a sly smile. "Bet if these folks are on the way to Vegas . . ."

New worry wrapped tension around Rider's spinal column and constricted it. "Yeah," he said, peering at the frightened young woman. "I might be able to get that tin can started, if these folks would be good enough to pass the hat?" He gave the bus driver a look filled with meaning. It was a strong suggestion to keep the wolves at bay using money as bait. Then he sighed theatrically when the bus driver nodded fast. "The man said there were a bunch of old folks on there—you know, the old dolls will travel across the country with one roll of quarters, man. They're nuts, like my mother. I ain't gonna do time for chump change. We've got a race to do, where the *real* money is."

Snake nodded and glanced at his squad. Bull's Eye sat on a stool. It made the others stand down, and then he looked at the bus driver. "Give Rider here enough to gas up the choppers, and we'll call it even. Your bus will get fixed, and we'll be on our way."

Rider could feel his shoulders drop two inches in relief. He eyed the girl and tried to send her a message to just stand still. No sudden moves.

"Uh . . . sure," the bus driver said fast, and began pulling the girl out of the bar behind him.

But she stopped, looked a little too long at Rider, and then dropped her gaze. "Mrs. Parker still needs—"

"Get the girl some water and something to eat for the old lady, for chrissake," Rider said, his nerves about to snap. He banged his fist on the bar, and pulled out a five-dollar bill. "I'm an artist under the hood and can't concentrate with all this crap." He looked at the girl, signaling her with his eyes that now would be a good time to leave. "I wish she'd just get on that bus and shut up. Geeze Louise. Can a man get a drink while he works?"

She nodded and scooted out the door with the bus driver. Her eyes said it all: *Thank you.*

Rider downed another drink as soon as the bartender had poured it, and he waited impatiently for him to return from the back room with some bread, an apple, and a beer pitcher filled with ice water. The men around him just grumbled and sat down hard on stools and waited. Nothing else was said as more drinks were poured and consumed.

"Money is money," Rider said, falsely complaining as they eyed him. "I'll come back with two hundred, then we're history."

Snake only nodded and slowly sipped his drink.

She accepted the outstretched tray with deep appreciation, and couldn't help again noticing the hazel eyes that glanced at hers, then looked away. They were more than kind eyes set in a ruggedly handsome face; they were gentle—albeit in a dirty face with a scruffy beard. She smiled and looked up at the dark blond hair caught in a long ponytail, as the one who had shown some mercy turned and walked away without a word, like he was angry.

He was tall, maybe six two, if her judgment was correct. The sun had burned his bare shoulders but had graciously turned his arms and face to a dark golden hue. He was indeed a part of the light, looked like he lived in it. She watched him pull his guitar off his back and set it down with care, leaning it against the front wheel of the bus. She glimpsed him from the corner of her eye, and let her gaze travel past the black leather vest he wore, studied the multicolored embroidered snake on it briefly, and then assessed the way his jeans hugged his narrow hips, hugged his behind as though it were cut stone beneath them, and then considered his hard, muscled thighs beneath the fabric and the pair of dusty black cowboy boots that were on his feet. All he needed was a hat, and he'd look like a rogue sheriff. What in the world was this man with a good heart doing riding with that mangy gang?

She smiled wider and then swallowed it away, taking the tray onto the bus for Mrs. Parker. Maybe her mother had been wrong? Maybe she shouldn't be frightened of every strange man she might meet along the way to her grandmother's house, visions, dreams, and superstitions notwithstanding. She was, after all, eighteen, and there was so much of the world she hadn't yet seen. So she'd had one bad experience. Her family's concept of being a cloistered healer was truly no way to live. If her grandmother could just fix one little mistake made in misguided passion . . .

Aghast that she'd actually gone into the tavern on a mission of mercy, the other passengers immediately bombarded her with questions. Each spoke in hushed tones.

"They're animals, Tara," one lady said, her whisper fervent. "They could have harmed you, or worse."

"They're not all bad," Tara said quietly, helping the lady she'd come to know on the ride as Mrs. Parker take a sip of water.

"Don't go back out there," an elderly man said, reaching past his seatmate. "You were just lucky."

Tara nodded. "We all were. But we have to pay the one fixing the bus."

"What!" another male passenger said too loudly, making the other passengers become even more nervous. "How much? We shouldn't have to pay. The bus company should."

Tara released her breath with strained patience while calmly cutting a piece of apple for her seatmate and placing it into her aged, shaking hand. "That's true, but we must deal with our circumstances."

"The girl is right," Mrs. Parker said. "If Tara hadn't been brave . . ."

"Perish the thought," another lady murmured and began digging in her bag for money. "Give him this." The action made others around her begin looking into their purses and wallets as well.

Tara stared at the crisp hundred-dollar bill and folded it away in her palm.

For the life of him, Rider couldn't figure out what was wrong with the bus. Sure, the radiator had overheated, but time and a little water would have solved the problem. The fan belt was shot, but still, a bus driver should have had enough road knowledge to fix something minor like that. It didn't add up. And why did the old buzzard keep looking over his shoulder and making the flashlight jump? The fellas weren't coming out of the tavern anytime soon. As long as he went in there with a representative knot of money in his pocket, then hey . . . everything would remain jakey.

Then there was that pretty girl who looked at him like she did. Made him want to buy her dinner at the next local diner, which was a foolish thought. As though a girl like her would be caught dead on the back of a bike, much less sit and eat with him. He knew better than that, and knew what the old folks on the bus were probably telling her. He focused on the engine, trying to see if the block had cracked from the heat. She was so damned pretty, so clean . . . had a voice that would make a man forget time. But those dark, troubled, mysterious eyes of hers drew him. They were the eyes of innocence, but also the eyes of someone trapped, and set in a face so pretty that a couple times he'd forgotten to breathe when she'd looked at him.

But all of that was stupid, anyhow. She wasn't his type. It had to be the heat, the road, and the boredom.

First off, she was too short, maybe five foot nuthin', a little bitty thing. She had no boobs to speak of, just a petite rise in her calico dress that didn't even offer a real cleavage—she was no Marianne. Her hips were very nice, he'd give her that . . . and, yeah, so okay, the perfect shape of her behind did nearly hypnotize him when she'd walked away, but she didn't have the full package he usually went for.

For instance, she didn't even wear makeup; no lipstick covered her lush, honey-brown mouth. Her long dark lashes didn't have that black stuff that came out of a tube caking them. All the women he knew wore that, even his mother. This babe wasn't even a blonde, he reminded himself. Far from it . . . far enough away to possibly get his ass kicked by the fellas if he treated her too nice, especially in this neck of the woods. Plus, she looked like she'd never been anywhere in the world . . . probably had the address to where she was going pinned to the hem of her dress, like a kid. Couldn't have been more than seventeen, maybe eighteen—if he stretched it—and with his luck, he'd get picked up by some sheriff on a statutory charge . . . were he so crazy to even attempt anything. So, what was the point? It had to be road dust and Jack Daniel's talking to him. Damn, it was hot out here.

Problem was, she'd come down off the bus again and had floated in his direction with a tray in hand and money in her fist. He could tell by the way one hand was balled up tight, like she didn't want to drop something important. He sighed. Then why'd she have to stand so close waiting for him to look up, smelling all good and like lavender? And dammit, why did she smile so sweetly, and flash him the whitest, most perfect row of teeth he'd ever seen when he bumped his noggin to stand?

He rubbed his head and looked at her hard. "You pass the hat?"

She nodded and extended her hand. "Two hundred and fifty for your trouble," she said shyly. "Thank you so much."

"Well, don't thank me yet," he muttered, taking the wad of bills from her. He paused as his fingers met her palm, the softness of it made him draw his hand away fast. He couldn't look at her, so he sent his attention to the bus driver. "Give it a try," he told him. "Gun the motor and see if this old battle-axe turns over. I don't know what the hell's wrong with it."

But the bus driver didn't move. He glanced at the tavern, and then at Rider.

"Okay, fine," Rider said, handing half the money back to the young woman before him. "Get on the bus, tell your driver to gun the motor, and if it doesn't turn over you can just pay me for taking the time to look at it."

She nodded and left the tray by his feet, and quickly fled back up the bus steps.

"Satisfied?" he grumbled to the driver. "So would you go try the engine?" Old people got on his nerves, especially tourists!

But before the driver could get up the steps, gunshots rang out. Rider turned and stared at the tavern. He heard several bike engines engage; voices escalate; glass break; grunts and snaps; more rounds fired. Shouts became frenzied yells, then turned into bloodcurdling screams. Voices of men carried on the night air and made him freeze where he stood, paralyzed as a hundred emotions slammed into him at once. Shit! Crazy Pete, or maybe Razor, had lost his cool. Maybe it was the bartender, but it wasn't a shotgun blast, it was a revolver. Snake was wild, but he wasn't out of his mind and Bull's Eye didn't make a move without Snake's okay. There was only one option. Run.

He snatched his guitar and headed toward his bike. He was *not* doing time if the fellas had held up the bar. He was not going to be locked in a cage because one of them had tripped out and had killed an old man for some change or a free bottle for the road. Hell no, he wasn't going to rely on some old bus passengers to vouch for his honor—they'd swear it was a set-up. They'd tell the authorities he'd kept them occupied while his boys robbed the joint. He'd be an accessory to sure murder; the robbery was secondary. They'd give them all the chair.

She pressed her hands to the bus window. "Oh, my God! What's happening? We have to get to a phone and call the police!"

"Calm yourself, child," Mrs. Parker said, eating the remains of her apple slowly. "They were animals, anyway."

"What?" Tara looked around the bus at the placid faces that stared at her. "There's an innocent bartender in there! I heard gunshots, a man being murdered! Didn't you hear that?"

"Oh, it's not murder, honey," an elderly man said with a

smile. "It's just an old place getting a little life back into it, is all. That's why we came, and they had so much vitality. It's the everlasting cycle of life." He nodded toward the tavern, and then glanced at the other passengers. "They'll be pleased. We did good this time."

"You think tonight will be the night they'll fulfill the promise?" Mrs. Parker asked, excitement brimming in her eyes.

"Fifteen strong, young males," the bus driver said with a smile as he entered the bus and came up the aisle. "Plus a girl? Yes. I think that would be enough to convince them we're ready."

New terror slammed into Tara as she looked at the insane expressions around her. Her heart almost seized when the bus driver reached for her. Brandishing the glass pitcher, a scream filled her lungs, then rent the air, and she swung it madly with her eyes closed tight. She could feel strong arms grasp her waist. Madness entered her ears above her screams as she left the bus floor kicking, yelling, clawing, fighting, but still moving forward and down a flight of steps. The old people were saying not to fight it, give in and be thankful that this was happening while her body was still young. Tears blinded her, choking her, drowning her cries. Her grandmother's visions were coming true. The nightmares she'd lived with all her life were coming true. She looked up and saw a man with a guitar on his bike, stomping his pedal.

"Don't leave me!" she shrieked, sobs wracking her body as she continued to fight. "Oh, God, they're crazy, don't let them take me inside! *Man with a good heart,* please, for the love of God, don't leave me!"

CHAPTER 2

A young woman's screams cut into his consciousness. Rider turned his head and glanced over his shoulder. His motor was running, the sound of it almost deafening. But what he saw was surreal, happened instantaneously and in slow motion at the same time. Crazy Pete's body was hurled out a window, shattering glass, landing almost at his feet. Rider looked down. Pete's jugular was ripped open. His body was still twitching. Blood spurted and turned the ground at Rider's feet muddy brown. He looked up and saw the girl over the bus driver's shoulder. Her hands were reaching toward him. Tears were streaming down her face. The bus driver was taking her into the middle of hell.

His guitar hit the ground. A .357 Dirty Harry was somehow in his hand. His arm was outstretched, and it trembled as he clenched the Magnum. He was going to jail, and wasn't even sure why. The center of the bus driver's skull had a bull's-eye on it, dead aim.

Blood and death and the stench of terror filled his nose and clung to the back of his throat, leaving a metallic taste as he swallowed thickly. Rider hocked and spat, but kept his gaze fastened on the man carrying the woman. The bus driver looked up. Their eyes met. Rider said nothing as he fired the first shot at the bus driver's feet. He stopped walking and smiled. The girl was still struggling. Old folks began coming off the bus.

His heart was racing; his ears were ringing. They were eyewitnesses who would remember things wrong. They were witnesses who were feeble, would not understand, and wouldn't give good testimony. Sweat was stinging his eyes.

The old people were shouting confusing things. One of them yelled, "Leave her. We have more than enough." What the hell did that mean? *Put her down!* his mind screamed, but his voice was lodged in his throat. Crazy Pete had freaking bled to death at his feet. Where was Snake! Another old bastard told the bus driver, "Don't be foolish. If he kills you, you'll miss the promise. She's so skinny, she won't yield much, anyway."

The girl was dropped, and she ran in Rider's direction before he could process what had been said. The inside of the tavern was suddenly too quiet. Ten bikes still sat in a row, undisturbed. When she came to Rider, he pushed her behind him, driven by instinct. He backed up, keeping her an arm's length in back of him. His motor was still idling. He couldn't turn away. He saw something in his peripheral vision that made him stare at the broken window, but he also kept the bus driver in his sideline view.

What appeared to be two gleaming red eyes flashed past the window. The metallic taste of death scored his throat. He shoved the young girl. "Get on the bike!" She ran ahead of him, and then leaned down for the guitar. "Leave it!"

She picked it up anyway and slipped the strap over her shoulders, and elbowed it to cover her back. More of those glowing orbs appeared in the window. The old folks were smiling, laughing, walking toward the tavern. Rider jogged backward, half hopping, half jumping, his eyes never leaving the window as he slid into his seat in front of the girl while still blindly pointing the barrel of his weapon in the direction of the bus driver's head. Instantly, he snapped his arm back, revved the engine—the gun affixed as a part of his hand—and left dust.

His chopper tore up dirt road, making everything on

either side of him a blur. He could feel his heart beating a hole out of the center of his chest, and hers thudding through his back. She'd buried her face so hard against his shoulder that it felt as if she were one of his shoulder blades. He could barely breathe, her arms were wrapped so tightly around his waist. That didn't matter, just as long as she took every lean and pivot with him and didn't make them wipe out. He wasn't sure how fast they were going; that didn't matter, either, until his engine coughed. Gas!

"No, baby, be good to Poppa. Please, girl, not now. Stay with me."

"Find a church," the girl clinging to him yelled. "We have to find sanctuary!"

He'd kidnapped an underage church girl? God, just make his bike keep eating up road. He'd give up drinking, smoking, making love to women whose names he didn't know . . . just one small act of mercy, that's all he asked.

"I'll take you to a church, and that's where you get off, love. You never saw me, cool?" And a church out here would have some vehicle he could siphon for petro.

He could feel her nod in agreement against his back, and his eyes scanned the blur of horizon. Everything was flat. It was pitch-black on the open road. Not a steeple in sight. His engine was beginning to knock. This was supposed to be God's country, Middle America, where was a damned church! Then his black and chrome baby sputtered, gave up the ghost, and simply died.

Tears of frustration stung his eyes as he coasted to a gentle stop. "Oh, screw *me*!" He jumped off his bike, made the stand come down with the heel of his boot, and did something he'd never done—kicked the front tire hard and pointed the gun at his engine. "You lousy, good for nuthin' whore! I'll kill you for dying on me like this! No, baby, not when I need you most!"

Then he dropped his arm, closed his eyes, raked his fingers through his hair, and walked in a circle. Trapped.

"We can't stay out in the open," a soft voice said.

He heard the girl dismount, her sandals hitting the ground as she neared him and touched his arm. He nodded, went to his bike, and spat.

Shoving his gun in the back waistband of his jeans he walked his bike into the tall grass. With his luck, some farmer had put up an electrified fence he wouldn't see until it was too late. What did it matter? He was going to prison sooner or later to fry, anyway. The only thing that helped was the fact that she seemed to be assisting, or at least had offered a good suggestion. But everything was just too damned crazy to sort out. Suddenly, he couldn't breathe.

Rider put both hands on the leather seat of his bike and heaved in air. Two soft palms rubbed his back. His road dogs had been butchered. He'd seen something that looked like it had slithered out of a horror movie. Not just one, mind you, but several. Old people were in on the deal, somehow . . . a young woman had been a temporary hostage, was gonna be sacrificed. He looked up fast, spun on her, making her back up. He only had one question.

"What the hell is going on?"

"It's hard to explain."

"Who are you to them, and what ambushed me and my squad?"

"The undead."

He blinked twice, drew his gun and leveled it at her. "Stop this crazy bullshit, and talk to me! In a minute, every highway patrolman in the state is going to converge on a scene where a bunch of bikers are gonna take the weight. We were just stopping for a drink and some grub. Whatever they find—"

"I know," she said, seeming unafraid of him. "That's why we must run."

Her eyes held such empathy that he couldn't stop looking at her. It took his brain a moment to transmit the command to his arm to put the gun away, but finally he did. She had knowledge of something he couldn't wrap his mind around. She'd seen it, too. So, if they both had the same story, then maybe they wouldn't put him away with the criminally insane.

"We have to find hallowed ground," she said again more firmly. "Soon."

He wasn't sure why he trusted her, but she was the only alibi he had at the moment. More than that, she was the only one in the world who'd been an eyewitness to the unthinkable. Neither said a word as they found a small path. She was at his side looking straight ahead. His eyes scanned everything, but he kept his gun hidden. All he needed was for some farmer to see a silver barrel, then shoot first and ask questions later.

"How do you know this is the right way?" he asked after they'd walked about a hundred yards.

"I'm a seer. I can sense the direction."

He'd heard about things like this, but wasn't buying it.

"Well, Madame Seer, tell me then, why didn't you see the firestorm coming our way?"

Her voice was patient as she spoke calmly. "I was on the bus because my mother came to me after she died. She said to go to my grandmother's . . . she'd have good medicine to help me. I was to learn the old ways from her, and to stay out of harm's way. I could feel evil coming." She stopped walking and looked at him hard. "I didn't know exactly when, or how, but I had a feeling—just like you can smell things."

He stopped walking.

"The cigarettes and other substances are hurting your sinuses. But your nose is still better than the average man's. You're supposed to be a tracker, a nose . . . a man with a good heart."

All he could do was stare at her.

"Where are you from?" she asked, her eyes holding his in a gentle gaze.

"Kentucky," he murmured, not sure why just looking at her made his voice drop to a reverent whisper.

She smiled. "Land of Tomorrow . . . my people, the Cherokee, named your state. That's what it means in our language, and that's where they said the tracker guardian with the music from his heart would come from." She shook her head and softly chuckled. "I just didn't think he'd look like you."

She took off his guitar and handed it to him. "This is a part of your destiny. That's why I couldn't leave it."

Now she was scaring him.

"All right. Point the way to a church," he muttered, accepting his guitar and slinging it over his back.

She just nodded and resumed walking. He followed her, numb.

It was a little clapboard structure painted gray and washed light blue in the moonlight. As soon as they stepped into the front yard, she sighed and dropped to her knees. They'd walked nearly two and a half miles in the dark toward nothing he could put his finger on. But for some strange reason, he also felt safe.

"So, what do we do now? Wait for daylight, or something?" He couldn't see squat in the darkness, save the light from the moon. But his eyes were adjusting as he urgently searched for a gas source.

She shook her head and glanced around. "They won't believe us."

"You got that right," he muttered, going toward a beat-up Ford that he'd finally made out. But her plan had merit. He could hot-wire the car, or maybe siphon some gas if it wasn't dead, too. No, screw taking the car. He was not leaving his bike.

Rider glanced around for a garden hose and to see if there was a container that could hold fuel. But he stopped when he saw this woman, whose name he still did not know, on her knees putting fistfuls of dirt in the pockets of her dress. "What the *hell* are you doing?"

"Getting hallowed earth to place a ring around us near the bike," she said calmly. "You'll need some to pack in your bullets, too, if what's after us is what I'm sure it is." She stood and gazed at him with such serenity that for a moment he was speechless.

"How about Plan B? I siphon this tank, and—"

"No, no! You must *never* steal from holy places."

He looked up at the sky and opened his arms wide. "Why are you torturing me? I know I've lived a wild life, but, hey, I'm only human."

"If you want to stay that way," she said in a tense tone, "you'd better listen to me and follow my lead."

"Listen, sister," he said, his nerves frayed beyond patience, "this is why I don't do religion—any of them. It breeds fanatics like we saw on the bus. Crazy people."

"It doesn't matter what religion or faith, as long as you believe," she snapped, gathering her dirt-filled skirt up as she stood.

He looked at this crazy woman before him who didn't know him from a can of paint, but had gone with him, trusted him—even with a gun in his hand—and who now had her white lace panties showing in a churchyard with dirt in her skirt. She was like nothing he'd ever encountered. Beautiful didn't describe her. It took him a moment to collect his thoughts as he continued to stare at her. He had to remember that his boys were either dead or in jail, most likely, and he was about to follow some religious nutcase down a dark road.

"It doesn't matter what culture," she said, pressing her point and not looking at him. Her gaze was on the stars. "There is good. There is evil. Tonight we have to make a stand."

She began walking back the way they'd come. For some unknown reason he found himself following her again. This was *not* the adventure he'd banked on.

"What's your name?" The question came out quietly as he tried to sort out what had just happened.

"Tara," she said. Her voice was so soft he almost hadn't caught it.

"Tell me you're not a minor."

He waited. She smiled.

"I'm eighteen. In some states I am, in some states I'm not. Like everything else, I'm caught in mid-transition."

"Yeah, well . . . I know what that's like—being trapped."

She let out a long breath and sighed. "I could feel that something wasn't right when the bus broke down. In my soul I knew it was starting." Her gaze went to the moon. "But I knew if I went inside to help someone, I'd be all right. It's always that way. Do you know what I mean? Good wins over evil."

What could he say? He truly didn't know what she meant. But he oddly liked the sound of her voice, no matter how strange what she said was.

"I knew you were a good egg, when I looked in your face," he admitted and resumed walking. "The fellas can get a little rowdy and out of hand, and I could tell you weren't the type that . . ." He paused and began the balance of what he had to say a different way. "I knew you didn't deserve how they were gonna behave." He fell quiet when she held his gaze. It nearly made him stop walking again. "I also knew when I heard you screaming that I couldn't leave you, don't ask me why."

He shook his head and looked forward at the dark path. Crazy Pete's face flashed into his mind. "I had a dead body at my feet. Never seen anything like it. Me and Pete never got along, but that's a whole nuther thing. I knew he was stupid enough to pull a knife, or make someone have to off him one day in self-defense . . . but to be sliced with his own bowie, or Razor's . . . damn."

He started walking faster. "Like I said, don't ask me why I couldn't leave you, but things weren't adding up . . . Then you called me, something familiar clicked—I can't even explain it. But I didn't kidnap you—be sure to tell them that, if we get caught."

"I know you didn't," she said softly. "You didn't leave me because you're a guardian." Her voice was so gentle that it felt like a caress.

He chuckled, suddenly feeling self-conscious. "No, darlin', you've got that wrong. I need a guardian, but I'm not one."

She laughed as they approached his motorcycle. "Don't you know you're part of a Legend?"

He laughed harder and found his stash of Jack Daniel's in his bike's side compartment, then gave her a sheepish look. "So my reputation got all the way out here?"

She shook her head. "Pick where you want to bed down for the night so I can ring you."

His jaw went slack. "Go figure. It's always the innocent-looking ones . . ."

"Find a spot where we can sit and make a fire," she said like a schoolteacher. But her smile was wide and warm.

"I knew that," he said, hoisting up his jeans to walk ahead of her. "I was just joking."

He watched her long process of walking in a wide ring around where they'd hole up while he built a fire. He didn't mind her prayers, or that she said two sets—one in her own native language and then the only psalm he'd learned from funerals, the twenty-third. He watched her carefully sit and wrap the remainder of the dirt in one of his bandanas. It was like watching a grown woman make mud pies, which messed with both sides of his already embattled brain. Then she crooked a finger at him with a gentle smile, crossed her legs in front of her like a yogi, and patted the ground for him to sit before her.

He gladly submitted. He was beginning to enjoy her strange company. "Now what, O learned one?" He was relieved that she laughed, because the sarcastic comment wasn't designed to offend.

She held a bit of earth in her delicate palm and gazed at him. "I need to put a little of this against your throat, all right? And then you can do me."

He didn't care that it seemed like superstitious mumbo-jumbo. Her hands could have been holding cow chips and he wouldn't have argued. He sat down cross-legged, remembering how soft her hands were. "Yeah, okay," he said without resistance, then waited for her touch, trying not to seem too anxious for it, yet wondering why that, of all things, would be on his mind—given everything that had just happened.

Cool earth and a soft caress warmed the sides of his neck. Dirt crumbled and fell to his shoulders and rained on his thighs and knees. Her seeking gaze captured his, and for the first time in his life he thought he could actually drown in a woman's eyes. The feeling was disorienting, if not totally disturbing, while also exhilarating. He could feel such caring enter him, yet he didn't even know who she really was. And as her empty palms slid away from his neck, it left an ache so profound that he'd almost taken her wrists to bring her hands back to where they'd been.

She had to steady her breathing and contain herself. The moment her hands slid against his throat it felt like a current had run through them. She could feel his pulse in her palms, could actually hear it thudding in her ears. And his eyes simply drank her in. This was such a good soul. Had he any idea what seeing him transform into an unlikely warrior had done to her? She tried not to let her hands tremble against his warm skin. He'd allowed her near his jugular, had offered her his throat with no resistance and with pure trust. Didn't he know how dangerous she was? But the fact that she could touch hallowed earth meant she still had a chance. Tonight she was still human, and alive, and had hope . . . and all because of him, she hadn't died the way the curse had predicted.

Rider studied the woman before him. Never had a simple touch ignited him like this. Nor had a pair of eyes ever held him for ransom.

"Now, you do me," she murmured, then signed the words with her graceful hands while speaking them softly: "man with a good heart."

His hands trembled as he reverently gathered a clump of dirt in them. This was the kind of woman a man would marry, for sure. She closed her eyes and leaned her head back, exposing her throat. For a moment, he couldn't move. Her thick, black lashes dusted her cheeks. The rich, deep color of her skin was warmed to a glow by the firelight. And for a second, his mind took a turn to envision that same expression on her face under different circumstances. What would she be like with her face flushed by passion, eyes closed, neck arched, breathing his name . . . An offering that he knew he'd never be able to refuse now, if she made it. But that was foolish, wishful thinking. Yet she was so trusting, seemed so good down deep in her gentle heart . . . Didn't she know he was a dangerous man out in the wilderness with a gun? But she sat there with only trust in her expression. Didn't she know what that was doing to him?

He brought the earth close to her neck, trying not to spill too much on her already dirty dress. He could feel the heat from her skin as his hands neared it. She was breathing in shallow sips of air, her petite breasts rising and falling ever so slightly, and it twisted his mind when he touched her and she shuddered.

That's when it really became difficult for him to catch his breath. Lavender and her light scent fused with earth and burning fire and open grassland. She was so damned soft . . . he had to fight to keep from leaning in to kiss her, or allowing his palms to run down her shoulders. But she wasn't that way, wasn't that type of woman. And for some very strange reason, he didn't want to offend or push her away.

Bits of dirt fell down her dress, and he followed it with his eyes. Blue calico had just become his favorite color. Flashy blondes a thing of the past. He had to stop touching her, and he did so abruptly. She slowly brought her head up, opened her eyes, and smiled. The look in her eyes drew him.

"Nobody ever told me I had a good heart before. Probably 'cause I don't," he said quietly. "And I've definitely never been called anybody's guardian." He forced a self-conscious chuckle and he rubbed his hands down his jeans.

"You're too hard on yourself."

"Madame Seer, you have got to stop messing with my head tonight. I've already had it blown, thank you very much."

"You really don't know the legend, do you?"

"No, but why do I have the funny feeling you're about to tell me?" He had to stop looking into her eyes and at that perfect smile of hers. He reached for his bottle and took out his cigarettes. "I know this ain't your thing, but I have to confess to being pretty messed up right now. So if you're gonna tell ghost stories around the campfire, after what we've just seen, indulge me."

She didn't agree, but didn't give him grief. He could deal with that. He leaned back on his elbows, took a healthy swig, set the bottle down hard, and brought a cigarette to his lips and struck a match. "All right. Shoot," he said, dragging as hard on the butt as he'd wanted to kiss her.

"What's your name?"

He stared at her for a second, and then laughed. "Oh, yeah. Jack Rider."

"Jack?" She frowned. "No. That's not right. It's really Jake . . . Jacob. A biblical name."

He sat up slowly, bottle in one hand, cigarette in the other. *Nooobody* knew that.

"You're scaring me again, lady. Honest to God."

She began drawing in the dirt with a twig. "There's a being coming that my people call the Great Huntress. She comes from a part of the Great Spirit's soul and is made of love and hope and faith. She's also known as the Neteru, they say. And from all walks of life, she'll draw people with special talents. Great warriors." She looked up. "A tracker is among them, a man with a good heart, named Jake."

"Aw, that's a buncha malarkey," he said, forcing himself to feel relieved. "A tracker. That's me, huh?"

"Yes. That's why you have the Nose."

He laughed and took a hard drag on his cigarette, making the end of it glow, then chased the exhale with a swig of Jack Daniel's. "I do have a huge schnoz, and snore like a buzz saw. All right. Say, for the sake of argument, that I go with this mystical legend. Then what?"

"They'll be seven around her, a sacred number. They'll come from all walks of life. Musicians . . . because music is a universal language that breaks barriers. It's also an art, but sound, like thunder, is something that comes from the sky, Heaven. Music can be felt, words are important, the sound takes harbor in the heart. You play guitar, right? You'll need it."

He relaxed and leaned back on his elbows, flicking his half-smoked butt into the fire. If she could understand that about music, then maybe she wasn't all that crazy, just a little touched. He could deal with that. He'd been around crazy people all his life—had been raised by them.

"Yeah, I play," he admitted. "Just mess around, from time to time. Won't ever make a living at it, most likely, but as they say, music soothes the savage beast."

She stared at him for a moment, suddenly understanding why musicians would be a part of the prophecy . . . to soothe the savage beast. She tried her best not to allow her gaze to rake over his lanky form, but lost the battle. He was a guardian. He had saved her from sure living death. And he was lying prone before her, relaxed, his warm voice coating her like a protective blanket and stirring something inside her that had never fully blossomed naturally on its own.

"You have a gift," she said. "Whatever people told you about it being less than that, ignore them. Follow your dream."

Her stare was so intense that he could barely hold it. He found himself swallowing hard. His mouth suddenly went dry. For a moment he couldn't respond. No one had ever looked at him with such utter confidence. No one had ever seen something in him beyond his dirty, grease-monkey hands that could fix an engine, or beyond his roughrider biker façade. And no one had ever told him to follow his dreams, not having heard him play a lick on his axe.

"Your guitar will get you in. It will also be your weapon."

Her voice caressed him and made his pulse race.

When he nodded, agreeing without understanding, she stopped breathing. Hope dangled by a thread. If he could understand, could read between the lines without thinking she was insane . . . and if he'd just kiss her, just once, before she couldn't even do that without risking his life . . . That's all she wanted—to experience the full range of human emotion, the depths of love, before it was too late. What had happened, before, was preternatural. It was a trick, an evil seduction. This was as right as sunlight, and had also been forecasted. And as she felt herself warm under his tender gaze, there were a hundred things she wished she could have done differently . . . anything to have waited for this unlikely knight on a black and silver charger.

"Jake, things are going to hunt you all your life. You have to learn so much."

Just when he thought he was talking to a rational person, he remembered that he was having a discussion with a chick who was certifiable. "You get put out for smoking too much peyote, hon? Since when—"

"You're supposed to fight vampires with the Great Huntress's warriors." Tears of frustration welled in her eyes. He was going to die if he didn't hear her.

He sat up. He didn't want to talk about this madness anymore. There was no such thing as the undead and this conversation was blowing the groove.

"How'd you wind up on a bus with a bunch of religious fanatics?"

"I got in trouble."

He sighed. Just his luck to be out in the wilderness, on the run, with a beautiful but crazy pregnant chick. Poof. There went hope. "So, you're going to your grandma's to have the baby?"

Her eyes got wide, then burned with outright indignation. "I'm not pregnant!"

He shrugged. "Hey, where I come from, when a woman says—"

"That's not what happened." She gathered her arms around herself. "Never mind. I should have known better. You took one look at me and assumed."

"Hey, don't get all touchy. I didn't think . . . I mean— hey, just tell me what happened?"

She shook her head and looked down. He'd never understand. She didn't understand it all herself, and hadn't truly believed until it was too late.

Now, he'd done it. He glanced at the bottle with disgust and screwed the cap back on tight. "Let's start again from the top, since we're sorta partners in some kind of crime— or crimes, plural, who the hell knows at this point? But I'm no choirboy, and I'm not throwing stones from my glass house. I've done enough crap to get put out by my folks, too. So, don't take whatever I said wrong. Cool? I'm not judging."

She nodded, but still denied him access to her gorgeous eyes.

"I'm sorry," he said again after a while, preferring the way she was before he'd offended her. "Listen, my pop was . . . nuts. Beat my mom. I was going nowhere fast. Loved rebuilding engines and working on anything that moved, but music is my first love. I've seen a lot of dysfunctional crap in my time. People dying in their own bodies, going to work in a hellhole they called a job. If you want to call that the undead, I'll go with you on that . . . and as for bloodsuckers, I've seen my dad work for vampires all my life. That's why I had to make a break for it."

He peered at her sidelong when she didn't respond, hoping to get the conversation back on a relaxed track. God, she was beautiful. His tone became more urgent as he tried his best to draw her out again. "So, if you did something to get away from a crazy situation, then what can I say? That's why I was on the road, myself."

"I did the unthinkable," she murmured.

Her eyes were on the horizon when she'd spoken. If she would just look at him to know he wasn't kidding around . . .

"What could somebody as sweet as you do that would cause unforgivable harm?" He truly meant what he'd said, and for his honesty her returned gaze rewarded him.

"I went off with someone I shouldn't have. He was tall, and handsome and mysterious and came into town from New Orleans . . . I'd never—" She glanced at him and then looked away, swallowing hard. "I couldn't resist him and it wound up killing my mother. She said that what I had become would shame all those from our Cherokee heritage who'd walked the Trail of Tears. My father, God rest his soul in peace, had been a good man. He was a Baptist, and

in the military, and would tell my mom that black folks
didn't deal with this mess. He would never have understood this, even though he and my mother were both
guardians. It was only one time, but it was enough."

What she'd said was too deep. She was a beautiful com-
bination of black and Indian, and her people had had a
problem with some foreign white guy that obviously blew
into town. That had to be the deal. He could relate. His
folks were the same way about differences. Sad, though,
that they'd put this poor girl on a bus for something as
minor as that—but where he'd come from, infractions
were often dealt with more severely. At least they didn't
burn a cross on her lawn. But it broke his heart to see her
still struggling with cutting ties to home.

"Yeah, well, my folks weren't big on interracial relationships, either," he said, studying the stars. "They didn't
want me to even play certain music, so I can dig it. Closed
minds, hey . . . whatcha gonna do? So you left. Cool. Just
did it myself, and I'm never going back. So, here we are,
Bonnie and Clyde, or the Odd Couple." He chuckled and
shook his head. "Who cares if they don't get over it? We'll
ride it out together. Cool?"

In that moment, Jake Rider became even dearer to her.
She watched him looking up at the stars, his mind open,
but not comprehending, his voice gentle, his spirit so fair.
She didn't care if he wasn't hearing what she was saying. It
didn't matter that it might take years before he truly understood. All she had to do was get to her grandmother's healing medicine to purge her system and she might not be lost
to the destiny she was supposed to have. She was to be one
of the guardians, too . . . whenever the Neteru came.

She looked at this handsome man, who had stood up to
pure evil on her behalf, and a knowing washed through her.
He'd never flinched, never wavered, just drew his weapon
on instinct like a warrior, and used his body to shield hers.
He didn't even know her name when he'd done it. A dead

man lay at his feet, but he'd had kept his goal singular—
protect an innocent . . . her.

The old men used to talk about this in quiet tones. Their
wise murmurs had also spoken of soul mates among the
newest Neteru inner circle. All she had to do was wait, but
she'd been so deceived when she had been so close. They
had told her she'd know by the depth of a man's eyes, but
had also told her not to look into every pair of eyes she'd
encounter.

Their messages were cryptic, and she'd been impatient
to taste a slice of life denied her. It wasn't fair, and the
Great Spirit could not forsake her . . . she'd prayed so hard
and so vigilantly, and the moment she saw the right pair of
eyes, she'd understood—a flicker of familiarity in a pair of
unlikely but kind hazel eyes that weren't dark, seductive,
or intense . . . they were eyes that didn't change into horrible glowing orbs. Jack Rider's mouth would issue a caress,
and never bear fangs. If only she'd waited . . . but how did
one stare at something like she had and not be seduced?

She almost wept as she listened to life all around her.
Music of the night, the cicadas, the crickets, the owls, a
mournful coyote's wail. She could already hear things she
shouldn't have been able to hear with normal human
senses, regardless of her gift. She could tell things about
this wild, but honorable man that should have been blocked
to her mind. It had only been one bite. It took three to completely turn a human. She hadn't even been bitten by the
master of the line, but by a lower-level lieutenant. Shame
filled her. Just one fateful, unfair bite, during an encounter
that should never have happened. Even her sensuality was
starting to change . . . a touch on her throat had scorched
her. She'd wanted Jake Rider to make love to her so badly,
she'd almost cried out. And that made no sense. She
needed time; he needed time—they didn't even know each
other, and her system had to be purged.

Tara wrapped her arms around herself. "My mother

came to me in a dream and she gave me an address—said to go to my grandmother, and meet up with the Creeks that had been through this before in New Orleans. There's a small group of them tucked away in the Navajo nation in New Mexico." She reached into her bra with two fingers and produced a small slip of paper.

He looked at her as she offered it to him, accepting it with caution.

"If something happens to me," she said quietly, "or if something happens to you . . . go to this man. He has a young son, José Ciponte. His mother never married his father, because she was afraid, too . . . she feared her son's destiny and had hoped she could keep him from it by staying away from his father, who would teach him. But she finally sent the boy there to learn and he saw the things that we did. They have different last names, but his father is a renowned Creek guide; his mother is Latina. You're going to Arizona, past New Mexico, right?"

He only nodded, stunned, because he'd never told her where he was going. Just like he'd never told her his name or about his ability to always smell things better than the average person.

"We should stay together, as long as possible. Those things in the tavern always try to separate the herd, get one off by themselves—unless they come in numbers, like they did there. Maybe we'll get to my grandmother in time." Her expression was sad as she glanced away. "You're a sharpshooter, too?"

He couldn't speak. How in God's name did she know that he'd spent nearly every afternoon of his life popping bottles at distances to the point where it was a local gambling diversion? He could hit a bottle at a hundred yards, dead drunk. "Yeah," he said slowly, his eyes searching hers for understanding.

"Pack your bullets with the earth I gave you . . . please do it for me. Humor me, even if you don't believe me, and don't go out alone, even for a pack of cigarettes, without it."

From a very remote place in his mind, everything she was saying, even the way the moon lit the side of her face, sounded and seemed too frighteningly familiar. He tucked the small slip of paper into his jeans pocket, knowing somehow that his adventure had only begun.

"Nothing's gonna happen to you—or me," he said, trying to convince himself. "What happened back there . . . was . . . there's a logical explanation." He pushed himself up and stood and began pacing, but was careful to stay within the hallowed-earth ring.

"My crew probably got restless. One of them probably rushed the bartender for a free bottle or his register, or he got jumpy and pulled a gun. The old dude may have had some hired help in the back, or something . . . yeah. And, uh, it got nuts—crazy. A couple of the guys riding with us did what was sensible, got out of Dodge." He stopped walking and looked at her for confirmation that never came.

"Tara, listen, honey, that's what makes sense. See, bikers get a bad rap. People always think we're just animals. And if the authorities came, we had illegal stuff on us, drugs, unregistered weapons—because the road is dangerous, we carry a lot of money, see. They would have pinned robberies across the state on us just to close the books so they'd have less paperwork. I mean, I've been temporarily locked up before for bar fights that I wasn't even involved in. But I had a Harley, so I went in overnight with the whole kit and caboodle. And, okay, Crazy Pete was crazy. Probably got his throat cut in the brawl. I'm sure the bartender had a knife or something, or one of his boys did."

Rider could feel his pulse quicken as he whipped himself up and raked his mind for a rational thought. He gestured wildly with his hands as he spoke, hoping that would invoke logic. "And it made sense for the bus driver to put you off the bus, because maybe he was just prejudiced—

you were the only different one on there—and he probably thought 'cause you were being nice to me, and everything, that he didn't want you with him . . . uh, yeah, because you'd tell the truth about what you saw, or didn't see, which would muddy up his open-and-shut version." He added, rubbing his jaw, "So the SOB was just gonna leave you with us."

He stopped walking, scratched his head, and started pacing again. "No, more likely, he was taking you to the winning side, the bartender. Sorry bastard probably didn't want to be detained for questioning or have to come back for a trial, with a busload of witnesses, so he did the punk thing and started his engine so he could roll. I pulled the gun because I didn't want you hurt by either side, and I was fixing the bus while it all happened, anyway. Before to-night, we never met each other, and I was just helping a damsel in distress. The eyes—cats. A rundown joint like that would have cats everywhere to chase away mice or rats . . . I didn't hear dogs bark, so that's what probably ran by the window fast. Cats move faster than dogs. Right?"

He stopped pacing, nearly winded, and stared at her. "I'm not putting you down, or your belief system down, or talking bad about your momma, your people, or whatever. I'm just trying to keep us as far away from the bodies that dropped as possible. We can't go telling this stuff that sounds like dementia to a sentencing judge, if we get caught up in a dragnet. If they try to pin a crime on us—believe me, an insanity rap ain't no day at the beach, and doesn't always work, anyway. So, if the police ask, *that's* the story."

"Okay," she said just above a whisper, standing and going to him. She looked into his eyes and touched his cheek. She could feel his hard pulse through her skin and almost kissed him. "If you say so, *that's* the story."

CHAPTER 3

A shiver ran through her as the adrenaline surging in his blood wafted toward her. The night was calling her beyond the protective ring, and a sudden hunger began to grip her. As long as she never took an innocent before the cleansing rituals were done . . . as long as she never polluted her system with human blood from a kill . . . before the teeth came, she had a chance. She walked away from him and sat down, rubbing her arms.

"I've got a blanket in my saddlebags," he said, not asking her if she wanted it.

She only nodded and closed her eyes tight. He had to stop being so kind. She could feel her gums thicken as he walked away, her will a shred of dental tissue from not being her own. She had to remember that she was still human, and hadn't died yet. That was the last phase.

"You hungry?" he asked, coming back to put a blanket around her shoulders. He set his guitar down inside the ring, but stood near her waiting for a response.

She clung to the rough fabric and wrapped it around her all the way up to her neck. She shook her head no. The question had made her shudder. He had to get away from her. She used her chin to motion toward his guitar. "Why don't you play? It's going to be a long night."

She relaxed when he slowly withdrew from her side. She could smell the blood and sweat on him.

"Like I said, I just mess around." He sat down and opened the case, glancing at her. "It's an acoustic. Don't always have a place to plug in an electric axe. But, one day, when I find myself somewhere permanent, I'm getting a Fender. The real McCoy."

"The one you have is beautiful," she said quietly, truly meaning it as she watched the fire bounce off the highly polished wood. "Where'd you get it?"

He paused and rubbed the body of the instrument. "Don't laugh. I got it from my mom." He looked at her, expecting her to laugh. But her eyes held understanding.

"Why would that make me laugh? Mothers will give you their life blood."

Maybe it was the tone of her voice, or that something he couldn't describe that glittered in her eyes, but she made him feel safe to tell her what he hadn't told another soul. "I told her I wanted it for Christmas when I was fifteen. I saw it in a window in town. I wanted this guitar more than anything. And she stole money from my dad—well, it wasn't really stealing, she just shorted the supermarket allowance, you know, ten dollars here, twenty dollars there, for a whole year so she could buy me this." He started tuning it as he talked, the memory hard to verbalize. "She got beat up that morning, and my dad threatened to break it. She stood the whipping, told me to run with it, and never look back. Took me six more years to heed her advice."

"I'm sorry," Tara murmured. "There are all kinds of demons . . . your mother sounds like a good woman."

"Don't be sorry," Rider said, chasing the memory with a swig of liquor and letting the pain fade. "But you're right. There are all kinds of demons, so maybe what your people believe isn't all that far-fetched." He played a little riff. "Yeah, Mom is a good woman. I'm going to send her some money to get away from my father."

He was glad that Tara didn't say another word while he picked up and down the bridge and tightened his wires, deciding. What would he play for her? He closed his eyes and listened to the night. He better understood the sad country songs he'd always shunned. But she wasn't country western . . . had something extra. Spanish guitar, a little funk, some blues, something Native American spiritual, something sensual, something honest, something that cut across all his known boundaries . . . she was something he'd never played before. He just let his hands work and follow her rhythm while they composed Tara on the fly.

Without a doubt, he'd wanted a woman before. But something about this one was different. Half of his mind wanted to pursue what that something different could be, the other half of it was rapidly losing perspective as the music hit his bloodstream and became her.

The way she watched him intently was something he could feel without opening his eyes. The heat from her stare entered his pores. He glanced up and saw her gaze rake down his throat so hotly that he almost closed his eyes, this time in pleasure.

Her expression was innocence and hunger. She licked her bottom lip. It made his mouth water and sent the burn racing across his skin, awakening erogenous zones he didn't even know he had.

He told himself it had to be the liquor talking, or the adrenaline still humming in his veins. But the look she gave him made him want to touch her so badly that the hairs were standing up on his arms. He could feel his nipples harden. They stung every time he took a breath and brushed the rough inside fabric of his vest. He was glad he had his axe on his lap. She didn't need to see the erection he was sporting. He didn't want to offend, scare, or disrespect her. He continued to play and his fingers almost stumbled when her gaze slid down his chest and settled on his hands.

She couldn't breathe. This man was stopping time with his beautiful music. She could feel the creative energy in his bloodstream, linking to hers and washing through her veins, creating an ache to lie with him. The beat of his pulse was maddening, driving another hunger within her to the surface. No, not him and not tonight. Never. This man with a good heart didn't deserve that. But soon she would have to leave him to feed.

The heat of her gaze settled like a molten ache in his groin. Yet he couldn't move toward her or away from her. He watched her lids lower to half-mast and his cock twitched. That's when he stopped playing, shut his eyes, and swallowed hard.

He carefully set aside his guitar and pushed himself up and walked toward her. He knelt before her and slid his fingers into her hair. He didn't care that they could both use a shower. He didn't care where she came from or where she was going. He didn't care what she believed in, or what color her beautiful skin was. All he wanted was her mouth, and whatever else she'd allow him.

"We can't," she whispered, as he leaned in to kiss her. "We have no protection against this."

Her hand found the center of his chest, but she wasn't pushing him away, just making him pause. There was no fear in her eyes, just a warning that he knew to be true.

"You're too decent a man to get trapped in a life like that," she said gently, shaking her head.

It was the truth; not that he felt he was a good man, but the part about being trapped. He'd never wanted to be the kind of man who had kids somewhere, a bounty for child support on his head, and guilt on his conscience. But at this very moment, all those issues seemed remote. She didn't understand that his sense of self-preservation and pride had been stripped, leaving him naked and aching before her. All rational thought had left him. The very fact that she cared about his future only caused him to want her more. But he also cared deeply about her future and he forced himself to pull away.

He dropped his hand away from her hair and sat back on the ground with a thud, looking at his boots. No woman had ever cared about his future. None of the others had ever given a rat's ass about anyone beyond themselves. And as his gaze found hers again, all he could think of was all the things a woman like her deserved. He wanted her to genuinely like him, respect him, not think he was just what people had said—some sort of lawless animal who lived only for the next thrill.

Then she got up and came to him, touched his face and traced his mouth with the pad of her thumb. Rider grabbed her wrist and kissed the center of her palm.

"I'll pull out. I promise." He looked at her, not breaking eye contact as he spoke, hoping that she'd work with their circumstances. The fact that she hesitated gave him a flicker of hope that there might be a chance, which only made his heart beat faster. "I *swear* to God."

She smiled and drew back her hand. "That's just the thing . . . I might not let you."

"I'll take my chances," he said after a moment and held his breath for her response. Oh, God, he'd never begged a woman like this in his life.

"I can't let you do that, man with a good heart. The result would kill you. Trust me, that much I know."

With that she stood and walked to the other side of the dying fire. She might as well have cut him and left him bleeding by the side of the road. He wasn't about to force her, had never done anything like that in his life. But he watched her intently, for a sign, any signal that she might change her mind. Please let her change her mind. Because, right now, if she wanted to trap him, she could. He'd go willingly down whatever path she wanted him to go.

She looked up at him like she'd just heard the thought. Unless his mind was playing tricks on him, he was sure he'd seen her shudder. He could sense her deep conflict. If she were feeling half of what was running through him, then she'd err on the side of reckless abandon and just go for it. He was ready to throw caution to the wind. Truth was, he'd jettisoned it about an hour ago.

Oh, Rider . . . you don't understand. Temptation tugged at her, nearly seducing her. To throw caution to the wind would be so irresponsible. But as he sat there, hope flickering in his eyes, his inhalations becoming shallow sips, she almost gave in to his offer. It took everything in her not to open the blanket for him to join her. She'd never been with a man before, not like this, when nature was simply taking its course. And with him under the stars, and his song still vibrating within her . . . She sucked in a deep breath, ashamed at the shudder of arousal that claimed her. Worry filled her as she watched it ripple through him, too. It was in his eyes, something that went beyond intense arousal. A knowing resonated in her core. If the man got up and came to her, she couldn't be held responsible for her actions.

"I'm ready to abandon caution," he finally said, more than hoping she had, too. It was more like a silent prayer, because if a beautiful brown baby came out of this, then he'd build a house and put her and his baby behind a white picket fence. The road wasn't all it was cracked up to be. He'd get over it. But one thing was for sure: he wasn't about to get over her anytime soon.

"When daylight comes, you'll feel differently."

He stared at her as he felt her retreat behind a very sensible wall. Trying to salvage some of his dignity, he just nodded and let it rest. "You're right. This probably just got intense because of what we've been through together. Warrior bonding." He made himself laugh.

But he thought, *Oh, God, let her change her mind.*

She laughed, nodded, and rubbed her arms under the blanket. *Oh, Lord, I want him.* The burn was so hot, she wanted to cry instead of laugh. Her body craved his touch.

He had to look away. Couldn't even watch the gentle slide of her hands up and down her arms.

"In the morning," he said, clearing his throat, "we'll walk back to the church. I'll see if they'll give us a lift to a gas station, then we'll refuel and head out. Why don't you get some sleep?"

"Okay," she said softly, "you, too."

Yeah, right. He got up and found the bottle of Jack Daniel's, opened it and took a swig, trying not to let her see his hands tremble.

He wasn't sure how long he had been asleep. He had slept like a dead man, but now had awakened with a start. He glanced around the circle, and jumped up in a panic. Tara was gone.

"Tara!" he hollered, his voice echoing back to him in the early predawn hours. If she'd left him . . . But that was crazy. What right did he have to feel this way? "Tara, honey, you there?" he called out again with less confidence. Then he saw her coming through the bushes not far away.

"Where did you go?" he demanded, rushing over to her. "You scared the crap out of me."

"I had to . . . relieve myself," she said with a smile. She sighed as she stared up at him. He was so sweet. But she was glad he didn't know the real reason she'd gone out into the woods alone.

"Yeah, okay, but you should have woken me up. There's things out there that—"

"I was fine," she said, kissing his chin. She wanted so badly to kiss him. She glanced down to fight the temptation. She clasped her hands together to keep from reaching up to trace the vein in his throat.

Rider gave her a quick hug, then let her go. "It'll be dawn, soon. Let's go get that gas."

"All right," she said, as he put his arm over her shoulders.

*   *   *

Dawn sounded so different from the night, especially in the springtime. It smelled different, too. Small birds began chirping, dragonflies buzzed. The frogs went quiet; a whippoorwill sent a lonely cry through the air. Dew brought the scents of the flowers and grass alive. Households slowly came alive in farm country at that hour. A bloodhound barked in the distance. His footsteps sounded heavy beside Tara's soft pad of sandals. He glanced at her and worry stole his peace. Her pallor was nearly gray now, her breathing labored. It was as though the cresting sunlight were sucking everything out of her. He hastened his steps, remembering how much she'd just been through.

As they approached the churchyard gate, he also remembered where he was—in a part of the world that had not changed since the Civil War.

"Sweetheart, stay right here, and let me go try to get us a ride," he said.

She nodded and leaned against the short fence, taking in small sips, breathing like she had asthma. Suddenly a stray dog rounded the corner, stopped when it sighted her, raised its hackles and snarled.

Before Rider could leap between her and the dog, Tara narrowed her gaze and hissed at the dog.

The large dog stopped advancing, turned tail and ran, barking hysterically.

Heart pounding, Rider pulled her in close to him.

"We need to get out of here. Can you make it for a short run?"

She shook her head no, as she clung to him for support.

He was about to sweep her up into his arms when he heard a deep baritone voice bellow, "Duke! Duke! Whatcha got, boy?"

Shit, his worst nightmares were coming true. He'd never outrun a hound and a man with a shotgun with her in his arms. He'd have to stand his ground and simply hope that this church didn't belong to a local Grand Dragon.

"It's going to be all right," he told her, holding her close. "I'll go talk to him, alone, and work it out."

"Be careful," she whispered. She raised her arm and shielded her eyes. "But hurry."

He reached in his vest pocket and gave her his shades. "Ten minutes." Then he jogged around the side of the church where a small house leaned. "Anybody home?" he yelled, announcing his approach, just in case someone had an itchy trigger finger.

A tall, broad-shouldered black man was standing in the doorway in his robe. He had a raggedy gray Afro, and was fumbling with a shotgun and his glasses.

"Whatcha wants 'round here, boy, at dis hour? We's God-fearing people, and I'm a minister. Don't want no trouble, ya hear?" He brought the gun up.

Rider held up both hands. "Just came to buy some gas, sir."

"Gas! Does dis look like a gas station? I'll tell ya what happened—ole Duke caught your thievin' ass trying to suck it out my car, right?"

"No, sir, honest. My girlfriend's sick, and I ran out of gas. I need to get her someplace where she can rest. And I have money." He reached for his pocket when he heard the distinctive click of a shotgun hammer cocking back.

"Reach slow, or lose your arm. Dis here is church property, and we don't need no junkies like you coming—"

"She isn't a junkie, and neither am I. Go see her for yourself. We just need a little help."

The minister glared at him before lifting the barrel slowly to the sky, gave Rider a hard scowl, then begrudgingly came down the steps. "C'mon, Duke," he said to his dog. "Let's go see what all the ruckus is about."

But the dog refused to budge.

The minister swung around to face Rider.

"Whatcha do to my dog?"

Rider held up his hands again.

"Nuthin', sir. Please. You can see I'm not armed."

"How I know it ain't a Klan ambush?"

"You don't," Rider said, defeated. He turned and walked away.

"You tell her to come 'round to the back, and I'll wait here. Won't call the sheriff right off, if everything's on the up and up. I don't like dealin' wit da po-lice, truth be tol', but I gots something fer ya, if yous a liar."

Rider nodded, relieved.

He found Tara where he'd left her, leaning against the fence. "Sweetheart, there's an old preacher back there who would like to see you. He's scared of an ambush."

She stared up at him and her eyes told him that she immediately understood. Without a word she took his hand and walked with him to meet the preacher.

When the preacher saw them his expression went from shock to fury in a matter of seconds. He rubbed the gray stubble on his dark walnut face and looked at Rider hard while addressing Tara.

"You need me to call the sheriff, baby?"

A plump older woman wrapped in a blue terry-cloth robe appeared at the door beside the preacher. "Oh, my Lord in Heaven, look at her. Clothes all tore up and dirty. Oh, baby, come on in. We'll he'p ya. We'll call yo' momma. Just give us an address, and we'll git you home. Sweet Jesus, he—"

"No," Tara said quickly. "I'm fine. He's a friend."

"How old are you, baby?" the preacher said, now completely focused on Tara.

"Eighteen, sir. And we just need some gas so we can be on our way."

"He got you on drugs?"

"No," she said. She took off the sunglasses and squinted. "I have a migraine, that's why I have on the glasses." Before she could say another word, she bent over and retched.

"You in trouble, girl?" the wife asked, coming off the porch.

Tara shook her head as tears spilled down her cheeks and Rider longed to hug her, but the situation was too fragile for that.

"No, ma'am, I'm not. I just ate something last night that didn't agree with me. That's why he's taking me to my grandma's. My momma died."

"I'm so sorry to hear about your momma, chile," the preacher said. "I got a gas can in the house. You all can come in, wash your faces, get some coffee or something to settle your stomach. Idell, you gots some aspirins in there for a headache, right?"

"Yeah, c'mon in here while my husband fetches some gas."

Rider glanced at the couple and the dog, then looked at Tara. "The dog, ma'am, it scared her."

"Oh, that old mutt . . ." The preacher's wife gave the creature a disparaging glance. "Shoo, you old thang. Git!" The dog scampered deep into the house and the wife let out a long sigh. "C'mon. It's all right, now."

"You go in and sit down for a while, all right?" Rider waited for Tara's response, noting her hesitation. "I have some money," he said and tried to hand a fifty-dollar bill to the preacher.

The man declined it with a wave and turned to go into the house and dress. "I'll be back in twenty minutes. You all go on up to the kitchen and set down. If she can stomach it, maybe a little breakfast?" He studied Tara. "Or maybe just some ginga tea to settle her stomach."

It felt like needles were stabbing her behind her eyes. All she could do was breathe deeply and put her head down on the kitchen table as the preacher's wife prattled on and on about who in her family had suffered migraines, and expounded upon her understanding of light sensitivity.

Then the older woman began going into the Scriptures about wanton behavior and the sins of the flesh. The four aspirin weren't helping. However, she was extremely grateful that the elderly couple had taken them in. Jake Rider nodded respectfully as he rubbed her back. He'd told the old preacher she was his girlfriend. Interesting. She liked the concept very much. But why had he said that?

Rider declined the tea, but downed two cups of black coffee. He intermittently forced her to take two sips of the wicked tea brew. All she wanted to do was get the sickening smell of the dirt off her. The walls of the tiny house felt like they were closing in on her, and an anvil-like pressure was caving in her chest. Her condition was getting worse, and she knew it. Soon she wouldn't be able to touch hallowed earth, or withstand the names of the Most High. Sunlight was draining, making black spots dance before her eyes. She wondered how long it would take them to get to New Mexico by bike?

When she heard the preacher's voice, and felt Rider stand, she pulled herself up. She watched them shake hands, and feigned a smile.

"Y'all need a lift to your bike?"

"Yeah. It's about two and a half miles from here, and I don't think she can make it until the aspirin kicks in," Rider said. "We appreciate everything you've done. Your hospitality's been a blessing." There was no fraud in his words as he looked at this older couple. He made his mind up right there and then to tolerate the initial misgivings Tara's family might have about him. If he had to run the gauntlet, so be it. His own father had called him worse names than anything they could dish out.

"That's what we's supposed to do—he'p each other," the wife said.

"Ain't too much trouble to he'p some young folks on they way," the preacher agreed.

"If everybody felt like that, the world would be a better place, mister." Rider threaded his arm around Tara's waist. That was the truth, if ever he'd said it. He just hoped that the old couple would take what he said as an apology, too, for all those who hadn't helped them along their way.

"Reverend Jones, son," the preacher said. "You ever come through dese parts, you come stop at my door, hear? Tell folks you wit Bible Tabernacle. Yous with Josephus and Idell's people—that'll give ya a temporary grace pass."

Rider nodded.

"Since you travelin' wit her, I'ma tell you some safe places to go, hear? Places dat you proba'ly don't know about. Some peoples might not understand, 'specially when you cross over into North Texas. Now, you heed my words, young fella. 'Less you in a major city, you best act accordingly. Don't take her into no small town when you gits supplies, and on this side of the county line, there's only one diner and one motel that's refuge. You listen to what I'm saying, hear?"

Rider extended his hand in friendship, understanding completely. "Much obliged, Reverend Jones."

The man at the motel front desk looked them up and down and pushed his girth off the stool, setting his newspaper on the counter with care. He frowned so deeply that the wrinkles in his ebony face made his white eyebrows touch. He gave Tara a look that lacerated both her and Rider. "You want it for how many hours?"

The question pissed Rider off so badly that he slid his hands into his jeans. "For the night," he said between clenched teeth.

The old man took his time, muttering something Rider was sure he didn't want to hear as he got a key, accepted the wad of bills, and thrust a register in front of him. "Mr. and Mrs. who?"

"Jones," Rider said, snatching the key off the counter.

"From Reverend Jones's church—Bible Tabernacle. We Josephus and Idell's clan."

The man shook his head. "Well . . . if Rev sent you, my name's Bennett and I ain't In-it."

Rider shut the door behind them, then walked over to the window and pulled the drapes as Tara flopped on the bed. "You okay?"

"Yeah," she said, feeling much improved as soon as the sun had been sealed out of the room. "Just don't turn on the lights, yet. The headache . . ."

"All right," he said. "Listen, why don't you take a shower, rest, and I'll go into town and get some supplies? When I come back, I'll knock three times, so you'll know it's me."

She smiled. It meant the world that he was trying his best to be a respectful gentleman. It meant the world that he had gotten a taste of her reality, and was dealing with it. It meant the world that he thought she was worth it. "Okay, but just be safe."

"I think we might be all right," he said, but his tone was unsure. "News should have hit by now. There wasn't anything in the newspaper that put the motel clerk on red alert, and the preacher and his wife didn't seem to know anything, either."

"Yeah," she said quietly, knowing full well that if bodies hadn't been discovered by now, they never would be. The things that hunted them were very efficient and had probably removed all traces of their presence. That was their way: to keep the humans in the dark. Ignorance was bliss.

"You want anything while I'm out? Anything specific?"

"Just some toothpaste and a toothbrush."

He nodded. "Cool. You got it."

She stood and walked to the bathroom, and closed the door.

*   *   *

The incident with the dog nagged at Rider's brain, but he had more important things on his agenda. Ammo. He'd find the local hardware store and go get hollow-point explosive rounds. Since she'd been dead aim on target about everything thus far, maybe he would pack some bullets with that dirt she'd collected and load his gun.

Hollow points made a small hole going in, but blew a hole the size of a barn coming out. Explosive rounds flattened when they went into something soft and sprayed the insides with whatever shrapnel material was packed in the shell. If he ever encountered what they'd seen again . . . shit, if she wanted him to make silver bullets, he'd do that, too. Kits were easy to buy, and he'd seen enough. That small precaution was worth it, just like she was.

She had lied for him; had thought fast on her feet. Had clung to him for support and protection, if there was ever a time in the world for her to make a break for it and save herself, it would have been back at the church with the old couple. They were her people . . . But she'd come to him, stayed with him, vouched for him, stood up for him. No one had ever done that with so much riding in the balance—and she seemed to know him even better than the woman who'd given birth to him.

He made short work of getting ammunition, then hit the corner drugstore. All right. Toothpaste. Toothbrushes. A carton of smokes. He bypassed the pharmacy with resignation. She was not that way, and wasn't interested in him like that yet. All right. He thought about her pretty hair, and found himself in an aisle looking at hairbrushes and combs. Crazy. He tried to remember the items he'd seen on ladies' dressers before. They had all sorts of potions and elixirs and lotions and junk. How did a man figure out what some woman needed in a motel room?

He studied the brushes and combs and just grabbed one of each. Motel soap, he knew from experience, was like laundry soap. On her pretty skin—no way. But what

the hell was he doing sniffing different lotions trying to figure out the closest thing to lavender? Nuts! But he so hated
that when she got sick she began to lose that lovely fragrance. She'd gotten this almost metallic scent like you'd
pick up in a hospital. He found a lotion, then went to find a
gentler scented soap. Then he thought about her hair . . .
no, she needed shampoo and that other stuff that went with
it. Yeah, conditioner. That's what they called it. Maybe that
would make her feel better. Maybe she'd want that dusting
powder stuff, too?

Rider cocked his head to the side as he looked at rows
of deodorants and antiperspirants. He chose one and tossed
it into the brimming basket in his hand. The thought of
deodorant made him stop, sniff himself, and cringe.
Christ . . . No wonder all she wanted was toothpaste and a
hot shower. He glanced in a mirror in the cosmetics section
and simply shook his head. How in the world was he supposed to take her to her people and withstand a family
inquisition with road dirt and gnats in his beard? Three
years of rebel pride since it grew in evenly, but it had to go.

Like a madman he started getting things he'd never
truly worried about before. Razors, his and hers . . . yeah,
ladies did that thing with their legs. Shaving cream. Damn,
when it was just him, he traveled light. The pharmacy
caught his eye again. Maybe?

CHAPTER 4

This was *not* the adventure he'd planned. Twenty-four hours ago he had been drinking with the boys, on his way to a race, had had money in his pocket, and been a free man looking for tail in a honky-tonk bar. One woman later, and he was nearly broke, was running from the law, was dealing with a minister who carried a shotgun to the door but gave him an underground passport, and he'd bought so much female junk that it wouldn't fit in his bike. Here he was, like a fool, balancing women's clothes on his lap and trying to ride slow enough not to lose his parcel. Not to mention, the wind was like a razor on his jaw, ever since he'd submitted to a bunch of old men in a barbershop who had brutalized his beard and had shaven his face as clean as a baby's butt.

Was he out of his mind? Yes. Was he pulling up to a motel with stronger headache medicine, hoping that the ruination to his life felt better? Yes. Did an hour away from her feel like a year? Yes. Did he almost go skinny-dipping with some chick he really didn't know, and not care that he didn't have a condom? Hell, yes. Oh, brother, he was in too deep. Best bet, the most rational thing to do, would be to give her all the stuff he'd bought, just hand it over at the door, let her buy a new bus ticket with the money he'd put in her new purse, give her an I'll-catch-you-later kiss, then ride like the wind.

That would have been employing common sense. So why was he standing at the door, knocking three times, and holding his breath for her to open it? Easy answer. He'd lost his mind.

"Hi," she said, peeking from behind the door and shielding her eyes.

"How's the headache?" he asked, coming in quickly and sealing off the sun's glare.

"Better," she said, nodding toward the one lamp that was on. "A good shower helped a lot. Thank you." Then she looked at him hard and slowly covered her mouth with her hand. "Oh, my goodness . . . you shaved?"

"Wasn't nuthin'," he said, dropping his parcels on the bed. He had to keep his eyes on the packages and not on her. She had wrapped a thin, white towel around her and her hair was dripping wet. It formed gorgeous, curly, jet-black tendrils about her shoulders and hung down her back. The fact that his new jawline pleased her had run all through him. Every minute under the barber's straight-edge razor had been worth it just to hear that appreciative gasp come from her.

"I just picked up some odds and ends." He looked at the chintzy towel around her, ready to kick himself for not buying a thicker, fluffier one of those for her, too.

"My dress was so dirty, I didn't want to put it back on. It was making me nauseous." She glanced down at her towel and held the corner of it tighter.

"Well, then, great minds think alike." He smiled at her from a sideways glance, and then thought about what he'd just said. "No, what I mean is—not that you made me nauseous . . . but I figured the dress was in pretty bad shape."

"It was." She laughed and he relaxed. "Man with a good heart, you're crazy, you know that?"

"Tell me something I don't know," he said, chuckling at himself. "Yeah, I'm out of my mind," he added, and began unpacking the first bag.

"This," he said, holding up extra-strength tablets, "is for those nasty, stress-induced migraines." He raised one eyebrow. "If I was with my boys, I'd have something much stronger than that to kill the pain, but . . . since I'm with Mother Teresa, we'll go with over-the-counter meds."

She held the edge of her damp towel harder and shook her head with a smile. "Thank you, Rider. These will be fine."

"But wait," he said, waving his hands over the bag like a magician, "there's more."

She watched in awe as he produced an array of every possible thing that could bring her comfort under the circumstances. She smiled as she looked at the brush and comb, knowing her heavy hair would break them. He had so much to learn about her difference, but it counted for everything that he'd tried. She looked away as the objects on the bed got blurry and he handed her shampoo and conditioner. For a man like him to go to all that trouble, and he didn't even know her, had already done too much, and had not harmed her in any way, but was so kind . . .

"Now, don't cry over lotion and shampoo. If I can't at least do that for you, then what good am I, huh?"

It was the tone of his voice and the way he looked her in the eyes, wasn't raking her body, that made her want to weep. Great Spirit, please don't fail me . . . this is *the one*.

"Well, look," he said fast, appearing self-conscious, "I tried my best to figure out your size, but I don't know anything about women's stuff. So, I hope you like the dress . . . and the jeans and whatnot are so we can ride hard and make time when you're feeling up to it."

He spread the dress out on the bed and placed a pair of jeans beside it, then dug around in his bags for other items, so that she had to slowly sit down.

"I got that ammo, too, like you suggested. I'll take a shower, we can go get something to eat, and before it gets dark, I'll pack some shells with dirt. Okay?"

All she could do was nod.

Then he took the bag away, and she could hear there was still more stuff in it. He gave her his back to study while he fished around and talked a mile a minute.

"Oh, yeah, got toothpaste, toothbrushes, a newspaper, uh, some shaving cream so I can look human . . . the rest of the bag is just junk. Nothing important. I'll, uh, just go outside and, uh, do some stuff while you get dressed. Cool?"

She nodded and opened the shampoo and smelled it. "You bought lavender?"

"Yeah, well," he said, shifting from foot to foot. "You said I had the nose . . . If you don't like it—"

"I love this fragrance. Thank you so much."

For a moment, neither of them said a word.

"I'm sorry I didn't have it before you washed your hair."

"That's all right. When you're done," she said shyly, "I may go in there and just try a bit . . . if you don't mind?"

Was she crazy? That's why he'd bought it—to please her.

"Gimme a minute," he said, moving to the door. "I'll be right back."

"Where are you going? I thought you wanted to get in the bathroom first?"

"I'm going to the front desk to get some cleanser."

"What?" Then her heart sank. Of course he'd want to clean the tub after her . . . some things hadn't changed since this country began. "I did leave a mess," she said, salvaging her dignity. She stood and gathered up her old dress.

He stopped and leaned against the door. "If you're going to wash your hair after I get in there . . . as long and as pretty as it is . . ." He laughed and looked at the bathroom door. "You think your dress made you nauseous, after I'm done, the tub will make you go running into the parking lot in your towel."

He loved the sound of her laughter and the way her dark eyes shone when she was happy. "In fact, the practical thing would be for you to go on in there and wash it first, I can wait. Then, I can wash your dress out with that para-military crap they call soap."

He watched her sit down with a smile, drop the old dress on the floor and reach over and pick up a pair of new lace panties. He almost didn't breathe as he watched her study them in her hand. He prayed she wouldn't get bent out of shape.

"You even bought these?"

"Yeah." He shrugged, hoping that she would understand by the color of them that he'd meant no disrespect. He'd purposely bypassed the reds and blacks and purples and all the colors he was used to seeing . . . hoping she'd understand what he'd meant. "I figured you'd be all clean and fresh after a shower, and that would be something a girl would like—if I did the wrong thing by buying 'em, it wasn't me trying to be fresh."

If she hadn't been sitting down, her knees might have buckled. She took a deep breath and pasted on her calmest smile. He was going to wash out her dress for her, clean the tub . . . had even thought of her down to her underwear? That he'd noticed every single detail about her was making it hard to breathe.

"Tell you what," she said carefully. "Why don't you go get the cleanser while I try to organize some of this stuff? You take a shower first, because I know how good one feels—it's relaxing, and we've both been through a lot. And if it's not too much trouble . . . when you're done, maybe you can help me wash this bird's nest?" She ruffled her hair and stared at him, hoping he'd clearly read what she was trying to tell him: he had a green light. She tried her best to casually make her signal clear. "You were so right. That hard soap just tangled it all up."

He didn't move for a moment; couldn't. Was she saying

what he thought she was saying, or did she just want him to wash her hair? And if it was the latter of the two options, that was fine by him, too, because he'd been wanting to run his hands through her thick tresses since the moment he'd laid eyes on her—yesterday it was a dream, today it was a near reality . . . and that meant other fantasies might also come true. He had to remember to breathe.

She smiled and looked at her lap when his expression went stone serious, and he slipped out the door without a word.

She would be calm, would sit quietly, and would seem platonically interested. Certain things took time, should progress slowly—the problem was, time wasn't her friend. Still, there was no real reason to feel all jumpy. The butterflies in her stomach would go away. He was a decent soul, biker or not; she was in the company of a true gentleman. The problem was, however, he was in the company of an almost vampire. But she had to stop being silly. She hadn't actually turned into one, yet. All she had to do was get to her grandmother's. So it was best that they both ignore the huge white elephant in the center of the room—the bed.

True, she had turned on the green light with her offer to allow him to wash her hair. But that was a signal with a caution flag to let him know she was interested, would like things to progress, and that she considered him a suitor . . . but . . .

Tara looked at the closed bathroom door and listened to the water. She briefly closed her eyes and let her mind wander, wondering what he looked like with suds running down his strong back and broad shoulders. The momentary fantasy produced a wave of desire, and she quickly opened her eyes. Oh, no, no, no, no, no—not until she was safe. This man had been so good to her, but he was in mortal danger and didn't even know it. Right now the best and most prudent course of action would be to develop the friendship, allow the courtship to proceed, get to Grandma's, then let nature take its rightful course.

But it was going to be challenging, especially when she could see him through the door in her mind. That new awareness made her tear her gaze away from his direction and cast it into the paper that she couldn't concentrate on to read.

She was getting stronger. More of the dark power was taking hold as the afternoon sun lowered. Yet, they said she was a seer. Maybe it wasn't the thing that would remain nameless within her. What if the fact that he was a guardian was increasing her sight?

Tara clung to that thought as her hands tightly gripped the newspaper.

He almost slipped and cracked his head in the tub, he was in and out of it so fast. He'd nearly blinded himself as he'd tried to scrub road dirt out of his hair while cleaning his fingernails, and brushing his teeth in the shower at the same time. He had to clean the tub, and dry the floor, and get on his jeans, and go out there calm, cool, act like this was just a walk in the park. Just another spring day. Couldn't let her see him behaving like a fool over the idea of washing her hair. But the finest woman he'd ever seen in his *life* was in the other room, sitting on the side of the bed, naked under a towel, still damp, reading the newspaper. He stumbled twice as he zipped up his pants, willing away an erection, trying to mop up the floor with his feet, using the towel.

"You ready?" he asked brightly, his voice almost cracking from anticipation as he burst out of the bathroom more eagerly than intended.

"Yup," she said, popping up from the bed and bringing the shampoo and conditioner into the bathroom clutched in one arm.

"Cool, uh . . . right," he said, coming into the bathroom

behind her quickly and turning on the tub, adjusting the water temperature as she got on her knees and leaned over the edge of it. He'd never done anything like this in his life . . . never washed a woman's hair. He'd done a lot of things, but this was too intimate. It was messing him up, big time. Then what was protocol—where was he supposed to stand? The tub was running, she was waiting. The practical position would be to straddle her and bend over, but that might seem too suggestive. Holy Moses.

She glanced up over her shoulder, and threw her mane over into the tub and leaned against the side of it deeper. It exposed the delicate nape of her neck, and her supple spine stretched and flexed when she did so. The sight was disorienting. The towel barely skimmed the back of her thighs. Her already wet hair formed little wisps and ringlets at the nape of her neck and before her ears. God, she was gorgeous, a stark contrast to the all-white glare in the confines of the tiny tiled room.

"Rider, the hot water is going to run out, if you don't hurry up."

"Yeah, sure," he said fast, wondering if there was some female code to what she'd just said. "Uhmmm . . . I'm not trying to be funny, but I need to stand a certain way, because your hair is so long."

"Go ahead, no problem. I trust you."

He swallowed hard and put one bare foot on either side of her and bent over to capture the heavy weight of her hair in his hands. For a second, he closed his eyes as the water fused with velvet in his palms. He suddenly became aware of how rough his hands were from everything he did in life. Working under a hood, working on motorcycle engines, playing the guitar, all of it made his fingers snag the silk he was holding and he was almost ashamed to even touch it. Almost.

His legs felt like steel on either side of her hips. She willed herself not to think about his sensuous stance, and refused to allow herself to consider the gentle way he stroked her hair. His tenderness was dissolving her into lather. She was practically a puddle on the floor. This was a bad idea. How in the world was she going to keep her distance from him if he worked on her like that?

"I need to wet it up good and then I'll put the shampoo in."

"Okay," she murmured and let out a slow exhale. She had to remember to breathe, and to not assume every word he said had a double meaning.

He almost dropped the bottle while trying to open it. It was the way she'd breathed out the word "okay." He poured way too much in his hands and the excess lather immediately created billowing white suds. The fragrance from it brought tears of anticipation to his eyes as he made gentle swirls with it.

A gasp was trapped in her throat, and she quickly swallowed it away. No, the gentle strokes had to stop or she'd never make it through the night with him. She had to just be calm, talk to him like they were doing something else, like watching TV.

"Oh, c'mon. You can do it harder than that. I'm not a baby, and I'm not tender-headed."

He paused with her hair in his hands, shampoo lather dripping in large globs into the tub as her words made him breathe through his mouth. "Cool," he said quietly, scrubbing her scalp a little harder. "Like that?"

"Yeah," she murmured, "harder, though." She'd meant her voice to stay light and cheerful, but when he stopped and took a deep breath . . . his voice had dropped to a low timbre that practically vibrated through his legs where they touched her hips.

He closed his eyes and let his hands work with the erotic textures under his palms. The way she'd asked for it harder . . . Okay, he had to pull himself together. This was ridiculous. He was simply washing her hair and needed to remember that. He added a bit more pressure but was unsure. "Like that . . . it's not too hard, is it?"

"Uh-uh . . . that feels *really* good," she said on a heavy exhale.

The response made him pause, then redouble his efforts. He couldn't think about the sound of her voice and the many ways what she'd just said could be taken. He made his fingers work out the frustration, scratching her crown, the sides of her temples, the back of her skull till she gasped. The moment the sound escaped from her, he wanted to drop to his knees behind her so badly that the muscles in his thighs were twitching. But he knew better than that, and stopped his own agony by rinsing out the suds. He could do this and remain cool. He had to.

Just rinse it and let me get up, she begged him in her mind. This was such a bad idea. The man had made her tremble with a touch, and it was time to put an end to it. She had to be responsible, she reminded herself. And she also knew herself well enough to realize that at this point, she couldn't take another soaping—not the way his hands felt.

Her hair squeaked as he stripped her long tresses of lather, and he watched it turn into long ringlets, just transform in his hands. Mesmerized, he wanted to do it again, just one more time. He was fascinated by the way it went straight under the flow of the water, then as soon as the air hit it, it became a thick mass of unruly curls.

But when he reached for the shampoo, she chuckled.

"I think my hair is clean," she said, "but it could use some conditioner."

"Right . . . right . . . that's right. You've already washed it once."

He straightened his back and locked his knees to give his legs a short rest. He was glad her head was in the tub, and was too embarrassed when he looked down at his blue jeans. He should have bought the black ones, then a wet spot in them wouldn't have been so obvious. This didn't make any sense. He grabbed the conditioner and slathered some into his palms and bent over her again.

However, the viscosity of the fluid in his hands was like straight sex. The way it slid down her hair, the slickness of it under his palms, the sound of it going on, made him shudder in earnest. She glanced over her shoulder, and he didn't even care. He was beyond worrying about appearances when her spine dipped so she could look at him.

"You okay? You need a break? My mom always said doing my hair broke her back." If he didn't need a break, she sure did. She hadn't expected the feel of the conditioner going in under his hands to melt her. She had to keep the conversation light. Yes, that was the only way. Her face was hot, her throat felt flushed, and he'd awakened other parts of her that she dared not admit to herself.

"No, I'm good," he lied, rubbing the slippery conditioner through her hair and reveling in the textures of her scalp, the fluid, and the curls, with the scent of her and the sight of her wearing him out.

"How long do you have to leave it in?"

"How long do you want it in?" he said hoarsely, his eyes closed against the sensations that were rocking him.

He felt her tense, pause, and turn her head.

"It says on the bottle, three to five minutes," he said quickly, trying to recover.

"Oh . . ." For a moment, she thought she'd lose it—had almost moaned. It was time for distance.

"How about five?" she said quietly, turning off the water. "It's really been a long time since I've done this right. Some things you just can't rush."

He stepped away from her, leaned against the sink, shut his eyes, and nodded. "Uh-huh. Know what you mean."

"You sure you're all right?" she asked, squeezing excess water out of her hair and turning so her tresses could hang over the tub, but so that she could lean against it while sitting on the floor looking at him. She would not read more into his expression than warranted. "You didn't hurt your back, did you? I mean, you ride that bike all the time, and could have—"

"I'm cool," he said, gazing at her, "but this *is* breaking my back."

"I knew it," she said with a sigh. "I'm sorry."

"That's not what I meant." He just stared at her.

"Oh . . ." She leaned over and turned on the spigot, then got on her knees. She had to stop looking at his intense hazel gaze. "If it's any consolation, it's breaking mine, too." She put her head under the water and closed her eyes. She turned the cold faucet on full blast. Oh, no . . . she hadn't misread him, had heard every word he'd said just as it had been intended. But the fact that he'd made her just say what was on her mind, so openly, made her cheeks burn. It sent the butterflies loose within her again, and then something imploded like a sudden heat.

While her admission was profound, if he was reading her right, it didn't help matters in the least, since it was obvious that she wasn't prepared to take things to the next level. If she had been, she wouldn't have turned on the water and begun washing the conditioner out. He watched her struggle to do it unassisted, loving the conflict as it unfolded, her towel sliding away, and then she'd grab it, trying to tuck it so it wouldn't fall while trying to get her head farther under the spigot.

"It hasn't even been three minutes yet. You're rushing it."

"I know," she said, almost out of breath. "It's hard to do it by yourself."

"Don't I know it," he said, finally going to help her. "Then why didn't you let it sit there for a few more, and wait it out? Patience is a virtue, I'm told."

"That's always been my weak point," she said, glancing up at him with a look that made him stop rinsing her tresses. "I'm trying to get this stuff out of my hair so it doesn't mess up the bed."

What was she doing! The words had just tumbled out of her mouth. Humiliation paralyzed her.

He blinked twice, then almost fell in the tub as he pulled her up, hair dripping, water still running, and kissed her hard. The inside of her mouth had the consistency of raw honey, mint hit his nose, and his tongue tangled with hers till he couldn't breathe. He broke away, took a huge gulp of air, and buried his face in her wet hair, then dragged his jaw down the side of her neck. Her immediate gasp blurred his vision, it hit his system so hard, just like her wet form molding to his bare chest did, her satin skin pure butter under his palms.

She almost passed out when he scored her throat where it had once been bitten. He didn't understand what he was about to unleash. But as his strong arms enfolded her, and he smelled so good . . . his pulse beat so hard, and Great Spirit help her, she'd never felt like this in her life. Her hands trembled as they slid up his back, the muscles within it pure cable. The way he tasted made her weak in the knees.

"Why didn't you just say so?" he murmured hotly against her ear, then captured her mouth before she could answer. Then she did something that almost made him pass out. She bit his shoulder and gently dragged her teeth up the side of his throat while her palms slid down his chest, one hand finding the middle of his back, the other finding the center of his groin, all in one fluid, graceful, feline motion. It forced the air from his lungs as her grip on his length tightened, and the sudden expulsion of air came out as a ragged groan combined with a gasp.

He didn't even feel it when his back banged the door on the way out of the bathroom. All he was aware of was her as he lifted her up and kept kissing her while walking, knowing his way to the bed blind. Her arms were around his neck, her legs wrapped around his waist, the attention she paid to his neck at the jugular was bringing tears to his eyes. He had read every signal wrong, but he was clear about this one. Caution was the wind itself, fleeting, unimportant, and something neither of them could summon.

They fell so hard they almost took out a slat in the bed. He fought with his jeans as her legs threaded around his and she arched. He felt a bite at his throat that made him see colors beneath his lids. He heard her whisper, "I'm sorry," and he couldn't even answer her, it felt so damned good. He returned the kiss hard, and then bit her neck even harder, and the sound she released almost made him release in his jeans.

She helped him push the barrier down to his knees, and when he entered her the sound of his voice was foreign to his own ears. The sensation was so immediately explosive that he had to look at a point on the wall for moment to hold back the inevitable. But when she leaned up and took one of his nipples into her mouth, his eyes literally crossed. The way she held his back made her part of his skin, and the way her pelvis worked in unison against his created pinpoints of light inside his head. He could feel them both sliding to the edge of the bed, about to go over the side of it as he began chanting her name on every other thrust. Then she called him by name, his real name, on a heave that became a shudder, which transformed into a jerking spasm that made him go blind for a moment when his body convulsed with hers so hard that he was sure he'd stripped a gear and had a hernia.

He couldn't even shout what his mind was screaming, it felt so good. Oh, God . . . Aftershocks were slamming him, her body was still moving, it was pleasure so profound that tears were running down the bridge of his nose. Jesus . . . *I've never felt anything like this in my life*. This woman had called him like that by name.

It took a while for him to stop panting and to get enough

air into his lungs. He looked at the tiny goddess under him
and kissed her forehead, too afraid of what her lush mouth
could do to him. Her eyes were closed; tears stained her
cheeks, her hands caressed his shoulders, then she sobbed
as she stroked his hair. Oh, yes, he was a blessed man. So
what that he'd never made it to the hidden box of protection in the bag? Yeah, he'd marry her. Whatever. All he
knew was, he wasn't letting this one go. Uh-huh, make it
last forever, baby.

She opened her eyes and peered at him as he petted her
hair while he was still lodged deep within her. "Oh,
Rider . . . this wasn't supposed to happen until—"

"Shush," he said, kissing away her words and banishing
them. "This had to happen."

"But—"

"Uh-uh," he murmured, sliding his hand up and down
her side and finding her breast. "Don't get nervous on me
now. I'm over the top and crazy about you. Whatever happens, happens."

"I'm crazy about you, too. That's the problem. But this
happened too fast."

"How is that a problem?" He looked deeply into her
eyes, loving the fact that he'd put tears of pleasure in them.

"Because I want to make it last forever."

He kissed the bridge of her nose, her face, and found
her earlobe. "Tell me how that's a problem . . . like I told
you in the bathroom, all you had to do was say so."

"I have to get something to eat. Soon."

He stared at her for a second, and then laughed. "Oh,
honey, I'm sorry. I forgot we were supposed to be getting
something to eat. It's just that when you came to the door
in that towel, wet, and then put that lavender dress up to
your pretty skin . . . then I touched your hair. I lost it."

"You promised you'd pull out." She smiled at him.

He closed his eyes. "Tara . . . I couldn't . . . so help me,
God."

He felt her cringe and knew that he'd messed up, knew that he should pull himself from her deep, warm valley to let her up, but that was next to impossible at the moment. And the thought of having to sheathe latex between him and that sensation, after knowing how good she felt, was going to be impossible, too.

"Rider, if I don't eat, I'll die."

"Okay," he said, bracing himself for the knife of cold air that would slice him when he pulled away from her. "All right. But when we get back to the room, please tell me you'll still feel the same way."

She touched his face and then kissed his cheek. "Once I eat and the sun goes down . . . I have this really dark side, sweetheart, that, uh . . . might make you feel differently. It might shock you."

He closed his eyes and flopped back on the bed, so grateful to be alive. His prayers had been answered. She was beautiful on the inside, gorgeous on the outside, was kind, gentle, funny, sexy, smart, passionate, *and* she knew how to handle herself on the back of his bike, plus loved music . . . she was trying to tell him that she had a little bad girl in her? Oh, yeah, he was definitely a blessed man.

"Let's get you something to eat, so we can get back here pronto and then you can shock me all you want."

She just looked at him for a moment, then her gaze went to the window. The sun was low, she could tell by the orange glow at the edge of the drapes. He didn't understand. She brought her hand to the side of her neck where he'd instinctively bitten her, as though he knew just the thing that would send her into a frenzy. But how could that be? No one uninitiated knew the secret. She let her breath out in defeat. A soul-mate would know, would have an instant roadmap to her body, just like he'd stumbled upon an immediate trail to her heart. All of it was working her mind way too hard.

He laughed when she sighed, trying to will his erection

away. This woman had him tied to her in a way no other woman ever had and he loved every minute of it. He laughed. She was going to be the death of him yet.

"The lady said she wanted it rare, not medium. If she wants the steak still mooing when you put the plate down, give it to her, so please take this one back."

"Thank you," Tara said quietly, ignoring the indignant look the diner waitress gave her. It was already late afternoon, and she sat in the local diner they had found and studied Rider. She'd bitten the man so hard that the side of his neck had a huge purple blotch on it. She was just thankful there weren't puncture marks. The sunglasses he'd bought her had helped, and every once in a while he would stare at her hard and ask if she was all right. It made her smile. She was flattered that he was so anxious to get back to the room that he was fidgeting with the silverware. She understood all too well, she could barely sit in the vinyl booth herself. His hair was still damp from the shower, and the heat in the diner and drips from his hair made his T-shirt cling to his torso. She watched the muscles in his shoulders work beneath the thin cotton fabric. Just looking at him was making her want to slide out of her seat.

Nobody had ever made her feel this way. At least not a man with a soul. He was a gift she wouldn't squander. She felt his caring all the way down to the bottoms of her feet. He was special. Suddenly she desperately hoped he'd be asleep by the time it got dark. Maybe the blood hunger wouldn't hit her so hard tonight. Maybe she could beat this thing and come out on the other side with a real life with someone who cared. As long as she didn't take his blood, they had a chance.

Lavender suited her. The dark rush of her skin against the pale color just twisted him in knots as he watched her practically inhale her steak. Just when he thought he had her all figured out, he learned something fabulously new about her.

He could almost see her coffee-brown nipples through the sheer fabric of her dress, could remember what every inch of her smooth skin felt like, and that scent, and the way she'd gathered up her hair into one easy-to-make-fall bun. He had to remember to stick his fork in his food and cut it, bring it up to his mouth, then chew it. Where she'd bitten him still burned and the signal resonated in his groin like reverb. It had been damn sexy. Suddenly he wasn't hungry anymore. Just watching her made a whole other hunger surface—the one he had for her.

But as he stared at her, many thoughts came to his mind. Reality was trying to blow the groove. He could hear them talking about rains hitting Texas soon. He was traveling by bike. Before her, that wouldn't have been a problem, yet there was no way he could put her on his bike in a driving rain. And if they had to hole up for a few days in a motel, that would eat into his shrinking budget.

The original plan had been to hit the races in Arizona, the money in his pocket was for incidentals, Snake was gonna cover his room and board . . . which meant that he needed a way to make some cash along the way to travel with her right. He couldn't take her to the roadside joints he and the fellas would crash at. He couldn't take her to some biker hangout trailer in the back woods where for a pound of weed they could stay for free and drink.

The preacher had had a point: they had to keep to the main highways, especially if they were on the move at night. And it wasn't about getting some side mechanic work around these parts—everybody knew how to go under the hood. Being a good mechanic was a matter of supply and demand. In L.A. there were a lot of cars and a lot of people who didn't know squat about how to fix them. But in no-man's-land, everybody could fix their car, do plumbing, carpentry work, hunt and shoot, and pretty much do whatever needed to be done—or they had a brother or cousin who could.

Rider rubbed his face with both palms. A cigarette was calling his name, so was Jack Daniel's. Since he'd put out the last butt before he'd gotten to the preacher's house, he hadn't even broken the seal on the carton he'd bought in town. He looked at Tara as she ate the last of her steak. Riding with a woman in tow was much more expensive, was much slower, but worth every damned minute. The question was, how to make it work?

"You look tired," she said, dabbing the corners of her mouth with a napkin.

"Just need a smoke," he said, stretching and trying to let his brain rest.

"I wish you wouldn't do that," she said quietly. "It's bad for your health, and I want you to live for a long time."

He wanted to lean across the table and kiss her, but thought better of it, given where they were. He smiled instead. "I'm going to live forever, don't you know that, darlin'?"

Her eyes held his, suddenly deadly serious. "Do you want to?"

Desire slammed him full force. "With you? Yes . . ." He could feel desire come back with a vengeance. "Let's get out of here. We can hit the road tomorrow morning."

"We might have to travel at night," she said with hesitation. "I'm better then, have more energy. Sometimes the sunlight saps my strength."

He smiled and allowed his gaze to rake her. Then he leaned forward and dropped his voice to a low, private murmur. "You don't need strength. You just hold on, baby, and leave the driving to me."

She just shook her head and smiled.

CHAPTER 5

She'd set a slow flame to every inch of him; had left no section of him unbranded. There had been moments during the night when he knew he was losing consciousness. She'd made obscure parts of him literally come alive in her mouth . . . the veins at his wrist, the insides of his elbows. When she'd nuzzled his femoral artery going down on him, he'd nearly blacked out. If this was what they taught healers, he'd convert to whatever religion her people espoused and would smoke peyote and live the quiet life. If she wanted him to go on a spirit walk in the wilderness, so be it, just as long as she kept loving him like this.

Even as he briefly slept, she was inside his head, calling him, loving him, arching under his hold. He'd ejaculated in his sleep, and had awakened to her kiss at his throat, which only started the whole crazy thing all over again. He couldn't stop if he'd wanted to; could no more reach for that damned box in the bag across the room if his life depended on it. Right now she was air. Right now she was the very blood in his veins. She was his pulse. Was his heartbeat, and the reason to draw another breath. Crazy about her didn't begin to define or do justice to what had happened. He'd lost his mind completely, and didn't care one whit that he had.

He pulled his mouth away from her neck, his hands

threaded through her dark tendrils as he peered up at her, exhausted.

"Are you all right?" she whispered, giving him a sexy, sated smile before gently kissing him. "I'm not scaring you yet, am I?"

"No," he murmured. "Just don't stop."

"I have to get some rest. It's going to be dawn in a couple of hours. You have to rest, too, if we're going to push on from here."

He flipped her to lie beneath him, looking down at her, his arms trembling at either side of her shoulders. "You are so beautiful," he whispered. "You have this effect on me that I can't explain . . . I'm sorry I lied to you when I said I'd pull out. Baby, I meant to every time, but couldn't. You're like an addiction."

She smiled and touched the side of his face, totally understanding what he was trying to say, and wishing with all her heart that she'd met him before. From the first time she laid eyes on him, she knew he was *the one*, just like his hazel irises now glittered with open desire. His pupils were dilated and every stroke of her hand made him shiver. Her gaze traveled down the broad chest, and her hands caressed his thick shoulders and trailed down his strong, trembling arms. And his hands . . . pure strength and yet gentleness resided within them. She'd lost her voice too many times to count at the mercy of those hands.

She rubbed her legs up against his hard ones, reveling in the sensation as she slid one delicate foot over the tight steel of his buttocks. She watched new tears form in his eyes as he closed them and allowed his head to hang back. There was so much that she needed to tell him, so much truth she'd already told him that he just hadn't heard.

"When you look at me like that, it just runs all through me. You have no idea . . ." His voice had come out on a ragged murmur as he began moving against her again. "Just one more time."

She let her body answer his request. She could feel his soul bound so tightly with her own that she couldn't speak. They had shared the same dreams; he was inside her mind and heart as deeply as he was inside her body. They had lived a similar life, being different, gifted with something special, misunderstood and feared, yet this man with a good heart had found her. They were opposites in so many ways, but so much the same. He was tall, she was short; she was dark, he was light; they were both on the run, had no family to speak of, were protecting each other, wanted a better life. Respect was the common glue, and she tried to siphon away all the hurt and pain and misery his life had been before her through her touch and her bites, without breaking his skin.

He'd tasted every part of her, had revered every inch of her skin, the heat of his mouth searing her. Every one of his shudders was hers. Every sensation traveling down his spinal cord, she felt. Every time he'd orgasm, he'd send her hurtling into a multiple spasm of ecstasy of her own. How was she going to disappear one night and leave this, leave him? They had to find a cure. Time was speeding up, and he was slowing it down as though he could stop it just for them.

Yet, as his hand covered one of her breasts and his lips found the other and he moved against her, the issue of time slid from her mind . . .

He blanketed her again and thrust hard. She gasped his name. He responded with a hard bite at her throat and she saw colors behind her lids. He moved against her smooth, controlled, slow, then he lost that control, his voice disintegrating into grunting chants of passion.

She couldn't stop her own panting, couldn't catch her breath, and couldn't stop the release that she was edging toward. She felt her incisors lower.

She arched hard, the crown of her head digging into the mattress, and she ran her tongue over her incisors to send them away, the razor edge of them cutting her tongue and drawing blood. Oh, no . . . It was starting, but she couldn't stop. He felt so good, her hands were shaking as she clutched at his back. Warm, salty blood filled her mouth. She screamed and he heaved in jerking spasms, then dropped on her like a dead weight.

It took her a moment to extricate herself from beneath him. She had to get out before he came back to himself completely. She needed to feed and she refused to feed from him.

Rider stirred, and blindly reached out for Tara, but drew his hand back, wanting. He slowly opened his eyes and looked at the clock. It was after checkout time. He pushed himself up slowly, yawned, and listened for her. Water was running. He relaxed and leaned forward on both forearms as his feet hit the floor. It felt like he had a hangover. Every inch of him was sore and reminded him of how much he'd abused his body. If he felt like that, then he could only imagine how Tara felt. Guilt swept through him. She was only a little, bitty thing, too. But heaven knew there was no way to control this wild relationship they had going.

He indulged his senses and pulled a deep inhale . . . The whole room smelled like her and sex.

The scent was staggering. It would always draw him to her like a bloodhound. He laughed—oh, yeah, he was whipped. She owned him. He'd heard about getting zapped with feminine mojo, but he'd never known it could be like this. He just hoped she felt the same way. Damn if he wasn't falling in love.

It took him two attempts to stand, and he squinted at the bright sunrays that were trying to push past the edges of the drapes. Yeah, he could understand her sensitivity to light.

He crossed the room and tapped on the door lightly. He rested his head against it, needing something sturdy to help hold him upright. "Tara, baby, I know this is a little strange, but I really need to get in there for a minute."

He waited, but she didn't answer. He knew women had delicate sensibilities about things like this, so he walked in a circle and tried her again.

"Honey, this is an emergency. Seriously."

"Okay," she said, her voice frail. "I'm in the shower."

Without hesitation he went into the dark room, not questioning the fact that the bathroom lights were out. That was a godsend, because his eyes couldn't take it, either. He put the seat up and stood before the porcelain throne holding the wall with one outstretched hand and holding himself as gingerly as he could, sighing with relief. There were some things a man could do blind, and he'd had plenty of practice taking dead aim the morning after a long night in a bar. He almost laughed at the thought; she was way better than Jack Daniel's, or anything else.

"If I flush, am I gonna mess up your water?" He'd even put down the lid. Oh, yeah, he was whipped.

"No, go ahead," she said quietly and turned off the tap.

"Good," he murmured, completing the task, then moving to the sink to wash his hands. Some breakfast, a cup of joe . . . more sweet lovemaking.

"Oh, what a night . . ." He almost fell asleep standing up at the sink with the water running. "I don't know if I can ride this morning; it's already past checkout, too." He leaned his forehead against the mirror, hoping that she'd understand his double meaning.

When she didn't answer he pushed away from the mirror, splashed some water on his face, and looked up. To his horror the only light in the room were two glowing orbs behind him that were her height. He froze.

"Don't be afraid," she said quietly. "But I can't go out in the sun anymore."

He spun so fast that he almost shattered the mirror with his elbow as he slapped on the light.

She immediately covered her eyes with her hands and turned away. "Turn it off!"

"Oh, *bull*shit," he said, backing toward the door and touching the sides of his neck.

Her body looked normal, except that she was shivering and had goose bumps covering her skin. His gaze scanned her frantically, while hovering in the doorway ready to bolt.

She turned to him slowly, and brought her hands away from her face in gradual increments. She looked like she was about to keel over. Half of him wanted to go to her; the other half of him was transfixed where he stood. She looked like a junkie. Her beautiful eyes had dark circles under them. Her gorgeous lips were nearly blue. Her once-fantastic coloring was ashen, and her hair looked wiry and brittle. He almost wept as he went to her.

"Oh, Jesus, what's the matter?"

She pulled away from him and cringed when his fingers trembled at her cheek.

"I'm so sick," she whispered. "I have to get there before it's too late."

She felt for his hand when he extended it, as though she were blind, and he helped her out of the tub and sat her down on the toilet seat, then lifted her chin with his finger and stared into her eyes. Her once-beautiful eyes had a bluish-gray seal over them like an old person's with cataracts.

"I'm blind," she whispered, feeling for his face. "I opened the curtain and the sunlight . . ." Her voice broke off with a sob.

He turned her throat to the side and saw two puncture marks on it and ran his fingers over the fresh wound. "Did I do that? Did I do that to you last night? Oh, shit!" He turned her wrists over, and then looked at the insides of her elbows, terror coursing through him by the second. Every major pulse point on her was scored, and witnessing it dropped him to his knees. His head found her lap. "Oh . . . baby . . . I swear I didn't mean to hurt you like that. I don't even remember."

"You didn't do it," she whispered, absently stroking his hair. "I went out last night while you slept."

Her confession snapped his head up and he looked at her blind eyes, holding her upper arms tightly. "What!"

"I needed human blood," she said quietly. "There are only a few ways to get it."

He stood slowly and then sat on the edge of the tub. There were no words. His mind couldn't process the madness fast enough. What was she talking about! Some crazy ritual?

"If I take an innocent, I'm damned. You're an innocent, Rider. Last night, I felt my gums rip. The teeth didn't come all the way down, and I haven't died, so I have time. But the hunger is like an acid burn inside your intestines that will eat them away until you satisfy it. The animal blood isn't working anymore. That's why I keep throwing up; even the steak didn't stay down. When the hunger came, I could feel it coming back up, so I left the room . . . I didn't want to hurt any of the townspeople—they're innocents, too. So I had to get real blood the only other way . . ."

"What the hell is that?" he said, standing quickly.

"I went to the one who made me like this, and fed from his veins."

The incomprehensible lodged in his throat. Irrational jealousy swept through him as he looked at her bite marks; the one by her femoral artery twisted him up the most. She instinctively knew where his gaze had traveled and she tried to hide the wound with her hand. He instantly understood her erogenous zones, and why a kiss at her throat would make her shudder. It was a painful comprehension that carved a section out of his brain. He didn't know how he knew, but he did.

His fist went through the bathroom door and came away bleeding. She swallowed hard, as though the scent were making her salivate. He now understood what she'd been telling him all along. He had some insight into how these things that were hunting her did a blood transaction. He watched her literally pull her blind gaze away from his bloodied fist and begin rocking.

Yet, the more she rocked with tears streaming down her face, the more his pulse points lit with a desire that was nearly beyond his will to fight. Her bottom lip quivered and the sensation made him want to offer her his throat. She pressed her knees together tightly and dropped her head back; he felt the phantom sensation of entering her sweep through his groin so brutally that he had to hold on to the edge of the sink and breathe through his mouth.

"I never meant to hurt you," she said on a choked whisper. "I tried to tell you, tried to warn you that you needed protection . . . and whatever you're feeling, it wasn't a feeding seduction. I wanted to make love to you for who you are, not for what you have . . . not for your blood."

A sense of violation spiked his fury, as he bitterly understood that there was a difference between an outright attack, and a seduction to feed. He wanted in the worst way to believe what she'd said, but as he began to hear his own pulse in his ears and she quietly moaned in a way that sent a hard spasm through his groin, he just couldn't.

"You want me to open up a damned vein, Tara? Answer me, now! Is that what you want me to do?" A sob cut off his words. He looked at her as she blindly followed the sound of his voice. "Because if that's what you need, baby . . . I'll do it—just ask, but you come to me." He wiped his eyes with the back of his hand. "Don't ever go to that sonofabitch again!"

He held his skull with his fists. What was he saying! Then he watched her wrap her arms around herself and begin crying so hard that all he could do was turn into the broken door and sob. That was when he knew he'd spend the rest of his life hunting down these demons. He'd devote his existence to wiping every one of them from the face of the planet. They'd taken the only thing from him that really mattered, and he was helpless to do anything for her but bring her to some old Indian medicine men in the hills. He pounded on the door and pushed away from it. He refused to give her up without a fight. This was war.

"Listen to me," he finally said, collecting himself. "If you rest by day, will you have enough strength to ride at night?"

She nodded and covered her face with her hands for a moment, then put them in her lap. "But only if I have blood." She gazed in his direction. "But it's not safe for you. My mother allowed me to drink from her when I first went into the fever. Then she and a small group went after these creatures, and . . ." Her voice trailed off. "She was killed. I can't have something like that on my conscience. I can't have it happen to you. You have to believe that you mean more to me than that."

Rider walked out of the bathroom and yanked on his jeans and his boots, then glanced at his pocketknife. She'd warned him; that was true. She could have ripped out his entire throat last night—he wouldn't have cared—and yet she never even broke his skin. Instead she'd gone to the one who had made her, rather than put him in harm's way.

Half of his brain told him to make a run for it. He paused, catching sight of himself in the mirror above the dresser. He saw the places where she'd bitten him but found no evidence of puncture wounds. He touched his throat, remembering the loving caresses she'd placed there, how she'd pulled away every time—unlike him. He hadn't been able to control himself nearly as well. Perhaps she'd been more responsible than him?

He picked up his knife and slowly walked back to the bathroom with it. He flicked it open with a quick flip of his wrist.

"What are you doing?" she asked, shivering.

"I'm feeding you," he told her, his voice quiet and strained as he made a fist.

She shook her head no and tried to stand. "If I take it right from your vein, I'll infect you, too. That's why I tried so hard not to all last night." Her voice had come close to hysteria. "Please. *Don't.*"

"Then I'll bleed it into a plastic cup," he said without emotion, taking one off the sink and pumping his fist. "You'll sleep in here so the daylight doesn't hurt you. I'll stand watch at the door. I'll give you the blankets off the bed. But as soon as night falls, we ride."

He ignored her tears as he made the cut, and couldn't look at her as the slow oozing color trickled from his wrist and made almost too loud slats into the plastic cup. He wrapped a used towel around his wrist and put the cup into her shaking hands. He left the bathroom as she brought it to her lips. He couldn't see for the tears as he swept up the blankets and sheets and pillows. The smell of her and them and their lovemaking made him bury his face in the bed linens. If she didn't come back from this, he'd die for her, for sure. He couldn't even think about it. He simply went back into the bathroom, made a small pallet on the floor, and turned off the light as he shut the door.

For the remainder of the afternoon, he made bullets, then dozed with his gun on his lap. As soon as the sun set, he heard the shower go on, but didn't flinch. His mind and soul were so weary that he just glanced up at her slowly when she came out and put on her jeans.

They packed only what was necessary. She reminded him to bring his guitar. At first, he tensed when she wrapped her arms around him after climbing on the bike, then he relaxed. This was still Tara, the woman he loved, an innocent who had been infected.

He was committed to her for better, for worse, for richer for poorer, in sickness and in health. All he had to do was get her down Route 666 in New Mexico to where the Navajo knew what to do. That's what he kept telling himself as he crossed the border into North Texas. That's what he told himself as he found a place to hide her before dawn. That's what he told himself when he became very afraid.

But each day was worse than the one before. It took more blood to rouse her, more effort to wake her at sunset. She was always cold now, her complexion always gray. By the time he hit the edge of the reservation lands, she could barely hold on to him as they rode, she was so weakened.

He swept her up in his arms and carried her to the first house he saw, but he didn't speak the old men's language and they just shook their heads. Dogs backed away. The old men sighed, and an elderly woman walked down the dusty path speaking in urgent unintelligible phrases.

Rider looked into her dark, leathery face, searching her deep brown eyes.

"I don't speak Navajo," he said, his voice breaking, but he held Tara close with one arm and dug into his jeans pocket and produced the paper she'd once given him.

The old woman shook her head and called out. A young boy no more than five or six appeared. Rider looked from the child to the elderly woman, confused, but desperate enough to try to learn whatever he could.

"She says her grandma moved to higher ground. Arizona."

The old woman said more words that Rider couldn't decipher while the child listened intently to her. Then the boy looked up at Rider.

"She left something for you and her." The child pointed to Tara's limp body. "Knew a guardian would protect her. Said a bad wind was coming." Then the child ran away.

"Where in Arizona?" he shouted to the old woman before him. Frustration and terror were making his ears ring.

She walked away slowly and met the young boy and took something dangling from his hands. Then she shuf-

fled back unhurried and looped a small leather pouch over
his neck and one over Tara's.

Rider stared down at what was given him. It was a
leather pouch on a long tether that had some type of herbs
and sandy-feeling stuff inside it. The outside of the bag
around his neck had silver and turquoise pieces inter-
spersed with long eagle feathers, short hawk feathers,
and what looked like some sort of animal tooth. On his
there was a jade cross, on Tara's there was a silver medicine wheel with turquoise and jade stones set in it. He
almost cried. He'd ridden hard for all those miles for an
asafoetia bag? This was bullshit. The child gave him a
crumpled-up piece of paper with the new address on it and
he tucked it away, then brushed Tara's forehead with a kiss.

Without a word, he trudged back to the first house
where the old men were sitting on the porch, produced a
twenty-dollar bill and pointed to the dilapidated truck in
the road and toward his bike.

"Where's the nearest medical center? A doctor?"

One of the old men chewed his pipe, stood slowly and
simply walked down the steps toward the truck with a sigh,
waving away Rider's money.

"How bad is she, Doc?" Rider said, clasping Tara's hand
and brushing her hair away from her forehead, and then
looking into a pair of old, wise blue eyes.

"There's probably some type of acid in that thing they
put around her neck, the way it's burning her chest," the
doctor said with disgust. He lifted it away from her skin
with two fingers, exposing a large red blister between her
breasts. "Take it off her and give it back to her family.
Superstition drives me nuts with these people." He raised
Tara's lids and looked at her dilated pupils and roughly
took the bag off, thrusting it toward Rider. "What's she
on?"

"Nothing. She has a blood disease," Rider said carefully, accepting the bag and putting it in his vest pocket. The wise eyes were failing him; total defeat had a stranglehold on him. This man didn't understand.

The doctor's eyes met his. "Do you think I'm crazy?" he snapped, pointing at the holes in her flesh and then at Rider's wrist bandages. "For the love of Christ, what's she shooting up on with you? If you want her to come out of this coma, you're gonna have to come clean and stop playing games and help us. Time is of the essence, young man!"

"I don't know what it is," Rider told him honestly. "But can you give her a blood transfusion, or something, to bring her back?"

"We're gonna give her a pint, because she's obviously anemic, then run some blood tests to determine what's in her system. She might be borderline OD, or have some sort of viral staph infection, or hepatitis from using dirty needles . . . but I've never seen injection sites so large. It looks like she was shooting up with a ballpoint pen."

He swished away from Rider, ordering the blood work and telling the nurses to give Tara a blood pint, and to keep her hydrated with an IV drip while on oxygen.

"Why don't you go have a drink and sit this one out?" a nurse said offhandedly, as she came into the room and began studying Tara's chart, but not looking at Rider when she spoke. "If she passes, does she have any next of kin?"

He just stared at the short, squat woman who had cold gray eyes. "I'm all she's got," he said just below a whisper.

"Fine job you did taking care of her." The nurse shut the chart with a snap. "How old is she?"

"Eighteen," he said, staring out the window.

"You two married?"

"No."

"Then you *ain't* next of kin." The nurse sighed with impatience. "You got insurance?"

He shook his head and dug into his pocket, producing two hundred dollars.

The nurse looked at him hard and accepted the bills, handing him back fifty dollars. "Put some gas in your tank and ride to wherever the hell her family is and go git 'em. That won't even cover the blood work, but by law, since she came in here under emergency conditions, we can't turn her away—even if she's a wetback."

"I'll go make more money and cover the bill. Just give her the best." He looked at the small form lying prone in the bed. "She has a grandmother that I have to go find. The old woman doesn't have a phone." He dug in his vest pocket and thrust the crumpled paper at the nurse. He'd already burned the new address into his memory.

"What's Tara's last name?"

He stared at the indignant woman before him and then headed toward the door. "Ma'am, I don't truly know."

A bad wind was coming, that was no lie. He knew it as soon as he'd put Tara on a gurney and the white coats had taken her away. But they were hooking up blood to her arm when he'd left—that was all he could do. At least she was somewhere safe, where there were professionals, where there weren't dust and rain and things that slithered in the night. Unshed tears stung the back of his throat and mixed with Jack Daniel's as he sat at the local bar, oblivious to the music, the crowd, everything.

Time had been his enemy. If he'd had more time, he would have sat out on a porch with her and brushed her lovely hair in the moonlight. If he'd had more time, he would have used his hands to build her that cabin she'd told him she'd dreamed about . . . the one in the woods, decorated with her people's art, the ancient ones. And still, time was preciously slipping away just like he could feel she was. The gun in his waistband felt so heavy. He'd have to go get her before morning, before the sun started to blister her beautiful brown skin, or blind her for good. But once he'd delivered her to what he thought was a medical sanctuary, time had sped up as the professionals around her slowed down, searching for answers that no one had.

A familiar voice laughed loudly and made him turn around on his stool easy. Crazy Pete was walking in the door with Snake and the rest of the gang, missing five. Rider stood slowly, trying to allow his mind to catch up to the images. He'd seen one of them die, and after what he'd been through, he knew the rest of them had died, too. He could now identify that metallic taste on the back of his throat. It was the smell of living death. Eyes that knew his met him, and heads nodded with sly recognition. He carefully set down his money for the bartender and glanced around for an alternate exit. As soon as he looked back toward the main entrance, they were gone.

The medical center stabbed into his temple. He moved toward the front door so fast that he nearly took out a waitress who'd been carrying drinks. He dashed toward his bike and then stopped as the shadows moved. Snake stepped out of the darkness with Crazy Pete, then Razor, and Bull's Eye, until his old squad formed a ten-man horseshoe ring around him.

"You left us, Rider," Snake said, his eyes glowing. "Thought we was going all the way to the limit, one gang, one road?"

"Plans changed," Rider said, the muscle in his draw arm twitching.

"There's only one way to save her, man," Crazy Pete said. "Don't knock it, till you've tried it."

It was reflex, not a thought. The light caught Pete's fang and made it glisten, Rider unloaded his revolver dead aim. Pete, Razor, Snake, center-of-the-skull hits, exploding them into ash and cinders. Two more of his boys lunged from either side, and took a bullet in the center of their chests on a quick pivot shot. Rider immediately spun, the hairs on the back of his neck registering the slightest movement, and he caught Bull's Eye mid-flight as he came down, burning.

"He's got that shit hanging on his chest. Don't reach for him, he's poisoned," one of the remaining creatures said, nodding toward the bag around Rider's neck. "Later, we'll settle up."

Later indeed. Rider was still pulling the trigger as they disappeared. Instantly he heard commotion behind him and knew it was time to ride. There were no bodies, just ash and the distinct smell of burning remains. He was gone before anyone could get a good look at him or his bike, and way before the sheriff's sirens ever sounded.

He reloaded his weapon and sat by her side all night, intermittently arguing with the authorities about at least allowing her to be in a dark room before morning came. Then security ushered him to the door with a brawl that drew the sheriff. He had one option: be cool, or do a night in a cage.

But all of that was for naught when the doctor came out and shook his head at dawn. Rider looked up. He was so defeated that he couldn't even cry. The only thing that made it all right was that they finally let him go in and see her. And she seemed so peaceful, like a sleeping baby. Her color was back, her beautiful eyes were shut, long black lashes dusting her high cheeks. Her once-agonized expression had disappeared as her facial muscles relaxed when she'd passed. He stroked her hair and it was velvet again.

"I'm so sorry that we ran out of time." He put his head on her chest and closed his eyes, hoping that she'd heard his whisper.

"We found something that we've never seen," the doctor said, his tone subdued. "There were no drugs in her system, and we'll have to send her work up to the Centers for Disease Control. If you can make contact with her family, they may have to wait for the body until we can determine that what she's carrying wasn't communicable."

"It wasn't," Rider said hoarsely. "Something bit her—that's the only way you can get what she had." He kept his back to the doctor as he drew away from her and just stared down at his heart—her.

Tears ran down his nose and splattered her face, and he kissed her so gently as he said a private goodbye in his mind. He branded her peace-filled expression into his memory, then stepped back, sucked in a ragged breath, and brushed past the people who wouldn't listen.

He rode hard and wild. The promised Texas rains did come and they also pelted New Mexico, but that didn't stop him. He found the Arizona door that had the number he was looking for in Sedona. He knocked hard and dragged on a cigarette and waited.

A striking woman with silver hair opened it. She could have been Tara's body double with wrinkles and an additional fifty pounds. He looked at her hard and cast away the smoldering butt with fury balled into his fists. The tears glittering in her eyes only made him angrier.

"I brought her to you!" Those were the first words out of his mouth. "But you moved and left her!" He thrust the medicine bag that had been around Tara's neck into the old woman's hands. "What about her destiny?"

The woman before him nodded and tucked the bag into her blue calico apron. The color of it nearly made him sob.

"She fulfilled her destiny," she murmured. "I didn't have the heart to tell the child what it was. Even my own daughter wouldn't listen, and tried to intervene . . . I lost her, too."

"What are you talking about?" he yelled, a sob catching in his throat as he opened his arms.

"The Ojibwa as far away as Wisconsin said the time is near when the rivers run with poison and the fish are no longer fit to eat. Each clan has their own version of the legend, all the ancient peoples know the truth. We Cherokee have a version. The stories are different, but the message is the same. The time is now. For fifty thousand years before the invaders came, there was harmony, and—"

"What the hell does that have to do with Tara and me!"

She continued to hold him in a calm, tender gaze. "Her destiny was to make you a warrior so that you can guard the Great Huntress. Every destiny is intertwined and woven together in the grand loom. Hers was to make you see your worth, your gift, and to show you the undead . . . and to make you understand how that beast functions so you can fight it one day for the Neteru as a part of that family . . . and yes, what I told her was true. She showed you the power of love, of hope, of faith in things unseen but known. Tara was your soul mate, but her destiny was to heal you and then leave you. Her purpose was to guide you to your destination, not to be your destination. Hers was an honorable sacrifice. She will be remembered as a guardian, too. Her body will never go to ash in the sun like the others. She was stolen. But I knew that by the time she got to New Mexico, it would already be too late. That's why we moved to higher ground to await you. Your purpose has just begun. Go to Los Angeles and play your guitar."

Tara's grandmother's calm acceptance of fate tore him to shreds on the porch.

"Don't you understand—*she* was my Neteru. She was my family. She was my breath. There is no other." He turned and walked away, headed down the steps. "She was my purpose, and the only one I'll ever guard," he said quietly. Right now, he couldn't even breathe.

"When she comes to you again, put her soul at peace. They gave her blood in the hospital and she died. They will never understand, but you must. She will come to you because she loves you so."

He looked over his shoulder as he walked off the last

step, but stopped and turned around. He couldn't take another minute of this crazy talk. Tara was dead and had never transformed into the creatures he'd seen. He flung the admission paper from the hospital on the ground. "You can get her body and bury it in hallowed ground. They wouldn't let me have it. I never got a chance to do the honorable thing and marry her like I'd wanted to. I'm not her next of kin."

The old woman nodded but didn't go near the paper as it blew away. "Remember the young boy who gave you my address?"

"Yeah. So?"

"His name is José Ciponte. Remember it. His grandfather gave you a lift to the doctor's. There are no accidents, no coincidences." She sighed and wiped her eyes. "If you ever encounter . . . if you should wake up one morning and the sun hurts your eyes, come to me, or the boy—during the day."

She left him standing in her front yard and went into the house, but left the door open.

One day's ride, and he was already out of gas. What did it matter, anyway, at this point? His plan was simple: hustle up a few dollars doing odd jobs, twenty dollars here, ten dollars there, sit in the town library and read as much as he could about this thing called a vampire . . . find a little hallowed earth to ring him and sleep in the wilderness. He didn't need food, just a bottle of Jack a day. Maybe God would be merciful and let him die of alcohol poisoning before he got to L.A.

By the third night stuck in the same sleepy town, the only thing that kept him sane was refining that song that he couldn't get out of his head. He didn't even look up when he heard a twig snap. If it was the rest of his old gang coming to settle a score, so be it. He had questions he wanted to ask them, anyhow, before he died.

"You're still playing," a soft female voice said.

He looked up fast but set his guitar aside slowly. He was on his feet in seconds, but then noticed that she stayed just beyond the ring. Tears of recognition stung his eyes and he swallowed them thickly, then went to the ring and opened a small path in it with his boot. He took off the bag that he always wore and cast it near his guitar.

"Don't do that," she said quietly, her eyes glittering in the firelight. "I've crossed over."

He nodded. "I know. I don't care."

"You always said that . . . and I'd always tell you that in the morning, you would." She smiled at him and shook her head, the tears in her eyes sparkling in the moonlight.

He stared at her as she backed away and he came outside the ring. "I've missed you so much that at times I've stopped breathing."

She stood very, very still. "I've missed you, too. More than you'll ever know."

For a moment they said nothing, then she came to him and placed both hands on his chest, but wouldn't let him hug her. Old desire fused with new desire, but it was all so fragile they handled it like fine china—too delicate to grasp tight. So they set it down easy between them and waited.

"You feel warm," he said, but wouldn't ask how that could be. He knew the answer, and left it alone. They were beyond that. It didn't matter.

"You have to stop smoking," she murmured, then inhaled deeply, coughed and spat.

He could feel where she touched him burn and then go cool.

"The addiction is gone. I love you and want you to live a long time."

"Don't take all of my human shortcomings away," he said with a sad smile, and traced her cheek. She was still so beautiful and gentle, no matter what she'd become.

"I didn't," she said, smiling. "I left Jack Daniel's alone."

"And the other one?" he asked, moving closer to her.

"I don't have a cure for that . . . we share that addiction."

"Good." He lifted her hair off her shoulders and stared into her deep brown eyes. "I'm going to build that cabin just how you wanted it. Might take me years, but it will be there for you . . . hallowed earth in a horseshoe, the front door never closed to you. Even if you only come there once a year on that date we met, I could live with that . . . just knowing you would be there." He brought his face closer. "I love you, Tara."

"I have to go."

He shook his head no. "You once asked me to make it last forever, now I'm asking you to do the same thing." He held her gaze and swallowed away the building emotion. "Don't leave me, because I can't ever leave you."

"I've never turned anybody into what I am . . . and if I do that to an innocent—"

"First off, I'm not just anybody. Second, as you know, I'm not so innocent. My choice." He kissed her gently, then deepened it, and scored her throat to make her gasp. "Don't you miss this? It's only been three nights away from you, and I feel like I'm dying . . . I'm not even counting all those days you were sick." He murmured against her temple as his hands slid down her arms and found her waist. "Without you, I'm already the walking dead. Can't you tell?"

Her fingers trembled as they touched the thick stubble at his jaw. "You still have the address that's just one day's ride from here?" she asked, nuzzling his neck as she melted against him.

"Yeah . . . your grandmother left the door open for me. So let's not lie to ourselves, or make promises about pulling out . . . how about if we compromise and just make it last all night."

* * *

She sat on the porch with an old man her age and a young boy, all three of them looking down the road. She stood calmly with effort as she heard the motorcycle before she saw it. She squinted against the sun; today was a very good day. Her dear friend chuckled as he hoisted the child off his lap and chewed the end of his pipe. He craned his neck but held the child's hand tightly.

"Today," he said in English to the boy, "we will learn how to heal a broken heart, and take out undead poison."

They said nothing as a young man with a black vest brought his bike to a wobbling stop and fell bleeding in the front yard dust. The threesome looked at the puncture holes in his neck, unfazed.

"The lost guardian is back," the old woman said with a chuckle and proceeded down the steps to collect the wounded. "And so it begins."

EPILOGUE

He took his time lathering his face with the barber's brush, then brought the straight razor to his throat, willing away the erotic sensation that was always there. Some things just took time and patience, or a man could get himself nicked. He listened to the lather make hard plops against the porcelain sink, but kept his focus on the razor as he removed the last of the blond and gray stubble from his jawline, then watched it all go down the drain as he turned on the tap. He bent and splashed his face with water and stood slowly, his eyes meeting the mirror, searching for the ones behind him in the master bathroom that were never there. Force of habit. Some things a man could never forget.

Everything still reminded him of her.

He dried his face and went into the next room, and glanced at the jade cross on his bedroom dresser, then touched the long eagle feather and short hawk feathers on the leather cord that held it. Spring always had the same effect on him, made him want to rush. But not today. He would take his time.

Rider went over to the wall-length mirrored closet and stepped into the spacious mini-chamber as he slid back the door and found a collarless black silk shirt, his black suede jacket, and pulled down a pair of black boot-cut jeans along with the Indian braided leather belt he only wore once a year. His custom-made Navajo black cowboy boots had already been polished. It was near time to ride.

He could hear the others moving about in the compound as he dressed, preparing to go into the studios to rehearse. Not today. He picked up his shoulder holster that held his old .357 and put it on after he buttoned his shirt. This was a process. A state of mind that required his total concentration. Getting ready always was. This was something the average human couldn't understand.

Rider ran a natural-bristle brush through his short hair, appraised himself with one glance, and put on his jacket. Checkbook in hand with the letters, he headed for the kitchen. He walked down the long corridor trying to keep his hands from trembling.

Thankful that there was no one else in the room, he sat at the huge oak picnic-length table of the guardian compound and finished writing out three checks; one destined to go to his mother, another his annual anonymous five-digit tithe to Bible Tabernacle in Oklahoma, and one destined to go to the woman who'd saved his life—Tara's grandmother. He sealed the letters with the checks inside them, gently tucking them away in his jacket pocket, then put on his black aviator sunglasses and headed down the hall to the music studio within the paramilitary-like complex.

"I won't be at practice tonight, gang. See you all Monday," he said in a somber tone, not fully entering the room. "I need to make a run."

Six sets of eyes looked at him and slowly put down their instruments. The one person he knew would protest was instantly on her feet. He just smiled. She was young, and had yet to begin to fathom how deep life and death could be. She wasn't even twenty-one, wouldn't be till summer, and was going to try to boss him. He could smell the fight coming. And she wasn't but an itty-bitty thing, trying to put her chin up to make herself seem taller, dark brown eyes blazing with frustration, long brown locks dancing at her shoulders as her head bobbed from side to side with her around-the-way-girl, East Side L.A. style . . . Was fussing at him like the daughter she'd become to them all. He knew her protest stemmed from love and worry. So he waited, with strained patience, knowing he'd been like her once. Uninitiated.

"Jake Rider, I'm serious. You are not getting on that motorcycle, gone for an entire weekend, without a way for us to get in touch with you. We've got this new CD to cut, a U.S. tour . . . might even get to go to Europe soon, if we play our cards right. At least take one of the fortified Hummers. And none of us deals with the night alone to risk a possible vampire attack. Ever. House rules."

"I'll be all right," he said, "just wanted you to know I was leaving so you wouldn't panic." This wasn't up for a vote; he was out. No convoy. This was a solo mission. Group consensus still sucked, even after all these years.

She glanced around the group for support, but found none from the older members of the team. Big Mike saluted him, José just gave him a cool nod, J.L. got up and stretched, Shabazz simply pounded his fist and started tuning his bass. Marlene stared at him, her wise, older-seer eyes appearing amused by the power struggle.

"Okay, now you're making me pull rank, Rider. As the Neteru," she said, putting her hand on her hip, "it's my job to make sure that all guardians make it through the night. Going up into the hills to wherever, alone, is crazy."

"Yep," he said, walking away.

"Yo, Damali, he's cool," José said. "It's something our brother has to do, you feel me?"

She sat down on a studio stool, hard. "I'd just *feel better* if he took more than that old Smith and Wesson when he went. The man isn't even strapped with a Glock, and won't wear a cell phone to save his life!"

* * *

Rider chuckled as he left Damali fussing and walked out into the bright, late afternoon sun. Freedom. It was an inalienable right that defied the requirement to explain.

He got on his old bike, and stomped down hard. His antique black and silver girl was still beautiful after all these years. He took good care of her, like he'd always promised himself he would. One day the young kid he was guarding would really understand what something like this was all about . . . she'd learn how to stop time for a moment and would appreciate the gift that that was.

The sound of the chopper became one with his pulse. Damali might be this era's Neteru, but there had definitely been one before her, to his mind. Her name was Tara. Only she didn't get to blow up the music charts with their band, Warriors of Light, or become a part of the nightly vampire-hunting team. Was a damned shame, but that was life. There was a pair of eyes missing from the group. The old Cherokee woman and her Creek partner had said seven were supposed to guard the Neteru. It still hurt his soul that it wasn't Tara's beautiful brown eyes begging him not to leave the compound.

But he chucked all that aside. Fate was what it was. The Native Americans had taught him to finally accept that.

Total freedom claimed him as the wind caught his jacket and whipped his clean-shaven face, but the helmet felt like an unnecessary black and silver anvil on his head. Long gone was his ponytail. The gray at his temples made some things passé. That, too, was fate. Time stopped for no man, that's why it was to be revered. Respected.

Everything from his era had changed, too . . . all the laws, even the women, unprotected sex could now kill you . . . drugs were no good—he didn't mess around anymore. It was too dangerous, worse than vampire hunting. Some things were worse than dying. He remembered telling Crazy Pete that with change came progress. Maybe he was wrong about a few things. But hey, what could he do? Too late to admit that truth to the bastard.

Rider kept his eyes on the road, wondering if the Ojibwa and Cherokees had been mistaken. Would there be anything left for seven generations to inherit after the people of peace took it all back?

Congested highways gave way to side roads, then narrow one-lane paths. Springtime was beautiful in the hills. He loved the way the grasses smelled, and as the scent of wild lavender caught him he almost sighed out loud. Heaven on earth. He found his private entrance to his secret property and rode a while, then stopped and parked his bike by his favorite tree by the lake.

It was a twenty-four-year old Indian redwood sapling that he'd put in as soon as he'd acquired the land, something that would live for at least a hundred years or more, like her. He crossed the ring of hallowed earth and knelt by it to say a quiet prayer, and then rearranged the bits of silver and jade and turquoise stones that formed a horseshoe border of hallowed earth in the mulch around its base. Maybe one night he'd finally have it within him to scatter her ashes by the tree that stood proud between his porch and the lake . . . just let her go free on a breeze . . . But not tonight. Some things took time to accept.

So he also took his time going up the front path of his cabin, trying to quell the nervous anticipation that ran through him on this same date every year. His gaze roved over the wide pine porch that he'd laid down by hand, one plank at a time . . . a twenty-year labor of love . . . a shrine to a memory, a promise kept the moment his money got right—the sacred place that still housed his old acoustic guitar and every bittersweet memory of her. His assortment of new electric Fenders could never replace the original, any more than a slew of flashy women on the concert trail could replace her.

Dead leaves were on the steps, and those had to be swept away, lest they'd blow across the hallowed-earth horseshoe from the sides and back of the house. The front path had to stay clear. Always. That, too, had been his promise, his superstition. It would be hours before sunset, and he'd have enough time to build a fire, light some candles, and go find his old acoustic guitar and relax, if that were possible. He just wished his old girl were there, too. Yeah, some things just took time to accept . . . it was a process.

Everything else, however, was just as he'd left it. He opened the door and punched in the alarm code, disgusted that he even needed such contraptions. But this was the new millennium. Indeed, much had changed.

Hours passed as he sat in a handmade oak rocker outside, tuning his axe, listening to the fire crackle through the screen, no porch light on, the fireflies enough for him. The rose-orange sun lit the lake; wild lavender from the flower beds along the front of the house and burning wood from the fireplace inside had enveloped him deep in thought, just like the music his hands softly stroked had. He listened to the crickets and the frogs, remembering the beauty the night held.

Where are you? he wondered. His hands coaxed her from his guitar, conjuring her from his memory using the one song that he'd never played for another living soul.

"You've gotten better each year," a soft voice said in the front path of the house.

He stopped playing and set his guitar down carefully, watching her materialize out of vapor as she walked toward him.

She signed his name as she came forward, her lush mouth practically breathing his name as she formed it with her graceful hands. "*Man with a good heart.* I missed you."

"I missed you last year, too," he said quietly and stood. "I thought something had happened to you." She'd worn a simple, elegant black sheath for him tonight. Each year as she matured she almost stole his breath. He signed the words as he spoke them in a soft rush. "I was *man with a broken heart* when you didn't visit." It was the bare truth, and he couldn't keep the tremor out of his voice when he said it. "Please don't do that to me again."

"We both live a dangerous life," she murmured, walking up the front steps. "There's a new master vampire in this region. I had to lay low, or become a part of his harem."

"Tell me where his lair is, and I'll deal with him like I dealt with that New Orleans problem you once had."

"I don't know where he keeps his main lair. I try to stay away from him, and don't even know his name. I'm low on the list; he has enough second- and third-generation females to keep him occupied before he senses me," she said quietly. "He hasn't called for me, yet." She let the last part of her statement hang in the air between them, trying to send him what that meant with her eyes; she hadn't violated their union. There was no one but him.

He knew it was irrational, but part of him was relieved and another part of him was offended. Tara was low on the list? And the word "yet" just jacked with his nerves.

"I'ma kill the bastard. You know that, right?"

"Yeah," she sighed. "But don't go after him alone."

"If he calls for you before I get to him, let me know. You might even make me get old-fashioned and pick up a crossbow for him, sugar."

"He's not a third- or fourth-generation like me, he's the real deal. Dracula era. Promise me you'll let this situation be. They say he is *literally* the fallen night."

Rider chuckled and cradled her face with his palm. "Remember, me and Mike did New Orleans during Mardi Gras, baby. Two-by-two detail; quick assassinations, then we were out. Don't worry. I'll be all right."

"I know, Rider, and thank you for everything. You didn't even have to do that. But to go after a master is something altogether different . . ."

"He made me miss my annual checkup," he said, grinning and warming to her stare. "The situation is personal now. The SOB has to go."

"Just be careful, honey. You're not as young as you used to be."

"Duly noted." Rider nodded and he could feel his smile fade as her hand touched the hair at his temple. Her gentle caress always had the amazing dual effect of relaxing him, yet also burning him. It was the same way with her eyes. "I am getting grayer every year, though. Thought that's why I didn't see you." He covered her hand and then kissed the center of her palm, turning into it, drawn to the irresistible softness of her skin.

"Your music gets better every year . . . I've been watching the magazines, you guys are hot." She chuckled and ran the ball of her thumb over his wiry eyebrow. "You can definitely shoot better . . . heard you're doing Glock nine millimeters with a clip when you guys go hunting these days. I'm impressed." She watched him remove his shoulder holster and drop his gun on the porch. "*Everything* you do has gotten better," she whispered, her voice becoming husky as he cast away the weapon that contained hallowed-earth shells. "Age brings refinement and finesse."

"But you were the first one who taught me how to load hollow-point shells," he said, closing the gap between them. "You're my first and only love. Time can't change that."

He coveted her smile and could tell that the honest admission meant a lot to her. "And twenty-four years have worn very well on you . . . you don't look a day over eighteen," he whispered, brushing her mouth and allowing his hands to slide down to her shoulders. "I also like what you've done with your hair," he added, filling his palms with her shorter, shoulder-length curls. He wondered what surprise she had for him under the black sheath. Two years ago she'd blown his mind with a white lace thong and garter combo. He never could tell what mysterious manifestation she'd gift him with.

She kissed him long and slow and wet and pulled back to look at him.

"I swear I feel twenty-one again when I'm with you, Tara."

"You always will be, to me . . . that way. Don't you know that by now?"

"Yeah," he said, chuckling as he draped his arm over her shoulder and led her into the house. He turned her to face him in front of the fire, loving the way it made her skin glow. "But I'm getting to be an old man. One night, you're going to have to fix that."

"Not tonight, though." She nuzzled his neck and enjoyed the light shudder it produced. "You've still got a lot of work left to do. Stop trying to seduce me."

"I've got Jack Daniel's in here . . . and in my system. Still got your grandmother's address. Even have an in-house guardian seer now, who's so good she detoxed my compound road dawg after he'd been to New Orleans with me on a hunt—although I do try to keep Marlene out of our business. So . . . you wanna talk about my retirement options over a drink?" He nipped her neck and made her sigh, then offered her his throat.

"Yeah," she said on a deep breath against his neck, "but let's not lock in that option for another twenty years. I'm not going there tonight."

She chuckled and nipped him, but didn't break his skin. "My grandmother is almost ninety-eight years old, and this wouldn't be a first-time-out bite on my first full night in the life. What I'd do to you would be coming from a forty-two-year-old woman . . . who's missed you terribly for two years—you want to give her a heart attack?"

The naked truth in her statement sent a hard wave of desire through him.

"Damn," he said on a heavy exhale as he nipped her shoulder. "I must be losing my touch."

"Oh, no, I guarantee you, you're not," she whispered, unbuttoning his shirt slowly.

"I keep waiting for you to lie to me, again," he said quietly, breathing in the fragrance of lavender in her hair and kissing her ear. "Keep waiting for you to lose it like you did that one time when we were kids in the woods . . . keep wanting you to tremble, close your eyes, drop fang . . . and whisper, 'Trust me, Jake, I'll pull out.' You make me lie to you like that annually, woman." He chuckled against her throat and listened to her swallow hard. "That's not fair."

They both laughed as she pushed him away from her neck, but not far.

"Cut it out," she said, a hint of fang now showing. "You're turning me on, and you know it. *That's* not fair. Don't dangle the temptation . . ."

He watched her run her tongue over her teeth and draw a steadying breath. The fact that he still had that effect on her after all these years twisted him in knots. He loved it. "All you have to do is ask . . ."

"Twenty-four years behind me, with eternity in front of me, has taught me patience," she murmured. "Now stop it, before I lose it and flatline you."

"As always, you're right. With age comes finesse," he said, now breathing through his mouth as he closed his eyes. "But I'm only human . . . and I love it when you get close to the edge like this. You have *definitely* perfected the art of patience. I'm still working on it."

It took a moment to stabilize herself. After twenty-four years he still knew how to make her hands tremble at his pulse points. Patience, have mercy; tonight she wasn't sure. She had to stop looking into his hazel eyes. It had been two years too long . . . if he didn't cut it out, she'd be in his bed every night—a very dangerous option to his destiny. But he wanted her so badly she could feel it through his skin. Hell, she wanted him so badly she was about to pass out.

Creating a diversion from the hunger in his eyes, she kissed down his chest and loosened his belt just to reduce the heat he created within her. But that didn't help much, either: it was supposed to put the whole situation on simmer; instead it had only turned up the flame. Damn . . . he smelled so good and felt even better. He'd aged *very* well. That was the last thing he had to worry about. She'd let him know in a way he wouldn't forget, would make sure he had no question that he'd become distinguished, more handsome, sexier. She dragged her nose across his muscular abdomen and felt it contract. She could hear his heart thudding faster as she'd done that, and it made her close her eyes tighter when they'd crossed beneath her lids.

"Let's compromise," she said in a hot whisper against his stomach. "I've perfected a few other things that take time." She looked up at him, pleased at the effect she was having on him. "I've learned how to make one night last forever."

He smiled as another shudder claimed him, thoroughly enjoying the effect he was having on her, just like old times. "Yeah . . . baby, so have I."

RED MOON RISING

LORI HANDELAND

CHAPTER 1

A red moon rising through a sultry evening sky is a rare and stunning sight. Such a moon will forever remind me of the first time I saw a skinwalker.

Staring at the nearly full moon lifting past the trees surrounding my isolated cabin, I shivered. I told myself I was spooked because I was alone. Growing up in a house filled with brothers, the word "alone" had never been in my vocabulary. Maybe that was why I chose to be a writer. I needed some quiet time.

However, living in Chicago, where every man in my family was a cop, I was lucky to get two minutes to myself. Another reason I'd escaped to Arizona.

Night pressed against the windows. I watched the trees and I waited. Something was out there, had been there every night of the seven since I had arrived. I'd never seen a thing, but I felt . . . watched. I might have blown off my unease as deadline fever, except every morning, in the damp earth at the edge of the clearing, there were tracks.

My cell phone shrilled, and I emitted a sound that was half gasp, half shriek. My heart thundered hard enough to make me dizzy as I punched the ON button. Before I could say hello, my agent started talking.

"Maya? Honestly, I've been waiting all day and half the night to call. I know how you hate to be interrupted when you're working. So, how's the book coming?"

I winced. It wasn't. I didn't have a word written. Hell, I didn't even have an idea. I also didn't have the advance I'd already been paid. I'd used the money to do a little thing I liked to call eating and sleeping off the streets.

I was in big trouble.

"Terrific, Estelle. Best work I've ever done."

"Uh-huh."

Estelle was no one's fool. Not even mine. Which was the reason I'd hired her.

"How many pages today?" she asked. "The book's due in a month, you know?"

I knew.

I glanced out the window again. The trees swayed. The moon pulsed. I was completely alone as I'd always dreamed of being. I had nothing to do but write. So why wasn't I?

Because my greatest fear had materialized. I'd lost it. Whatever the "it" was I'd had in the first place that allowed me to write some twenty action-adventure novels under the name M. J. Alexander.

I made a living. Kind of. I wasn't rich, and probably never would be, but I had a job I loved. Or at least I had until last week.

"I don't know why you felt the need to fly all the way to Arkansas," Estelle said.

"Arizona."

"Whatever."

Estelle, a born-again New Yorker, originally from New Jersey, was vague on the details of any place west of Trenton.

"You're so isolated there."

"I'm at the edge of the Navajo nation. There are thousands of people a stone's throw away."

A very long throw, to be honest. I hadn't seen a single Navajo, or anyone else for that matter, but she didn't need to know that.

"Don't they keep them behind a fence or something?"

"A reservation isn't a prison." Even though Estelle couldn't see me, I rolled my eyes. "The government granted the Navajos their homeland long ago."

Unlike many tribes that had been relocated to much crappier land than that which they'd been driven from, the Navajo resided on their traditional homeland. Damn near a miracle considering the U. S. of A.'s record in Indian affairs.

"I don't understand you anymore, Maya. You're not the adventurous type."

True. I'd always been safety girl, never take a chance, never rock the boat. I didn't ski; wouldn't own a skateboard. I drove the speed limit at all times. And skydiving? Yeah, right.

I'd behaved out of character by selling everything I had and moving halfway across the country. This was probably the biggest adventure I'd ever have, and I was already sick of it.

I liked my life to follow a plan; I didn't care for any surprises. Which was probably why my sudden writing block was freaking me out.

My family faced danger every day, so I preferred mine on a page, safely tucked away in a book. My mother had been killed going to the store for milk. She'd stepped off a curb and *bam*—out went her life. How's that for adventure?

Since I was six, whenever the phone rang, whenever someone knocked on the door, I caught my breath, expecting the worst. So what in God's name was I doing here?

I was desperate. I had to do something to jump-start the muse, and moving to the middle of nowhere was the most excitement a woman like me could withstand.

"I'll be fine, Estelle," I murmured, even though she wasn't really asking about me but the book, and I doubted the book would be fine. Still, I wasn't ready to admit that. Not yet.

I hit the END button, cutting off my agent mid-word. Then I powered down the phone and threw it onto the couch, before sitting down at the desk.

Blah, blah, blah, I typed onto the empty blue screen of my laptop.

"Well, at least I wrote something."

I'd taken to talking to myself a lot over the past week. If that kept up I just might be certifiable. At least then I'd have a reason to miss my deadline.

I picked up the headphones I always wore when writing. Listening to instrumental music kept out the real world and helped me focus on the fantasy one. Or at least it used to. Lately, I'd found myself hearing the music and not the magic.

Tossing the headphones onto the desk, I left the laptop behind, drawn again to the window. Tinged the shade of fresh blood, the moon made me uneasy. Was it an omen?

I snorted and rubbed my arms against the spreading chill of the night. Despite what I'd believed about Arizona, evenings were cool in the northern part of the state, at times reminiscent of the biting wind that blew off Lake Michigan even in the summer. I was used to cold, but that didn't mean I liked it.

A flicker of white in the night made me lean closer to the window. For an instant I thought I saw my own reflection, until the apparition on the other side of the glass grinned, exposing long, crooked, yellowing teeth that weren't my own.

I blinked and the face was gone. I couldn't breathe. Had that been my imagination or . . .

I glanced at the door, trying to remember if I'd locked it. The knob rattled, but didn't turn, answering both my questions. Not my imagination and I had locked the door. A better question might be: Why in hell hadn't I brought a gun?

Because I couldn't carry one on the plane. And that was good. That was right. But I'd give unimaginable amounts of money for the weight of a Glock in my hand.

Backing away, I worried the window might shatter, and then what would I do? I grabbed the fireplace poker and held up the iron rod like a bat.

The knob rattled again. "Who is it?" I shouted. "What do you want?"

A scratching came at the door, followed by pathetic, doglike whining. While what I'd seen through the glass hadn't looked completely human, the face hadn't been canine, either.

I crept closer to the door, heard a whisper, as faint as the trees rustling in the breeze, a word I couldn't quite make out. I was drawn closer and closer. I reached for the knob. The chill of the brass made me straighten and snatch back my hand.

"Uh-uh," I muttered. "I saw that movie."

As well as every other teen scream flick boasting an idiot heroine who opened the door and went outside, or down into the basement, maybe up the steps into the attic, where she met her horrific and bloody doom.

"I'll just stay in here with my cell phone and my fire-place poker, thank you."

As a kid, I wasn't supposed to watch those movies. But whenever my dad had been at work, my brothers had ruled, and they'd loved them.

An uneasy glance around the room and my eyes lit on my cell phone. I could call someone, but who? My family was thousands of miles away. Nine-one-one wasn't an option in this neck of the woods. I could dial the nearest sheriff's office, but what would I say?

I'd seen a face, heard a whisper. By the time the authorities arrived, whatever had been on the other side of my log-cabin walls would be gone.

I pulled a chair into the middle of the room and sat where I could see both the window and the door—for the rest of the night.

Morning came, along with my sanity. I *couldn't* have seen a face. Even if I had, it was probably some kid playing a joke. I refused to consider what a kid would be doing so far out in the wilderness. Right now, I didn't know what *I* was doing here.

Opening the door to bright sunshine, I kept the fireplace poker in hand. Just because idiot heroines got killed in the dark didn't mean I wouldn't get killed in the daytime. Still, I couldn't sit in the cabin forever, as much as I might like to.

I walked around to the window, knelt and discovered the clear impression of a man's bare feet in the dirt.

The prints led to the front door, then across the yard toward the woods. At the edge of the clearing they mixed with the wolf tracks that had become more abundant with every passing night.

How did I know they were the tracks of a wolf? Because no dog I'd ever met had feet that big.

I knelt again, touched my fingers to the dirt, which appeared damp, though it hadn't rained. When I lifted my hand, my skin was tinged with mud the shade of the moon I'd seen last night.

I stared at it for several beats of my heart before I understood that the earth beneath my sneakers was awash in blood.

CHAPTER 2

A hair-raising growl made me slowly lift my head. I came nose to snout with a black wolf. His lips were pulled back, exposing sharp, discolored teeth. There was something odd about the eyes, but I couldn't figure out what.

I had a hard time thinking straight, even before his breath washed over me, bringing the scent of meat. I fought the gagging reflex. Right now I really shouldn't move.

I tried to remember every tidbit of information I'd read about wild animals. What to do? What to do?

Was I supposed to play dead? No, that was for a bear.

Run? That was for animals unable to catch me, of which there were very few.

Wolves? The old memory banks were as empty as the pages of my next book.

Suddenly the beast snarled and I shrank back. I was going to die. I should close my eyes, but they seemed glued wide open.

Instead of tearing off my nose, the wolf swung his head to the side, his eyes narrowed at a spot behind me.

"Down!" a voice shouted.

My inertia fled and my face hit the dirt. A gunshot exploded above me. My ear pressed to the earth, I heard paws scrambling, feet pounding. I could see nothing, because at last I'd closed my eyes, and now I couldn't get them open.

I needed to race inside where I could call someone, anyone, preferably a SWAT team, Special Forces, the cavalry, so I lifted my head—and discovered I was alone. A few feet down an overgrown path I saw a pile of . . .

My mind shied away from identifying whatever the flies were so interested in. I got up, ran into the house, slammed the door, locked it, and shoved a chair under the knob for good measure. Nothing would get in through there. But—

I glanced at the window, which was much too small for man or wolf to fit through. Still, what I wouldn't give for a set of storm shutters similar to those covering the windows of my father's hunting cabin in Upper Michigan.

I'd put them on my wish list. Storm shutters, Glock, Uzi, rocket launcher.

I needed to leave this place, jump in my car, speed down the road to a town where I could surround myself with hundreds of people, but I couldn't go anywhere like this.

I smelled the tang of blood on my skin, tasted the rusty flavor of fear at the back of my throat. After a final glance at the locked and barricaded door, then the too small window, I hurried into the bathroom.

There I stripped and removed every trace of blood with a washcloth, then brushed my teeth until they tingled. All the while keeping my ears cocked for any out-of-the-ordinary sounds from the other room.

As clean as I could get without an hour-long shower and a visit to the dentist, I stared at my stained clothes and sighed. I'd have to burn them. Wrapping myself in a towel, I left the bathroom.

Someone grabbed me.

I had an instant to register that the front door was wide open before the towel fell to my ankles. I drew in a huge breath and a hand clamped over my mouth.

Training kicked in. A girl didn't grow up with four brothers and not learn how to fight and fight dirty.

My heel went for his instep, but it wasn't there. My

elbow jabbed back, aiming for the throat. He dodged. I tried to swing around to face him, the heel of my hand speeding toward his nose. He grabbed my wrist and twisted it behind my back.

"Very nice," growled the same voice that had shouted, "Get down."

Well, who else could it be?

I wanted to ask, but he had managed to keep his hand over my mouth. I struggled, but that only served to reveal that having a naked stranger in his arms made this man very happy indeed. I froze as either a gun, or something else, poked me in the rear end.

"That's better," he murmured, his breath brushing my ear, before he nuzzled my hair and took a deep sniff at the curve of my neck. "Now, if I let you go, will you be good?"

I had a bad feeling I knew what "good" meant, and I wasn't giving in gracefully. I nodded, and as soon as his grip loosened, I spun around, ramming my knee toward his crotch.

But he wasn't where I expected him to be, and my leg hit air. I nearly fell on my face. Catching myself, I snatched up the towel and wrapped it tightly around my body.

The man lounged against the wall, arms crossed in front of his chest as he watched me. He was some kind of soldier, or a wannabe. His T-shirt was camouflage, so were his pants. Face blackened with greasepaint as dark as his eyes, he'd covered his hair with a knit cap that matched the outfit.

I couldn't tell what he looked like beneath all that paint, but he was big—over six feet four inches of corded muscle and taut, sun-bronzed skin. Not an extra inch of flesh anywhere, unlike me.

I pulled the towel closer to my chest, but there wasn't a whole lot of material to spare. Small and petite, I wasn't.

At my movement, his gaze dropped to my breasts,

slipped to the lowest edge of the towel, where the vee of my thighs was most likely visible.

I cleared my throat. "Hey, pal, I'm up here."

He met my eyes and smirked. I wanted to slug him right then and there. "What kind of man gets a hard-on after scaring a naked woman half to death?"

"That's a rhetorical question, right?"

My temper, one of the many curses of being a redhead, ratcheted up a notch. "Who the hell are you, and what are you doing in my house?"

The man pushed away from the wall, and I took a single step backward before I could stop myself. I couldn't let him see how unnerved I was.

But instead of grabbing me again, he strolled to the window and stared out at the bright sunlight. "You have brothers."

I gaped. "What?"

He lifted one shoulder, then lowered it. "I've got sisters. Y'all fight like girls."

"Yeah, we're funny that way."

I stared at his back and pondered. I hadn't heard "y'all" since traveling to Alabama for a book signing. In the Midwest we said "you guys" or, as my brothers often did, "youse guys." "Y'all" marked this man as Southern even though the rest of his words had been as Yankee as Boston beans. The discrepancy made me even more suspicious of him than his breaking into my home had done.

Nevertheless, my temper had cooled a bit, as had my fear of him. Despite his obvious "interest" he hadn't thrown me to the ground and ravished me. Yet. He'd saved me from the wolf. Maybe he was one of the good guys.

"Get dressed."

"Excuse me?"

He turned away from the window. "Now. I can't think with all that skin and those . . ." He waved a vague hand at my chest.

"Breasts?" I supplied. He didn't bother to answer. "You act like you've never seen a naked woman before."

"Not lately," he muttered.

"You've been in the bush? On assignment? In Iraq?"

"Something like that. No hot water, no MTV, no nookie. It's been rough. So get dressed, Maya. I've got no time for bullshit."

I tilted my head. "How do you know my name?"

"I know a lot more than your name. Get. Dressed."

The last two words were spoken low, with a tinge of desperation. I was reminded of the vicious snarl of the wolf only moments before. This man was barely civilized, and I was poking him with a stick.

A thrill of awareness rippled down my spine, shocking me. I'd never been attracted to guys like this—wild, rough, dangerous. Studious, staid, safe was more my speed.

My last date had been a stockbroker, the one before that an accountant. My brothers tried to fix me up with their friends, but I needed another cop in my life like I needed a bigger ass.

As if he'd heard my thoughts, the stranger's gaze drifted, narrowing as if he had X-ray vision. I decided getting dressed wasn't a bad idea.

When I'd moved to Arizona, I'd left all my city duds behind. I'd bought jeans a size too big so when I sat at my desk nothing puckered and pinched. No one out here cared if I wasn't a perfect size ten.

T-shirts or flannel, heavy socks or bare feet, I owned one pair of tennies and one pair of boots. My underwear drawer boasted fourteen new pairs of granny undies, with three bras shoved all the way to the back. I'd hated bras since I'd first had to buy one while my dad slunk around the outskirts of the unmentionables section at Sears.

But today called for as much armor as I could don, so I dug out my C cups, then covered them with a bright yellow T-shirt and royal-blue plaid flannel.

When I stepped back into the living room, the first thing I saw were the guns. How I could have missed them earlier, I wasn't quite sure. Of course, I *had* been a little preoccupied with the man holding me captive.

A Beretta rode his hip, a Ruger was strapped to his thigh. Both an automatic and a revolver; he wasn't taking any chances, and I had to wonder why. Propped next to the door was what would appear to be a machine gun to the common man, but I recognized a Wilson combat carbine, the latest weapon of choice for the urban police department. The days of being outgunned by the bad guys were at last in the past.

"What are you expecting?" I asked. "Armageddon?"

At my question, he turned from the window, and my breath caught. He'd washed off the greasepaint and removed his hat. High, hollowed cheekbones, square jaw, wide forehead. He'd never be a model—unless you counted those posters that urged Americans to "be all that you can be."

I understood why he'd covered his hair. Blond, it would shimmer like a beacon in the night, even though he'd shorn the strands to near crew-cut length. The style went very well with the camo, the boots, and the weaponry.

His eyes widened, their inky hue a complement to his sun-bronzed face. "Jesus, why don't you paint a bull's-eye on your back?"

I frowned. "What?"

"Yellow? Electric blue? You'll stand out like a neon light."

"Stand out where?"

He opened his mouth to answer, and the window behind him shattered.

"Watch out!" I dived for the floor.

I'll give him credit, he hit the deck without question as something thumped to the floor, bumped a few times, then rolled.

"Shit!" He hauled me to my feet, shoved me out the door, dragged me across the yard and fell on top of me as everything I owned in the world exploded.

Debris thunked all around us. I lifted my head, he pushed me back down. But not before I saw a wolf streaking through the cinders and ash.

Struggling against his hold, I managed to raise my eyes again. I saw nothing—not a man, not a wolf. We were alone with what was left of my cabin.

The guy rolled off me and onto his feet. Ruger in hand, he scouted the trees.

"That way," I managed, my voice not much more than a croak.

He cast me a sharp glance. "What did you see?"

"Wolf." I coughed. "What exploded?"

"Grenade," he said in the same tone I might say "orange juice."

"Grenade? Grenade?" My voice was shrill and loud and caused me to cough again.

"Relax," he murmured, holstering the Ruger. "It wasn't meant for you."

CHAPTER 3

Oh, gee, that's a relief. The grenade wasn't meant for me. Tell it to my house. My cell phone. My—" I caught my breath. "My computer," I wailed.

"Everything will be replaced."

"That's it!" I clambered to my feet, swayed a bit. It wasn't every day I narrowly missed being blown to smithereens by a grenade. If I was a little wobbly, a little hysterical, I was justified. "Who are you? *What* are you?"

"We don't have time." He grabbed my arm and pushed me in the direction of his characteristically black SUV, which he'd parked half-in, half-out of the brush behind the cabin. "Get in the car."

I snorted. "I haven't gotten in a stranger's vehicle in . . . Well, let's just say forever. Not on your life."

He drew the Ruger, cocked it and pointed the barrel at me. His head jerked toward the passenger door.

"Oookay." I got in.

I wasn't scared—much. If he'd wanted me dead he could have left me in the house, or left me to the wolf. Still, I wasn't about to argue with a Ruger.

He climbed behind the wheel and spun the SUV in a circle, tires spraying dirt across the ruins of my brand-new diesel station wagon. I'd parked a little too close to the house for its comfort.

"Do you have a name?" We bounced over a rut at far too

fast a clip, and my head nearly banged against the ceiling. "A driver's license?"

His mouth was set, his eyes intense, as he tried to keep the car from flipping off the narrow path. "Clayton Philips. Clay."

"And you're what? Special Forces?"

His gaze flicked to me, then back to the road. "Sure."

Sure? Does anyone but me see "lie" written all over that?

"How do you know my name?"

He opened his mouth, and the wolf bounded directly in front of the car. I gasped, braced myself, expecting him to hit the brakes. Instead, he hit the gas.

The wolf was quicker than any wolf I'd ever seen—not that I'd seen very many—and leaped into the brush mere centimeters ahead of the SUV's fender.

At last Philips used the brakes, and I was thrown forward, then back, with such force my head struck the seat and my breasts got an overenthusiastic hug from the seat belt.

"Hey!" I shouted, but he was already out of the car, gun drawn.

"Lock the doors," he said, and then he was gone.

"Creep. Jerk."

My gaze went to the ignition. No keys.

"Asshole!" I muttered, unbuckling the seat belt and reaching for the door. Fingers on the handle, I hesitated. I could go back to the cabin, but why? No house, no phone, no freaking car. I got mad all over again.

I glanced down the trail. What if I walked to town? Twenty miles away. *Ha.* I hadn't walked a *mile* since high school, and then only because the Nazi gym teacher had made me. Besides, Philips would catch me, then we'd have the dragging and the threatening and the guns all over again.

Still . . . I gazed longingly at freedom.

A wolf slammed into the passenger window. I shrieked and scuttled back.

The animal slavered, snarled, snapped, trying to get to me despite the barrier. Red-tinged drool ran down the glass. Aw, hell, had Philips gone and gotten himself killed?

The wolf disappeared, and my eyes widened as the latch thunked. I smacked my finger onto the button and all the doors locked with a satisfying *thwack*. There was something very strange about this wolf.

Living in Chicago, I didn't come across many wild animals, but even I knew they weren't very good at opening car doors.

I couldn't see the wolf, couldn't hear him any longer. Maybe he was gone.

The front of the car dipped. He stared through the windshield, snarling. Where was my rescuer now?

As if he'd heard the question, the wolf's head lifted, cocked. He glanced toward the trees, then back at me.

A sudden sweat, icy cold and dizzying, broke out on my skin, as I stared into brown eyes surrounded by a whole lot of white. I suddenly understood what had bothered me about the wolf.

I blinked and looked again. Yep. People eyes, wolf body. I tried to get my mind around the concept, but I kept coming up short on an explanation.

Then several things happened at once. The wolf's mouth opened; a breeze ruffled the trees, and swept through the car. I'm not sure how, since all the windows were closed. But my hair fluttered, the sweat on my skin tingled, and I heard a single, muffled word that sounded like—

Philips burst out of the woods. He pointed the Ruger at the wolf on the hood, and I ducked. Holding my breath, I waited for the glass to explode, then shatter all around me.

Nothing happened.

I didn't want to lift my head and risk getting it blown off by my new pal, the gun-happy psycho. Instead I twisted on the seat so I could see through the windshield. The wolf was gone.

The sudden release of the door locks made me yelp. But it was just Philips with the only set of keys. He narrowly missed sitting on my head as he climbed behind the wheel, then took off while I was still struggling to fasten my seat belt.

Silence settled between us as he stared intently through the windshield. Speeding like a bat out of hell and hitting every bump on the road must require complete concentration.

"What was that?" I asked.

"What do you think?"

Was he being a smart-ass? I couldn't tell. Considering my penchant for sarcasm—blame the behavior on my brothers; biting wit was the only weapon I'd had against their superior strength—it was surprising I couldn't recognize the same in him.

"Skinwalker," I said.

His foot slipped off the gas and the car jerked, but he managed to recover the next instant. "Where did you hear that?"

I opened my mouth, closed it again. How was I supposed to explain that the wind had spoken inside the car?

Obviously he hadn't heard anything, so the wolf hadn't talked, the wind hadn't whispered.

I thought Philips was crazy? He needed to get in line. Behind me.

"Around," I mumbled.

The car slid to a stop. He put the transmission in park. "Around where?"

From his reaction, the word meant something to him. I wanted to know what.

"You tell me what 'skinwalker' means, then I'll tell you where I heard it."

He made an aggravated noise. "Maya, we don't have time for this."

Which reminded me . . .

"How do you know my name?"

He sighed and put the car into gear. "Fine. I can drive and talk."

"Walk and chew gum, too, I bet."

Philips' lips twitched, and he shot me a quick sideways glance. Dark eyes wandered over every inch of me just as they had when I'd been wearing nothing but a towel. I shivered, though the air in the car was more hot than cold.

I'd been kidnapped by a handsome, mysterious stranger. Some women would be envious. I was . . . highly stressed.

This entire scenario resembled one of my books—books in which I safely orchestrated adventures for people who didn't exist outside my own head. There was a reason for that. I was no good under fire, and I never would be. Every time I took a chance, I got burned. Life, love, the pursuit of happiness—none of those adventures had gone very well for me, so I'd stopped trying.

I'd had a dozen jobs before I'd found writing. I'd failed at every one. Another reason I was panicked at the thought of failing this time.

Boyfriends? They never lasted. Happiness either. Just ask my mother.

I dragged my eyes from Philips and pointedly stared out the window. His sigh held both disappointment and resignation.

"Do you know anything about the Navajo?" he asked.

"They live . . ." I frowned and glanced at the sun, gauged our direction and pointed. "Thataway."

Philips snorted. "Anything else?"

I shook my head. "You've heard the extent of my knowledge on the Navajo nation."

"Yet you know we're chasing a skinwalker."

"We are?"

He looked at me out of the corner of his eye.

"Gotcha," I murmured. "What's a skinwalker and why are we chasing one?"

"A skinwalker is a Navajo witch who thrives on destruction, murder, mayhem."

I flashed on an image of the smoldering remains of my house and car, the face at the window, the grenade. None of this added up.

"I thought witches were peaceful, that hags stirring cauldrons were just a myth."

"Modern-day witches *are* peaceful. Their creed is to harm none. Skinwalkers aren't modern. They're ancient and very pissed off."

"Why?"

"No one knows. The Navajo are extremely close-mouthed about the dark side of their culture. Most live in harmony with their world. They don't kill animals or humans for the sake of killing. The skinwalker wants to inflict as much pain and misery as possible just because it can."

"Nice guy."

"Not a guy."

"Girl?"

"Not exactly."

"*What* exactly?"

He shook his head. "I kept my part of the deal. Where did you hear the word 'skinwalker'?"

I sighed. "This is going to sound nuts—"

"Tell me something that doesn't today."

"Fair enough. While you were in the woods and the wolf was on the hood . . ." I paused.

"What?"

"Well, I heard the word on the wind. In a closed car." I glanced at him, but he continued to stare out the windshield. "You don't seem surprised."

"I've seen some mighty surprising things in my life."

"Maybe you can tell me what the hell is going on then."

"Did the wolf appear strange to you?"

I nodded, remembering the human eyes. I considered all that I'd seen, all that had happened.

The face at the window, the rattle at the door, the canine whimper. Then the man's tracks blending with those of a wolf. A whisper when there was no one around but me and a wild animal. None of it made any sense.

"A skinwalker is both a witch and a werewolf," Philips said, "and this one seems to have a hard-on for you."

CHAPTER 4

M e? You said the grenade was meant for you."

"It was. Ever seen a wolf toss a grenade?"

"I've never seen a wolf before today."

"You didn't see a wolf today either. That was a—"

"Werewolf. Right. Do your handlers know you're loose?"

"Joke away. I'm all that's between you and that thing."

"And just who are you?"

"Clayton Philips."

"I know your name, jerk-off, *what* are you? Cop? Soldier? Psycho?"

"I'm a *Jäger-Sucher*."

I'd taken German as a foreign language. Don't ask me why. The only time I'd ever had any use for it was now.

"Hunter-searcher?" I translated.

He glanced at me with surprise and some interest. "Right."

"What does that mean?"

"We're a division of the government—"

"Never heard of it."

Reaching the main road, we bounced from dirt onto pavement.

"A secret division," he continued.

"Why, yes, Virginia, there is an X-file. If it's a secret why are you telling me?"

"You need to know what we're up against."

"A Navajo werewolf."

"You don't believe me?"

"Should I?"

"I've been tracking and killing werewolves for ten years. I'm not making this up."

"Oh, that's convincing."

Annoyance flickered across his face. "Since the skin-walker slipped off the reservation three people have died. You appear to be next."

"What about you?"

"The man wants me—hence the grenade. Considering his behavior of a few moments ago, the wolf wants you."

"If I believe your delusion, the man and the wolf are one and the same."

"Which explains why the skinwalker didn't care overly much if he blew you up along with me. Still—" He broke off and shook his head.

"What?" I asked, though I probably shouldn't have encouraged him.

"Werewolves kill quickly," Philips continued. "They aren't big on self-restraint. They don't hang around watching people like this one has been watching you."

Unease trickled along the back of my neck. "How do you know what he's been doing?"

"I was called to investigate a death about a week ago not far from your place. I followed several sets of wolf tracks. There was one that kept circling back to you. I couldn't figure out what he was up to."

"Why didn't you just shoot him?"

"I never saw anything but tracks. Until I found the kill on your property—"

"What kill?"

"There was a body about a hundred feet from the house, or what was left of one."

The blood, the unidentified pile, the flies. I'd blocked

that out. At this rate I wouldn't remember my own name by tomorrow.

"Female," he continued. "They've all been female. But the similarity ends there. Young, old. Silver-haired, blond." He glanced at me. "Redhead. No rhyme or reason."

"To a werewolf? Why am I not surprised?"

"Exactly. Werewolves kill indiscriminately, they don't have a plan, so why didn't he kill you?" He shook his head. "The tracks, the spoor—at least five days' worth. That isn't like a werewolf."

"Maybe it *is* like a skinwalker."

He glanced at me and interest lit his dark eyes. "Maybe it is."

"You don't know?"

"This is the first skinwalker case we've worked on. The Navajo usually deal with renegades themselves. They're considered an embarrassment."

"I can imagine."

He frowned. "You need to take the situation seriously, Maya. I know I sound crazy, but I'm not."

"So says every crazy person."

"I promise the skinwalker won't get you as long as you're with me."

He was so earnest, I found myself nodding. Nevertheless I'd attempt escape at the first opportunity. Grab a phone, call the cops, send Clayton Philips to the nearest padded cell. He might be hot, but he was crazier than the craziest person I'd ever met.

"Where are we going?" I asked.

"There's a man I'm supposed to talk to on the reservation."

"If the Navajo are so closemouthed about skinwalkers why did they call you for help?"

"They didn't."

"Then how did you find out there was a skinwalker loose?"

I couldn't believe I was playing along with him, but it did pass the time.

"The *Jäger-Suchers* have connections everywhere. Several dead bodies in the same area, mutilated beyond recognition by wild animals, we get a fax."

"Uh-huh. Explain how this skinwalker changes from man to wolf and back again."

"He wears the skin of a wolf."

I frowned. "So he isn't really a wolf? He's a guy running around with a carcass on his head?"

"You saw the wolf. Did it look like a real wolf to you?"

"Except for the eyes—yep."

"The one physical difference between wolf and werewolf is the eyes. As for the skinwalker, the man is a witch. He combines magic and an animal skin—"

"How?"

"No one knows for sure. The process is as secret as the identity of the skinwalker."

I glanced out the window. As we'd been talking, he'd been driving. There wasn't a neon sign that said, WELCOME TO THE NAVAJO RESERVATION, but I still knew the instant we crossed over. The land flattened out; the dust kicked up. Trailers and hogans—the traditional dwellings of the Navajo—dotted the horizon. The shades of the desert, brown, tan, chocolate, blended toward tabletop mesas and sculpted sandstone in the distance.

The first time I'd driven to this area I'd experienced déjà vu. Despite never having set foot west of the Mississippi, I'd seen Monument Valley before.

Once I read up on the region I understood the sense of familiarity. Many John Ford westerns had been filmed here. The Navajo lived at the heart of an American icon.

Philips turned into a dirt lane, which led to a small house with nothing around for miles but sand and buttes. If we kept traveling in one direction we'd run into the White Mountains, in another we'd hit the Painted Desert, still another would lead us through a dense woodland. Visitors were shocked to hear that Arizona had more mountainous regions than Switzerland and more forest than Minnesota.

The house appeared deserted. No one stepped onto the porch, no dogs ran out to greet us. The hair on my arms prickled.

"Whose place is this?"

"Medicine man."

"Right."

He cast a quick glance in my direction as he stopped the car. "There *are* medicine men and women. Most Navajo still take part in the Blessingway."

"Which is?"

"Rites to promote happiness and wisdom. They also have sings or chantaways to promote health."

"And that's what this guy does for a living?"

I contemplated the house. There didn't appear to be too much cash in the venture.

"As well as hunting the occasional skinwalker."

I looked at him. He wasn't kidding. What else was new?

Philips climbed out of the car. "Hello?" he called. "Joseph Ahkeah?"

No answer. Not a flicker of the curtains. Nothing.

"I've got a bad feeling about this," I murmured.

"Joseph is an expert on skinwalkers. He'll know what yours is up to with the stalking and the not killing, even though you've been a sitting duck."

The image was disturbing. I'd been alone. Staring at my computer, listening to my music, obsessing over a deadline.

Considering the last few hours, a book was hardly worth the worry. I still didn't believe we were dealing with a werewolf, but there was something funny going on. The guy who'd been playing peekaboo at my window was nuts at the very least. He'd blown up my house, melted my car.

Even if Philips was on the fruity side, too, he hadn't tried to kill me. Yet.

He knocked on the door. We listened, but all we heard was the wind. He peered into the window.

"You're asking to get your head blown off."

He glanced at me. "My boss was supposed to call Joseph and tell him I was coming. I don't understand why he isn't here."

Philips reached for the doorknob, and at his touch the portal swung open. Shrugging, he stepped inside.

"Hey!" I hovered on the porch. "Is that legal?"

"What if he slipped in the tub, cracked his head? What if he's fallen and he can't get up?"

"Rationalize much?"

"Every damn day."

Since I did, too, I followed him into the medicine man's home.

The cabin was small, dark, hot. Stuff lay all over. Joseph really needed a housekeeper, although most women would never touch what I saw spread around.

Bones, large and small, the skull of an unidentified animal, skins of every shape, size, and color. *Uh-oh.*

Philips made a beeline for them. I was right behind him until I stepped on something crunchy. Looking down, I discovered what appeared to be the thigh bone of a—

"Ew!" I skittered after Philips so fast I slammed into his back. "Is that human?"

"Not anymore."

He pulled his Beretta and quickly checked the house. There wasn't much to see. A single living area with a kitchen, small bedroom, an even smaller bath. No sign of anything alive.

The skins were spread across several tables at the north side of the room. In contrast to the rest of the house, they were organized and labeled with anal precision. A small piece of paper had been taped beneath each one.

"Fox. Bear. Coyote," I read. "What's with that?"

In the midst of reading the top sheet on a huge stack of papers, Philips looked up. Eyes unfocused, at first he didn't appear to see me. I waved my hand in front of his face until he blinked.

"What? Oh, a skinwalker can take many shapes."

"I thought it was a werewolf."

"Right now. Most likely for endurance and tenacity. Wolves have the ability to run for miles, then accelerate. They're quick, smart, and they can be vicious when provoked. But a skinwalker could become a fox, a bear, a coyote." He spread his hand, indicting the skins in front of us. "All he has to do is change his skin."

"You're telling me that this thing could have morphed into another animal?"

"Possibly. The fox is for cunning, the bear for strength, coyote for speed and agility. Still, from what I've been able to gather in my studies, most skinwalkers stick to the one animal they identify with."

"In this case, a wolf."

He grunted, already returning his attention to the books and the papers.

With nothing to do, I wandered down the row of skins. Deer. Elk. Raven. Eagle. The display was quite creepy.

"The sturgeon moon," he muttered. "Hell. That's soon."

"The what-who?"

He lifted his gaze. His eyes were all dreamy again—lost in the book. Funny, I never would have pegged him for a scholar.

"Back when the Indians owned the earth, they gave each full moon a name. The wolf moon was in January because the wolves howled with hunger in the middle of winter. There's the harvest moon in September. The blood moon is October—"

"Sounds like one we want to avoid."

Philips gave a small smile. "Also called the hunter's

moon, because in that month meat was stockpiled for the winter."

"I take it the sturgeon moon is August."

"Bingo. The fishing tribes christened that one because the fish are easily caught at this time of year. But the August moon carries other names, too, from other tribes. The green corn moon, the grain moon . . ."

"What happens under the sturgeon moon?"

He held up a hand and kept reading, only to curse again seconds later. " 'Any human who hears the skinwalker whisper in the time of the red moon is chosen.' "

Our eyes met. We'd both seen the moon. It was very red indeed.

"Let me guess, 'red moon' is another name for 'sturgeon moon.' "

He nodded. "Most werewolf lore is attached to the full moon."

"For obvious reasons. When is it?"

"Tomorrow night."

Terrific.

"What does 'chosen' mean?"

"Not sure. But when dealing with monsters, I've never found 'chosen' to be a good thing."

"Better and better," I muttered.

Philips continued to read. " 'In the month of the red moon, the skinwalker roams the land of the Glittering World. Murder and mayhem give him strength for the task ahead.' "

"What task?"

" 'When the full, red moon rises over the Canyon of the Dead the skinwalker will reveal himself to the chosen one, and the world will tremble before him.' "

"Also not good."

He clapped the book closed and walked the length of the table, his fingers brushing the skins.

"That's all?"

"A lot of these Indian legends are . . . vague."

"To hell with vague. I want to know why I'm chosen. What that means. Where the hell is the Canyon of the Dead and how far away from it can I get?"

"Maya," he said softly. "I won't let him touch you."

"I'm sorry if your assurances don't make me feel all warm and cuddly."

"Don't you trust me?"

"You break into my house, scare me to death, let a lunatic blow up everything I own in the world, then kidnap me. You say he's after me. Mr. Philips, I think you're crazy."

I headed for the door; he snagged my arm and dragged me back. My momentum was such that I slammed into his chest, stumbled and nearly fell. He caught me around the waist and hauled me flush with his body.

"I'll take care of you," he ground out. "I swear."

"I can take care of myself."

I meant to say so with strength and courage. Instead my voice came out a breathy, girlie whisper.

His gaze dropped to my breasts. His eyes heated; so did my skin. I had a flash of him and me entwined on black silk sheets. He'd be both gentle and rough. Needy, desperate, unbelievably skilled.

What was it about this man that made me think of such things at the most inappropriate times? I shouldn't even like him. He reminded me of my brothers—overconfident, overmuscled, oversexed.

My cheeks flamed—the curse of being a redhead. I blushed far too often and too well.

His eyes narrowed. I waited for him to shove me aside and tell me to fend for myself. Instead, his arm tightened and his mouth crushed down on mine.

I'd been trained to fight, to claw and scratch and bite if I had to, anything to keep a man from overpowering me. Right now every trick I'd been taught fled as blinding lust rocketed through my body.

His mouth was hard; his tongue soft. He bit my lip, yanked my shirt from my pants and scraped his nails across my back. I gasped, bowed, rubbed the front of me all over the front of him.

My hands dived under his shirt, touching his skin, gauging his muscles, skimming his ribs.

He groaned into my mouth, the vibration against both my lips and fingertips a dual sensation that set my pulse pounding. He skated his teeth across my jaw, then latched on to my neck and suckled.

I arched, and he buried his face in my breasts, filled his hands with my ass and lifted me so I could wrap my legs around his hips and ride his erection along another pulsing, pounding, mindless part of me.

The door slammed and we both froze. His breath brushed the damp spots made by his mouth. My nipples tightened. My body throbbed.

"Just the wind," he murmured. "We're okay."

Funny, I didn't feel okay at all.

He let me go, and my legs slid down his. My feet touched the floor, and my cheeks flooded crimson again. I tried to turn away, but he hauled me back into his arms, leaning down and pressing his forehead to mine.

"Maya," he whispered in a shaky voice. "What was that?"

"A kiss?"

Clay let out a harsh bark of laughter that tapped our heads together hard enough to make me blink. "That's like calling dynamite a firecracker."

He ran a hand over my hair, then kissed my cheek. "Bad idea. I'm sorry. I don't know what got into me, except—"

"Except?"

"I've wanted to kiss you since you walked out of the shower and tried to beat the crap out of me."

I smiled. "You get off on that, huh?"

"Looks that way."

"I suppose you'll come if I kick you where it counts."

He lifted a pale brow. "Let's not find out."

I'd lived too many years in a household of males not to be blunt in both my language and my behavior. Probably one of the many reasons I was still alone. Most men found me too much like one of the guys. None had ever found me as intriguing as Clay appeared to.

My gaze lowered to the bulge in his jeans. Yep, he really, really liked me.

I took a step toward him and he stumbled back. "Bad idea, remember?"

"Seems like a good idea to me."

"Maya, no. The last woman I—"

He scrubbed a hand through his hair, making the bright strands stick straight up, then whirled away, leaning over the table full of skins and hanging his head. "The last woman I cared about got killed. Badly."

"Is there a good way to be killed?"

"I suppose not. But Serena—Well, let's just say there wasn't much left of her to bury."

He sure knew how to kill the mood.

"She was a *Jäger-Sucher* like me."

"A werewolf killed her?"

"No. She had a different specialty."

"I don't understand."

"Different divisions, different monsters."

"You're telling me there's more in this world than werewolves?"

He took a deep breath, let it out slowly. "A lot more."

I opened my mouth to ask what, then decided I really didn't want to know.

CHAPTER 5

Suddenly Clay straightened. "Uh-oh."

"What's uh-oh?"

"The wolf skin is missing." He pointed to the table in front of him.

I hadn't gotten that far down the display before I'd become creeped out by all the dead things. Otherwise I would have noticed the great big empty space—that had a label. A label that very clearly read "wolf."

"Son of a bitch!" Clay twirled, "Joseph Ahkeah is the skinwalker."

"Maybe he just decided to throw on a wolf skin and take a little walk. Traveling a mile in someone's moccasins, so to speak. That doesn't mean he's an evil, soulless killer."

"Just throwing on the skin won't make a skinwalker. Both the skin and the magic are necessary. A man like Joseph would know very well what he was doing."

"You have no idea what kind of magic he'd use?"

Clay had been stalking around the room as if searching for something. He stopped with his hands full of loose newspaper clippings. "Kind?"

"A spell? A sacrifice? Mystic powder? A wand?"

"That's what I wanted to talk to Ahkeah about." He shrugged. "I guess it doesn't really matter *how* he became one. What matters is *when*—he dies."

I rolled my eyes at the line straight out of a John Wayne movie. My brothers talked like that, and it annoyed the hell out of me. Why did I find the same behavior in Clay kind of cute?

Cute? Clayton Philips was a lean, mean, crazy fighting machine. Just because he could kiss better than any man I'd ever locked lips with didn't make him sane.

Still, I had to admit that being in this house, seeing Joseph's collection, hearing the curse of the red moon rising had made me lean a little bit closer to Clay's side of the fence.

An ear-splitting explosion erupted outside. The ground shook; I swore I heard a flame thrower. I raced Clay to the window and discovered there *were* flames and they *were* being thrown. Toward the sky, from the hull that had once been his SUV.

But that wasn't the sight that made me stare, blink, rub my eyes, then stare some more.

The naked Indian man was still there.

The air wavered with heat. Smoke blew in waves, obscuring, then revealing him again. He stood about fifty yards beyond the flaming car.

His hair was loose, long, and black. He wasn't tall, but he was muscular. He looked as if he'd been lifting small trucks as a hobby.

"Ahkeah," Clay muttered.

The man cocked his hand behind his ear, like a major league pitcher. His black hair swung. So did other, non-black parts a little farther south.

He threw whatever had been in his palm. Something small and dark wafted end over end in our direction. Going by previous experience, I should have started running.

But he bent down and picked up what appeared to be a fur cape, with a snout. He positioned the head on top of his own, and the fur settled over his shoulders. Lifting his hands to the sky, he spoke, though I couldn't hear the words. However, I heard the howl that followed very well.

The sound was so loud it made me blink, and when my eyes opened a wolf stood where the man had been. He was sleek and dark; I'd seen the animal before—outside my cabin. But how could he have gotten here so quickly?

Clay grabbed my arm and dragged me toward the back door muttering, "Another fucking grenade. Do you believe this guy?"

I did now. I'd seen him change with my own two eyes.

Clay shoved me outside. "Run!"

He didn't have to tell me twice. I was getting very good at dodging grenades thrown into the houses I occupied.

We weren't more than thirty feet from the porch when the place blew. The heat was intense. The pressure lifted me up and tossed me several feet before depositing me, face first, into the desert dust.

There was a thump to my right, which I certainly hoped was Clay and not the skinwalker.

I managed to turn my head, open my eyes. Clay was already on his feet, gun drawn. I moaned and closed my eyes again.

"Maya?" He dropped to his knees. His hand touched my neck. "You okay?"

Nothing felt broken. I ached, my palms burned, my cheek too. I'd live. Again.

"We have to move. The fire will spook him for a while, but he'll be back."

That got me up—almost. I made it to a crouch before my head spun. I fell on my butt, and Clay shoved my face between my knees. "Breathe," he ordered.

A few minutes later the ground stopped spinning, and I tentatively lifted my head. "That was the same wolf."

"Yes."

"But it was at my cabin. We drove here . . ."

"I've heard a skinwalker can run as fast as a car. There've been reports of people riding along desert highways and seeing a wolf race past them, then disappear. Considering what just happened, I'll have to believe the hearsay."

"Why do you think he's coming back?"

"For you."

How could I forget? I was chosen. Special, special me.

"But why . . . ?" I indicated the fireball that had once been a house and a car. "If he needs me on the night of the full, red moon, doesn't it defeat his purpose to blow me into itty-bitty pieces?"

"Maybe he doesn't need you alive."

I lifted my brow, which felt a little singed. "You're quite the cheery fellow, aren't you?"

Clay shrugged. "I don't know what he's up to, why he needs you, what he's planning. All I know is that I'll make sure he's dead before we are."

I stared into his nearly black eyes, and I knew several things for certain. He meant what he said. I trusted him. And he *wasn't* crazy.

Clay and I were in this together now. No going back. Not if I wanted to live.

"We need to leave, Maya."

Clay clapped his palm against mine and hauled me up without any trouble. When I was on my feet, he kept holding on, and I let him.

His gaze drifted to my lips. I swayed, and I wasn't even dizzy. I wanted to kiss him, right there in the middle of another burning wasteland. We should be running for cover, calling the cops; instead we were staring into each other's eyes and puckering up.

Clay dropped my hand and stepped away. At least one of us had some wits left.

"He'll be back as soon as his people brain overrules his wolf fear of the flames."

He started walking toward a distant butte. I hurried after him. "Where are we going?"

"We can't stay here. We've got no cover. He blew up my car." Clay shook his head. "I really liked that car."

Just as I'd liked my house, my clothes, my computer. But I kept the thought to myself.

"I'd head to another house," he continued, "but this is the middle of the reservation. Joseph is a leader. I doubt anyone would help us."

I considered that they might do worse than *not help,* and agreed with his rationale. We were strangers. Outsiders. We didn't know who our enemy was. He could be anyone or anything.

"We'll find a place to hide. Set a trap. I wish we were near the mountains. I'm better in the mountains than the desert."

"You're the expert," I said. "Let's just steer clear of that canyon-of-the-dead thing. I don't suppose you have a map."

"In the car. Along with my rifle and extra ammunition."

I stopped. Clay kept walking. More had been lost than some of my hearing. We were in the desert with nothing but a Beretta, a Ruger, the bullets still in them, and each other.

How would I write one of the heroes in my action-adventure novels out of a situation like this?

I had no idea. My muse was still deathly silent.

"What are we going to do?"

"I told you. Set a trap. Kill him. Then file a report."

I giggled, and the sound held a tinge of hysteria. Clay must have heard it because he cut a quick glance in my direction, though he never faltered.

"I've done it before, Maya."

"You said this was your first skinwalker."

He shrugged. "A werewolf's a werewolf."

"You sure about that?"

"No."

I suppressed the return of the hysterical giggle. "Don't sugarcoat it, Clay. I can handle anything."

His face creased in concern. "Don't worry. I can."

"Worry? *Moi?* You can't be serious."

How did Clay know that worry was my middle name? Because he knew everything about me, or so he said. I wanted to know everything about him, or at least as much as he'd tell me. Besides, talking passed the time and might make me forget to look behind me every few seconds so I could see the wolf before it snapped at my heels or tore out my throat.

"Why are you better in the mountains?" I asked.

"I'm from Appalachia."

I recalled his use of "y'all" when we'd first met, but other than that, I'd never heard a trace of an accent.

"When did you leave?"

"Long, long time ago."

"Why?"

"There was nothing left for me there."

His words fell into a deep silence. I understood what he meant. I'd left behind family, friends, a condo. Still, there'd been nothing for me in Chicago either.

"Your family?"

"Dead."

The way he said it made me wonder, but the strained expression on his face wouldn't let me ask. I should have known he'd answer anyway.

"They were killed by werewolves. All of them."

"And you?"

"I wasn't."

"So you became a hunter."

"I was always a hunter. We needed to eat. I was out hunting the day—" He took a deep breath and walked faster. "The day they died. I came home and followed the tracks. I thought it was just wolves, though wolves don't behave like these did."

"How's that?"

"They were an army. Alpha general, foot soldiers, military movements."

I frowned. "How old were you?"

"Sixteen."

"And you knew what they were doing?"

"Not then. I learned later how common the behavior was—in regular werewolves out for a little fun and food."

"Regular werewolves? Isn't that an oxymoron?"

He smiled, but the expression held little joy. How could it when he was recounting something so horrific? I was tempted to take his hand, but after the flare that had passed between us the last time we'd touched, I was scared to, as well.

"There are countless monsters. Some you've heard of, some you couldn't even imagine. Then there are variations of them—mutations, new strains and old. The skinwalker is ancient. A lot of the monsters are. Then there are the ones made by the Nazis."

"Nazis? I hate those guys."

Clay laughed at last, which made me smile. He'd been so sad, I'd been contemplating ways to make him happy—each involving various sexual practices I'd only read about.

"My boss, Edward Mandenauer, was a spy during World War Two. He discovered a secret lab in the Black Forest where Mengele was doing a lot more than experimenting on the Jews. But, by the time Mandenauer reached the hidden laboratory, all the monsters were gone. He formed the *Jäger-Suchers,* and he's been hunting them ever since."

My smile faded. "You expect me to believe there've been monsters engineered by the Nazis spreading throughout the world since World War Two?"

"You saw the skinwalker."

"He wasn't made by the Nazis."

"True. But if you can believe in him, why can't you believe in the others?"

I did believe, and it only made me want to glance over my shoulder all the more. Safety girl had just discovered that her cacophony of worries were minor when compared to the supernatural terrors she'd never even known about. It's hard to accept that the little bubble of security and harmony you'd been constructing since your mother hadn't come home one day was only an illusion.

Amazingly, I was a lot less upset about my bubble bursting than I would have thought. Perhaps because Clay was by my side. So far, he'd kept me alive. And while I'd never been much for adventure, except on the page, he was fast becoming the best time I'd ever had.

We reached a set of low-lying indigo hills as the sun met the western horizon. I'd been sweating like a sow beached in the desert sand. The instant the sun disappeared and shadows spread across the land, everything went gray, still, and cool.

A rumbling growl was my only warning an instant before something slammed into me from behind. I kissed dirt, again, but I had bigger worries than a fat lip.

This wolf meant to kill me.

CHAPTER 6

I covered my head with my arms, attempting to protect my neck with my hands. The wolf sank its teeth into my wrist.

If you've ever been bitten by a dog, you know what that feels like. I screamed and suddenly the weight on my back was gone. The thunder of a gun exploded so close my ears rang.

Something wet rained down all over me. I had a bad feeling I was now wearing more than sweat. I flipped over, cradling my bitten arm.

"Aw, hell," I muttered. "Am I going to grow fangs?"

Clay stared at what was left of the reddish-brown wolf. Smaller than the black wolf I'd seen several times before, this one also had longer ears and a narrower muzzle.

When Clay lifted his gaze, I reared back at the violence roiling his eyes, but in the next instant the expression disappeared. He fell to his knees beside me, reaching for my injured hand. "Wasn't a werewolf. You're safe. From fangs anyway."

Blood dripped down my fingers. He tore a strip from the bottom of his T-shirt, baring a band of taut, bronzed skin, then wrapped my wound with an expert twist.

I tore my gaze from his stomach. Was I dizzy from the sight of his abs or the loss of blood? I shook my head and focused on more important matters. "How do you know it wasn't a werewolf?"

"Didn't explode."

I glanced at the remains. "Looks like an explosion to me."

"Werewolf plus silver equals fire shooting toward the sky. This one just . . . died."

"There are silver bullets in your guns?"

"Did you think there wouldn't be?"

I hadn't thought about the need for silver at all. Such concerns were foreign to my world.

"Are there two skinwalkers?" Panic made my heart thunder so hard it was difficult to speak past the pulse in my throat. "What do I turn into when one of those bites me?"

"That wasn't a skinwalker."

"Once again I have to ask, how do you know?"

"Legend has it that when a skinwalker dies the skin separates from the body."

"Ew."

"The animal skin. If this were our skinwalker, we'd have a dead man and a wolf skin, side by side." He frowned. "I'm not sure if either one of them explode at the touch of silver. I guess we'll find out."

"If that isn't a skinwalker, what is it?"

"Red wolf. Native to the Southwest." He frowned, shook his head. "Only rabid wolves attack."

"I saw *Old Yeller*," I muttered. "I so don't want to go there."

"Relax. No weaving. No drooling. I've seen rabid animals. This one wasn't."

"Then what the hell?"

Clay lifted his eyes and scanned the steadily encroaching darkness. "The skinwalker's controlling the wolves."

As if they'd heard him speak, a chorus of howls rose

toward the rising red moon. A heated haze made the orb appear wobbly.

"Controlling how?"

"A skinwalker is both witch and werewolf. I have no idea what the extent of its powers might be." He stared at the horizon for several moments. "We'd better find a cave."

"Is that where they hide?"

He jerked his head in the direction of the howls. "Does that sound like they're hiding to you? They're coming after us. We need a place where our backs are protected and I can set a trap. You ready?"

I jumped to my feet without his help. "Let's go."

Clay led me over rocks—no tracks, little scent—to the east, then the west. I was exhausted by the time he found a cave.

We squeezed through a hole that opened on a room just large enough for us to lie down and move around a little. The fit was far from ideal, though Clay said he couldn't have constructed a better place for us to make a stand. There was even a small puddle of water near the back of the hollowed-out cavern, a miracle at this time of year.

The howls had faded as we hurried through the night. Clay set up his ingenious trap in front of the entrance—something with sticks and rocks that looked like a child's game from the Stone Age. He covered the tiny entrance with brush, leaving an opening at the top for the nearly full moon to shine through.

"Anything trotting by in the dark should just keep on keepin' on," Clay said, as he bathed my wolf bite with water from the puddle.

"Do you think we lost them?"

"Maybe." He lifted his eyes to mine and shrugged. "Did you want me to lie?"

"Yep."

He smiled and smoothed my hair. "I promised I'd protect you."

His smile faded when his fingers brushed the scrape on my cheek. I reached up and put my hand on top of his, pressing his palm to the reddened skin. "I know you will."

For a minute I thought he might kiss me and I caught my breath. But he slipped his hand from beneath mine and busied himself tearing another strip from his T-shirt.

The garment barely covered his pecs. I had a hard time focusing on anything but smooth, rippling skin until he tightened the bandage on my wrist with a little too much force. "Hey!"

"Sorry." He let his hands fall to his lap. "I haven't done a very good job of protecting you so far."

"You saved my life. Several times. I'm sticking with you, Clay. Alone I'd be meat. Together, we'll be all right."

He stared into my face, as if trying to gauge my sincerity, then patted the elbow of my injured arm. "As long as that doesn't get infected, we're all set."

Infection. What a pleasant thought.

"Lucky you got bitten by a wolf." Scooting closer to the entrance, he drew up his knees and rested his wrists on top. He held both the Ruger and the Beretta. "In ancient times domestic dogs, the descendants of wolves, licked their masters' wounds. Their mouths held healing properties."

"I should be okey-dokey then."

"As soon as we get you some antibiotics. Go to sleep, Maya. That's the best thing you can do."

I took off my flannel shirt and used it for a pillow. The cave warmed from the heat of our bodies, but the ground was hard and always would be. I didn't expect to sleep, but I did.

I awoke to an earsplitting chorus of howls. The sound reverberated through the small cave. I sat up with a gasp. The moon had shifted; the cave was dark.

A hand clamped over my mouth. I would have struggled, even screamed, except Clay's touch, his scent, his very taste was familiar.

My tongue darted out to meet his palm, and he started, then pulled away as if I'd burned him.

Paws padded outside. Noses snuffled, tracing the ground for a hint of our scent, but none came close to where we hid in the darkness.

A solitary howl in the distance was answered by the others nearer our hideaway. The snuffling ended, the paws retreated. We were alone.

"They're gone," Clay whispered, his breath warm, arousing, along the sensitive skin below my ear.

I turned my head, our noses brushed, and the next instant our mouths met. Who kissed whom? I have no idea. I only know that I'd never wanted anyone as I wanted him. I didn't care how close to death we'd come, how close we might yet come. Perhaps that was even the reason behind our desperation. If tomorrow was the end, at least we had tonight.

The complete darkness surrounding us was as arousing as the texture of his skin beneath my fingertips and the taste of his mouth against mine. I kept my eyes wide open, yet I couldn't see a thing. Every touch a surprise, each caress was a mystery.

I let my hands drift over the stomach that had tantalized me, allowed my fingernails to scrape the pectorals I'd fantasized about. What was left of his shirt disappeared, as did every stitch I now owned. The only strip of cloth on my body remained wrapped around my wrist.

Nudity had always embarrassed me. I wasn't small. Too many hours spent with my butt in a chair meant I wasn't toned. I'd never be tan. Men had wanted me, but they had never yearned. In the darkness, I was a goddess and Clay was my slave.

I sensed him above me, like a great dark bird—hovering, hunting, waiting to swoop.

I liked the not-knowing, the aura of danger that clung to him like cologne, the possibility of death just beyond the realm of our cave.

What had happened to safety girl? She'd died in the flames that had consumed everything that was left of her life.

I wanted to run naked through the trees, skinny-dip in the ocean, make love on the beach, the grass, the desert floor. I wanted to do every one of those things with him.

Was I experiencing kidnap dementia? Bonding to my tormenter? Falling in love with a man who could never be any more than a one-cave stand? Maybe. But I'd worry about that after he made me come.

I hunted for the zipper of his camouflage pants and couldn't find one. I did find an impressive erection, which I explored through the coarse material.

His guns weren't in their holsters. He'd no doubt held them while the wolves prowled outside and left them . . . Lord knows where. Oh well, one less thing to remove.

I slipped my hand into the waistband of his pants, filled my palm with smooth, hard flesh, then stroked and kneaded him to greater heights.

I wanted to feel all of his skin against all of mine, so I tried to locate that zipper again but had no better luck.

"Are these locked?" I murmured into his mouth.

He reached between us, fumbled a bit and the waistband gave way in my hands. Seconds later he was naked, too, but instead of letting me run my fingers all over his toned, tanned skin, he traced his lips down my neck, over my breasts, along my belly, then my hip, performing amazing, innovative tricks with his tongue and his teeth.

My fingers toyed with what was left of his hair. His tongue swept across me once, then dodged back and lingered. I arched, and the rocks of the cave floor scraped my back. I couldn't focus, didn't care. He pushed me harder and harder, faster and faster, until I was moaning, begging for release.

As I flew over the edge, the first contractions of my orgasm making my insides clench and spasm, he slid into me. Like a surfer catching the wave, he rode mine, drawing out the pleasure. Slowing down, then speeding up, playing me until I was limp, satisfied, exhausted. Only when he kissed my eyelids, nibbled my nose, did I realize he was still hard and hot, still ready to go.

Aching, sensitive, I didn't think I had another round in me, but I was wrong. He laid his head on my chest and his breath chilled my sweat-slicked skin. My nipples hardened as he nuzzled the underside of my breasts.

He licked one tight bud in a lazy, possessive swirl, then bit the edge lightly before drawing me into his mouth to suckle in a copycat rhythm to the slide of our bodies—in and out, shallow to deep, tip then full hilt.

The friction began again. With skillful manipulation he brought me to a second climax, and this time he followed me there. The pulse of his ejaculation made my own release linger. By the time my body stopped dancing, his movements were languid as he rolled to the side, tugged me off the ground and into his arms.

I was almost asleep when Clay shifted, reaching for something. The scrape of metal on stone, he drew his gun closer, holding the weapon in one hand and me in the other. I liked the sense of safety in that image, and I drifted off.

Sometime later, I was jerked awake. Disoriented, I tried to sit up, but Clay held me too tightly.

The cave was still dark. I couldn't see a thing. But I felt him trembling.

CHAPTER 7

"What's the matter?" I whispered, placing my hand on Clay's chest. His heartbeat raced beneath my palm.

"Nothing," he said harshly. "Go on back to sleep."

As if I could when he was so upset.

His voice had slid south, the accent he'd lost found again. I lifted my fingers to his face, stroked his temple, played with his hair. Inch by inch he relaxed, but he didn't fall asleep.

"Nightmare?" I asked.

He snorted.

"Wanna tell me about it?"

"So you can have nightmares too?"

Just like that, his voice had returned to the flat, cultured tones that told no one where he'd come from, gave no hint of where he'd been.

"Like I don't already have them?"

He shifted, as if to see my face, but he couldn't in this darkest hour that always preceded dawn.

"What do you dream, Maya Alexander?"

He was asking about the bad dreams—the times when I awoke gasping and panicked, the nights I relived my mother's death, I'd added twenty years to my age, but those dreams of a little girl left alone had never gone away.

I'd be damned if I'd share past nightmares while we

were fashioning new ones. Here, in the dark, in his arms, was the time for sharing happy dreams.

"I dream of the *New York Times*."

"You want to own a newspaper?"

"The list. Books? My job?"

"Ah," he said, though I could tell he didn't understand. Non-writers rarely did.

The *New York Times* Bestseller List was a rare accolade aspired to by every author who put pen to paper, or fingers to keyboard. Not only did the list mean prestige and fame, it meant money. While I enjoyed the writing, I enjoyed the food, the clothes, the shelter too. Or I had until they'd gone *boom*.

On any other day I'd have been worried sick over the loss of everything I owned. Since I'd be lucky to get out of this alive, and would therefore have no further need of *stuff*, I experienced a sense of freedom I couldn't recall having since long before my mother had died.

"What else do you dream of?" he asked.

"A cabin in the woods."

"Oops."

"Yeah. I hate the thought of running home to Daddy."

"I'm sure he wouldn't mind."

He wouldn't, but he'd never let me forget it, and neither would the bozos I called brothers. They'd already started a pool on when I'd call it quits. I'd put ten bucks on the space marked "not in this lifetime." However, if I was sent home in a pine box, did that mean whoever had the space nearest the date of my death got the money? Oh well, I wouldn't be around to be pissed off about it.

"Ever dream of a husband, a family?"

"No," I lied. Because I had—an eon ago when I'd still believed the line they fed little girls. That there's someone for everyone. One man, one woman, for all time.

I was two inches short of six feet. I weighed a hundred

and sixty pounds. My hair was long and red, my skin white, except for the freckles. And I talked, daily, to people who didn't exist. Or at least I had before the damned writer's block hit.

"So there's no irate fiancé who's going to kick my ass?"

"Don't worry. Your ass is safe with me."

He chuckled, appearing to have forgotten the nightmare, which was exactly what I'd had in mind. But appearances are deceiving, because Clay suddenly stiffened and withdrew from my arms.

"What's the matter?" I asked.

"I didn't use a condom. I've never done that. Never. Hell, I didn't even think about it until now."

I hadn't either. No big surprise there. All I'd been able to think of, practically since we'd met, was getting him inside me. Now he'd been there, and left a little something behind.

My mind whirred, counting backward, letting out the breath I'd been holding. "We should be all right. The days are wrong."

"There's still a chance—"

"There's always a chance."

A tiny flutter began in my belly. I think it was hope. Or hunger. I hadn't eaten since yesterday. Which probably explained the light-headedness, but the stupidity was all my own. My mind was suddenly full of pink ribbons and blue bicycles. English stone cottages and wedding bells. I forgot who I was dealing with.

"This can never happen again, Maya."

"Barn door wide open, horse running down the street," I mumbled. "Or maybe up the stream."

"This isn't funny!" he snapped.

I jumped, wrapping my arms around myself as tears stung my eyes. Even though I'd just denied any need for home and family, his reaction hurt. I'd believed for just an instant that he saw me differently than other men, that he found me funny, pretty. That he might even consider me special.

"I'm sorry if the idea of making a baby with me is so disgusting."

"That's not it." He took a deep breath, which caught in the middle. "I tried to be normal once, tried to love someone and have a life. She was the one who paid."

"Serena," I whispered.

"You asked about my nightmare. This is it. I let someone get close to me, then the monsters take them away. They'll use you against me, and I can't let that happen."

"You could quit."

"No. I vowed over the bodies of my grandparents, my parents, my sisters, my brother, then Serena that I wouldn't stop until every werewolf was dead."

"You could be alone for the rest of your life. I doubt your family, or Serena, would want that."

"If I quit, people die. The survivors get my nightmares. I can't live with that either. I've lost those I loved twice. I wouldn't survive being a three-time loser."

"So you have nothing, love no one?"

"It's the only way I can go on."

Silence settled between us. When I finally slept, my dreams weren't happy, and when I awoke my cheeks were tight with dried tears. I was alone, just as I'd been in those dreams.

Gray light filtered through the scrub across the entryway, illuminating my clothes strewn across the floor of the cave, revealing Clay's silhouette near the door. When he'd left me to stand watch again, I had no idea, but his absence had seeped into my subconscious, creating loneliness even though he was only a few feet away.

I got up, gathered my clothes, got dressed. I had just tied my flannel shirt around my waist and slipped into my shoes, when the snap of a twig and the ping of stone on stone made us freeze. Clay held up one hand indicating I should stay back, even as he reached for his Beretta with the other.

His trap had been sprung. Something lurked outside our cave. But what?

We'd heard no howls, no pitter-patter of tiny feet, not even the thud of great, big paws. Nothing until the snap, crackle, ping. Could a skinwalker fly?

I recalled the skins of the eagle and the raven in Joseph's cabin. I had a very bad feeling that it could.

"Hello, the cave. Anyone there?"

Clay frowned and his gun dipped a bit. The voice had been gruff, wobbly—the voice of a very old man.

Joseph? I mouthed.

Clay shook his head and leaned over to whisper in my ear. "Mandenauer said he's about my age."

"Hello?" the voice repeated. "You need help?"

Clay crept to the side of the entrance and peeked through the tiny hole in the covering. His shoulders relaxed at the sight.

"Ancient white guy," he told me.

"Sounds like a new rock group."

His lips twitched. I liked it that he found me funny. I liked it that he'd found me at all. Just my luck he'd sworn off women along with his life.

Clay tore down the covering with a sweep of one hand and crawled into the daylight. I followed, standing stiffly at his side. We'd slept longer than I thought. The brush over the entry had shaded the rising sun amazingly well. From its position in the sky the day was well past noon.

My first sight of our visitor made the word "ghost" whisper through my head, and not because he was pale. His skin was as sun-bronzed as Clay's and showed the wear of countless years. His hair was long and white, his clothes had seen better days. Perhaps in the year 1895.

He looked like the poster boy for a gold rush—grizzled

prospector complete with six-guns and a mule. His pack animal pulled for all it was worth—which couldn't be much considering the gnarled forelocks and swayed back—at the very end of its tether.

"Stop that, Cissy." The old man yanked on the rope. "We'll be off in a bit."

He grinned at us, several black gaps appearing where teeth should be. "I'm Jack."

"Clay Philips. Maya Alexander. We *could* use a little help, Mr.—"

"Just Jack, boy. No need to 'mister' me."

"Jack, then. How close are we to a town?"

"Depends what kind of town yer lookin' fer. Ghost towns all over the place. Real town?" He shrugged. "Fifty miles 'r more."

"How about a phone?"

"That I got. Back at my place."

"Could we borrow it?"

"Sure. Follow me."

The old man headed toward the slowly descending sun. As he passed Cissy she brayed and skittered backward. Jack pulled on her lead, but she couldn't be budged. He scratched his head, squinted at the animal.

"I don't know what's gotten into 'er." He tethered Cissy to a juniper and lifted the saddlebags from her back. "I'll just let her think on things a while. Fetch her later."

Slinging the pack over his own shoulders, he strode off. Clay and I fell in behind.

"Why do we need a phone?" I whispered.

"I'm going to have one of my colleagues pick you up and take you somewhere safe. Then I'll go after the skin-walker."

I didn't like the idea of a babysitter. I liked the idea of Clay facing the skinwalker alone even less, and I told him so.

"I've done this a hundred times before, Maya."

"You've killed a hundred skinwalkers?"

He scowled. "You know I haven't, but someone has to handle the situation."

I'd heard the same explanation from my father and each one of my brothers. Why are you a cop? Someone has to be. I didn't like the rationalization any better from Clay than I had from them.

"You don't know what you're facing."

"I know my job. I'll do a better one if I'm not worrying about you."

"Will I ever see you again?"

He didn't answer, which was answer enough.

We continued to walk. Jack was ahead of us by quite a few yards. The old guy could really make some time. Clay brought up the rear, watching the horizon with suspicious eyes.

"Aren't wolves nocturnal?" I asked.

"Doesn't mean they can't come out in the sunlight. They aren't vampires."

"What about werewolves?"

"Most can't change until dusk."

"Then what are you nervous about now?"

"A skinwalker is a special type of werewolf. One that can pad around anytime it puts on the skin."

Suddenly I was watching the horizon, too.

We'd been walking for over an hour when Clay asked, "How far away do you live, sir?"

"Not far now. Keep your pants on, sonny."

"I wish I had," Clay muttered.

I flashed him a dirty look, which he ignored. We continued to walk for another three-quarters of an hour.

I wasn't sure if it was the heat of the sun, the lack of water, the absence of food—but I started to see things. Shadows at the edge of my vision that disappeared when I glanced their way. Moisture hovering above the desert sand. A mountain where there hadn't been one before.

Skinwalker.

I stopped as the wind whispered, except there wasn't any wind.

"Maya?" Clay stared at me with a worried expression.

"Did you hear anything?"

He tilted his head. "No."

I shrugged and kept walking.

Cañón del Muerto.

My Spanish was as nonexistent as my next book. I ignored the voice I didn't understand.

Maya.

Hell. The wind that wasn't now whispered my name.

Jack disappeared around an outcropping of rock. I followed, then halted so fast Clay slammed into me from behind.

"What the—"

A huge canyon opened in front of us. Towering walls, rocky ledges, buttes the shade of the sun and the sturgeon moon.

"Welcome to Cañón del Muerto," Jack said in a low voice that was no longer his own. "The Canyon of the Dead."

CHAPTER 8

J ack yanked me in front of him and pressed a gun to my
  temple. Clay, who had been reaching for me, too, let his
hand fall to his side, where it rested atop his Ruger. The
Beretta was already aimed in the general vicinity of Jack's
head, which was, unfortunately behind mine.

Shadows fluttered past my face, seemed to touch my
skin and whisper. There was more here than the living.

"Let Maya go."

"Can't do that." The old man's voice no longer wobbled
and wheezed but had become deep, melodic, with an
accent I couldn't quite place. "The red moon will rise, and
I'm going to need her for the ceremony."

"You're the skinwalker?" Clay asked.

"Got it in one. I heard you were a bright boy."

I didn't understand. I'd seen the Navajo man turn into a
wolf, so who was this guy?

"If you're a skinwalker, then tell me something," Clay
continued. "How does a witch become a werewolf?"

"A chant in the language of the people, followed by the
cry of the beast. Wear the skin and—"

"Poof," I murmured.

"Exactly."

"How do you change back?"

I wanted to tell Clay to save his questions for a different

time, preferably one when I didn't have a gun to my head. But he slid his gaze to mine. I could read the intent in his eyes. He was trying to buy time.

"Changing back is the easy part," Jack explained. "Walk as a beast in the sun, walk as a man beneath the moon, and vice versa."

"The rising of the sun or the rising of the moon triggers it."

Jack's head was so close to mine I could feel him nod. "Now the red moon rises and the ultimate power will be mine. I will no longer be forced back into my body at the whim of the elements. The change will be mine to keep or discard."

"How?"

"Blood, death, sacrifice." His arm tightened across my chest in what would have been a hug, if he wasn't planning to kill me. "Of the one who is chosen."

"Why Maya?"

"She heard me whisper. Only the chosen can."

"What about the others? Why did you kill them?"

"The legend says the chosen one will have hair the shade of the moon."

I recalled the skinwalker's victims—both silver-haired and blond. But what about me?

"I don't remember anything about this in the book I read," Clay said.

"Book?" Jack's voice was scornful. "You can't learn magic from words on a page. There is more to legends than what is written."

"Why were all the victims women?"

"To birth the power there must be yin and yang. Male and female. Harmony first. Chaos later."

He nuzzled my hair. "Your death, Maya, for my ever-lasting life."

"Well, as long as that's all."

I couldn't believe I was joking at a time like this. But it was better than crying. Maybe.

"I still don't understand why you hung around her place and watched her. The others you killed the instant you knew they couldn't hear the whisper of the beast."

"She hardly ever came outside. All she did was stare at her computer and listen to music with her earphones on."

My block had been good for something at least. It had given Clay time to arrive.

"You took a chance waiting around until she could hear you. You had to know I'd show up eventually."

"Once I saw the moon turn red, then I saw . . ." He shifted, taking a deep, loud sniff of my auburn hair. "I couldn't leave."

Voices came out of nowhere, swirling around me. I couldn't make out the words.

"What is that?" I asked.

"You hear them?" He rubbed the barrel of the gun along my temple like a caress. "I knew you were special the first time I looked at you. Those are the spirits of the dead, trapped in the canyon that carries their name. Only the Dineh, the Navajo, hear them. Only the Dineh and—"

"The one who is chosen," I muttered.

I'd never been psychic, though being a writer, hearing voices in my head, having stories spill out my fingertips, is a magic of sorts. However, the ghosts were new to me and not altogether pleasant—even without the promise of imminent death by sacrifice.

"If she's your chosen one," Clay asked, "why have you been trying to kill her?"

"I needed to get her to the Cañón del Muerto. I didn't think she'd just stumble on it by herself."

"But—"

"Doesn't matter *when* she died, just that she died. Once her blood touches me beneath the moon, in this sacred place, I'll have what I desire. To become in truth what I must now wear a skin to achieve."

"A wolf?"

"Much, much more. Combine a witch with a werewolf, add the ceremony of the red moon rising, and I will become a *chindi*—a witch, a human wolf—greater than legend has ever foretold. I won't even need the skin, all I'll have to do is—" He snapped his fingers. "Can you imagine the power in that? Today I rule the beasts, tomorrow—"

"The world," Clay finished. "Why does everyone want to do that?"

"Not everyone," I said. "Only the crazy people."

"True." He shook his head. "You're no different than any other freak of nature I've ever met."

"There you're wrong. Skinwalkers are superior to our werewolf kin. We can become anything just by a change of our skin. We exist beneath both the sun and the moon, and we aren't insane with the blood lust."

"Could have fooled me," I murmured.

"You've never encountered one of the bitten. The virus makes them mad. They think of nothing but the kill. A silver bullet is the best thing for them. Once I complete the ceremony beneath the red moon, nothing, and no one, can destroy me."

"Let's find out." Clay sighted down the barrel of his Beretta.

"You won't shoot me. You could hit her. Just like Serena."

Clay stiffened.

"I thought Serena was killed by . . ." I wasn't sure what. "Monsters?" I supplied.

"Ultimately. But only after Clayton shot her trying to save her. Then she was devoured while she lay screaming. Isn't that right?"

Clay lowered the gun. "How do you know so god-damned much?"

"I never leave anything to chance. I knew that as I

searched for the chosen one, the unworthy would die. And the *Jäger-Suchers* would come."

"Aren't you supposed to be a *secret* society?" I muttered.

Jack's chuckle made the gun at my temple shudder. There was also an unpleasant scent rising from him that wasn't sweat but something worse.

"Secret to the world at large but not to the ones they hunt. Not anymore. We know *Jäger-Suchers* exist, only their identities are a secret—for the most part."

"How did you find out about me, about my past?" Clay asked.

"That's *my* secret."

Clay's eyes narrowed. I could almost hear the word going through his head, because it went through mine too.

Traitor.

Someone in the *Jager-Sucher* ranks was selling information to the enemy. But I really didn't have the time to worry about that, and neither did Clay.

The sun was falling, which meant the moon was rising. Clay didn't have much time to do . . . whatever it was he planned on doing. I hoped Clay had a plan, because I didn't. I'd run out of ideas the second Jack had put a gun to my head. I seemed to be having that problem a lot lately, even without the gun.

"A skinwalker is a Navajo witch," Clay blurted. "You aren't."

"Appearances are deceiving. A skinwalker takes the shape of the skin he wears. Be it beast or man."

Suddenly I understood what the nasty smell was. And Cissy, the mule, had known it too. Animals can smell death long before humans. Cissy hadn't cared for Jack, because Jack was no longer alive. The skinwalker was wearing the skin of an ancient white man.

"You *are* Joseph Ahkeah," Clay stated. "I thought you were Mandenauer's friend."

"Friendship means nothing in the face of power. If Edward could feel what I feel when I run as a wolf, he wouldn't be so eager to kill me."

"He'd be first in line."

Jack . . . Joseph—hell, I didn't know what to call him except nuts—sighed. "Edward has a most annoying need to be a hero, and he can't help but hire people just like him."

"I can think of worse things to be than a hero," Clay said.

Ahkeah merely laughed at him some more.

"You were a hunter," Clay insisted. "You've seen the evil and destruction these things can bring to the world. How can you become one of them?"

"I've been tracking and killing monsters for years. There are always more. I got tired of fighting a losing battle. I wanted to be on the winning side. We will win, Clayton. It's only a matter of time."

"Not if I have anything to say about it."

"Sadly, you won't."

I'd been planning to point out to Clay that Ahkeah was being far too accommodating in answering all his questions. The villain only blabs his plans to those he intends to kill—it's in every bad movie. I wasn't the only one who would die tonight if the skinwalker had his way.

The spirits murmured, louder this time. The very air seemed to vibrate with their presence. Ahkeah took a deep breath, as if to drink in the dead.

Help me. I thought. *Not him.*

The spirits spoke at once in a hundred different languages. Dizziness washed over me in a mind-numbing wave at the same time my stomach rolled. I slumped, and the gun slid from my temple into my hair.

Jack struggled to hold me upright, but in this instance being a big girl was a good thing. He wasn't strong enough, and my knees slammed into the ground.

The moon, red and full, burst over the horizon. The earth began to shake, and a gunshot sounded.

I caught the scent of sulfur, right before agony burst across my cheekbone. I ate dust when my face smashed into the rocky terrain of the Canyon of the Dead.

CHAPTER 9

I must have passed out because the next thing I knew I was staring at the huge red moon blazing in the sky above me. I heard whispers again—soft as the wind, though the air was cool and still.

Everything came rushing back, and I sat up too fast. My head spun, something warm and wet ran down my cheek. My palm came away slick with blood.

"Clay?"

"I'm right here." And suddenly he was. His dark gaze skittered over my face. "Damn, Maya, you're bleedin' like a stuck pig."

His accent was back. I must have looked even worse than I felt.

Clay yanked off what was left of his shirt and pressed it to my cheek, then sat back to stare at me solemnly. Poor guy, if he hung around me much longer, he wouldn't have a stitch left to wear.

"It's over," he murmured.

I glanced toward the two shadowy bumps lying a few feet away, then got to my feet, slowly. Once there I was steady. The world no longer shook and neither did my knees. My stomach was steady and so was my head.

One lump was nothing but skin. The other appeared to be what was left of a thirty-something Navajo male. I guess skinwalkers exploded just like werewolves when shot with silver, but . . .

"I thought a silver bullet wouldn't work."

"If I remember correctly, it wouldn't work once he completed the ceremony."

"I'm not dead, so he is." I lifted my gaze to Clay's. "He was going to murder me, and you too."

"I nicked your cheek." Clay's head lowered. "Another centimeter to the left and—"

He didn't have to finish. Another centimeter and the world would have been Joseph's, not ours.

Once upon a time the realization of how close to death I'd come would have paralyzed me. Now it made me act. I crossed the short distance between us and slipped my arms around Clay's waist. He stiffened in my embrace, but he didn't pull away.

"You had to take a chance, Clay."

"I'm too reckless. Always have been. That's how Serena died."

"But I lived. Because of you."

Hope lit his face, until he saw mine.

"You need a doctor. Preferably a plastic surgeon. And your wrist." He yanked off the dirty bandage, then cursed some more. "Doesn't look good."

I'd forgotten about the wolf bite. Compared to our other problems, it was minor, but Clay was right. The torn skin was red and warm to the touch.

Clay opened Ahkeah's saddlebags. "That son of a bitch." He lifted a cell phone from inside.

"Like he'd let us use his phone and waltz off before we got to Cañón del Muerto."

Clay turned on the phone, frowned at the display, then glanced up at the towering stone walls. "I'll be right back." He headed toward the center of the canyon.

The instant he was gone, the whispers returned. Indistinct, they rippled across the air like wind across calm water.

I cast an uneasy glance at the skin and the body, but neither one moved. When the skinwalker spoke to me, I understood his words. When the spirits of this canyon murmured, I could make no sense of them at all.

But they'd heard and helped me, causing me to create a diversion so Clay could come to the rescue.

"Thank you," I said aloud.

As if a great switch had been thrown, they were gone. The night was still and I was alone.

A short while later, the distant whir of a helicopter filled the canyon. Clay, who'd been on the phone the entire time, ran toward me just as the searchlight burst over a stone wall.

"Let's go." He grabbed my elbow and pulled me toward the hovering craft.

"How did they get here so fast?"

Clay lifted a brow. According to him, *Jäger-Suchers* were everywhere. They must have a budget that just wouldn't quit.

I climbed into the helicopter and less than an hour later I was being stitched up by the best plastic surgeon in Phoenix. The ER doctor wanted to keep me overnight, probably because I appeared as if I'd had the crap beaten out of me. Besides the crease in my cheek, kissing the dirt far too many times had given me a fat lip and black eye.

I had countless other scrapes, bumps, bruises, but my wrist wasn't infected. If the wolf that had bitten me turned out to be rabid upon testing—Clay had already made arrangements to have the body brought in, along with what was left of the skinwalker—I'd get a rabies shot. Not exactly pleasant, but not the life-threatening occurrence it had once been.

I wanted to sleep in a clean bed—with Clay. All I had to do was convince him that he wanted that too.

Clay took one look at me when I walked out of the emergency room and winced.

"It only hurts when I laugh."

He didn't answer, and I wished I'd kept my big mouth shut.

We stood in the waiting room, the silence stretching between us for far too long. I had to say something. "Now what?"

As soon as the words were out, I wanted to take them back. I'd given him the perfect opportunity to say goodbye, and I wasn't ready.

"I—"

"I want champagne," I blurted. "A shower, food, not necessarily in that order."

"I can arrange that." He whipped out a new cell phone with the speed of a gunslinger at high noon. Minutes later a limo slid to a stop at the entrance of the hospital.

Champagne peeked out of an ice bucket. Crackers and cheese lay on a crystal tray. I'd never seen anything so wonderful, or tasted anything so wonderful either. Sitting back, I let my gaze wander over the car and the driver.

"J-S sent him. He's trustworthy."

My eyes widened as I realized Clay's life was in danger from every monster on the planet. There was a leak at *Jäger-Sucher* headquarters.

"Where are we going?" I asked.

"The Biltmore."

"Really?"

The Arizona Biltmore was a landmark designed by Frank Lloyd Wright. Nestled at the foot of Squaw Peak, the place was gorgeous—and expensive. I'd never be able to afford a night there on my own. But on the *Jäger-Suchers*? What the hell.

"You can't leave me alone tonight."

Clay opened his mouth to refuse, I could see it in his

eyes, and I blurted the first lie that came to my lips. "I need to be woken up every hour. Concussion."

His mouth closed with an audible snap of his teeth. "Of course."

Guilt swamped me, but I shoved it away. I was going to seduce him—a first for me, but hey, so was getting shot at and kidnapped and any number of things that had happened in the last forty-eight hours. My life was one adventure after the next these days. I'd have a spectacular story to write just as soon as I could find a pen and some paper.

Would the ending be happy? I stared at Clay over the rim of my champagne glass. It would if I had anything to say about it.

An hour later I was squeaky clean from a shower and pleasantly tipsy from the champagne. I sat in a big, plush chair in the first suite I'd ever set foot in, writing down everything that had happened to me before I forgot it. As if.

Clay was using the shower, and the thought of slipping in behind him and letting the water seduce us both pulled me out of my story.

The bathroom door opened, and a soapy-scented mist poured out. Clay appeared through the fog, a towel looped around his hips, his skin moist, shiny, hot.

My pen and paper dropped to the floor. His head jerked up and his gaze shifted to my shadowed corner. "You should be in bed."

"I know."

I walked toward him until I was close enough to feel the warmth of the steam. He stepped back, and I caught him by the towel, then yanked.

"Maya—"

My hand closed around him. He was already hard. I drew him closer.

"We can't," he protested.

I pumped my fist several quick strokes, and he leaped in my palm. "I think we can."

"Not *can't*." He groaned as I continued to work his skin back and forth against the shaft. "Should. I mean shouldn't. I'm not thinking straight."

"Good. When you think straight, you think stupid."

"It's not stupid to stay away from you. I'm a dead man. It's only a matter of time."

"I won't let you die."

"You don't have anything to say about it."

"I love you."

Shock flashed across his face. "You can't love me. You just met me."

"Are you saying you don't love me?"

I held my breath. I'd been taking a chance to put my heart in the open so he could crush it. But I believed Clay cared about me, otherwise he wouldn't be trying so hard to leave me behind.

"If you can look me in eye, right now, and tell me you don't want me I'll—"

"Obviously I want you, Maya. You can feel that in the palm of your hand."

I could, and it was unbelievably erotic to be talking about both love and death as he pulsed and grew at my touch. What had happened to safety girl? I'd left her in the desert with the snakes.

The thought should have made me panic, instead it intrigued me. My life, until now, had been staid and predictable. What if I took a chance, faced the world, courted death instead of fearing it?

I guess we'd find out.

I kissed his neck, his jaw, ran my tongue up to his ear, and sucked the lobe between my teeth. The pulse at the base of his throat throbbed. I put my lips there, and his blood beat in time with mine.

I stroked him again. He showed me what he liked—how hard, how soft, how fast.

I wanted to taste him as he'd once tasted me. Sliding down his body, I took him in my mouth.

"Maya—" he murmured.

Protest or encouragement? I didn't know, didn't care. He was warm and alive. He filled me, and I no longer felt alone.

He tasted like a desert night. Hot, salty, dangerous. You could die in the desert. We almost had.

But we'd survived together and that had to count for something. Together we could do anything, face anyone.

His hands cupped my head, urging me on. He wasn't thinking of the past now, but then, neither was I.

Suddenly he reached down and grabbed my arms, yanking me to my feet and kissing me, long and deep, with a hint of desperation that only made me want him more.

Past, present, future? Whatever.

My robe slid from my shoulders. I wore nothing underneath. I had nothing anymore but him.

My skin tingled at his touch. His fingers fluttered everywhere. He soul-kissed me as he backed me toward the bed. My legs hit the mattress, and we tumbled onto the sheets.

His palm smoothed the skin of my thigh, my rear, my spine. Lifting his head, he stared into my face. Only when his gaze darkened, and he started to inch away did I remember what I looked like.

Scrapes, bruises, black eye, stitches. He believed I'd been hurt because of him. He was wrong. Without him I'd be dead. I had to make him understand that I needed him. Forever. I knew only one way to do that.

Lacing my fingers behind his neck, I drew him closer and made him kiss me again. The hand/blow job had excited me as much as him. I arched, and he slid along the part of me that cried out for a man—this man.

"Now," I whispered into his mouth. "Please."

He didn't hesitate, just lifted his hips and plunged all the way home. I was wet, tight, excited. Only a few deep strokes, and I shattered, squeezing and contracting around him. The pulse in his neck jumped as he came, and I latched on to his skin, tasting him as we both shuddered with a release that went on and on.

When he stilled, I nuzzled him behind the ear. I loved the scent of his hair, the taste of his skin. He kissed my unmarked cheek, then gently brushed his fingers over my black eye. "I'm sorry."

I sighed. My plan hadn't worked. He still didn't see how much we needed each other to survive. I'd have to be more direct.

"I'm not. I don't regret a single thing that brought us together. I didn't realize how alone I was."

"You've got four brothers. You were never alone."

"I was alone in a crowd, until I found you."

"You didn't find me. I was sent."

"Even better."

He made an exasperated sound and rolled to the side. I'd have been insulted, if he hadn't caught my hand and held on tight. "Are you always so happy?"

"No." In fact, I couldn't remember a time when I hadn't been downright cranky. "You make me this way."

He laughed, and I laid my head on his shoulder. His breath brushed my temple, slower and slower until he was asleep.

I dreamed of blue booties and pink hats, cabins in the deep woods and a love that could survive anything.

Nevertheless, when I awoke it took me only an instant to understand that Clay was gone and he wasn't coming back.

CHAPTER 10

He'd left his Beretta and a cache of silver bullets. Nothing says "I love you" like guns and ammo.

I held the weapon in my lap, stroked the metal, absently checked the load. When the door of the suite burst open and a strange man flew inside, I flicked the sheet over both myself and the pistol. The guy had a crazy look in his eyes, but he didn't have a gun or a knife that I could see.

"Where's Philips?" he demanded.

"Never heard of him."

"You came with him. I saw you. I've been waiting."

He was breathing heavily. Sweat dotted his upper lip and his brow. He opened the curtains, and the silver sheen of the just-past-full moon streamed in. He bathed in the light as if it were cool water in the heat of a sandstorm.

"Who are you?" I demanded.

He turned toward me and his eyes glowed. Ah, hell. He leaped onto the bed, onto me, and I stifled a scream.

"Brendan Steiger. I wonder if Philips will even remember why I spent my life savings to buy his."

"Buy his what?"

"His *name*. His picture. His whereabouts." Steiger's voice, half man, half beast, scraped against my skin like a razor. "He's not here? I'll just kill you. Payback."

His head lowered, and he sniffed my neck, licked me

from collarbone to cheek. I caught the scent of blood. He'd already been a busy boy.

The man's face began to change. His nose lengthened, his teeth grew, fur sprouted from his pores, but his eyes remained human.

"Even better," he snarled. "I'll make you like me. Then he'll have to hunt down his lover and put a bullet in her brain." He laughed and the sound melded into a howl. "I wish I could be here to see it."

"Too bad you won't be."

I shot him right through the sheet. Flames erupted from the wound, and his howl went on and on. I shoved the body away, but not quickly enough. I was covered in blood and my palms were burned. Nevertheless, I sat on the floor unable to move as the half man, half beast sizzled on the king-sized bed. This hotel was not going to ask me back.

Footsteps pounded down the hall. Clay stumbled into the room. One glance at me and he fell to his knees. "What happened?"

I didn't bother to answer. The mess on the bed should be answer enough.

"Come on, Maya. Into the shower."

I let him lead me from the room and urge me beneath the heated spray.

"You left me," I said.

"I had no choice. You wouldn't survive in my world."

"I've done pretty well so far."

Silence met my statement. Had he run off again?

I peeked around the shower curtain. He leaned against the sink, head down, shoulders bowed. I hated to see him so defeated.

"Why did you come back?"

He glanced at me, misery all over his face. "I tried to go, but I couldn't. I—"

"What?"

"I was worried. And I was right."

"How you figure?"

"The werewolf."

"I did just fine without you."

He scowled at the gun still clutched in his hand. "Dammit, Maya, I love you."

"Don't sound so happy about it."

"Just because I didn't leave tonight, doesn't mean I don't have to in the morning."

"Like hell."

I was feeling better minute by minute. Sure, it had been a shock to have a man break in, turn into a werewolf, and try to eat me, but I'd handled it. Everything would be all right, unless Clay really left.

I shut off the water, wrapped myself in a towel, took the gun out of his hand. "We're together, and that's the way we'll stay."

"You almost died. Because of me."

"I lived because of you. Time and time again. We're better together than apart. When are you going to see that?"

"You fainted at Cañón del Muerto. Not that it wasn't a good thing at the time, but— It was too much for you."

"Wait a second, you think I fainted because of Jack? Joseph? Hell, whoever?"

"Well . . ." He shrugged. "Yeah."

"No, Clay. The spirits spoke. There were so many of them, I got dizzy. I asked for help and *bam*, out went the lights."

I expected him to scoff at my talk of spirits, but I'd forgotten who I was dealing with. If he could be a Special Forces werewolf hunter, the fact that I could hear spirits wasn't anything to write home about.

"You didn't swoon in terror?"

"Sorry, no. But you did rescue me. My hero."

"Knock it off. I can't stop seeing you covered in blood."

I spread my hands wide. "Washed right off."

His gaze narrowed. "Your hands are burned."

"They'll heal. Next time I'll know better."

"Next time?" He shoved his fingers through his hair. "There isn't going to be a next time."

"You know that's not true."

He made a sound of frustration and yanked open the door. I followed him into the bedroom. The first thing I saw was the man sitting in the wing chair reading my notes.

"What is this, Grand Central Station?" I pointed the Beretta at his head.

"No." Clay put a hand over the barrel and gently shoved the weapon down.

The intruder lifted his gaze from the papers to my face. "You should never shoot a werewolf in mid-change," he said, his German accent so heavy it would have been comical under different circumstances. "That leaves too many questions and a very big mess."

"I'll keep that in mind. Who the hell are you?"

"Maya, this is Edward Mandenauer."

I stared with renewed interest at the former spy and present leader of the *Jäger-Suchers*. Most likely a handsome man in his day, he now owned every one of his eighty-plus years.

He'd seen many things and all of them haunted his faded blue eyes and sagging, drawn face. He was scarecrow thin and basketball tall. His hands were gnarled, spotted, his fingers crooked from breaks that had never healed right.

"You cannot publish this." He lifted my notes in one hand and a lighter in the other.

"Wait!" I sputtered, but he brought the two together and flames licked at my hastily scrawled words. I sighed. "Have you ever heard of freedom of speech, private property, the public's right to know?"

"Yes." He dropped the rapidly decomposing paper into a tin trash can.

"How are you going to erase the memory from my head? Same way?"

"Put a sock in it," Clay muttered. "He might look like your favorite granddad, but he isn't. He's dangerous."

I glanced at Mandenauer, who shrugged. "I am."

I wouldn't have believed either one of them, except there was something in Mandenauer's eyes, something in Clay's voice, that convinced me.

"Fine." I threw up my hands. "I'll keep quiet."

I wondered if McDonald's was hiring. Because that was the only other job I was qualified for.

"Can we trust her?" the old man asked.

"What do I have to do?" I asked. "Write it in blood? Let you cut out my tongue?"

"If you don't mind—"

Since he said the words with a completely straight face, I didn't think he was kidding. Clay must not have either because he moved in front of me.

"Leave her alone. She's been through enough."

"Precisely. You should never have involved her, Clayton. You know better."

"The skinwalker blew up her house. I didn't have much choice but to take her along after that."

"And Joseph? Was he of any help?"

We exchanged glances. Mandenauer frowned. "What?"

"Joseph was the skinwalker."

"Impossible. He's been a trusted colleague for years."

"He got sick of being on the losing side. It's happened before."

The old man sighed and his shoulders slumped. If possible he appeared older than before. "Even the strong ones succumb. The allure of power is a human failing. Sometimes I think it would be easier to . . ." His voice drifted off.

"To what, sir?"

"Never mind." Mandenauer stood and crossed the short

distance to the bed with a military bearing. "Any idea who this was?"

"Brendan Steiger," I said.

Both men glanced at me with a frown. I shrugged. "He was chatty. Something about payback."

Clay shook his head. "I don't remember the name."

"Why would you?" Mandenauer asked. "They don't wear dog tags while running through the forest." He waved a hand at the remains. "I will get rid of this. You must be going."

"Where?"

"Take Maya home."

"I don't have a home. Your pal Joseph blew it sky high."

Mandenauer's expression was both exasperated and exhausted. "Take her somewhere safe. We have a traitor in our midst."

"Steiger said he bought Clay's name and photo, his background and his whereabouts."

"*Jäger-Suchers* are turning up dead all over the country," Mandenauer murmured. "Now I know why."

"How many?" Clay asked.

"One is too many. But three, so far."

Clay cursed and I slid my hand into his. The old man lowered his gaze to our joined fingers. "What is this?"

"Holding hands. Show of affection. You should try it sometime."

"I have. It leads to more serious shows of affection." He studied us for several ticks of the clock. "Which I can see you've already sampled." He lifted his gaze to the ceiling and tapped his foot. "Agents are dropping like flies. If they aren't being killed, they're falling in love. What is the world coming to?"

"Oh, no. People falling in love. What a tragedy."

Mandenauer glanced at Clay. "Is she always like this?"

"Pretty much."

"Good. She'll need spunk to survive life with you."

"Spunk?"

Clay shrugged. "He knows a lot of words."

"I was alive when most of them were invented," Mandenauer said dryly.

"What's my next assignment, sir?"

"Disappear."

"I'm sorry?"

"The monsters know your name, face, and Social Security number. Until we find the traitor, you're in danger." His eyes met mine. "And everyone around you is too."

I tightened my fingers on Clay's and moved closer to his side. "You're not leaving me," I said.

"I can't." Clay motioned to the bed with his free hand. "They probably know about you too. Damn, Maya, I'm sorry."

"I'm not. I'd rather be in danger with you, than safe all by myself."

Clay searched my eyes. He must have found the truth there because he kissed me, sealing the bargain.

Together we left the hotel, then Phoenix, behind. We disappeared. *Jäger-Suchers* are good at that.

They still haven't found the traitor and a few more agents have died. We may have to stay hidden indefinitely.

At first Clay was antsy, then Mandenauer found him a new job. The far-reaching arm of the *Jäger-Suchers* needs a whole lot of fingers. The Internet has made Clay into a cyber-searcher. Tracking monsters online may not be as exciting as shooting them, but as he told me once before, someone has to do it.

I didn't have to apply at McDonald's, which was lucky, since we live a long, long way from any golden arches. Though the voices of the spirits remained behind in the Canyon of the Dead, hearing them, even for a little while, jump-started my muse. I can't write fast enough. Estelle says my next book should be a runaway hit.

It's the story of a spy during World War II. He discovers a secret lab in the depths of the Black Forest. You wouldn't believe what he finds.

And those dreams of pink ribbons and blue bicycles? They aren't just dreams any longer.

Don't miss sneak peeks at upcoming sexy paranormal tales from

SHERRILYN KENYON,
L. A. BANKS,
AND LORI HANDELAND!

Turn the page to find out more!

FROM

SEIZE THE NIGHT

SHERRILYN KENYON

Coming January 2005

Valerius pulled at the edge of his right leather Coach glove to straighten it as he walked down the virtually abandoned street. As always, he was impeccably dressed in a long black cashmere coat, a black turtleneck, and black slacks. Unlike most Dark-Hunters, he wasn't a leather-wearing barbarian.

He was the epitome of sophistication. Breeding. Nobility. His family had been descended from one of the oldest and most respected noble families of Rome. As a former Roman general whose father had been a well-respected senator, Valerius would have gladly followed in the man's footsteps had the Parcea or Fates not intervened.

But that was the past and Valerius refused to remember it. Agrippina was the only exception to that rule. She was the only thing he ever remembered from his human life.

She was the only thing *worth* remembering from his human life.

Valerius winced and focused his thoughts on other, much less painful things. There was a crispness in the air that announced winter would be here soon. Not that New Orleans had a winter compared to what he'd been used to in D.C.

Still, the longer he was here, the more his blood was thinning, and the cool night air was a bit chilly to him.

Valerius paused as his Dark-Hunter senses detected the

presence of a Daimon. Tilting his head, he listened with his heightened hearing.

He heard a group of men laughing at their victim.

And then he heard the strangest thing of all.

"Laugh it up, asshole. But she who laughs last, laughs longest, and I intend to belly-roll tonight."

A fight broke out.

Valerius whirled on his heel and headed back in the direction he'd come from.

He skirted through the darkness until he found an opened gate that led to a courtyard.

There in the back were six Daimons fighting a tall human woman.

Valerius was mesmerized by the macabre beauty of the battle. One Daimon came at the woman's back. She flipped him over her shoulder and twirled in one graceful motion to stab him in the chest with a long, black dagger.

She twirled as she rose up to face another one. She tossed the dagger from one hand to the other and held it like a woman well used to defending herself from the undead.

Two Daimons rushed her. She actually did a cartwheel away from them, but the other Daimon had anticipated her action. He grabbed her.

Without panicking, the woman surrendered her weight by picking both of her legs up to her chest. It brought the Daimon to his knees. The woman sprang to her feet and whirled to stab the Daimon in his back.

He evaporated.

Normally the remaining Daimons would flee. The last four didn't. Instead they spoke to each other in a language he hadn't heard in a long time . . . ancient Greek.

"Little chickie la la, isn't dumb enough to fall for that, guys," the woman answered back in flawless Greek.

Valerius was so stunned he couldn't move. In over two thousand years, he'd never seen or heard of anything like this. Not even the Amazons had ever produced a better fighter than the woman who confronted the Daimons.

Suddenly a light appeared behind the woman. It flashed bright and swirling. A chill, cold wind swept through the courtyard before six more Daimons stepped out.

Valerius went rigid at something even rarer than the warrior-woman fighting the Daimons.

The summer I discovered the world was not black-and-white—the way I liked it—but a host of annoying shades of gray was the summer a lot more changed than my vision.

However, on the night the truth began I was still just another small-town cop—bored, cranky, waiting, even wishing, for something to happen. I learned never to be so open-ended in my wishes again.

The car radio crackled. "Three Adam One, what's your ten-twenty?"

"I'm watching the corn grow on the east side of town."

I waited for the imminent spatter of profanity from the dispatcher on duty. I wasn't disappointed.

"You'd think it was a goddamned full moon. I swear those things bring out every nut cake in three counties."

My lips twitched. Zelda Hupmen was seventy-five if she was a day. A hard-drinking, chain-smoking throwback to the good times when such a lifestyle was commonplace and the fact it would kill you still a mystery.

Obviously Zelda had yet to hear the scientific findings, since she was going to outlive everyone by smoking unfiltered Camels and drinking Jim Beam for breakfast.

"Maybe the crazies are just gearing up for the blue moon we've got coming."

"What in living hell is a blue moon?"

The reason Zee was still working third shift after count-less years on the force? Her charming vocabulary.

"Two full moons in one month makes a blue moon on the second course. Very rare. Very powerful. If you're into that stuff."

Living in the north woods of Wisconsin, elbow to elbow with what was left of the Ojibwe nation, I'd heard enough woo-woo legends to last a lifetime.

They always pissed me off. I lived in a modern world where legends had no place except in the history books. To do my job, I needed facts. In Miniwa, depending on who you talked to, facts and fiction blurred together too close for my comfort.

Zee's snort of derision turned into a long, hacking cough. I waited, ever patient, for her to regain her breath.

"Powerful my ass. Now get yours out to Highway One-ninety-nine. We got trouble, girl."

"What kind of trouble?" I flicked on the red lights, con-sidered the siren.

"Got me. Cell call—lots of screaming, lots of static. Brad's on his way."

I had planned to inquire about the second officer on duty, but, as usual, Zee answered questions before they could even be asked. Sometimes she was spookier than anything I heard or saw on the job.

"It'll take him a while," she continued. "He was at the other end of the lake, so you'll be first on the scene. Let me know what happens."

Since I'd never found screaming to be good news, I stopped *considering* the siren and sped my wailing vehicle in the direction of Highway 199.

The Miniwa PD consisted of myself, the sheriff, and six other officers, plus Zee and an endless array of young dis-patchers—until summer, when the force swelled to twenty because of the tourists.

I hated summer. Rich fools from Southern cities traveled the two-lane highway to the north to sit on their butt next to a lake and fry their skin the shade of fuchsia agony. Their kids shrieked, their dogs ran wild, they drove their boats too fast and their minds too slow, but they came into town and spent their easy money in the bars, restaurants, and junk shops.

As annoying as the tourist trade was for a cop, the three months of torture kept Miniwa on the map. According to my calendar, we had just entered week three of hell.

I came over a hill and slammed on my brakes. A gas-sucking, lane-hogging luxury SUV was parked crosswise on the dotted yellow line. A single headlight blazed; the other was a gaping black hole.

Why the owner hadn't pulled the vehicle onto the shoulder I had no idea. But then, I'd always suspected the major-ity of the population were too stupid to live.

I inched my squad car off the road, positioning my lights on the vehicle. Leaving the red dome flashing, I turned off the siren. The resulting hush was as deafening as the shrill wail had been.

The clip of my boots on the asphalt made a lonely, ghostly sound. If my headlights hadn't illuminated the hazy outline of a person in the driver's seat, I'd have believed I was alone, so deep was the silence, so complete the still-ness of the night.

"Hello?" I called.

No response. Not a hint of movement.

I hurried around the front of the car, taking in the pieces of the grille and one headlight splayed across the pave-ment. For a car that cost upward of $40,000 it sure broke into pieces easily enough.

That's what I liked about the department's custom-issue Ford Crown Victoria. The thing was built like a tank, and it drove like one, too. Other cities might have switched over to SUVs, but Miniwa stuck with the tried and true.

Sure, four-wheel drive was nice, but sandbags in the

trunk and chains on the tires worked just as well. Besides, nothing had an engine like my CV. I could catch damn near anyone driving that thing, and she didn't roll if I took a tight curve.

"Miniwa PD," I called as I skirted the fender of the SUV.

My gaze flicked over the droplets of blood that shone black beneath the silver moonlight. They trailed off toward the far side of the road. I took a minute to check the ditch for any sign of a wounded animal or human being, but there was nothing.

Returning to the car, I yanked open the door and blinked to find a woman behind the wheel. In my experience men drove these cars—or soccer moms. I saw no soccer balls, no kids, no wedding ring. *Hmm.*

"Are you all right?"

She had a bump on her forehead and her eyes were glassy. Very young and very blond—the fairy princess type—she was too petite to be driving a vehicle of this size, but—I gave a mental shrug—it was a free country.

The airbag hadn't deployed, which meant the car was a piece of shit or she hadn't been going very fast when she'd hit . . . whatever it was she'd hit.

I voted on the latter, since she wasn't lying on the pavement shredded from the windshield. The bump indicated she hadn't been wearing her seat belt. Shame on her. A ticketing offense in this state, but a little hard to prove after the fact.

"Ma'am," I tried again when she continued to stare at me without answering. "Are you all right? What's your name?"

She raised her hand to her head. There was blood dripping down her arm. I frowned. No broken glass, except on the front of the car, which appeared to be more plastic than anything else. How had she cut herself?

I grabbed the flashlight from my belt and trained it on

her arm. Something had taken a bite-sized chunk out of the skin between her thumb and her wrist.

"What did you hit, ma'am?"

"Karen." Her eyes were wide, pupils dilated; she was shocky. "Karen Larson."

Right answer, wrong question. The distant wail of a siren sliced through the cool night air, and I permitted myself a sigh of relief. Help was on the way.

Since the nearest hospital was a forty-minute drive, Miniwa made do with a small general practice clinic for everything but life-threatening crises. Even so, the clinic was on the other end of town, a good twenty minutes over dark, deserted roads. Brad could transport Miss Larson while I finished up here.

But first things first. I needed to move her vehicle out of the road before someone, if not Brad, plowed into us. Thank God Highway 199 at 3:00 A.M. was not a hotbed of traffic, or there'd be more glass and blood on the pavement.

"Ma'am? Miss Larson, we need to move. Slide over."

She did as I ordered, like a child, and I quickly parked her car near mine. Planning to retrieve my first-aid kit and do some minor cleaning and repairs—perhaps bandage her up just enough to keep the blood off the seats—I paused, half in and half out of the car, when she answered my third question as late as the second.

"Wolf. I hit a wolf."

FROM L. A. BANKS'S

THRILLING VAMPIRE HUNTRESS LEGEND SERIES

THE BITTEN

Coming February 2005

THE LAIR IN ST. LUCIA...

Tell me your darkest fantasy," she murmured against his ear, gently pulling the lobe between her teeth.

Carlos smiled with his eyes still closed, too exhausted to do much else. Damali sounded so wickedly sexy, but why did women always go there—searching for answers to questions they really didn't want to hear in bed? "I don't have any, except being with you."

"Tell me," she pleaded low and throaty, her voice so seductive that he'd swear she was all vamp.

No. He was not going to go there, no matter what. He was not going to stare into those big brown eyes of hers and get hypnotized by them. Dark fantasies. She had no idea what went through a master's mind. Despite himself, his smile broadened, although he was still not looking at her. The things he'd seen ... Had she any concept of the lifetimes of male vampire knowledge he'd acquired from Kemet through Rome and beyond, just by being offered a Council seat?

He stroked her still damp back, his fingers reveling in the tingling sensation her tattoo created as he touched the base of her spine, hoping she'd let his love be enough to satisfy her.

"You're my fantasy," he finally said to appease her when she became morbidly silent. But he'd also meant what he'd said, albeit skillfully avoiding the question she'd really asked. "You're this dead man's dream come true, baby."

Her response was a chuckle, followed by an expulsion of hot breath down the shaft of his ear canal. "Liar," she whispered, as she slid her body onto his. "I know where you want to go."

"D . . ." he murmured, too tired to argue with her, and much too compromised by her warmth to avoid being stirred by her butter softness. "C'mon, girl . . . stop playing."

His hand continued to stroke her back, finding the deep sway in it that gave rise to her firm, tight bottom. He allowed his fingers to leisurely play at the slit that separated its halves, enjoying the moistness that he knew he'd created there. Her immediate sigh made him shudder and seek her mouth to kiss her gently, half hoping to shut her up, half hoping to derail his own darkening thoughts. Without resistance, she deepened their kiss, rewarding his senses with a hint of mango, the merest trace of red wine, and her own sweetness fused with his salty aftermath as his tongue searched the soft interiors around it.

Damn, this woman was fine . . . five feet seven inches' worth of buff curves packaged in flawless bronze skin, lush mouth, brunette locks that kissed her shoulders, and a shea oil scent that was working him. It always did. He breathed in the fragrances held by her still-damp scalp, vanilla, coconut oils, and then there was also the scent of heavy, pungent sex hanging in the air.

"You always smell *so* good," he murmured, kissing the edge of her jaw. He could still taste her on his mouth when he licked his lips, "Hmmm . . ." Sticky, sweet-salty, female. The way she breathed against his neck, and her head found the crook of his shoulder, she fit so perfectly, like a handmade blanket on him. Even exhausted, her slick wetness made him want to move just to maintain their friction, their pulse. Merely thinking about it made him hard again.

"I know you have to eat," she said in a husky tone against the sensitive part of his throat, her tongue trailing up his jugular vein, causing him to tighten his hold on her.

"Yeah, I do . . . in a few," he admitted quietly, now too distracted to go out hunting at the moment.

The way she tilted her hips forward, ever so slightly, a tease, an offering, just a contraction of the muscles beneath her bronze skin fought with the hunger and was winning.

"What's *your* darkest fantasy?" he said smiling, turning the question on her, and not caring that a little fang was beginning to show with his smile. He passed his tongue over his incisors, willing patience as he played the game that she seemed to be enjoying.

Damali brought her head up to stare into his eyes with a mischievous smirk. "My darkest fantasy is fulfilling yours."

He laughed low and deep and slow. "Yeah?" He raised an eyebrow in a challenge. "But I don't have any really dark fantasies . . . this is all I need."

"Liar," she said again, chuckling from within her throat and planting a wet kiss on his Adam's apple in a way that made him swallow hard. "I bet I know what it is, even if you won't tell me."

"Curiosity killed the cat," he told her, arching, trying to penetrate her without success.

"But satisfaction brought her back." She lifted her head and stared at him hard, her smile strained with anticipation, her expression one of unmasked desire.

For a moment, neither of them spoke. The exchange was telepathic, electric, and he found her neck, kissed it hard, then her shoulder, licking a path down her collarbone. When she moaned, he almost lost it and bit her.

"Tell me what you want," he murmured hot against her breast, before pulling a taut nipple between his lips.

Whatever she asked for, he'd give her one last time before dawn. Didn't she already know, *por ella seria capaz de cualquier cosa?* Yeah, he would do anything for her. "Tell me," he whispered, "and it's done."

"I've already told you," she said in a rasp, moving to allow him to slip inside her, then contracting around him before withdrawing.

"You have no idea . . . what you're doing to me." That was the pure truth. A scent that had been locked in the deep registers of his mind filtered into his awareness, gradually at first, and then stronger until it was all-consuming. Every inhalation now was riddled with the maddening aphrodisiac that he'd sworn he'd forget—had to—but it moved his body, banished a portion of his control. Master or not, Neteru was entering his system and slaying him.

Her skin had a sheen of perspiration on it, and she slid against him like water flowing over rocks, liquid fire motion, hips undulating in a slow, rolling current, with eddies that spontaneously spun, lurched, took him in to the hilt, then washed him ashore. His tightening grip would each time be enough to summon his return to her warm, wet center, only to be cast ashore by her fickle tide again and again, until he flipped her on her back and was done playing.

"Enough." There was no play in his tone. He was beyond games as he stared into her eyes; saw a glow of red reflected back from her dark brown irises, knowing it came from his. Her scent bathed him, made him shut his eyes tight as he breathed in deeply and entered her hard. "*This* is what I want."

His fingers tangled in her velvet spun locks, and her arches finally met him in a rhythm they both knew by heart—no stopping, no teasing, just hard down, uninterrupted returns until he felt his gums give way to the incisors he could no longer hold in check, no more than he could hold back the inevitable convulsion of pleasure that was about to rip through his groin.

Nuzzling his throat, her fingers wound through his hair, and he was surprised by the force of her pull, that her fingers had made a fist at the nape of his neck, and that one of her palms slid against his jaw to push his head back, her breath on his throat in the way he'd always imagined. Trembling with need, the sensation was so damned good . . . if only . . . she could . . . just once . . . *Oh, baby* . . .

Then she suddenly shifted her weight, her legs a leveraging vise, and rolled on top of him. Her strength came from nowhere. It happened so quickly. A sharp strike as fast as a cobra's tore at his throat, making him shut his eyes harder, his gasp fused with a groan that transformed into a wail, and the pull that siphoned his throat sent the convulsion of ecstasy throughout his system, emptied his scrotum until his body dry heaved, made his lashes flutter from the rapid seizure, where every pull from her lips erupted hot seed from him into her. Sheets gathered in knots within his fists before his hand again, sought her skin, shards of color ricocheted behind his lids while he cradled her in his arms, stuttering through tears, *"Don't stop . . . take it all."*

His body went hot, then cold, minutes of unrelenting pleasure—her hold indomitable, a physical lock of sheer will, as she moved her hips in a lazy rhythm, ignoring his attempt to rush her with deep thrusts and staccato jerks, his voice foreign to him as it reverberated off the walls of the lair, echoed back, and taunted him . . . a master vampire . . . done for the first time, for real, by what could only be a female vamp. *A master female.* One conjured from his darkest fantasy, riding him with more than skill, precision, working his ass to the bone—slow torture that he couldn't stop, even if he'd wanted to.

Winded, siphoned, turned out, he could barely open his eyes—but he had to. Which one of them had taken Damali's place, stolen her form? Daaayum, his territory had some shit with it . . . but never in his wildest dreams would he have imagined it to be like this. If Damali ever found out . . . and how did this female get in here? Where was D!

She smiled, looking down at him, and wiped her mouth with the back of her hand.

"Who made you, baby?" Dazed, that was all he could ask.

"You did," she said, chuckling low, and pressing an index finger over one of his streaming bite wounds to seal it. Then she slowly licked her finger and smiled before sealing the other so he wouldn't entirely bleed out.

Carlos blinked twice, staring. "Damali?" Two inches of fang glistened crimson in the moonlight within her lovely mouth, and a thin red line of blood had dribbled down her chin between her breasts. He resisted the urge to sit up and lick the dark trail up to her stained lips.

"Who else?" She shook her head, sat back with him still in her, and folded her arms over her chest. "Oh, so you had some other Jane on your mind while I was working?"

"No . . . oh . . . shit . . ."

He grabbed her by the hips, and extricated himself from her to stand, stumbling a bit, but he needed motion—fatigue and the siphon, notwithstanding. "No, no, no, no, no—this *cannot* be happening."

He could feel panic bubbling within him, and he had never been a brother to outright freak about anything. But this, of all the things he'd seen and been through so far, was scaring the shit out of him.

"No!" he said fast, walking in a circle, then going from the deck back to the side of the bed, gesturing with his hands in a naked frenzy. "Something went wrong. I have to get you back to the guardians—to Marlene, your Mom . . . baby, you're turning—"

"Turned," she sighed with a smile, "and I love it. Relax. What's done is done."

"Oh, my God, D—"

When she hissed and held both sides of her head and

glared at him, he could feel hot tears begin to form in his eyes. He could call on the Almighty, but the Neteru couldn't? What the hell had he done?

Visit www.vampirehuntress.com for more.

And don't miss the other books in the Vampire Huntress series:

Minion
The Awakening
The Hunted

Available now